THE CHINESE
LANTERN

Harry Bowling

HEADLINE

First published in 1997 by
HEADLINE BOOK PUBLISHING

First published in paperback in 1998
by HEADLINE BOOK PUBLISHING

10 9 8 7 6 5 4 3

ISBN 0 7472 5545 8

Typeset by Palimpsest Book Production Limited,
Polmont, Stirlingshire
Printed and bound in Great Britain by
Clays Ltd, St Ives PLC

HEADLINE BOOK PUBLISHING
A division of Hodder Headline PLC
338 Euston Road
London NW1 3BH

To Chu and Frieda,
my friends at The Blue Heaven.

Prologue

21 May 1929, Bermondsey

It had been a long and terrifying night, but now at last it was all over, and as the first light began to filter through into the quiet bedroom Ruby Neal carefully eased back the swaddling-cloth with the tip of her finger to gaze down in awe at the new life by her side. The baby screwed up its face at the intrusion and gave out a tiny sound of protest before settling again, and Ruby sighed deeply as she sank back on to the cool pillow.

The muted sound of iron wheels over cobblestones and the clatter of a dustbin in a nearby backyard gave way to silence once more as the young mother closed her eyes and mouthed a thankful prayer to the God who had delivered a miracle.

'The heart's struggling! I'll need to cut!'

'There there, Mrs Neal. Just breathe deeply. You'll be fine.'

The large bloated face of Nurse Morgan had looked grotesque beside the ashen countenance of Dr Swain as she sought to reassure, but her officious tone of voice only served to aggravate the sense of panic and Ruby cried out in agony as her eyes flashed to the elderly doctor leaning over her. *The heart's struggling.* The words echoed over and over in her mind. Whose heart, hers or the baby's? Was she going to die in labour? Were they both going to die?

The doctor's brow was bathed in sweat and his shirt-sleeves were turned back to the elbows exposing thin hairy forearms as he prepared to set to work with the scalpel. Even through her pain Ruby noticed that his double-breasted waistcoat had spatters of what appeared to be food down the front of it. She appealed to him with eyes full of terror to free the breeched baby quickly and let it live, let them both live.

Firm footsteps on the stairs and the door opening gingerly brought a tired smile to Ruby's pale face. Four times in the last half hour Jim had peered into the bedroom and crept over to her with a happy grin on his handsome face to kiss her forehead and gaze down at his son, but this time he had his coat on.

'I must go now, I'm gonna be late,' he told her. 'Will yer be all right?'

She nodded. 'Mrs Allenby's stayin', an' the nurse is comin' back soon.'

'Are you sure yer'll be all right?'

'I'm sure. Get ter work, Jim. Yer mustn't be late.'

She heard him leave and lay there quietly, listening to the normal, everyday sounds of domesticity as Bel Allenby busied herself in the scullery downstairs.

The sun was climbing steadily in the early morning sky, and the bright rays that shone through the net curtains and bathed the small bedroom were like a blessing from above. Ruby glanced up and focused her eyes on the thin crack running across the ceiling as again dustbins clattered outside and iron wheels ground past over the cobblestones. Everything was right now. After two years of marriage it was high time to start a family, and they had both longed and prayed for this moment. The baby boy they had secretly hoped for had been delivered safely, and now on this new morning the young woman looked back on the pain and suffering of the breech birth and considered it a small price to have paid. Jim would cope for a few days, she thought, with the help of Mrs Allenby, and soon everything would be back to normal. Must remind her to dust the parlour though, and throw out the old newspapers. Jim had an irritating habit of hiding them under the cushions. Better remind Mrs Allenby to sweep the front. Oh, and the net curtains should be changed too. People would be visiting and it wouldn't do to let them see dirty curtains up at the windows.

Heavy footsteps on the stairs and the creaking floorboards of the landing heralded Bel Allenby and Ruby eased herself up against the pillows. Must remind her not to miss the coalman, she thought. The evenings were still chilly and the baby would need plenty of warmth.

21 May 1929, Shantung Province

Warm rain fell from a sky heavy with dark clouds as the women toiled into the late afternoon. In an endless cycle, rice shoots had to be replanted, cultivated and harvested, and with their bare feet sunk in the yellow, muddy water and their garments sodden, the peasants were resigned to their lot. Mei Ching had been warned to stay in the village until the doctor arrived later that week, but she ignored the advice. The rewards of toil were little enough already, but at least a good harvest would mean full bellies, something that had become a rarity of late, due to diffident weather and drying rivers which failed properly to irrigate the paddy fields.

The twinges had become more frequent as the day wore on, and suddenly an excruciating pain coursed through her, doubling the young woman up.

'It's going to be early,' an old woman said. 'She was told it would be.'

'Get her to the side of the field,' another ordered. 'Get some sticks to build some shelter over her.'

Mei Ching gave birth as the evening rain beat down and the old woman shook her head. 'It's very weak and puny. It won't live.'

'It's a six-months' baby, they seldom do,' the other woman replied.

'We must get her back to the village.'

'She's bleeding badly.'

'Leave her. Let her rest here,' someone said quietly. 'She doesn't have long.'

The women knew there was little they could do, and one of them gently bathed the dying peasant's fevered forehead in the same water which had soaked her thin body for years and rotted the nails from her feet.

Li Fong's contented features changed as he came along the path by the paddy field and saw the group of people gathered together on the dry knoll. He frowned as he reached them and saw an old woman holding the tiny bundle.

'The mother died,' she told him, 'but the baby's still alive. For the moment.'

The travelling trader put down his large bundle with extreme care. Along with the supplies he was delivering to the English mission was another ginger pot which would be reverentially installed in his house. He had sought after it for some considerable time and to break it now would make him a clumsy, careless fool. Had he not dreamed of the day when he would own the complete set of six Ming ginger pots, exquisitely made copies of the original Ming pots of the Hsuan Te period which bore the divine, smiling Sian Buddha, and which graced the Emperor's palace? He had only two so far, but if trade picked up he would travel across to Hopeh Province where he had heard there were individual ginger pots on sale at the weekly antique market in the village of Chang Lu.

'We can take the mother back to the village later,' the old woman said. 'There's no hurrying for her any more, but what about the baby? It's a girl, and none of us can suckle her, though it probably wouldn't help. Look for yourself. Feel the faint heartbeat. She's finding it hard to breathe.'

Li Fong looked down as she opened the rag covering and he felt something catch at his heart. Another day, another time and he would have shrugged his shoulders and gone on his way. The infant was bloody and mud-streaked and looked like a tiny skinned rabbit which would hardly have been noticed at the family meal. Today, however, it was different. He had his pot, and supplies for which the mission would pay handsomely.

'I could take it to the mission,' he suggested.

The old woman shook her head. 'It's five miles away,' she replied. 'It'll be dark before you arrive.'

'If it's her fate, the child'll live,' Li Fong told her. 'I'll put her inside my coat next to my skin. She'll be warm at least.'

'The mother's name was Mei Ching,' she told him.

'And the father?'

'Some young man from the travelling theatre I've no doubt,' the old woman said. 'She was a pretty girl and could turn many a young man's eye, though you'd never guess it, seeing her lying there.'

Li Fong picked up his large bundle of supplies and slipped his arms through the canvas straps, then when it was comfortable on his shoulders he opened his coat and took the tiny bundle from the woman. With a nod he started off, and after a while he turned round and saw that the women were back tending the shoots. 'I know your belly's empty, little one,' he murmured, 'but tonight it'll be full and you'll sleep in a warm crib by the fire. Take another breath for me, little one.'

The flat fields gave way to a steady incline, and as the darkness descended Li Fong took deep lungfuls of the colder air and used his heavy staff to aid his climb. There was no time to rest now, no time to take refreshment; he would waste precious minutes, and reach the English mission too late to save the baby. It was still clinging on to life, he could tell.

That night, after his trading was over and he had eaten at the mission table, Li Fong slept curled up tightly on the stone floor. His dream was crystal clear, so much so that he was sure he was awake. He was in a faraway land

and the beautiful young girl by his side was causing much excitement amongst the young men in a large palace. 'No, she's not my wife,' he told them with a smile. 'No, she is not my daughter. I am her guardian Li Fong, and her name is Mei Li.'

Early next morning the mission doctor came to the sleeping trader and woke him. 'Everything possible has been done but the baby is still struggling to live,' he said. 'Now there is only prayer. Pray to your gods too, Li Fong.'

Chapter One

May 1950

Ruby Neal stood at the deep stone sink, distracted from washing up the breakfast things by a blackbird that had suddenly appeared on the fence in the small garden. She noticed that early flowers were coming into bloom, and the recently turned soil was drying in the heat of the sun. Everything looked neat and tidy. The paved pathway had been swept and the stack of flowerpots hidden away from view, which she was pleased about. Ruby liked order and tidiness and, like the house, when the garden was neat and tidy she was happy. Her long-time friend Bel Allenby often remarked that tidiness was an obsession with her, but it was said in the nicest way and they laughed together about it. Bel sought to keep her home spick and span too but she smoked, a habit picked up from the war years, and the ashtray was usually in need of emptying. Newspapers tended to clutter the parlour too, and they were a few days old before they were thrown out, but all in all the older woman's house was tidy enough.

The blackbird flew off, disturbed by Lizzie Roach's mangy cat which was on the prowl again, and Ruby grabbed the broom standing by the scullery door and went out into the garden. The tabby crouched down on the fence in an act of defiance, but as the woman approached menacingly along the path, armed with the broom, it thought better of it and disappeared down the other side. Ruby looked around and then swept a sprinkling of earth back into the tiny flowerbed before returning to her chores.

Life had been very kind to her, she thought. She had her health, and she was happily married with two grown-up children. Her husband Jim was hard-working and contented with his job at Madeley's Food Factory in Dockhead, where he was employed as a maintenance engineer, and her son Paul was home again after his National Service in the RAF. He was doing well at his job as a telephone linesman, and in a few days he would be celebrating his twenty-first birthday. Her daughter Kay was nineteen, blue-eyed and flaxen-haired and as pretty as a picture. Unlike Paul, who had a serious nature, Kay was inclined to be carefree and frivolous, but Ruby hoped that with a little bit of prompting she would pay more heed to her future and then things would turn out for the best. Richard Mills was steady and reliable, and from good, hard-working folk who had seen to it that their only offspring had received a good education. He was very keen on Kay, it stood out a mile, but he was inclined to be reticent and he sometimes seemed a little overawed by Kay's bubbling enthusiasm. He was coming around though, with encouragement, and if all went according to plan he might well take the bull by the horns and make a proposal before much longer.

There was little more to do about the house and it was nearing ten o'clock so Ruby hurried up the stairs to the front bedroom to get ready for her part-time job at Dr Ambrose's surgery in Grange Road. She had promised to look in on Lizzie Roach that morning and she wanted to have a quick word with Bel too. There would be enough time if she hurried. The surgery was only a short walk away but she would have to be careful not to get into a lengthy chat with Lizzie. The poor old soul did go on at times.

Outside in Tanners Alley the sun was hitting the school wall across from the six little cottage-type houses and before noon it would be shining down on the tiny front gardens and the flowerboxes and tubs set out on the fenced patios. Along the way there was a Victorian gaslamp and beyond it the back door of the leather works, where the alley snaked right and left and out into Abbey Street.

Tanners Alley served no obvious purpose as a short cut. Other turnings running from Grange Road linked the main thoroughfare with Abbey Street and over the years local folk had grown reluctant to use the alley to any large extent, partly because they saw it as an intrusion. The six terraced houses there were fronted with waist-high fences and garden gates, setting them apart from the usual backstreet homes which opened straight on to the pavement. The rear gardens too were unusual for the area. Most of the houses had backyards that rarely caught the sun. All in all Tanners Alley was a pleasant place to live, and Ruby Neal was forever grateful that Jim had been given the opportunity to rent number 2 a few months after they were married.

During the Blitz the houses were spared, although they suffered blast damage when the old buildings backing on to them took a direct hit, and now in the sunshine they looked spruce and welcoming. Lizzie's house had ivy growing up the front wall and Bel Allenby's patio had a small circular flowerbed in the centre. At number 1 the Wilsons had flowering bushes in wooden tubs, one on each side of the front door, and Ruby was envious. Connie Wilson never ever tended the plants but they seemed to flourish and every year the berries grew large and plentiful. Ruby was often tempted to water them when she was tending her own flowerboxes but she thought it might be taken the wrong way and she left them as they were.

Bel Allenby was standing by her front door at number 6 and she smiled as Ruby came out. 'Lizzie just asked me ter bring 'er chair out,' she said, nodding at the tatty rocker with its even tattier cushion. 'I expect she'll be rockin' away till the sun goes down.'

'I won't be a minute,' Ruby told her. 'She wants me ter collect a prescription for 'er.'

Bel pulled a face as Ruby slipped the gate latch of number 5. 'What's it this time, 'er back?'

Ruby briefly raised her eyes to the heavens before knocking. ''Ello, Lizzie, are yer decent?' she called out.

The door was soon opened. 'Come in, gel,' the old lady beckoned, mouth cracked in her usual toothless grin.

Ruby followed her into the parlour, caught sight of the iron range and wondered when it had seen its last application of blacklead. 'I'm gettin' yer prescription this mornin',' she told her.

Lizzie nodded. 'Seen the papers?' she asked.

'I've been too busy,' the younger woman replied.

'They're talkin' about puttin' up National Service ter two years,' Lizzie informed her. 'I bet yer glad young Paul's finished wiv it.'

Ruby nodded. 'I see yer gonna take the sun,' she remarked.

'Yeah I am. Bel put me chair outside. Good as gold she is.'

'Well, don't fall asleep wivout yer cap on,' Ruby reminded her. 'Yer remember last time.'

'Do I,' Lizzie said with conviction. 'Bad fer a week I was. Sent me blood pressure right up. Tell yer the trufe I thought it was me lot.'

'Where is yer cap?'

'Under the stairs.'

'What's it doin' under the stairs?'

'I frew it there ter frighten the mouse.'

'I'm sure that would frighten it,' Ruby grinned. 'It's more likely sleepin' in it right this minute.'

'Don't say that,' Lizzie shuddered. 'I can't stand 'em. Mrs Wilson's boy keeps tame mice in a cage. I've seen 'em. I looked over me garden fence an' saw 'im cleanin' the cage out. "'Ere, Freddie, don't you go lettin' them get out," I told 'im. Didn't take a blind bit o' notice 'e didn't.'

'I shouldn't worry. Maybe it wasn't a mouse after all,' Ruby said in an effort to calm the old lady.

'White ones they are,' she went on. 'Tiny little fings, but they do smell. I could smell 'em from where I was standin'. I wonder Connie Wilson allows that boy of 'ers to 'ave 'em in the 'ouse. If one got loose she'd die o' fright.'

Ruby went into the passage and retrieved Lizzie's cap. 'If yer worried about mice why don't yer buy a mousetrap,' she suggested.

Lizzie looked horrified. 'I can't stand 'em but I couldn't kill 'em,' she said with a shudder.

'Are yer sure there's nuffing yer want me ter get yer?' Ruby asked her as she made to leave.

'Only me prescription,' Lizzie replied as she eased her frail frame from the armchair with a groan. 'I need it fer me back. Playin' me up somefing terrible it is. I've tried Sloan's liver pills an' that unction from Cheap Jack's stall but they didn't touch me.'

'Well the unction wouldn't, would it,' Ruby said laughing. 'It's s'posed ter be fer coughs an' colds.'

'Well it could be a cold in me back,' the old lady said defiantly. 'Anyway, Cheap Jack said it's good fer lots o' fings. 'E said it's good fer nursin' muvvers an' anaemic children.'

'Yeah well 'e would,' Ruby replied. 'You stick ter what Dr Ambrose prescribes. 'E knows best.'

'Yeah, when 'e's sober,' Lizzie snorted. 'When I went ter see 'im 'e wanted me ter take me shift orf so 'e could feel me back. "No fear," I told 'im. I wasn't 'avin' 'is 'ands all over me. Dirty ole git.'

'Dr Ambrose is the best round 'ere,' Ruby told her firmly. 'You take notice of what 'e says.'

'Yeah well, I ain't strippin' orf fer 'im or anybody else at my time o' life,' Lizzie went on. 'Whatever next.'

Ruby smiled in resignation. 'I'll pick yer prescription up an' slip in the chemist on me way 'ome,' she said in a placatory voice. 'An' don't ferget yer cap.'

'Yer a good gel,' the old lady replied, her face becoming cheerful once more.

Bel was still at her front door when Ruby stepped out

from number 5. 'She's a scream at times,' the grey-haired woman said grinning. 'When I got that chair out for 'er I told 'er not ter ferget ter wear 'er cap an' she told me she'd mislaid it. Said she was gonna wear 'er best bonnet instead. 'Ave yer seen that bonnet? Gawd 'elp us, it looks like a nest o' robins on a bush.'

'I found 'er cap,' Ruby told her. 'Under the stairs it was. She said she frew it at a mouse.'

'Got time fer a cuppa?' Bel asked, already knowing what the answer would be.

'Maybe later. Gotta dash now,' Ruby replied. 'She kept me chattin'.'

Bel watched her friend hurry along the alley into Grange Road and shook her head slowly. For Ruby, getting to the surgery a couple of minutes late was unthinkable. Bel knew that she would have been up early as always and after organising her protesting family and getting them off to work on time she would have gone round that house of hers with a fine tooth comb before leaving. Poor Jim, she thought. He still dotes on her but how he suffers. I bet he's the only husband in Bermondsey who has to take his shoes off in the passage. He was a handsome man who had cut a fine dash in his uniform. Never had eyes for anyone except Ruby, Bel recalled. She should think herself lucky. Another man wouldn't put up with the way she carried on. But that was being nasty, she chided herself. Ruby was kind and considerate and the first to help anyone, as the neighbours would all be quick to testify. She was a smart woman too. A nice figure still and looking nowhere near her forty-four years. She had been very supportive too when Jack was ill, and there had been no one more helpful and comforting than Ruby when he died. She was a good woman and a good friend, despite her irritating ways.

'I got me cap on,' Lizzie announced as she came to her front door and made herself comfortable in the rocking-chair.

'Yeah, so I see. Well keep it on, or yer'll get sunstroke again,' Bel told her sternly.

Ruby hurried along Grange Road and as she was about to climb the few steps to the surgery she saw Mrs Mills approaching. There was time for a few words, she decided.

''Ello, Pam. It's a nice day.'

'Very nice. 'Ow's young Kay? I 'aven't seen 'er fer a few days.'

'Very well. 'Ow's Richard?'

'Very well.'

'They seem ter be 'ittin' it off,' Ruby remarked. 'I'm pleased. Richard's a nice respectable lad.'

Pam Mills smiled at the compliment. 'Richard's 'opin' ter get a promotion very soon. Wiv a bit o' luck 'e'll be workin' on valves.'

'Oh? Is that good?'

'I should say so,' Pam said staunchly. 'Yer see, this office Richard's workin' in does all the drawings fer the big 'eavy machinery, but the ovver office upstairs is where all the important drawings are done. The valves are much more complicated an' yer gotta know what yer doin' in that office. That's 'ow Prentice 'imself started, in the upstairs office, an' now 'e owns the firm.'

Ruby started to feel a little agitated. 'Look, I'd love ter stop fer a chat, but I'm gonna be late. I'll see yer later.'

Once settled at her desk and with the patients' records neatly in order Ruby allowed herself to dwell on what Pam Mills had said. It seemed strange that the woman hadn't seen Kay for a few days. Richard had called round and he and Kay had gone out together, and their evenings usually ended up at the Millses' house for a short while before Richard walked Kay home. She must remember to mention seeing Mrs Mills when her daughter got home that evening.

Dr Ambrose's surgery was well organised. He and his assistant Dr Phelps were highly thought of in the area and their waiting room was always neat and tidy and smelling of furniture polish. The small room where Ruby worked led off from the waiting room, and to the side of her desk doors opened into the doctors' rooms.

Normally everything went like clockwork and the three hours flashed past but Ruby soon realised that today was going to be somewhat different. Dr Ambrose had managed to mislay a document and he mumbled irritably to himself as he hurriedly searched through the filing cabinet by Ruby's desk. Mrs Caulfield had brought her young son to the surgery with the croup and she wanted to jump her turn. Albert Walburton, moreover, was suffering from an ingrowing toenail and he wasn't too pleased when the young lad reached for a magazine from the table and stepped on his foot.

'Bloody 'ell!' he groaned. 'Can't yer keep 'im still, missus?'

''E only wants somefing ter read,' the harassed woman replied sharply.

'I'm sure *Country Life*'ll interest 'im,' Albert growled. 'An' anyway ovver people 'ave ter read those magazines. Nice ain't it, what wiv 'im coughin' an' splutterin' all over it.'

'Put it down, Billy,' Mrs Caulfield told him.

The young lad did as he was bid and once again stepped on Albert's foot.

'Fer Chrissake!' Albert called out. 'That kid should be tied ter the chair.'

Mrs Childs had come to the surgery for some more cough medicine and she tutted loudly. 'Don't be such a miserable ole sod,' she said with a hard look. ''E's only a boy.'

'Bloody 'ooligan more like,' Albert growled as he lifted his troublesome foot.

'You can go in now, Mr Walburton,' Ruby told him.

Billy had another fit of coughing and against her better judgement Ruby quickly juggled the records. 'Dr Ambrose'll see yer now, Mrs Caulfield.'

'An' about time too,' the woman said puffing loudly.

''Ere, I should be first,' Mrs Childs protested, following Ruby into the office.

'I was worried about your chest, Mrs Childs,' Ruby told her with a serious look. 'I didn't want that lad coughin' all those germs over yer. It's so easy ter catch fings when yer've got a weak chest.'

The explanation served to satisfy the old lady and things finally got back to normal at the surgery.

'I wouldn't do that again, so help me,' Ruby told herself as she hurried back to Tanners Alley at two o'clock. Order and propriety were everything. Cut corners and act lax and it courts trouble. God! she thought suddenly. I've forgotten Lizzie's prescription. This is going to put me behind today, she fretted as she retraced her steps.

Chapter Two

Jim Neal slid out from under the wrapping machine and hauled himself to his feet. 'It's the belt, Mary,' he said, running his fingers through his dark wavy hair. 'It's snapped. I'll need ter change it. Shouldn't take long.'

The forelady gave him a saucy smile. 'What would we do wivout yer,' she said mockingly.

He grinned back at her. 'Better tell that ter the manager. I need ter get on the right side of 'im.'

''As 'e bin on yer back?' Mary asked.

'Nah. I'm s'posed ter be strippin' down a machine next weekend but I can't make it. There's a reunion on Saturday night.'

'That sounds good. Can yer take me along wiv yer?' the forelady joked.

'I'm afraid it's men only.'

'Don't your Ruby mind?'

'Nah, she doesn't drink much, an' besides, it's only service talk,' Jim told her. 'She'd be yawnin' 'er 'ead off inside five minutes.'

'I wouldn't be,' Mary remarked, her eyes flashing. 'I fink you airmen were very brave. I was only readin' the ovver

21

night about the losses on those bombin' raids. Wasn't you on those Wellin'ton bombers?'

'Lancasters,' he corrected her. 'I was a rear gunner.'

Mary was getting interested and she leaned on the side of the machine with her chin resting in her cupped hand. 'Did yer go on many raids?' she asked.

'Twenty in all.'

'Wasn't yer scared?'

'Terrified.'

'Go on. I bet yer wasn't scared at all.'

'Believe me, Mary, I was really petrified. We all were,' he told her, his eyes widening slightly.

'I went out wiv a pilot officer one night durin' the Blitz,' Mary confided. 'There was nuffing in it mind. We just went dancin'. I was lonely what wiv my Stan bein' away in the army. I could 'ave got serious, ter be honest. 'E was very 'andsome, but I resisted the urge. It wouldn't 'ave bin fair ter Stan. I was glad too. The war broke up so many marriages.'

'Yeah it did, but I was lucky,' Jim replied. 'I was stationed in East Anglia an' I got 'ome quite often.'

Mary spotted the foreman approaching and she stood up straight. ''Old tight, there's Ugly Features.' As he drew near she raised her voice for his benefit. 'So it's only a small job, then?'

'An hour should do it,' Jim said.

The hawk-faced foreman gave him a searching look and then turned to Mary. 'I want yer ter replace Mrs Springer,' he told her. 'She's gone 'ome sick.'

Jim hurried away to the maintenance store for the necessary part and while he was waiting for the storeman to fetch it he slumped down at a long wooden table and rolled a cigarette. Ruby had never smoked and she had been on at him to give it up. It was proving to be very difficult, but he had found a happy medium by not smoking at home, which went some way to placate Ruby, he thought with a trace of a grin. At least she wouldn't be following him about the house to empty the ashtrays. Come to think of it they had suddenly disappeared. Maybe he should be a little less accommodating. Kay certainly thought so. Ruby's obsession with keeping the home spotless irritated her and she often made her feelings felt. Paul on the other hand suffered her idiosyncrasies in silence. But then he was a tidy lad himself. Most of the time he had his face buried in a book or the newspapers, and things tended to go over his head.

'There's the belt, Jim,' Nobby Smith said as he came out from the caged stores. 'I dunno what yer doin' wiv these. That's the third one this week. I'll need to order some more terday or we'll be runnin' out, an' that won't please ole Bradley.'

''Ave yer seen 'im this mornin'?' Jim asked him.

''E's not in,' Nobby replied. ''E'll be in termorrer though. By the way, Angela wants ter see yer. I dunno what it's about.'

Jim noticed the sly grin that had appeared in the corner of the storeman's mouth. 'Annual 'olidays,' he said with emphasis.

'She certainly fancies you,' Nobby remarked, the grin growing.

'She fancies everybody,' Jim told him dismissively.

'I wish she fancied me,' the storeman replied. 'What a

dish. She's got legs like Betty Grable, an' those . . .' He held his hands up in front of his chest.

'She's married, Nobby, an' so are you,' Jim reproached him. 'It don't do ter play away from 'ome.'

'I'd chance it if she gimme the word,' Nobby called out as Jim went back to work.

Kay Neal left the typing pool of National Supplies in Aldwych and walked towards Waterloo Bridge in the evening sunlight. It was nice to get out from the incessant clacking of typewriter keys and the stuffy, oppressive atmosphere into the open air, even if it wasn't that fresh with the rush-hour traffic fumes. There was a welcoming tang in the air on the bridge, and as she waited for a number 1 bus Kay fished into her handbag for the note one of the typists had discreetly passed to her that afternoon. It was an advertisement for young women to apply for posts as NAAFI assistants and Kay smiled to herself as she read the part that said candidates must be prepared to work abroad. Just imagine. An oasis in the desert where young servicemen came to eat and relax. Romantic nights under a star-filled sky with wind-carved sand dunes stretching away into the lonely distance, and the occasional passing camel train silhouetted against a blood-red horizon. It might be the steamy tropics though, with wild beasts calling out in the night and the buzz of mosquitoes outside the protective netting. The free days would of course be spent visiting the ancient temples and climbing above oven-like valleys into the cool hills to gaze down over steamy jungles and twisting yellow rivers.

Kay hurriedly put the newspaper cutting back in her

handbag as the bus drew up. It all sounded very exciting, she thought, but what about the possibility of working in some godforsaken army camp like Catterick during a freezing January. Or even Aldershot? It conveniently didn't mention places like that.

'Five only standin' inside,' the conductor called out as the bus pulled away from the stop. 'Plenty o' room on top.'

Kay leaned back in her seat on the upper deck and gazed down at the river. The cranes along the waterfront were stilled and a brace of laden barges rode at anchor in midstream ready for unloading the following morning. A lone swan drifted along on the ebbing tide, and upriver beyond Westminster Palace the western sky was catching fire. Tonight Richard was taking her to the pictures but she could raise no enthusiasm. He was thoughtful and very court-eous, and one day he would make someone a good husband, but his main effects on her were to dampen her spirits and test the limits of her tolerance. The young woman sighed miserably. Their meetings had become nerve-jangling. She knew more about pressure-reducing valves, compensating bypass switches and the new thermodynamic contraption that was set to revolutionise the whole engineering industry than she did about what the colour was to be this autumn, or what was new in make-up. It couldn't go on. She would have to finish it before she became trapped in the marriage stakes with someone she could never love. Already her mother was hinting about an engagement and Richard's mother was almost as bad.

Kay found herself staring at the back of the young woman seated up front as she wallowed in her misery and suddenly realised how beautiful her long raven hair was. It was parted on the centre of her head, combed down closely then drawn forward one side of her neck to hang down at the front. The girl turned to glance out of the bus window and Kay saw that she was Oriental. Her face was finely chiselled and pale, with high cheekbones and a small pointed chin.

The conductor came along the aisle and Kay handed him four pennies. 'Grange Road, please,' she said.

The conductor punched the ticket and handed it to her without comment and then the girl in the front seat held out her hand. 'Grange Road, please,' she said in perfect English.

She must be visiting the area, Kay thought to herself. She looked Chinese and there were no Chinese families living in that part of Bermondsey as far as she knew, apart from the Chinese laundry that had opened last year in Cater Street. That was it, she was visiting someone there.

The bus passed Waterloo Station and carried on towards the Elephant and Castle and Kay took out the small newspaper cutting from her handbag. Maybe this was the answer, she mused. At least it was a chance to get away from her mundane existence, away from the claustrophobic surroundings of Bermondsey and see some of the world. She smiled as she thought about her mother's reaction.

'Mum, I'm leavin' 'ome.'

'Leavin' 'ome?'

'I'm joinin' the NAAFI.'

'You can forget that right away, my girl. Yer can put that idea clean out o' yer 'ead.'

'I'm sorry but it's done. I leave fer trainin' termorrer.'

'But 'ow yer gonna survive? Who's gonna look after yer?'

'I'll look after meself.'

'But they could send yer anywhere.'

'I've applied fer the Far East.'

That would be the point where Mum fainted away from shock. Paul would smile and understand, and Dad would put on a show for her mother's benefit but he'd wink at her secretly and he too would understand. Poor Richard. He would tell his mother, and ask her to have a few words.

The Chinese girl was reading a fashion magazine and Kay noticed how delicate her hands were as she flicked the page. Her nails were long and painted with a transparent varnish. She seemed engrossed in the article and Kay became more intrigued. Had she been born here, or had she travelled from China or maybe Hong Kong? The elderly man sitting next to her was smoking a pipe and although Kay winced at the smell of the strong tobacco the Chinese girl appeared not to notice.

Kay put the clipping into her bag once more and stared out of the window at the tenement block in New Kent Road. Washing was hanging from balconies and women in pinafores stood in the entrances chatting together. Children were playing close to hand, and then as the bus pulled away from the stop Kay noticed a young woman pushing a pram into the grounds of the building. Two youngsters clung to the handle of the pram and another, older child followed on sucking what looked like a toffee bar. Normally Kay would have smiled at the scene and forgotten it without much thought, but this evening it made her feel strangely sad and empty. Her mother was keen for her to get married, and by the way she was acting it seemed Richard Mills was an ideal choice. Whose choice though? It certainly wasn't hers. It had been an arrangement, carefully manipulated by her mother and Mrs Mills. Together they had made the introduction and she had been snared.

'I've decided we're gonna 'ave a demob party fer Paul,' Ruby said.

'That'll be nice,' Jim replied.

'I'll invite a few neighbours an' we'll see if Amy an' John can make it,' Ruby went on.

'You 'aven't seen that sister of yours fer ages,' Jim remarked.

'I'll write to 'er,' Ruby persisted. 'Bel's sure ter come, an' the Wilsons.'

'What about the Thompsons next door?' Jim asked.

'I know they're a scruffy pair but I can't leave 'em out,' Ruby told him.

'Well it's up ter you,' he said resignedly.

'I'm gonna invite Mrs Mills too,' Ruby went on with a sly grin.

'Mrs Mills? Who's she?'

'She's a nice woman. 'Er 'usband's a nice bloke too. Their son Richard's doin' very well. 'E's a draughtsman.'

'Ruby, I asked yer who she was, not whevver she an' all 'er family were nice or not,' Jim said with irritation.

'I first met 'er at the market,' Ruby explained. 'We were in the bread queue tergevver an' we got talkin'. You know 'ow it is. We talked about our families an' I told 'er about you an' the children. Paul 'ad just started 'is National Service an' I told 'er 'ow worried I was, what wiv the way fings were.'

'But 'e was only in Middlesex,' Jim said with a despairing look.

'Yeah but I didn't know where they were likely ter send 'im, did I,' Ruby replied. 'Anyway we got ter talkin' some more an' she told me about 'er boy. Apparently they'd turned 'im down fer the services 'cos of 'is flat feet, an' Mrs Mills was well pleased. She told me about 'ow well 'e was doin' at this engineerin' factory. 'E's a draughtsman, like I said. Anyway we walked back tergevver an' she invited me in fer a cuppa an' showed me this picture of 'er Richard. 'E looks a nice lad.'

'Are yer gonna invite 'im as well?' Jim asked.

'Well of course.'

'Ruby, you ain't gettin' no ideas are yer?'

'About what?'

'About our Kay.'

'She could do a lot worse,' Ruby replied indignantly. 'It worried the life out o' me when she got in tow wiv that barrer boy.'

'There was nuffink in it,' Jim told her.

'Anyway I'm gonna invite Pam an' 'er boy, an' I'm gonna let 'er know that Kay 'asn't got a boyfriend at the moment,' Ruby said firmly.

Kay was still imagining how the whole conversation would have gone when the bus drove into Tower Bridge Road and pulled to a stop. The Chinese girl had finished reading the magazine and was idly staring out of the window. Kay thought about the evening ahead. The picture was a Western and Richard had told her how much he liked cowboy films. They would sit in the back row together and after a while he would shyly put his arm around her, not taking his eyes from the screen for a second. There would be no encouragement for her to snuggle up to him and exchange clandestine kisses in the darkness, not that she wanted to, but he would be sure to infuriate people sitting in the immediate vicinity by opening a bag of sweets at the wrong moment. Richard was inclined to sweat when he had his arm around her, and he had to remove it occasionally to polish his tortoiseshell glasses on an ironed and folded handkerchief, which he removed from his top pocket and flapped open with determination.

God, it was no good. She would have to cry off this evening. But what could she say, apart from telling him she was finished with him? Pretending she was under the weather with a cold wouldn't serve any useful purpose. Richard would call back with a bunch of grapes and expect to sit with her, urging her to keep well wrapped up like an old maid.

The number 1 bus turned into Grange Road, and as it slowed down at the second stop Kay slid out of her seat behind the Chinese girl who was getting off. She stepped down on to the pavement and set off towards Tanners Alley, her fellow traveller still ahead of her. The girl wore a long black coat and high heels that complimented her shapely legs. She walked with a confident sway of her body and Kay could see that she was about the same height as herself. The girl suddenly turned to look for traffic and then hurried nimbly across the road to disappear into Cater Street. She was obviously going to the Chinese laundry, Kay thought.

As she turned into Tanners Alley Kay had the answer. After tea she would suddenly develop a bad migraine and be forced to lie down in her room. It was the only way, for the time being. Richard would get over it. His mind was more likely focused on compensating bypass valves anyway, she thought uncharitably.

Chapter Three

Jim Neal let himself into the house and kicked off his shoes in the passage. His slippers were there as always, placed by the foot of the stairs, and as he slid his feet into them Ruby called out from the scullery.

'Is that you, Jim?'

'No, it's the bailiffs,' he replied with a smile.

Ruby turned her head sideways for his kiss as he walked up to the stove. 'Wash yer 'ands, I'm just about ter serve up,' she told him. 'I've made a steak pie fer tea.'

Jim grabbed a cake of soap from the metal holder standing on the draining-board and went through the ritual. The last thing he always did before leaving work was to clean the grease and grime from his hands but he had long since realised it wasn't worth the hassle of mentioning it. Come to think of it, it wasn't worth Ruby mentioning what was for tea. It was Friday, and for as long as he could remember Friday was the night for steak pie.

'Did yer get yer 'olidays sorted out?' Ruby asked as she reached into the oven.

Jim grabbed the small towel from the back of a chair. 'I went in the office about it an' I've gotta pop in again termorrer,' he told her. 'They're gonna let me know if they can fix up the first two weeks in August.'

Ruby placed the hot pie dish down on the oven top and put her hands on her hips in a show of petulance. 'I shouldn't 'ave thought there'd be any problem,' she said quickly. 'After all, yer've been there fer years.'

Jim shrugged his shoulders. 'Trouble is there's only four of us on maintenance,' he replied, 'an' they've gotta take school 'olidays into account. Joe an' Benny 'ave both got children at school.'

'An' I s'pose they both want your weeks,' Ruby said puffing.

'I dunno,' Jim sighed. 'Anyway I'll sort it out termorrer.'

'Go in an' sit down,' Ruby told him. 'It looks like Paul's gonna be late again. I'll 'ave ter put 'is meal in the oven.'

Jim walked into the parlour and found Kay already seated at the table, gently massaging her temples with the tips of her fingers. 'Are you all right, luv?' he asked.

Kay looked up at him, her pale blue eyes narrowed. 'I got a muzzy 'ead,' she replied.

'Is Richard comin' round ternight?' he asked.

She nodded. 'We were gonna go ter the flicks, but I don't fink I can face it, Dad,' she sighed.

Jim smiled in sympathy. Richard Mills irritated him. The man seemed to have a holier-than-thou attitude, and Jim was well aware that Kay was unimpressed with her young suitor. He could see it and so could Paul, but Ruby appeared to be doing everything to encourage the courtship, such as it was. 'Send 'im on 'is way ternight,' he told her with a smile.

Any chance to probe a little further was lost as Ruby

came into the room carrying three plates of food on a large tray. 'Now get on with it before it gets cold,' she ordered.

Jim ate in silence, his mind dwelling on the afternoon that had just passed. When he had called into Angela Stapleton's office she invited him to sit down and make himself comfortable while she thumbed through the holiday book.

'I know it's a bind, Jim,' she had said with a friendly smile, 'but as you know it's a company policy to give priority to employees with children of school age.'

'Yeah I know,' he said, returning her smile.

'Look, leave this to me. I'm sure we can accommodate you,' she went on. 'Are you planning on anywhere nice?'

'I'm tryin' ter get Ruby interested in goin' down ter Devon fer a week,' he replied. 'It'll certainly make a change from that caravan in Bognor. We've bin goin' there fer the past three years.'

'Devon sounds very nice,' she said, leaning forward on the desk. 'Will it be just the two of you?'

Jim nodded. 'My daughter Kay goes on those Government farmin' 'olidays every year, an' now that Paul's demobbed 'e'll be goin' off somewhere fer a week wiv a few friends.'

'So it could be a second honeymoon for you two then,' Angela said with a wicked smile.

'Well, it'll certainly be a change o' routine,' he replied with a cynical edge to his voice.

'Yes I know the feeling,' Angela remarked, studying her long painted fingernails. 'Unfortunately we never had children, and Laurie spends most of our holidays bird-watching.

This year it's Eastbourne, and Laurie's already reading up on sea birds. I'm sure one of these days he's going to walk over the edge of a cliff while he's looking through those bloody binoculars of his.'

Jim laughed aloud. 'An' 'ow do you spend your time?'

'I knit, read, and sometimes I walk round the shops,' she explained, turning down the corner of her mouth. 'I shouldn't be telling you this, Jim, but I usually end up feeling glad when the holiday's over. Do you ever feel like that?'

Jim saw the pained look in her large dark eyes and he shook his head. 'I don't exactly wish the holiday over, but sometimes I do get a bit peeved if it's rainin' or chilly an' we end up spendin' the day traipsin' round shops.'

'I could think of plenty of better things to do on a rainy day,' Angela said with a meaningful look as she leaned back in her chair and smiled at him. 'The rain and cold weather don't seem to worry Laurie though, as long as he's got those stupid binoculars strapped round his neck.'

Jim could see the outline of her large firm breasts beneath her white frilly blouse and he looked up quickly into her face. She was a very attractive woman, he thought. She had a full figure, large expressive lips and tiny ears beneath thick reddish hair that she piled on the top of her head. Her two-piece mustard-coloured suit looked expensive, as did the gold bangle hanging loosely on her right wrist.

The telephone shrilled and Angela paused with her hand on the mouthpiece. 'Can you call in tomorrow, Jim?' she asked him. 'About the same time?'

He got up quickly and nodded. 'Thanks, Angela,' he said as he turned to go.

The company secretary flashed him a wide smile and he left her office feeling strangely elated.

Ruby pushed her plate away and glanced across the table at her daughter. 'Yer've not finished yer meal,' she remarked.

Kay was playing her role masterfully. 'I've 'ad a bad 'eadache all day an' it's makin' me feel sick,' she replied.

'Take a couple o' my tablets,' Ruby urged her. 'They're very good.'

'It's not a time o' month 'eadache, Mum,' Kay told her quickly. 'I've got a flashin' in front o' me eyes.'

'Sounds like migraine,' Jim interjected. 'You should go up an' lie down wiv the curtains drawn.'

'What about Richard?' Ruby reminded her.

'When 'e calls just tell 'im I can't make it ternight,' Kay said, getting up from the table.

As soon as their daughter left the room Ruby turned to Jim. 'I bumped inter Mrs Mills this mornin',' she said with a frown, 'an' she told me she 'adn't seen anyfing of Kay fer a few days. I thought Richard took 'er back fer a cuppa an' a chat wiv 'is muvver before bringin' 'er 'ome.'

'P'raps she didn't wanna go back there,' Jim suggested irritably.

'I dunno what's got inter that gel,' Ruby said sighing loudly. 'Richard's a nice lad, an' 'e's a good catch. 'E's far better than that Joey Westlake. 'E's a bad 'un. I know fer a fact 'e's bin in trouble wiv the police.'

'It was only fer fly-pitchin' at London Bridge Station,' Jim replied quickly. 'That's nuffing terrible.'

''E was too flash,' Ruby argued. 'I didn't like the look of 'im right from the start.'

At that moment the front door sounded and Paul walked into the parlour. He was a broad-shouldered young man of average height with short fair hair that tended to curl when it was wet.

'I can smell meat pie,' he said sniffing loudly.

'Well yer better clean up before it's all baked up,' Ruby told him. 'Just once in a while I'd like us all ter sit down fer a meal at the same time.'

'Sorry, Ma. We 'ad a bit o' trouble wiv the cable,' he explained.

'Don't call me Ma,' Ruby said, hiding a smile. 'Yer make me sound like an ole woman.'

'OK, Ma,' he replied with a quick glance at his father. 'At least yer the best pie maker in Bermondsey. Possibly in London.'

'Don't flannel me,' she said, nudging him on the arm as she went out to the scullery.

'Where's Kay?' Paul asked his father.

'She's gone ter lie down,' Jim told him. 'She's got a bad 'eadache.'

Paul sauntered up the stairs and tapped softly on the door of Kay's back bedroom. 'Are yer decent?' he called out.

'Yeah, come in,' Kay answered.

''Ow's the migraine?' he asked with a knowing smile as he sat down on the edge of the bed.

'It's not too bad,' she told him straight-faced.

'Don't you worry, I'll tell Dicky boy that yer indisposed.'

Kay put her hands behind her head and looked up at him, and seeing the mischievous look on his boyish face she shook her head. 'Let Mum tell 'im,' she replied.

'I dunno why yer don't give 'im the elbow,' Paul went on. ''E's enough ter give anyone the 'orrers.'

Kay forced a smile. 'Don't worry,' she said. 'I'm just bidin' me time.'

Paul playfully patted her arm. 'Well, I'd better get downstairs fer me tea,' he told her.

As he made himself comfortable at the table Ruby came into the room with a loaded plate. 'Ain't yer gonna wash yer 'ands first?' she asked him.

Paul grinned as he picked up the knife and fork. 'I'm not eatin' wiv me bare 'ands, Muvver,' he declared.

'What about 'andlin' the bread?'

'I can pick it up wiv me fork.'

Jim spotted Ruby's look of disgust and he gave his son a quick grin. Paul was the only member of the family who seemed to get away with it. Maybe it was because he was too placid to get roused over trifles and Ruby knew only too well that she was wasting her time trying to change him. He always had a humorous answer to her criticisms.

Ruby gathered the dirty crockery together and dabbed at the spot of gravy Paul had splashed on the blue chintz tablecloth.

'Yer should 'ave left that, Ma, I was gonna lick it up afterwards,' he said with a disappointed look.

'Yeah, I believe you would at that,' Ruby retorted as she strode out of the parlour.

Jim reluctantly got out of his armchair and went into the scullery to go through another household ritual. 'I'll dry. Where's the teacloth?' he asked.

'You sit down an' relax,' Ruby told him. 'It won't take me long.'

Jim nodded and went back to his favourite chair. Ruby never let him help with the washing up, but if he hadn't offered she would have certainly made him aware of the fact.

Paul finished his meal and proceeded to wipe his plate with a piece of bread stuck on the end of his fork. Finally satisfied that it was all gone he leaned back in his chair. 'Are yer gonna go ter the reunion next week, Dad?' he asked. 'It is next week, ain't it?'

Jim nodded. 'I got the invite yesterday,' he replied.

'Yeah, I just saw it on the mantelshelf,' Paul told him. 'I could see the emblem on the envelope. I thought fer a minute they was callin' me back.'

'I don't fink the air force is short o' clerks,' Jim said smiling. 'Now if they wanted me back I could understand it. They're always in need o' sergeant gunners, especially tail gunners.'

Paul went over to sit facing his father. 'D'yer fink it's gonna come to it?' he asked.

'Anuvver war, yer mean?' Jim queried. 'Nah. Anuvver war would be the end of everyfing.'

'I dunno so much,' Paul replied. 'It only takes one lunatic ter press the button.'

'It ain't as simple as that,' Jim told him. 'There's safeguards built inter the Russian system as well as ours. And no sane leader is gonna start a war.'

'It makes yer wonder though,' Paul went on. 'Look at all that stuff the Government send out about buildin' atomic shelters. Did yer see that one the ovver day about wrappin' silver paper round yerself an' sittin' under the stairs in the event of an atomic attack? Christ, it's bloody stupid. I fink

I'd find out where the bomb was gonna land an' go an' wait there. I'd sooner stand in the street an' get fried like a crisp. It'd be all over in the blink of an eye anyway.'

'Shut up, Paul, yer givin' me the creeps,' Jim said frowning.

Ruby looked in the room. 'I'm just poppin' along ter see Bel fer a few minutes,' she announced. 'If I'm not back by the time Richard arrives tell 'im Kay's very sorry but she's got a terrible migraine. And don't let 'im go up ter see 'er. I've just looked in an' she's sleepin'. An' besides, I 'aven't changed that bedspread yet.'

Jim nodded, and when the front door slammed shut he closed his eyes and sighed deeply. Ruby was a good wife who put her family's welfare before her own, and there were certainly many men who wished they were in his shoes, but he could not escape the fact that her fastidiousness and obsessive preoccupation with seeing that the house ran like clockwork were beginning to get under his skin. Even their love life had become like a ritual, not that they indulged all that often lately. Most wives would have relied on the timeworn excuse of a headache, but with Ruby it was more dramatic. Her back was aching after standing at the copper for most of the day, or she was too emotionally drained after a bad day at the surgery. Was it his fault? Was he losing his appeal? Was she bored with him after all these years they had spent together? Maybe it was her time of life.

The rat-tat on the front door made him jump and Paul pulled a face as he bounced out of his chair. 'That'll be Dicky Drippin',' he said.

'Go easy on 'im,' Jim called out.

Paul opened the front door and found the bespectacled

youth standing on the step. 'Kay can't come out ternight, pal, she's got a terrible migraine,' he said, relishing his task. 'As a matter o' fact she's gone ter bed.'

Richard was clearly disappointed. 'Didn't she say anything?' he asked quickly.

'About what?' Paul replied caustically.

'About when she wants to see me.'

'Nah she just groaned and moaned an' then said she was off ter bed.'

'Will you give her a message?' Richard asked, fishing in his coat pocket and producing a fountain pen. 'Have you a piece of paper I could use?'

'I got a fag packet,' Paul said mockingly.

'I want to write her a note,' the young suitor replied.

'All right, wait there,' Paul said puffing. After a minute or two he came back to the front door with a used envelope. 'That's all I could find. Write on the back.'

Richard Mills looked disdainfully at the envelope before scribbling a short message. 'Will you see that she gets that, please,' he said officiously as he folded the envelope in half and handed it back.

'Will do, pal,' Paul replied. 'Be seein' yer.'

Richard hesitated for a moment. 'Goodbye then.'

'Piss off,' Paul mumbled under his breath as he closed the front door.

Chapter Four

The folk living in Grange Road and the neighbouring backstreets were lucky that they had two very good markets within short walking distance. Tower Bridge Road market was on one side, where everything could be bought from pins and needles and patent cough medicine to lengths of cloth and pots and pans, as well as fresh fruit and fish brought daily from the nearby wholesale markets of Billingsgate and the Borough. Apart from the stalls, Tower Bridge Road market boasted various locally renowned food shops that sold pie and mash, fish and chips, freshly cooked jam doughnuts and delicious apple pies, as well as clothes shops, shoe shops and the inevitable pawnbroker's. In the opposite direction, and about the same distance away, was the market which was known by everyone as 'the Blue'. It took its name from the Blue Anchor pub which faced the long line of stalls, and like the other local market the Blue sold just about everything you could think of, and a few other things besides. The Blue was where Kay had decided to go on Saturday morning to get a birthday card for her brother Paul. He would be twenty-one the following day and she wanted to buy him a special card. There was a stall at the end of the market which was noted for having unusual ones and Kay was happy to stand and browse through the large selection on that warm and sunny day.

'Sort 'em out, gels,' the stall owner said in a loud voice. 'Finest choice in London. Buy four an' get one free.'

Kay found two which she thought were appropriate for Paul; and while she was debating over which one to buy she saw the Chinese girl. She was browsing through the pile of cards with a concentrated look on her pale face.

'They're all tenpence on that pile,' the elderly stall owner said as Kay caught his eye.

She handed him a card along with the money and he slipped it into a paper bag with an envelope which he took from a cardboard box by his side.

'There we are, sweet'eart. Now what about you, luvvy. Found anyfing suitable?'

The Chinese girl flushed slightly as she smiled at him and Kay noticed her perfect white teeth. The man pointed to the pile nearest to her. 'Seven an' a tanner the lot,' he said, and seeing the two red patches growing on her cheeks he laughed. 'Only kiddin' yer, darlin'. Those are elevenpence each.'

The girl handed him the card in her hand and fished into her purse for the money. She counted out some coins then bit on her lip in consternation as she took out a pound note. 'I'm sorry but I've only got ten pennies,' she said apologetically as she handed him the note.

The stall owner looked a little irritated as he slipped his hand into the canvas money pouch tied to his front and Kay immediately took a coin from her purse. 'There's a penny,' she said.

The Chinese girl smiled gratefully as she handed over the coins. 'You're very kind,' she said in a quiet voice.

'It's only a penny,' Kay said smiling back.

They walked away from the stall together and the girl touched Kay's arm with the tips of her fingers. 'When I next see you in the market I'll repay you the penny,' she told her.

'It's all right,' Kay reassured her. 'A penny's nuffing these days.'

'But it was a kind gesture to a stranger,' the girl said smiling.

'We are neighbours, at least I fink we are,' Kay replied. 'I live in Tanners Alley.'

'I live in Cater Street,' the girl told her.

'I saw you on the bus yesterday evenin',' Kay went on. 'I was sittin' just be'ind yer.'

The Oriental girl looked surprised. 'I work in Aldwych,' she said.

'That's funny, so do I,' Kay replied.

'A coincidence, yes,' the girl said smiling.

'Yeah I s'pose it is,' Kay said grinning back. 'I work at the Government typin' pool.'

'I work for the Government too,' the girl told her. 'I'm employed as a translator at the Ministry of Information.'

They passed by the line of stalls and Kay pointed to a café. 'I usually go in there fer a coffee when I'm shoppin'. Would yer like to 'ave one?'

'If you let me pay.'

'OK,' Kay said smiling.

They took their milky coffees to a small marble-topped table, and when they were seated the Oriental girl held out a tiny hand. 'I'm called Mei Li, Mei Li Ching. I'm very pleased to make your acquaintance.'

'I'm Kay Neal, an' likewise.'

Mei Li sipped her coffee and put the cup down in the saucer, looking amused as Kay practised her name. 'Mei Ching was my mother's name, though I never knew her. She died when I was born. My middle name Li is after my guardian, Li Fong.'

'Li Fong,' Kay said carefully. 'Excuse me fer askin', but is Li Fong the man at the Chinese laundry in Cater Street?'

Mei shook her head. 'No, that's my guardian's brother Ho Chang,' she explained. 'He's been in England for many years. He was once a seaman and he decided to stay here after he married. He lived in Chinatown until last year, but circumstances forced him to move away from the area and he chose Bermondsey.'

'Chinatown's by the Millwall docks isn't it?' Kay queried, and Mei Li nodded. 'My dad took me over there when I was little. I remember the name Pennyfields.'

'Pennyfields is near the street where Ho Chang had his laundry,' Mei told her.

Kay finished her coffee and reached into her handbag to look at the card she had bought. 'I 'ope Paul likes this,' she remarked. 'Paul's my bruvver an' 'e's twenty-one termorrer.'

Mei Li's eyes widened and she delved into her own handbag. 'I'm twenty-one tomorrow too. Do you like my card?'

Kay looked confused. 'You bought yer own card?' she said frowning.

Mei laughed. 'Yes. My guardian speaks English fairly well but doesn't read it. I had to buy a card with words he would like and then he and his brother and his family will all sign the card to me.'

Kay laughed aloud. 'Well, at least that way yer'll be certain of gettin' a card.'

'Yes I will, though in China very little is made of a twenty-first birthday, especially when it's a girl,' Mei Li told her. 'Even the boys are considered mature adults at a much younger age.'

''Ave yer bin in England very long?' Kay asked her.

Mei Li drained her coffee and stared down into the dregs for a moment or two. 'Two years,' she replied.

'An' you were born in China?'

She nodded. 'In a north-eastern region called Shantung.'

'I'm sorry, am I bein' too nosy?' Kay asked self-consciously.

'Nosy?'

'Askin' too many questions.'

Mei smiled disarmingly. 'No of course not. We have a saying: "To know just a name is like turning a blank page".'

'Let me get us some more coffee,' Kay offered.

'You have the time?' Mei Li asked.

'It's Saturday. Terday I 'ave all the time in the world.'

With their coffee cups replenished Kay leaned forward on the table with her hands clasped together. 'You asked me about my time, what about yours?'

'I have a room upstairs in the house next to the laundry,' Mei Li told her. 'On Saturdays and Sundays I spend a lot of time there reading, working on a tapestry and just resting. I share the Chang family's table but there are no, umm . . .' she frowned with concentration as she searched for the word. 'Constrictions on my leisure time. I'm very happy to talk.'

Kay gave her a warm smile. The young woman made her feel at ease, and she felt almost as if she had known her for a long time already. 'Tell me a bit about when you were a child,' she urged her. ' 'Ow did yer learn ter speak English so well?'

'I was brought up in an Anglican mission,' Mei replied. 'Li Fong told me I was born on the edge of a rice field and my mother had died giving birth to me. I was premature and not expected to live out the day but Li took me several miles to the mission nestling beneath his coat. He was a trader you see, and he made regular trips around the area. The doctor there managed to save my life and when Li Fong called the next time he agreed to become my guardian, my godfather, as you might say here. He donated some money each time he called to the mission. The money helped them. They were good Christian people and struggling desperately to survive.

'When I was eight years old the Japanese soldiers came down from Manchuria and overran much of Shantung province. We heard many terrible stories about their brutality and the people at the mission decided to join the many thousands who were fleeing westwards. I was at school there learning English and although I was only eight I can still remember that trek clearly. We climbed up through the mountain passes, forded rivers and crossed barren plains. Maybe you learned about the Long Trek at your school.

It wasn't only refugees. Whole industries were dismantled and transported on that long journey. Li Fong came too. By that time he had built up a thriving business trading with American and English companies.'

'An' that was 'ow 'e learnt ter speak English,' Kay prompted.

Mei Li smiled and took a sip of coffee. 'We finally arrived in Chungking and the mission was set up there. It was then that Li left for nearly two years on a long trip that took him through Burma and Malaya and on to Singapore, where he had business contacts. I was ten years old when he returned and by that time the Japanese were bombing Chungking. I finally said goodbye to the good people at the mission and went with him on the long journey to Singapore, where he put me into a very good school so that I could continue with my English language studies.'

'All that travellin' fer a young child,' Kay marvelled.

Mei smiled. 'The travelling was only just beginning. When the Japanese were about to invade Singapore my guardian managed to get us both passage to San Francisco along with an American company that was leaving the island.'

'So you grew up in San Francisco,' Kay said.

'Yes, and when I was eighteen I got a job as a translator with the United Nations in New York. It meant another long journey across America, but I was now a woman and quite capable of travelling alone. Li Fong was not happy for me to make the journey, but very proud that I had found such a good post. I stayed with a Chinese family for one year and then the chance to work in England came up. Li Fong was pleased. If I could manage to get him a visitor's permit he would be able to see his brother who he had not met up with for over twenty years. Anyway I did manage the permit, and we arrived in Liverpool in the summer of nineteen forty-eight.'

'An' yer lived in Chinatown?' Kay said, draining her cup.

'Li Fong and I moved into Cater Street a few weeks ago to be with his brother Ho Chang,' Mei told her, 'but that's another story which would take too long to tell now. Already I've taken up all of your time.'

'No, no,' Kay said firmly. 'I've bin fascinated listenin'. So much travel fer someone so young.'

'I'm twenty-one tomorrow,' Mei said laughing aloud.

They made ready to leave the café, and once out in the bright sunlight Kay held out her hand. 'I'm very glad to 'ave met yer, an' fank yer fer tellin' me all about yerself.'

'I've enjoyed it too,' Mei Li said, taking Kay's hand in hers.

'Are yer walkin' back ter Cater Street?' Kay asked.

Mei nodded. 'Li Fong will be wanting the card to sign.'

'Well then, let's walk back tergevver,' Kay suggested.

'Yes, let's.'

They left the noise and crowds of the bustling market behind them and strolled along the curving thoroughfare towards Grange Road, two young women from opposite sides of the world and different cultures chatting away like sisters: Mei Li dark-haired and petite, Kay fair and shapely.

'Look, I have the opportunity to get some complimentary tickets to an exhibition organised by the Chinese Cultural

Society,' Mei explained. 'It's to be held at the National Gallery in Trafalgar Square next weekend. Would you like a ticket? I could let you have two if you'd care to take a friend.'

'Yes, I'd like that very much,' Kay replied. Then she looked a little puzzled. 'Is it paintin's an' . . .'

Mei Li smiled. 'The idea of the exhibition is just to give people an idea through paintings and pieces of artwork, of the Oriental culture and history of China, ancient and modern. There'll be a Chinese theatre with very old plays and miming, and music of course. It should be very interesting. I should tell you also that I'm to be one of the guides, explaining the scenes painted on ancient pottery.'

'After what yer've told me about yerself I'd love ter come,' Kay said smiling.

'Would you like two tickets?'

Kay paused for a moment before answering. The thought of Richard Mills accompanying her made the young woman shudder, and then as she was about to ask for just one ticket Mei Li made a suggestion. 'Perhaps your brother would like to come along too? I'll be very busy and there'll be little time for us to talk. He'll be company for you. Shall I get you two tickets?'

'Yes, that'll be lovely, Mei. Fanks very much.'

They parted on the corner of Cater Street, shaking hands once again, and Kay walked into Tanners Alley smiling to herself as she imagined Paul's reaction when she told him what she had planned for him next week.

Chapter Five

Paul stood in the saloon bar of the Swan public house on Sunday evening chatting with Joey Westlake, who looked a little sorry for himself.

'Well, if yer wanna put fings right between yer you gotta do it yerself,' Paul was going on, 'yer can't expect me ter do it for yer.'

'Yeah, I know,' the barrow boy replied as he picked up his pint of beer. 'I really like 'er, Paul, yer know I do, an' it was all so stupid. Now she's got 'erself in tow wiv that dopey-lookin' git Mills. What a plum.'

Paul grinned. 'Kay said she might look in later, after the pictures.'

'Not wiv 'im,' Joey groaned as he subconsciously pinched the knot of his striped tie. 'Fer two pins I'd deck 'im.'

'That'd do a lot o' good wouldn't it,' Paul said quickly. ''E wears glasses an' 'e can't 'old 'is 'ands up. Yer'd be takin' a right liberty. Besides, if yer really wanna get back wiv our Kay yer gotta start actin' a bit less flash.'

'Flash? Who's flash? I ain't flash.'

Paul grinned as he looked the stocky barrow boy up and down. 'Yer dress smart, yer look smart, but you act flash,' he told him. 'There's a difference, Joey.'

'What, just 'cos I said I'd like ter deck the geezer?'

'Exactly.'

'I wouldn't do anyfing like that in front o' Kay, now would I?'

'No, but yer'd do it outside in the karsey.'

'Course I wouldn't,' Joey said, looking hurt. 'It's just a figure o' speech.'

'What yer gotta remember is, don't go sayin' yer gonna thump everyone who upsets yer,' Paul urged him.

Joey took a large gulp from his glass and then ran his hand through his thick dark hair. 'I can't do right fer doin' wrong, can I?' he groaned.

'All yer gotta do is act all calm an' collected when Kay an' Richard show up,' Paul told him. 'Our Kay's not too 'appy, ter tell yer the trufe. Play yer cards right an' you could be back in the frame, that's if yer don't . . .'

'Act flash,' Joey finished for him. 'Leave it ter me, Paul, I'll be a real cool geezer.'

Paul drained his glass and put a ten-shilling note down on the counter. 'Same again, Joey?'

'Yeah, cheers, pal.'

Paul leaned on the counter idly watching as the barman refilled the glasses. ''Ere, what yer fink, Joey,' he said with a grin. 'Our Kay wants me ter go wiv 'er ter this Chinese exhibition next Saturday. It's over the Art Gallery.'

'A Chinky exhibition? Bloody 'ell, that'll be a bundle o' laughs,' Joey remarked with a sideways glance. 'What'd yer tell 'er?'

'I said yeah, why not,' Paul replied. 'I could do wiv gettin' a bit o' culture, an' so could you.'

'I got enough culture, fank you very much,' Joey growled.

Paul slid a full glass along the counter to him and sighed. 'Well, well. I'm twenty-one terday an' I got the key o' the door,' he said smiling broadly.

'I remember my twenty-first very well,' the barrow boy replied.

'An' so yer should. It was only six months ago,' Paul said grinning.

Joey pulled on his tie again. 'This tie don't look flash, does it?' he asked suddenly.

'Nah, course it don't.'

'What about me shirt? It goes wiv the suit don't it?'

'What's wiv yer ternight?' Paul said quickly. 'Yer a bundle o' nerves.'

'I wanna create a good impression when Kay turns up,' Joey replied.

'If she turns up,' Paul corrected him. 'Richard ain't one fer drinkin'. 'Alf a shandy's about 'is limit.'

The two friends stood at the counter chatting for a while, and when the bar started to fill up they moved along to the end farthest from the door. At nine o'clock a broad-shouldered young man ambled in and looked over. He came towards them grinning, with a big gap where his two front teeth should have been. ''Appy birfday, Paul. Wotcher, Joey,' he accosted them in a deep voice. 'What'll it be?'

Paul waved his hand. 'I'm in the chair, Butch. It's my shout.'

'Fanks, pal. I'll 'ave the usual,' Butch said, rolling his shoulders and pulling on the cuffs of his white shirt. 'What'd yer get fer yer birfday then?'

'Me mum an' dad bought me an electric shaver an' Kay got me a shirt,' Paul told him.

'All I got was a card when it was my twenty-first,' Joey complained.

'What yer talkin' about?' Butch said quickly. 'Me an' Paul an' Sonny Rowland stood yer drinks all night. We wouldn't let yer put yer 'and in yer pocket. You come out this gaff pissed out o' yer brains an' we 'ad ter carry yer 'ome.'

'Oh no yer didn't,' Joey replied firmly. 'I distinctly remember walkin' 'ome.'

'Yeah, wiv me an' Paul 'oldin' yer up.'

'Anyway, apart from you boys I didn't get any presents.'

'That's 'cos nobody loves yer, 'cept us,' Butch remarked, breaking into a loud guffaw.

'I know, it's 'cos I'm flash,' Joey replied.

'You flash?' Paul cut in, trying to keep a straight face. 'You ain't flash. 'E's not, is 'e, Butch?'

'Well, only a little bit,' the big man said.

Joey decided it was time to divert attention away from himself. 'Bin workin' terday, Butch?'

'Yeah, I done West Street Buildin's this mornin',' Butch told him. 'I tell yer what, it ain't that easy winder cleanin'. I'd sooner be on the broom. That job road sweepin' on the Council was a doddle.'

'Nah, but it wasn't you,' Paul said, giving Joey a crafty wink. 'A young lad like you shouldn't be sweepin' streets.'

'Well, it was still better than poxy winder cleanin'. 'Cept now an' then.'

'Like when it's rainin',' Joey remarked.

'Nah, when certain fings 'appen,' Butch replied mysteriously as he picked up his drink.

'Come on, pal, don't keep us in the dark,' Joey prompted.

Butch looked left and right in an exaggerated way and then leaned sideways on the counter. 'There's a tasty-lookin' sort livin' in Riverside Buildin's who performs,' he said, waiting for a reaction.

'What d'yer mean, performs?' Joey queried, taking the bait.

Butch laughed, the wide gap showing prominently between his large white teeth. 'She puts on a bit of a show.'

'Like 'ow?'

'Like strippin' off in front of yer.'

'I can't believe that,' Joey said, shaking his head dismissively.

'It's the trufe, sure as I'm standin' 'ere,' Butch asserted. 'Last week I was doin' 'er winders an' there she was, in the room stripped off ter the waist washin' in a bowl on a chair. I could see it all. She was only a few feet away. Then she turns round an' gives me a big smile as she's dryin' 'erself. So I calls frew the winder, "'Ere, luv, I'll do that for yer." She just grinned an' stuck 'er blouse on, then what yer fink?'

'I ain't got a clue,' Joey replied.

'She puts these stockin's on right there an' then in front o' me eyes, an' she clips 'em on 'er suspender belt, like they do, an' I tell yer, if I'd 'ave bin up a ladder instead o' standin' on 'er balcony I'd 'ave fell off fer sure. What a sort. She looked like a cross between Betty Grable an' Lana Turner.'

''Ave they got any vacancies fer winder cleaners on your firm, Butch?' Joey said grinning.

The pub pianist started to plonk away on the keys and the bar had become packed as the friends stood chatting together. Suddenly Paul nudged Joey. ''Old up, there they are,' he whispered.

Joey looked over and saw Kay coming towards them followed by a young man in grey flannels and a navy blue blazer, sporting a blue-spotted bow tie at the neck of his white shirt. 'Will yer take a look at that prat,' he hissed.

Kay looked a little uneasy as she came up to them. 'I thought we'd find yer 'ere,' she said, nodding to Butch and giving Joey a quick look.

'Can I get you two a drink?' Joey said smiling blandly. 'Er, port an' lemon, Kay? Shandy, Richard?'

'Yes please,' Kay said, nodding.

Richard slipped his hands into his trouser pockets and looked short-sightedly at the group. 'Just a half, please.'

Joey put Paul between him and Richard as he looked towards the barman. ''Ave yer clocked that poxy bow tie,' he growled out the corner of his mouth to Paul. ''E only wants a banjo. 'E'd go down a treat on Southend Pier.'

'Take it easy,' Paul muttered. 'All calm an' collected, remember?'

'Bin ter the pictures?' Butch asked Kay.

'Yes. Quite a good film,' Richard answered for her. '*Johnny Eager*. It was one of those smouldering gangster films.'

'A lotta gunsmoke yer mean?' Paul said sarcastically.

Kay gave him a hard look but the sarcasm was lost

on Richard. He shook his head. 'No, more the moody style of gangster. It was a very good film as a matter of fact.'

Kay had yawned all the way through it and she gave her brother a tired smile. 'Yeah, it was OK,' she sighed.

Joey handed the drinks around, saving Kay's till last. He moved a little closer to her. 'There we are, Kay. 'Ow are yer?' he asked.

'Fine,' she said quickly.

Richard was looking anxiously from Kay to the young barrow boy and Paul moved in front of them. 'By the way, we're goin' on ter the Gregorian later. There's a band there on Saturdays. Fancy comin'?' he asked him, knowing the answer.

'No I don't think so,' Richard said, trying to see what was going on over Paul's shoulder.

'It'll be a good night. We're celebratin' me birfday.'

'No I'd sooner not.'

'What about Kay?'

'She's still got the remains of that migraine I'm afraid,' Richard informed him. 'We're going back to my place for a bite of supper and then I think she should get an early night.'

Joey leant close to Kay. 'Look, I'm very sorry about that night,' he said sincerely. 'It wasn't what yer thought.'

'I know what I saw,' Kay told him sharply. 'I saw yer kiss 'er.'

'It was just a peck,' Joey pleaded. 'She'd just got the new job an' she was all excited. It was over between us before me an' you started goin' out. Gospel, Kay.'

Richard had squeezed past Paul and he took Kay's arm.

'Mother'll be expecting us, Kay. We should make a move soon,' he said, giving Joey a quick, meaningful look.

'Yeah, OK. I'll just go an' powder me nose,' she told him.

'It looks fine to me,' Richard remarked.

Paul and Joey exchanged glances of despair as Kay walked through the bar towards the toilet.

'We're goin' on the piss, cocker. Comin'?' Butch asked, putting a large arm round Richard's shoulders.

The young man looked uncomfortable. 'No. I've told Paul we won't be going.'

''Ere, I was tellin' the fellers about this woman in the buildin's,' Butch said, still with his arm around Richard's thin shoulders.

Joey could have kissed the big man as he ambled casually along the bar holding on to Richard and moving out of their view, and when Kay came back through the door he was waiting. 'Look, Kay, I want yer ter come back,' he told her. 'I promise yer'll never 'ave reason ter regret it. I want yer ter be my gel. I can't stand ter see yer wiv that jumped-up little ponce.'

'Richard's a decent feller,' Kay said protectively.

''E don't know 'ow ter treat a gel. 'E dunno what it's all about.'

'Oh, an' I s'pose you do.'

'Yeah I do, Kay.'

'Look, I gotta go.'

'Wait just a minute. Give me anuvver chance, kid.'

'Richard's lookin' over this way. I gotta go.'

Joey touched her arm. 'Fink about it, Kay. Give 'im the elbow.'

The pianist was into his stride now as Kay and Richard said their farewells, and it seemed strangely quiet as they stepped out into the balmy night and walked along the deserted Grange Road. They hadn't spoken for a few minutes and Kay could see that Richard was looking a little peeved.

'Yer didn't mind takin' me in there ternight, did yer?' she asked.

'I'd have preferred not to,' he replied. 'It's not the pub, it's their clientele. That Butch Wheeler is very crude and I didn't want you to have to face Joey Westlake again.'

''E was quite pleasant as it 'appened,' Kay retorted.

Richard turned to give her a hard look. 'I saw him talking to you at the other end of the bar.'

''E was just askin' 'ow I was,' Kay lied.

'Well, I don't want us to go in there any more,' Richard said firmly.

Kay felt a strong urge to scream aloud but she took a deep breath and quickened her pace. 'We can't 'ide from people you don't like,' she said with passion. 'My bruvver uses that pub an' it's nice ter meet up fer a drink now an' then at weekends.'

Richard matched her pace and took her arm. 'We'd better cross here if we're going to have a bite of supper with Mother,' he said.

Kay flinched from his touch. 'Richard, I don't really feel like it ternight. Just take me 'ome.'

'But Mother's got some of those crumpets for our supper. They're lovely toasted,' he told her.

'No truly. I'd sooner not.'

He puffed loudly. 'If you insist.'

They reached Tanners Alley and Richard planted a kiss on her cheek. 'I'll tell Mother you're still feeling unwell,' he said as they parted.

Kay walked away towards her house. 'You can tell 'er what yer like fer all I care,' she mumbled to herself.

Chapter Six

Ruby hurried home from the surgery on Monday afternoon and breathed a sigh of relief to see that there were none of her neighbours about. She couldn't afford to stand chatting that afternoon. She had promised to take Lizzie Roach to the Mothers' Meeting at the Methodist Hall in Tower Bridge Road at three o'clock and there were things to do in the house before then.

With the mats beaten over the clothes-line and the copper emptied, Ruby hurried up to her bedroom. Everything was in order and there were a few minutes to spare, she thought, as she combed out her short blonde hair at the dressing-table. It was good that Jim had managed to get the two weeks' holiday he had put in for, and Kay had shaken off her migraine, though she had still looked a little washed out on Sunday. Richard was a gem. Another lad wouldn't have thought to get her home early after her not feeling too well. She would do well to remember that. Joey Westlake wouldn't have been so considerate. Never mind, she was well rid of him. Anyway, she thought, to the job in hand. Better go now and knock for Lizzie. The mission was only a few minutes' walk but the old lady had to take her time. She didn't get out much these days, and though she could be a trial at times she was really a sweet old thing. Lizzie had had a sad life too. According to Bel Allenby, she had brought up three children with little help from her beer-guzzling husband who ended up killing himself through the drink and now she hardly ever saw them. On the rare occasions when they took it on themselves to call they couldn't wait to leave, but Lizzie wouldn't have a word spoken against any of them.

It was twenty minutes to three o'clock when Ruby knocked at number 5, and after a lengthy pause the old lady opened her front door to announce that she'd changed her mind.

'But why?' Ruby asked her. 'You were so keen ter go when I spoke ter yer last night.'

'The cat's pissed in me bonnet,' Lizzie said. 'Bloody well ruined it. Bin sleepin' on it as well.'

'But 'ow could the cat get in yer wardrobe?'

'I took the bonnet out ter brush it an' left it on the bed.'

Ruby gave her an encouraging smile. 'Look, yer don't need yer bonnet,' she told her. 'I'll brush yer 'air out an' lend yer my beret. Yer'll look nice in that.'

'I gotta wear somefing on me 'ead in church, but I don't fancy that beret,' Lizzie grumbled. 'I'll look like Greta Garbo.'

'So what,' Ruby replied. 'I wish I looked like Greta Garbo.'

'I don't, not at my age,' Lizzie told her sharply. 'Bloody mutton dressed up as lamb.'

'Look, it's quarter ter three, so yer better make yer mind up,' Ruby sighed in exasperation.

Lizzie stroked her chin. 'I'd like ter go. I wonder if Bel can lend me 'er 'at.'

'Get yer coat on then an' I'll see if she's in.'

Wearing Bel's black satin hat the old lady felt quite smart as she took Ruby's arm and stepped out into Grange Road.

''As any o' the kids bin round lately?' Ruby asked her.

'Mary's s'posed ter be comin' round next week some time,' Lizzie told her, 'but I don't know about the ovver two. They're so busy wiv their own kids.'

'Ain't we all,' Ruby said under her breath.

They reached the Tower Bridge Road and crossed the busy thoroughfare to the hall. The old Methodist building was very welcoming inside; it felt cool after the walk in the bright sunlight. The walls had been freshly painted in white, which contrasted with the varnished wooden pews and the arched beams in the lofty ceiling. There was a high, panelled dais at the far end with a pulpit extending forwards at the centre, draped in a purple and gold cloth. Reverend Goodright was already in position as Ruby and Lizzie joined the congregation and took their places in the back row.

'I can't see very well from 'ere,' Lizzie said just as the minister cleared his throat. 'Can't we move down the front?'

'C'mon then, quickly,' Ruby told her.

'Whenever I look down on this filled hall on Monday afternoons I take comfort,' Goodright began.

Lizzie and Ruby slipped into their seats two rows from the front. 'I couldn't see back there,' Lizzie explained to the old lady next to her.

Goodright looked over his glasses at the mumbling before he continued. 'I take great comfort that in your busy, hurried lives you find the time to come to this house of God to give thanks.'

'I didn't 'ave much else ter do,' Lizzie told the woman next to her in a voice loud enough for the minister to hear.

Ruby pulled a face. 'Be quiet, Lizzie,' she hissed.

'And when we stop to think about it, it is all about time,' the cleric went on. 'Time to give to our neighbours, time to share our happiness and sadness with our friends, and time to do the little things, not for monetary gain, but out of love and caring.'

'She's like that,' Lizzie said in a proud voice, nudging the old lady next to her. 'Do anyfing fer 'er neighbours she would.'

'Be quiet,' Ruby growled.

'We all know the parable of the good Samaritan. He cared. He cared enough to stop at the wayside when others had passed by, and he administered love and care.'

'If it wasn't fer 'er I wouldn't be able ter get 'ere,' Lizzie went on. 'I ain't too steady on me ole plates o' meat an' I'm terrified o' crossin' that busy road.'

'Do you mind. I'm tryin' ter listen ter what's bein' said,' the woman replied irritably.

'Sorry I spoke,' Lizzie said sharply. 'I was only tryin' ter be friendly.'

Ruby wanted the ground to open and swallow her up. 'Lizzie,' she muttered. 'Everyone can 'ear yer.'

The old lady slipped her hands into the sleeves of her coat and looked up at the minister. Goodright stared at her for a few seconds and then he gripped the rail of the pulpit. 'Now I'm going to tell you a story about a man called Frederick Charrington,' he went on. 'His father owned the large East End brewery of that name.'

'That's a Charrin'ton's pub opposite, ain't it?' Lizzie remarked.

Ruby gritted her teeth and nodded her head tensely.

'One cold winter's night the young Charrington chanced to walk through a cobbled lane and he saw something which totally changed his whole life,' the minister continued. 'There, on the corner of the lane, he saw a young mother holding her baby to her, and the child was crying pitifully. She was standing outside a pub and she was calling through the door. "Please, Albert, even if you care nothing for me, at least give me some money so that I can buy some food for the child".'

'Sounds like my ole man,' Lizzie cut in, which raised one or two quiet chuckles.

With a brief, thunderous look in her direction, Goodright took a deep breath before elaborating. '"Be off with you, woman," the man told her with a cuff that sent her and the baby sprawling in the gutter.'

'I'd 'ave opened 'im if 'e'd 'ave done that ter me,' Lizzie said firmly.

Goodright pretended he hadn't heard. 'The young Charrington who had witnessed the terrible deed hurried to the woman's aid and helped her up on to her feet,' he continued in a loud voice. 'And then he chanced to look up at the pub and saw that it was called the Rising Sun, and what was more it bore his family name. He gave the poor woman money to feed the child, and from then on he began a crusade against strong drink.'

Feeling that the woman next to her had got the hump Lizzie turned her attention to the old lady sitting immediately in front of her. 'I always say a little of what yer fancy does yer good, in moderation,' she said, leaning forward.

The woman totally ignored her but Ruby shook her by the arm. 'C'mon, Lizzie, I can't sit 'ere any more, yer showin' the two of us up.'

''Ere, I bet the ole boy Charrin'ton wasn't very pleased,' Lizzie chuckled as she was hustled from her seat. 'Fancy yer own son turnin' against yer.'

Ruby held her head low as she took Lizzie's arm and escorted her along the aisle and out of the hall, knowing that everyone's eyes were battened on the two of them. 'I've never felt so embarrassed in all my life,' she berated the old lady as they stepped out into the lobby.

'I was only passin' a few remarks,' Lizzie replied indignantly. ''Ere, we ain't goin' 'ome yet are we? When the service is over they serve tea an' biscuits. Last time I came 'ere they 'ad fairy cakes. Ain't we gonna wait an' see what they got?'

Ruby struggled to keep her composure. 'No I fink we'd be better off 'avin' a stroll frew the market,' she told her with an exasperated sigh.

Myrtle and Ron Thompson lived at number 3 Tanners Alley. Myrtle was a buxom, ginger-haired woman with freckles and Ron was short, slightly built and wiry with a mop of unkempt grey hair. Only a few months ago the last of their offspring had flown the nest, much to their delight.

In sharp contrast to Ruby Neal, Myrtle didn't worry too much if the mats didn't get beaten every week or the ashtrays weren't emptied constantly, nor if the doorstep wasn't whitened every Saturday morning like the rest in Tanners Alley. Both she and Ron kept themselves personally clean and tidy, and they tried to remain on good terms with their neighbours, but the chores were indeed chores as far as Myrtle was concerned. However, she was aware that even in the most casual and slap-happy of households some things needed to be done, and done quickly.

'I'm tellin' yer now, Ron, those ole bedsprings 'arbour bugs.'

'We ain't got bugs, yer scatty mare,' he rounded on her. 'Bugs breed in that tongue-an'-groove what people 'ave round the walls an' I got rid of it all last year.'

'Yeah I know that, luv,' Myrtle replied with a smile, 'but bugs can be blown in frew the winders in summer. What's more they can walk in yer place. It only wants one. Them ole bedsprings is the sort o' place they lay their eggs.'

'So what's on yer mind?' Ron asked, fearing the worst.

'I fink we should get rid o' Danny's bed an' buy one o' them nice divans,' Myrtle told him. 'After all, Danny's married now an' 'e won't be usin' it.'

'I thought we was gonna chuck that ole bed of ours out an' use Danny's ter sleep on,' Ron said scratching his head.

'Yeah, we'll still chuck our ole bed out, but won't it be nice ter sleep on a nice new bed what don't make our backs ache?'

The look in her eye and the way she put it won him

over. 'Well, I'll leave it ter you, but yer'll find those new beds ain't cheap.'

'Don't you worry about anyfing, let me do the worryin',' Myrtle said, slipping her arm around his waist. 'I've just cleared up the tally man, an' there's some nice beds in 'is catalogue. I was lookin' at 'em only yesterday.'

Ron was finally sold on the idea and he pulled on his chin. ''Ow do we get rid o' Danny's bed? The dustmen won't take it.'

'You just get it out the front an' I'll sort the rest,' Myrtle reassured him. 'Ole Mutton-eye comes round on Tuesdays an' 'e'll be glad ter take it away fer nuffink. 'E'll make a few bob on it. 'E only lives in Cater Street so I'll put a note frew 'is front door.'

'So yer want me ter do it right away.'

'Well, 'ow the bloody 'ell is it gonna get done if yer don't do it now, yer silly git? Yer out of 'ere at six every mornin'.'

'Say no more, Muvver, I'm on me way,' Ron told her.

Myrtle made herself a cup of tea and sat down in the armchair to study the catalogue while her husband banged away upstairs. It was convenient that Ron was on early shift at the brewery that week. His coming home at two o'clock enabled her to get things moving.

As she sat poring over the glossy pictures in the thick book her neighbours Ruby and Lizzie walked into the alley.

'Now d'yer want me ter come in an' make yer a cuppa before I go?' Ruby asked.

The old lady shook her head. 'No, I'm much obliged already,' she said. 'An' I'm sorry if I upset yer at the church.'

Ruby smiled at her. 'Don't give it anuvver thought. We enjoyed the walk frew the market anyway, didn't we?'

Once in her house Ruby made a cup of tea and decided she had earned the luxury of putting her feet up for ten minutes. Meanwhile Lizzie Roach had decided that a glass of stout would do her more good after the tiring trip out and she reached down in the hearth and picked up a bottle. A few minutes in the sun wouldn't do her any harm either, she thought, but unable to carry the heavy rocker outside she took a kitchen chair instead, put a cushion on it and made herself comfortable. The sun felt nice and pleasant on her face and the beer tasted good. She closed her eyes, feeling at peace with the world, until she heard Myrtle Thompson's high-pitched voice through the open front door two houses away.

'What the bloody 'ell yer doin' up there?'

'I can't shift the bloody bolts.'

'Well, tap 'em wiv an 'ammer.'

'What the bloody 'ell d'yer fink I'm doin'?'

'Sounds like yer knockin' the poxy ceilin' in.'

'Shut up, yer silly mare.'

'Want me ter give yer an 'and?'

'No fanks.'

'Well, sod yer then.'

'Yeah, an' sod you too.'

Lizzie closed her eyes again now that it had gone quiet, but her reverie was short-lived.

'Lift it from the bottom. No, not like that, yer got me bloody fingers trapped.'

'Tilt it.'

'I am tiltin' it.'

'That's it. No, mind the ceilin'.'

'It's 'eavier than I thought.'

'That's it. Yer got it now.'

'Get out o' the way, woman.'

'I'm only tryin' to 'elp.'

'Go in the parlour out the way, yer gettin' under me feet.'

'I'm tryin' to 'elp an' shit's me fanks.'

The scraping noise grew steadily louder and Lizzie saw Ron emerge, dragging a heavy iron bedframe out to the front of the house where he let it fall.

Lizzie got up and leaned on the low wooden fence. 'They're awkward fings them,' she remarked, but the man seemed a bit deaf. 'I say they're awkward fings to 'andle.'

'Yer can say that again, gel,' Ron puffed. 'Proper game I've 'ad wi' that.'

'Gettin' rid of it then?'

'Nah, I'm playin' silly buggers,' he mumbled under his breath, then he grinned at her. 'We're gettin' a new bed.'

'That still looks a strong bed.'

'Yeah, but these type breed bugs.'

'What yer say?'

'Bugs.'

'Bugs?'

'Yeah, they lay their eggs in the wire mesh springs.'

Lizzie could feel herself starting to itch and she stared nervously at the bed. 'You ain't leavin' it there, are yer?' she said quickly.

'Only till the mornin'. Myrtle's gettin' Mutton-eye ter shift it termorrer.' With that Ron went in to put his feet up.

Lizzie returned to her chair but she couldn't settle. She frequently glanced over at the bed and began to imagine all sorts of things. An army of bugs was coming her way, just like ants, to take up residence in her house. Before long she would be overrun. Ruby would no doubt give her a hand to disinfect her bed but the bugs would be everywhere and they'd be climbing all over her again in no time and she'd never get rid of them. The only thing to do then would be to get the Council to fumigate her place, and if that happened she might as well put her head in the gas oven. The shame would be too much to bear.

The sun had disappeared behind the rooftops and still Lizzie sat staring over at the discarded iron bedsprings. It's no good, I'll have to see Ruby, she decided. I'll never be able to sleep with that thing stuck in the front. Ruby'll know what to do. She'll soon tell that Ron Thompson to shift it.

Ruby was stirring the gravy when a distraught-looking Lizzie knocked. 'Whatever's wrong?' she said quickly.

Lizzie sniffed into her handkerchief. 'I'm worried sick,' she said tearfully. 'Just sittin' there's made me feel ill.'

'What yer talkin' about?' Ruby asked frowning.

'That silly git Ron Thompson's chucked a bed out on 'is front an' it's runnin' alive.'

'Runnin' alive?'

'Yeah, wiv bugs.'

''E wouldn't!'

'Well 'e 'as.'

''Ow d'yer know it's bug-ridden?'

''Cos 'e told me.'

'Show me,' Ruby said.

The evening meal was ten minutes late that evening but Ruby had had a chat with the Thompsons and managed to clear the misunderstanding up. Hopefully Lizzie would sleep peacefully in her bed that night, she thought. What with the performance at the Methodist Hall, the old lady had had quite a good innings today.

Chapter Seven

Kay Neal had hoped to meet up with Mei Li again on Monday evening at the bus stop on Waterloo Bridge but she was disappointed. She thought that maybe Mei had caught the bus at the stop before the bridge and she scanned the faces of the other passengers as she boarded the vehicle, but there was no sign of her new-found friend. Perhaps her hours of work varied, Kay thought, or maybe she was off sick.

Each evening Kay looked out for Mei Li and by Thursday she had still not met up with her. After work that evening the young woman strolled unhurriedly through the home-going workers, taking her time in the hope that maybe Mei Li had been catching a later bus, but there was still no sign of her. It was a shame, Kay sighed. Mei had promised her two tickets for the Chinese exhibition and it now looked as if she wouldn't be able to go.

The bus trundled on and Kay sat deep in thought. She had seen nothing of Richard so far that week. Normally he would call round on Tuesday but on that morning his mother had slipped into the surgery and reported that her son was feeling under the weather with a summer cold but would probably be much better by the weekend.

Kay was glad of the respite and she had flatly refused to take him round some grapes as her mother had suggested. The thought of feeding him grapes while he spluttered and snorted filled her with horror. She began to think about the newspaper advertisement which was still tucked down inside her handbag but she had to admit that the initial surge of enthusiasm had faded. Somehow she couldn't see herself being happy serving teas and buns to servicemen in some garrison town. There must be something better.

At the Elephant and Castle Kay glanced out of the bus window and noticed a fruit stall standing on a corner by the Trocadera cinema, and her thoughts turned to Joey Westlake. He had apologised to her in the pub on Sunday evening but really it was all a storm in a teacup. She was stupid to have made so much of what Joey swore was an innocent kiss and she should have been more mature. It had not warranted the row it caused, and her storming off, saying they were finished. Maybe she should have trusted her own intuition, instead of allowing herself to become suspicious of Joey by listening too much to what her mother had to say. Ruby didn't like the young man and had been quick to say so. Joey had been good fun to be with though, and how different he was from Richard Mills, who was beginning to bore her to distraction.

By the time she stepped down from the bus in Grange Road Kay had succeeded in disliking herself intensely. What was wrong with her? Why couldn't she just tell Richard that he wasn't for her? She was too soft, too timid to do anything about it, and before long if she didn't hurry up and do something there would be wedding bells ringing. God forbid, she sighed.

As she walked into Tanners Alley Kay saw Mrs Wilson standing at her front door and the grey-haired woman gave her a crooked grin. ''Ere, luv, I gotta tell yer,' she said.

'Tell me what?' Kay asked frowning.

'This Chinky bloke knocked at my door this mornin'.'

'Chinky bloke?'

'Yeah, 'im from the Chinese laundry in Cater Street,' Connie Wilson told her. 'Frightened the bleedin' life out o' me 'e did.'

'What did 'e want?' Kay asked her.

'You.'

'Me?'

'Yeah, 'e asked me which 'ouse you lived in,' Connie went on. ''E mumbled somefing an' pointed ter this letter 'e 'ad, an' I could see it was your name on it, so I told 'im which 'ouse was yours. I 'ope I done the right fing. Yer gotta be so careful wiv those Chinks. They'd slit yer froat as soon as look at yer.'

'Connie, they're no different from us,' Kay admonished her. 'Lots o' people use that laundry an' from what I've 'eard they're a very nice family that run it.'

'P'raps they are,' Connie said, looking a little abashed, 'but I can't 'elp feelin' scared of 'em. My George told me a few fings about what goes on over Chinatown. 'E knows, 'e's worked in the docks over there, an' 'e told me there's a lot o' gamblin' dens where they smoke opium in pipes an' gamble right frew the night. George said that they drug young women an' take advantage of 'em.'

'I fink your George is tryin' ter scare yer,' Kay told her.

'Anyway, you just be careful 'avin' anyfing ter do wiv

77

that lot,' Connie warned her, slipping her hands into the pockets of her clean apron and nodding knowingly.

Ruby looked puzzled as she handed the letter to Kay and she stood beside her while the young woman tore it open. The single sheet was folded in half, enclosing two pink tickets which Kay passed over while she read the note:

Dear Kay,

I'm sorry not to have seen you this week. I have been working at the exhibition hall, helping to set things up ready for Saturday. I do hope you are able to come. I will look out for you with much anticipation.

Your friend,
Mei Li

Ruby looked even more puzzled. 'Chinese Cultural Exhibition? What's this all about?'

'Yer remember I told yer that I'd met this very nice Chinese girl down the Blue last Saturday,' Kay began. 'Well, this letter's from 'er. Read it.'

Ruby sat down at the table to read the note then she looked up with a smile. 'I'm sure Richard'll be pleased ter go,' she remarked. 'That'll be right up 'is street.'

'Oh no,' Kay said with emphasis.

'What d'yer mean, "Oh no"?' Ruby queried.

'Richard is the last person I'd want to inflict on Mei Li,' Kay told her.

'I don't understand. Why ever not? Richard an' you are . . .'

Kay sat down facing her. 'We're nuffing, Mum. 'E's

borin', self-opinionated, an' inclined ter be domineerin' as well. I'm gonna finish wiv 'im.'

'Well, I'm shocked as well as disappointed, ter say the least,' Ruby said quickly. 'The young man's got a very good job an' 'e's polite an' respectful, despite what yer say. Anyone can see 'e finks the world of yer.'

'It's not enough, Mum,' Kay sighed. 'Richard's twenty-one goin' on fifty. There's no sparkle in 'im, no adventure, just an obsession wiv that job of 'is an' it's turnin' me into a nervous wreck. I just can't stand it any more. Just ask me about valves. Go on.'

'What yer talkin' about?'

'Valves, bloody valves,' Kay went on in anger. 'Did you know that the new compensatin' bypass valve is set to revolutionise the engineerin' industry? Did you realise that the calibration on the new multi-valve bein' tested fer submarines can be set an' changed by electrical impulse?'

'I don't understand what you're talkin' about,' Ruby said shaking her head, 'but if Richard is so keen ter tell yer about 'is work you should be only too glad ter listen. Mrs Mills seems ter fink 'e'll go right ter the top, an' it'll mean a good life for both of yer. There'll be no scrapin' an' schemin' ter make ends meet. When yer married yer'll be able ter move out o' Bermon'sey, maybe inter one o' them nice new 'ouses they're buildin'.'

'Mum, yer gotta get it inter yer 'ead I'm not gonna marry Richard,' Kay replied firmly. 'I don't love 'im an' that's the crux of it.'

'Love? Don't make me laugh,' Ruby said disparagingly. 'You young gels seem ter go around wiv blinkers on 'alf the time. Yer can't see what's in front of yer. Would you be 'appy married ter some feller who works in a factory an' brings 'ome a pittance every week? There'd be 'im strugglin' ter provide an' you saddled wiv kids an' not knowin' which way ter turn.'

'If I loved the feller I'd cope, like everybody else does round 'ere, an' be 'appy doin' so,' Kay retorted sharply. 'I wouldn't care if 'e swept the streets fer a livin'. Look at you an' Dad. 'E doesn't earn big wages, but it doesn't matter, as long as the both of yer love each ovver.'

'Yer farvver's got a responsible job, an' there's a chance of 'im gettin' the foreman's job when Percy Bradley retires next year,' Ruby replied quickly. 'An' yes, we do love each ovver, but it's not the sort o' love you're referrin' to. You youngsters nowadays expect bells ter ring an' yer wanna be swept up an' carried off ter some dreamland. Life's not like that, not fer the likes of us anyway. Me an' yer dad didn't 'ear bells ringin', but we felt comfortable an' 'appy bein' tergevver from the very beginnin'. Love grows fer most of us, it doesn't come up an' slap yer across the face.'

'Well, there's no chance of it growin' on me an' Richard,' Kay countered. 'You just said it was comfortable bein' wiv Dad at the beginnin'. I don't even feel comfortable, only irritated, so there's no sense in prolongin' the misery, 'cos that's what it is. It's not bein' fair ter Richard eivver. 'E'll meet somebody else in good time, somebody who'll be glad to 'ear all about 'is work an' spend Saturday nights chattin' about valve calibrations an' engineerin'.'

Ruby shook her head slowly. 'So I s'pose yer'll be gettin' back wiv that Joey Westlake again,' she said.

'I dunno, I might even take a job away from London,' Kay told her.

'Away from London?' Ruby queried with a shocked look. 'Like where, doin' what?'

'The NAAFI's advertisin' fer gels ter work all over the country,' Kay explained. 'There's a good chance too of workin' abroad.'

'NAAFI indeed,' Ruby scoffed. 'Yer'd soon wish yerself back 'ome, me gel. If the job was that good they wouldn't 'ave ter put advertisements in the papers, there'd be a waitin' list.'

'Look, Mum, I don't wanna argue wiv yer,' Kay replied wearily. 'It's just makin' me un'appy the way fings are at the moment.'

Ruby brushed an imaginary crumb from the linen table-cloth. 'It's your life,' she sighed, 'but just remember what marriage is all about. It's about makin' a good 'ome fer yer 'usband an' lookin' after 'im. Men are the breadwinners an' they've gotta be looked after if yer want a regular wage on the table. Then there's children ter fink of. It's the woman who brings 'em up, not the farvver. It's the muvver who wipes their noses an' sits up at night when they're ailin'. It's the woman who makes the 'ome a place 'er man's 'appy ter come back to every night. My parents were strict. My muvver was a very proud woman who kept the place spotless. Never anyfing out o' place, an' we 'ad ter be tidy as kids. She an' me farvver were regular churchgoers. They were God-fearin' an' respectable people who were looked up to. That's why I expect all o' you ter respect the place an' not use it as a slop-'ouse. It's all about settin' standards, an' it was drummed inter me as a kid. I didn't appreciate it at the time, but I'm grateful now, an' so will you be when you get married an' get yer own place.'

Kay was about to respond but a knock on the front door stopped her. Ruby got up to answer it and soon came back frowning. 'Kay, light the gas under the greens, will yer,' she said quickly as she reached on the mantelshelf for a key. 'I gotta go in ter Lizzie's. That was Nora Mason. She said Lizzie's bin tappin' on 'er bedroom wall.'

'Shall I come wiv yer?' Kay volunteered.

'No, you do as I said,' Ruby told her, 'an' check those spuds, they should be ready by now.'

As Ruby hurried out of the house she saw Bel standing on Lizzie's doorstep. ''Ave yer knocked?' she asked her.

'Yeah, but there's no answer,' Bel replied. 'She must 'ave 'ad a fall.'

Ruby twisted the key in the lock and the two women hurried up the stairs. Lizzie's front bedroom door was open wide and when Ruby looked in she saw that the bed was made and the lace curtaining was pulled back neatly. Of Lizzie Roach there was no sign.

'Let's try the back bedroom,' Bel suggested.

Ruby pushed open the door and she and Bel looked at each other in confusion. 'This is just a junk room,' Ruby said.

'Well, where the bloody 'ell is she?' Bel puffed frustratedly.

They quickly went down the stairs and searched through the parlour, the small back room that smelt of mildew, and finally the scullery. Bel pointed to the bolt which was drawn across the door leading into the overgrown back garden. 'Well, she ain't out there,' she said scratching her head.

'She wouldn't be, she's just bin bangin' on the bedroom wall,' Ruby replied.

The two women stared at each other for a few moments and then it hit them almost simultaneously. 'I bet she's fell down the back o' the bed,' Ruby said in alarm.

Once again they hurried up the stairs and as Bel leaned over the bed they heard a grunt. Ruby got down on her hands and knees and saw the diminutive figure stretched out under the bedframe. 'What the bloody 'ell yer doin' under there?' she said angrily. 'Yer've frightened the bleedin' life out of us.'

'Never mind about that, just get me out,' Lizzie growled. 'I'm 'ooked up on the springs. I bin bangin' on that wall fer hours wiv me pisspot. It's a good job I emptied it this mornin'.'

Ruby reached under the bed and with some difficulty she managed to free the old woman. Together she and Bel dragged her clear and helped her on to her feet.

'Lizzie, beds are s'posed ter be slept on, not under,' Bel told her, grinning widely.

'That's right, take the piss,' Lizzie grumbled. 'Yer've all gotta get old one day.'

'It's nuffing ter do wiv gettin' old,' Bel said, trying to look straight-faced. 'I would 'ave got 'ooked up under there. What we'd like ter know is what made yer get under there in the first place?'

Lizzie had slumped down on the edge of the bed. 'I come up 'ere first fing this mornin' an' I changed the bedclothes, put fresh curtains up me daughter ironed fer me an' 'ad a good dust round, an' then I got me mop an' done under the bed, but I knew it wasn't enough. I 'ad ter do what I 'ad ter do.'

'What yer talkin' about, Lizzie?' Ruby asked with a note of exasperation in her voice.

'That's what I'm talkin' about,' the old lady said quickly as she pulled up the sleeve of her black dress. 'Take a look at that.'

'I can't see nuffink, 'cept a couple o' spots,' Ruby told her.

'I bin scratchin' 'em all night,' Lizzie went on. 'I got bugs. That's where they bit me.'

'They're not bug bites, yer silly cow,' Bel said laughing aloud. 'They're gnat bites. Yer must 'a' got bitten sittin' out the front yesterday. You 'ad yer sleeves pulled up, remember?'

'Are yer sure they're not bug bites?' Lizzie asked her.

'Sure as Gawd made little apples.'

'Well, I'm relieved.'

Ruby reached under the bed once more and removed a box of matches and some thin waxed tapers. 'You was lucky,' she said, making a serious face at Lizzie. 'If yer'd caught the bed alight yer'd 'ave burnt ter death before we found yer. Yer s'posed ter strip the bed before yer use lighted tapers.'

'I know that,' the old lady said haughtily. 'I wasn't born yesterday. I couldn't strip that fing again though, not after just makin' it.'

'I'd better make yer a cuppa before I go,' Ruby sighed, shaking her head slowly.

'That'd be nice,' Lizzie said with a toothless grin.

'An' I'd better go an' tell Mrs Mason yer OK,' Bel added.

'Don't mention bugs, fer Gawd's sake,' Lizzie told her anxiously. 'It'll be all down the Grange Road in no time.'

A few minutes later the old lady sat in her comfortable parlour, sipping her tea with relish. 'If I 'ad 'ave found a bug yer know what I would've done?' she asked.

'Tell me,' Ruby said.

'I'd 'ave put it in a matchbox an' dropped it frew that scatty Myrtle Thompson's letterbox,' Lizzie growled.

'Well, there was no need after all,' Ruby replied as she got up to leave.

As she reached the parlour door Lizzie called her back. ''Ere, you *certain* they ain't bug bites?'

Chapter Eight

Jim Neal gave Angela a friendly smile as he placed his canvas tool-bag down by the leaking iron radiator. 'I 'ope this isn't gonna disrupt yer too much,' he said.

'No, it's nice to see you again,' she replied with a sweet smile. 'I enjoyed our last little chat.'

Jim set to work dismantling the ancient rusting radiator, his back to the desk where Angela sat smoking a cigarette. 'It'll be nice when the office is finally finished,' he remarked as he searched for his wrench.

'It's about time they got round to doing something about it,' the young woman said, tapping the ash from her cigarette thoughtfully. 'It must be at least two years since it had a coat of paint, and I've even been allowed to choose the wallpaper, would you believe.'

Jim freed the locking nut and used a small spanner to loosen the pipe connection, suddenly aware that Angela had left her desk and was standing behind him. He looked up and smiled self-consciously. 'The new radiators are much less bulky,' he said quickly, 'an' we're goin' ter see if we can 'ide some o' the pipin'.'

'That'll be good,' the young woman replied with an amused expression. 'Do you always take your work so seriously?'

'It's professional pride,' Jim countered.

Angela walked round to stand at the side of him as he set about releasing the second locking nut. 'Is it to be Devon this year?' she asked.

He shrugged. 'We've not really discussed it since I first suggested it, but I expect it will be Devon.'

'Lucky you.'

Jim leaned back on his haunches, feeling a little embarrassed as he looked up at Angela who stood with her legs slightly apart and her hands on her hips in a posing stance. He could not but notice how tightly her olive-green blouse fitted her and how well her calf-length grey skirt showed off her shapely figure. Her red hair was neatly fixed around her ears and she looked very attractive as she gave him another sweet smile.

'It'll be a good rest at least,' he said simply.

'Do you know you've got a few grey hairs coming,' she remarked suddenly.

''Ave I?' he replied.

'I like to see a few grey hairs on a man,' Angela told him with a suggestive look. 'I think it makes a man look mature and attractive.'

'Yeah, I s'pose it does on some men,' Jim said, fumbling.

'It does on you,' Angela went on, revelling in his discomfort. 'Laurie's as bald as a badger. He lost his hair when he was very young. You're about the same age as him but you seem to have kept all yours.'

Jim leaned forward and moved the freed radiator back and forth on its brackets. 'This should be easy ter shift now,' he said.

'I'm sorry if I'm embarrassing you,' she said, her smile gently mocking him again.

Jim drew a deep breath, realising that she was expecting him to respond to her game. Why not, he thought, if it made her happy. 'No, I'm pleased you said what yer did,' he told her, leaning back on his haunches again. 'It's nice ter work up 'ere in the presence of an attractive woman. Usually I'm surrounded wiv girls in white overalls an' caps when I'm fixin' the machines.'

'Do you really find me attractive?' she asked.

'Yes I do, an' it's a little off-puttin'.'

'Would you like me to take my work into another office?'

'No, I'd prefer it if yer stayed put.'

'Then I shall.'

Jim stood up and gripped the radiator, finding it more difficult than he thought to lift it off the brackets. 'That wall needs plasterin' first,' he remarked as he picked at the crumbling surface.

'I'm going to make us a nice cup of tea, you've earned it,' Angela said smiling easily.

While she busied herself in the small room that led off from her office Jim set to work removing the length of piping which ran along the wall beneath the window.

'Do you take sugar?' Angela called out.

'Two please.'

'A sweet man, eh?'

Jim smiled to himself as he rummaged through his tool-bag for the large screwdriver. Angela was certainly coming on strong, and it made him feel good. He would have to be careful though. Overstepping the mark might spoil the game. Better play it nice and sensible.

The wall brackets were soon removed and the length of piping dismantled and stowed next to the radiator by the time Angela came in carrying two mugs of tea. 'I hope you won't think I'm being unladylike drinking out of a mug,' she said as she put the tea down on her desk. 'Draw up a chair, Jim.'

It was a fine day outside and the bright sunlight was glaring into the small office. Angela got up and pulled on the strings of the sunblinds. 'There, that's better,' she remarked as she swayed back to the desk.

Jim sipped his hot tea, and when he raised his eyes over the mug he found Angela staring at him. 'How long have you been with Madeley's now, Jim?' she asked. 'Nineteen years isn't it?'

'Twenty-three,' he corrected her. 'It's broken service though. I 'ad four years in the RAF.'

Angela had seen his employment file and knew all the details, but she wanted to draw him into talking about himself. 'It all counts though,' she said quickly.

'I started 'ere as a grease monkey back in twenty-seven, the year I got married,' he told her.

'And now you're a fully-fledged maintenance engineer who might well be the next man in charge of the department when Percy Bradley retires.'

'I don't know about that,' Jim replied modestly. 'There's ovvers wiv good credentials.'

Angela smiled. 'You forget I'm the company secretary and I get to hear things,' she reminded him in a confiding tone of voice. 'Your name's been mentioned for the post, but of course it's early days yet so I shouldn't take it for granted.'

'I wouldn't dream of it,' he replied.

Angela set her mug down on the table. 'Will you be working overtime in the office this weekend?' she asked him.

Jim shook his head. 'No, I've managed ter squeeze out of it. I'm goin' to a reunion on Saturday.'

'RAF?'

'Yeah, our bomber squadron,' he told her. 'It's at the RAF Association in Piccadilly. We'll get tergevver an' chew over ole memories.'

'And all your conquests, no doubt,' she said, looking at him with mischief in her large blue eyes.

'No, just shop talk.'

'I bet you all get very drunk.'

Jim chuckled. 'I went last year expectin' to 'ave a good time an' it ended up bein' a really miserable occasion, fer me at least. Names came up, one after another, the names of 'ole crews who were shot down over Germany. There were too many people not there, too many good pals, an' I got very depressed all of a sudden. Silly really but I expect it was the drink. We were all pretty well drunk by then. Anyway I left early an' strolled along Piccadilly an' down frew Trafalgar Square ter the Embankment. I sat on a bench by the river fer what seemed ages, an' then I caught the tram 'ome. Ruby was surprised I was 'ome so early, but I fink she understood. I 'ope it won't be such a morbid gavverin' this year.'

'Well, if it is you must leave very early and call round for a chat on your way home,' Angela told him with a gentle tap on his wrist, which brought a shy smile to his handsome face.

'I couldn't do that. What would Laurie think?' he reminded her.

'Laurie's got other things to do this weekend,' Angela replied, briefly raising her eyes to the ceiling for effect. 'He's going to Devil's Dyke with the Surrey Ornithological Society on Saturday morning until Sunday evening. It's something to do with identifying and cataloguing a rare species of corncrake, would you believe.'

Jim smiled. 'If I did leave early I wouldn't be much company anyway,' he told her.

'Just you let me be the judge of that,' she replied quickly. 'All you need to do is hop off the tram in the New Kent Road at the stop before the Bricklayer's Arms. You'll see Brant Street to your left. Just down on the right-hand side are some old Victorian houses. I live at number thirteen. Just remember, lucky for some. I wouldn't want you knocking at the wrong door, especially when you're feeling down.'

Jim felt a sudden thrill of excitement run through him. The game was hotting up, he thought. 'I might take you up on that,' he said.

'I'd like you to,' Angela replied in a low voice. 'You'll find I can be a very good listener, if nothing else. At least then you'll arrive home to Ruby a little less miserable.'

'I'll remember that,' he said as he stood up. Just then there was a tap on the door and Percy Bradley put his head inside the office.

'Jim, we got an emergency,' he croaked breathlessly. 'The main fillin' machine's jammed. There's a right ole mess, there's jam an' cream all over the place.'

'OK, Percy, I'm on me way,' Jim said quickly as he grabbed up his tool-bag.

Angela followed him to the door. 'Don't forget what I said, Jim,' she called out as he hurried along the corridor.

Bel Allenby thoughtfully stirred the tea and then almost as an afterthought she handed the cup to Ruby. 'She's young, luv, yer can't run young people's lives,' she remarked.

'She's my daughter, Bel, an' she's inexperienced,' Ruby said ardently. 'Richard Mills might not 'ave bin at the front o' the queue when looks were given out but 'e's got all 'is marbles. 'E's polite, thoughtful, an' very 'ard-workin'. What's more 'e comes from a respectable family.'

'Ruby, it don't add up to a plateful o' beans,' Bel told her kindly. 'If she can't feel anyfing for 'im it's best she makes the break now.'

The younger woman slid the bottom of her cup over the edge of the saucer before taking a sip, then sighed sadly. 'I was sure they'd get on well tergevver,' she went on. 'Now I s'pose she'll be back wiv that flash barrer boy.'

'Joey Westlake ain't that bad,' Bel rejoined. 'At least 'e's 'ard-workin'. When I was doin' that early mornin' cleanin' job I often used ter see 'im on 'is way ter the Borough Market. An' yer gotta remember, 'e's out in all weavvers.'

'I'm not sayin' 'e's lazy,' Ruby replied, 'it's 'is attitude. 'E's too worldly-wise fer our Kay. I could see 'er gettin' inter trouble while she was wiv 'im an' I breavved a big sigh o' relief when they split up.'

Bel smiled and shook her head slowly. 'Ruby, yer

got some funny ideas,' she said. 'Kay's more likely ter get pregnant by someone like the Mills boy than Joey Westlake.'

'I dunno so much.'

'Well, *I* do.'

'Kids. They're a worry when they're toddlers an' a bigger worry when they're grown-up,' Ruby groaned.

'I dunno about that. I wasn't lucky enough to 'ave any kids o' me own,' Bel replied as she put her cup and saucer on the table. 'Jack would 'ave loved 'em but there yer go. We never get everyfing out o' life. We just gotta be fankful fer what we 'ave got.'

'I'm sorry ter go on,' Ruby said with a warm smile, 'but I needed ter talk ter someone an' I always come ter you, don't I?'

'Yer can say that again,' Bel replied with a chuckle. 'Remember the time you was 'avin' Paul? There was me goin' round wiv a big list that you wrote out fer me. An' when yer finally made it downstairs I actually 'eld me breath in case yer spotted anyfing I'd fergotten ter do.'

'I wasn't as bad as all that, was I?' Ruby asked frowning.

'What d'yer mean, "wasn't"?' Bel said mockingly. 'You still are. Yer've never changed from the first day yer moved in the alley. Who else along 'ere bashes their mats every week wivout fail? Who else changes the lace curtains twice a week? Who else . . .'

'Bel, yer makin' me feel like a tyrant,' Ruby cut in. 'You know me. I put great stock in keepin' the place spotless. Jim an' the children don't wanna come in to a shit-tip. Besides, I get pleasure out o' keepin' me 'ome nice an' clean. I'm never bovvered about who comes in, 'cos I know they can never find fault.'

'Yer gotta ease up a bit, Ruby,' her old friend said kindly. 'Do yer really fink people visit just ter see the state o' the place? Most o' the time people who call do so 'cos they've got troubles, an' the last fing they'd notice is the state o' your curtains or a speck o' dust on yer carpets.'

'I can't 'elp it,' Ruby persisted. 'It's the way I've bin brought up. We all 'ad chores ter do. Me an' our Amy 'ad ter scrub the 'ouse out every week an' our muvver worked like a Trojan ter keep the place spick an' span. She set good standards an' I just got used ter seein' a spotless place.'

'A few papers lyin' around an' a dirty cup an' saucer on the table don't make the place filfy, gel,' Bel remarked. 'Wiv you it's an obsession, an' ter be honest, if you'd bin married to our Jack you would 'ave copped it.'

Ruby looked a bit downcast and Bel gave her a sympathetic smile as she picked up the empty crockery. 'I'm gonna make us a fresh cuppa,' she said. 'I don't want you sittin' there lookin' all mean an' 'orrible. Cheer up, Kay won't let yer down, but yer gotta let the gel make 'er own decisions.'

Jim Neal walked home from work thinking a little guiltily about that afternoon. Angela Stapleton had really got to him and he knew it was wrong. He should not have encouraged her. But then again she didn't need any encouraging; she was making a play and the offer was there. She had invited him to her house this coming Saturday and made it clear that Laurie would be away at the time. Even an imbecile would put two and two together.

Jim bought the evening paper and crossed into Grange Walk, feeling strangely elated. The young woman's interest in him had boosted his morale and worked on his ego, he had to admit. She was very attractive and she had hinted heavily enough that her marriage had become stale and unfulfilling. He had been careful not to let her know that he was unhappy with his sex life, and had been for some time now, but he was certain she could tell just by looking at him. Women seemed to guess these things.

As he walked into Tanners Alley Jim saw Connie Wilson standing by her front door. ''Ow's George?' he asked her.

'Dr Phelps give 'im anuvver week off,' she told him. ''E's up anyway. I got 'im sittin' in the chair. Mind you, 'is back might be a lot better but I can't say the same fer 'is temper. Dr Phelps said 'e should apply fer a lighter job. 'E said that disc could go again at any time. These doctors make yer laugh. 'Ow can a docker apply fer a light job?'

'Give 'im my regards,' Jim said as he slipped the latch of his garden gate.

As usual his slippers were at the foot of the stairs, and after putting them on he went into the scullery to greet Ruby. Partly in a show of amorousness but also because of his guilty feelings he slipped his hands round his wife's waist as she turned for her usual peck on the cheek.

'What's got inter you?' she said with a questioning look.

'I just feel like it,' he told her.

'Mind, Kay's in the parlour,' Ruby said quickly as she pulled backwards.

Jim picked up the cake of soap and proceeded to wash his hands. ''Ow did it go terday?' he asked.

'Same as always.'

'No more excitement?'

'No, just the normal day.'

'I might not bovver ter go ter the reunion this Saturday,' he remarked.

'But you always go.'

'Yeah, but it's gettin' ter be a bit of a muchness really.'

'Well, it's up ter you.'

Jim dried his hands on the towel and went up to her as she stood stirring a large pot of stew. His hands slipped round her waist again and he nuzzled her ear. 'I could take you out instead,' he said in a low voice. 'We could go fer a drink, an' then maybe 'ave an early night.'

'Jim, will you stop messin' about,' Ruby said sharply. 'I don't like plannin' those sort o' fings. It should be spontaneous, not somefing yer put in yer notebook.'

He released her and stood back a pace. 'I like it ter be spontaneous too, but it never seems ter work out like that, Ruby, does it?' he said quickly.

'You don't do so bad,' she chided him.

'It's not about me, it's about us,' he replied, feeling anger building up inside him. 'Fer months now whenever I get near yer I've bin gettin' the cold shoulder. Eivver yer too tired or it's too late at night.'

'What about last Saturday,' Ruby countered, 'or 'ave yer forgotten?'

'That wasn't very satisfyin' fer eivver of us,' he reminded her. 'Yer said as much yerself.'

'I couldn't relax after that bad day at the surgery,' she

replied. 'You was tired too, or are yer sayin' it was all my fault?'

Jim put his hands up in resignation. 'All right, luv, I'll say no more. I thought yer might like a Saturday night out fer a change. Just a thought.'

'We'll 'ave ter wait an' see,' Ruby said irritably.

Kay was reading the paper when Jim walked into the parlour and she gave him a welcoming smile. 'I've bin sent in,' she whispered.

'Why?'

'When I came in Mum started goin' on about Richard again, an' then she came out wiv a funny question.'

'Oh?' Jim said as he slumped down in the chair facing her.

'Yeah. She asked me if I thought she was a martinet.'

'An' what did you say?'

'I said she was, sort of.'

'I bet that went down well.'

'She told me she could manage the tea quite well enough on 'er own,' Kay said with a furtive smile.

'Well, if it's any comfort I just got a blank meself,' Jim told her.

Kay looked a little worried. 'Maybe Mum's started ter go frew 'er change.'

'Yeah, it could explain it,' he said sighing.

'It could last fer some time,' Kay reminded him.

'Yeah, I s'pose it could,' Jim said as he closed his eyes and recalled how Angela had stood over him seductively, with her shapely legs spread apart and her large breasts straining against her blouse.

Chapter Nine

On Saturday Kay had been up since early morning, and after her usual trip to the market she sat sipping a cup of tea in the parlour. Paul was still recovering from a hangover and he was unshaven as he sat at the table contemplating his mug of tea.

'I 'ope yer gonna spruce yerself up a bit,' Kay told him firmly. 'You look like Bill Sykes wiv that stubble.'

'Don't worry, Sis,' he replied in a hoarse voice. 'By the time I'm ready I'll look like Errol Flynn.'

'We'll need ter set off at two o'clock,' she reminded him. 'It starts at three o'clock, and the doors are open at two-thirty.'

'There's plenty o' time,' he groaned. 'I need ter get me 'ead tergevver first.'

'You shouldn't 'ave drunk so much last night,' Kay chided him. 'I expect Joey Westlake's feelin' the same as you this mornin'.'

'Worse I should fink,' Paul replied. ''E was well on the way before I walked in the pub. 'E's carryin' a torch, Kay.'

'Over me?'

'Who else?'

'Did 'e say anyfing about me?'

' 'E never stops talkin' about yer.'

'Yer 'avin' me on!'

'No I'm not, it's true.'

Kay gave him a doubting look. 'Yer'd better wash yer dirty self an' get a shave,' she told him sternly. 'Remember I'll need ter use the scullery fer a wash-down soon.'

Ruby came in carrying a laden shopping-bag and refused the offer of a cup of tea. 'I'll 'ave it later,' she told Kay. 'There's queues at every stall down the Blue, an' I need ter go ter Tower Bridge Road market as well. I've got some bits 'ere fer Lizzie. I'll 'ave ter take 'em in later, I don't wanna get delayed chattin'.'

The sun was high in the sky and a light refreshing breeze was blowing as Kay and Paul stepped out of the house that afternoon. The young woman was wearing a lemon-coloured dress with a high turn-back collar and a lightweight white jumper, with stockings and her best high-heeled patent shoes. Paul wore his grey suit and a blue shirt open at the neck. His short fair hair was brushed back from his forehead and he had dabbed on a liberal amount of aftershave.

They walked through the backstreets and caught a number 38 tram in the Old Kent Road, and as they settled themselves on the upper deck Paul broached the subject. 'So what yer intendin' doin' about glamour boy?' he asked her. 'Are yer gonna give 'im the elbow or not?'

'I said I was,' Kay replied quickly.

'Yer keep sayin' yer will, but yer never do.'

'I'm doin' it ternight.'

'Can I tell Joey?'

'It's up ter you.'

'Then I will. 'E'll be very pleased.'

'I 'ope 'e don't get the idea I'm comin' runnin',' Kay was quick to point out.

'I tell yer, Kay, Joey's a changed man,' Paul said soberly. 'I 'ad a word wiv 'im the ovver night about bein' flash an' I fink the penny's dropped. Yer 'ave ter realise it's just 'is way. Joey's a right decent bloke, an' yer gotta remember 'e's bin on 'is own fer a few years now. It's a shame really. 'E told me 'e gets very lonely at times. 'E said you was the best fing that ever 'appened to 'im.'

'Then 'e should 'ave minded what 'e was doin', shouldn't 'e,' Kay retorted.

Paul chuckled. 'Ter change the subject, what's this friend of yours like?'

'She's very sweet,' Kay told him.

'Yeah, but what's she look like?'

'She's Chinese,' Kay said with an amused smile. 'She's got long raven 'air an' a very pretty face.'

'Slanty eyes?'

'They do slant a bit, yes, but it adds to 'er attraction.'

'Does she talk in pigeon English?'

'She speaks perfect English, a lot better than you do.'

''Ow tall is she?'

'Just wait an' see,' Kay said in exasperation. 'Yer like a little kid at times.'

'Only askin',' Paul remarked with a disarming smile as he took a packet of Player's Weights from his coat pocket.

'Since when 'ave you bin smokin'?' Kay asked frowning.

'I smoked when I was in the RAF,' he told her.

She watched him light his cigarette with some amusement. 'I bet yer wouldn't smoke indoors,' she said.

'It's not werf the aggro,' he replied. 'There'd be Muvver followin' me all over the 'ouse wiv an ashtray.'

'She can't 'elp it,' Kay said in her defence. 'I fink she's on 'er change.'

'Yeah, more than likely,' Paul agreed.

The tram clattered over the quiet river and along the Embankment, grating to a stop by the Obelisk. The two young people hurried over the tree-lined thoroughfare and into Northumberland Avenue. Up ahead they could see the tall, imposing pillar of Nelson's Column with the four sitting lions guarding the naval hero. Pigeons fluttered around the fountains and flew up on to the hands and shoulders of visitors who held out food for them.

'Those bloody fings scare me,' Paul confessed as he steered Kay around the edge of the square.

They climbed the flight of wide steps and passed under the portico into the large vestibule of the National Art Gallery. There was a prominent sign pointing to the exhibition and Kay handed over both tickets to a smartly dressed young Chinese man as they turned into a long corridor. A door led off to the left and as they entered Paul sniffed the air. Burning joss-sticks were standing in upright bunches in pots strategically placed around the large marbled room and there was a huge poster pinned to a board on the wall. Paul stood just behind Kay as they read the history of the Cultural Society and studied the small watercolour pictures of typical Chinese scenes. Music played softly from a speaker set high on the wall above the poster, with muted cymbals and strange reed instruments transporting the two young people far away from the familiarities of London.

'There's Mei Li,' Kay said suddenly, tugging on Paul's arm.

Other people in the room were moving forward and Paul could not get a clear view of her.

'Welcome to the Chinese Cultural Exhibition,' she said in a soft but confident voice. 'My name is Mei Li Ching and I'm appointed as your guide. People coming in after you will be escorted around the exhibition by other guides, so to prevent any delay to them I suggest we start off now. If you will follow me.'

As she smiled sweetly and turned to lead the way Paul caught a full glimpse of her and he whistled softly to himself. 'She's very pretty,' he remarked to his sister, 'an' she's got a stunnin' figure,' he added to himself.

Kay was sure that Mei Li hadn't noticed her and Paul, but as they walked along behind other people Mei turned briefly and smiled as she caught her eye.

They entered a smaller room adorned with pots and receptacles of all shapes and sizes, and Mei Li walked behind a heavy rosewood table with a purple and gold cloth spread over it. The group gathered in front of her and saw the line of pale blue porcelain pots, six in number and varying in size. They were intricately decorated with images of small wooden bridges, flowers and birds in flight, as well as Chinese people in traditional dress, some toting large bales. Mei Li gently turned one pot around and Kay studied the artwork, but Paul was looking directly at the young Chinese girl, captivated by her sheer beauty and elegance.

'These are a set of ginger pots and they are very valuable,' Mei Li began as she leaned her hands on the table. 'I have to tell you though that they are not Ming. They are copies, made at a much later date, and hereby hangs a tale. For hundreds of years the art of porcelain flourished in China and was well known to the West. The shapes, artwork and glazing changed distinctively throughout the various dynasties, but in the eighteenth century in particular, there was a tendency to over-elaborate, and in consequence the sheer beauty of a simple design was lost. It was then that a Chinese potter called Cho Tsung decided to make limited sets of pots which recaptured the older style that was slowly being lost to over-adornment. He produced twenty sets of pots during the year seventeen eighty-five and then he disappeared. No one ever found out what happened to him, but it was said he left China in fear of his life, having displeased the Emperor by daring to copy the originals which stood in the palace. Ladies and gentlemen, you are looking at one of the twenty sets of copies Cho Tsung made.'

There was a murmur of voices and an elderly man in gold-rimmed glasses coughed nervously. 'Do you know where the other sets are?' he enquired in a reedy voice.

Mei Li gave him an easy smile as she laid her hand on one of the pots. 'One set is on display in the Metropolitan Museum of Art in New York, one set in the Museum of Antiquities, Paris, and another in Oslo,' she told him. 'The others are either split up and held in ones and twos or were destroyed during the Sino-Japanese wars. No one knows for sure, but the search goes on to acquire a complete set of these Tsung ginger pots. It should be understood that, because of the skill and artistry of Cho Tsung, and his decision to produce a limited number of sets, the value is much greater than would be expected for other porcelain objects of similar design made in the same period.'

Paul could barely take his eyes off Mei Li, watching every movement she made and fascinated by the sweetness of her soft yet firm voice. 'She's gorgeous,' he whispered to Kay.

Mei Li picked up the smallest of the pots and revolved it slowly in her tiny hands. 'Painted and preserved on these pots is an unfolding story,' she went on. 'In olden days throughout China the story of the lantern was told to every child. In the West it would be called the story of the Chinese lantern, so that is what we shall call it.

'In ancient China the Taoists were revered as sages who had penetrated the secrets of life and death,' she began. 'Taoist masters went far and wide to enlighten the populace, and they visited inns and tea houses throughout the Shantung region to liberate people from illusion. They knew that the inns and tea houses were always full of travellers, and it was on one bitterly cold night, on a mountain pass which led down into the Husan valley, that a solitary mystic who was called Chi Liang visited an inn called the "Shining Light". He entered and saw that it was full. It was warm and welcoming, with camphor logs burning in the huge hearth and green tea being served with a rice dish laced with freshwater fish caught that very day from the fast-flowing river. Chi Liang settled down to rest awhile, and after he had warmed his body and filled his stomach he set about his self-appointed task. He was very well received, and the inn owner, being a very shrewd man, decided to invite him to stay for a few nights.

'Word of Chi Liang's wisdom and intuition soon spread, and the Shining Light was full to capacity two nights later when a young traveller called Fu Ching arrived. Fu was a trader who made the regular journey over the mountains to the Husan valley below, and as he listened to Chi Liang's teachings Fu Ching realised that he was a very learned man who would surely be able to give him the answers he needed so desperately. Biding his time until most of the travellers were bedded down for the night, Fu Ching finally approached Chi Liang. "I left my village today for the Husan valley," he informed him, "and I am laden with supplies. I should be happy, for I will do a very good trade, but my heart is as heavy as the yoke of an ox."

'Chi Liang nodded knowingly. "If your heart is as heavy as that then it can only be one of three things, my son," he replied. "It is either health, wealth, or unrequited love. As you are fit enough to make this hazardous journey it cannot be health. Wealth is the product of many laden travels and in the years ahead you will surely acquire wealth, which leaves just one thing."

'"You are right," the young traveller told him. "In my village there is a girl called Wu Shan who is in full flower. I am hopelessly in love with her, but she spurns me, preferring my cousin Hsi. Today I saw her on the bridge. I gave her the look of love but her eyes were empty, until she looked beyond me to the village gate where my cousin stood."'

Paul stared fixedly at Mei Li as she related the ancient story, his heart pumping. The expressive movements of her delicate hands were hypnotising him, and the lilting cadence of her voice echoed like a ringing in his heart.

'The sage nodded again, edging closer to the fire as the wind howled like a demon. "Listen, and listen carefully," he said. "Inside every man's soul are three essences: one of love, another of cherishing, and the third of honour for family and ancestor. They are gifts which accompany every birth. Inside the woman's soul is a lantern, and it too is a gift that comes with life. The lantern remains unlit, until it is fuelled with the three essences. Together, and only together, the three essences fuel and kindle the lantern till it burns brightly and emits its glow from the window of the soul, the eyes. The light is unmistakable, like the glow that shines out from this inn, warming the snow outside and welcoming to the traveller. So you see, my son, when next you see Wu Shan you must remember that to look at her in love alone is not enough. You must also give her the look that tells her you will cherish her. Also, you must not forget to let her know by your look that you will honour her family and ancestors whence she sprang."

'Fu Ching slept peacefully that night, and when he arrived back in the village four days later he saw Wu Shan, once again standing on the bridge. His look was filled with all his feelings for her and he knew in his soul that the three essences were passing from him to fuel her lantern, but her eyes turned away from him and he knew that his cousin Hsi was there by the gate once more. A few days later he left the village on another journey and on the first night he reached the inn of the Shining Light. There were many faces he recognised, but of the mystic Chi Liang there was no sign. Fu Ching could not bear to return to his village, and for many months he wandered abroad buying and selling throughout the region. With money in his pocket the young trader finally returned home, only to learn that Wu Shan was no longer there. She had married his cousin some four months earlier, but now Hsi was dead, poisoned by Wu Shan, who had run away with an old, fat and very rich mandarin.'

Mei Li turned the smallest pot in her hands. 'See there the young traveller climbing the mountain,' she pointed out. 'Here on the second pot is the Shining Light inn with the travellers gathered around the mystic to hear his Taoist teachings.'

People moved forward to take a closer look, and Mei Li took the opportunity to smile warmly in Kay's direction. The visitors were eager to hear the story's conclusion and they stood silent while the young Chinese girl composed herself.

'The next day Fu Ching left the village for the Husan valley once more,' she went on, 'but this time vowing never to return. When he arrived at the inn he saw Chi Liang sitting at a table sipping green tea and he approached him. "I did what you told me to do," he said, "but still the lantern in the soul of Wu Shan never burst into flame."

'"If the three essences truly moved between you both, then the woman was certainly not for you," the Taoist told him. 'A black soul would prevent the flame from kindling the lantern."

'"You are very wise," Fu replied. "That woman poisoned my cousin to death."

'"You must go back to your village," Chi told him. "There a new love awaits you and she will become the love of your life. All you have to do is let the essences flow but this time let them flow between touching fingertips and you will see the light of the lantern shining in her eyes."

'This time Fu Ching hurried back to his village sure of everything, for he knew just where he had to look.'

Mei Li paused and the atmosphere seemed strangely charged as she awaited some reaction.

'Did the man find the love of his life?' an elderly lady asked her.

'Yes he did,' Mei Li told her.

'And did he see the light?'

'He went to the house of Kansu to seek out the daughter Yung Lo and he held out his hand to hers,' Mei explained. 'Fu Ching felt the essences flow as their fingertips met and there was a light shining in her eyes, even though she was totally blind.'

The elderly lady looked about to cry, and the man in the gold-rimmed spectacles coughed nervously again.

'That, ladies and gentlemen, is the ancient legend of the Chinese lantern,' Mei Li said smiling. 'Now you are free to wander around as you will.'

The time had gone so quickly, Kay thought. Paul had been walking round the rest of the exhibition as though in a trance, and when she chanced to speak to him he just mumbled a reply. She slipped her arm through his. 'Come on, dreamer, there's a tea room where we came in.'

They saw nothing of Mei Li and Kay guessed that she would be kept busy until closing time. Paul was still very wrapped up in himself as they sipped their tea and chewed on hard dry rock cakes.

'Wasn't that a lovely story,' Kay remarked.

Paul nodded. 'I've gotta see 'er again, Kay,' he said with feeling.

'She's pretty, isn't she? Did yer like 'er?' she asked him.

'Like 'er? I'm in love wiv 'er,' he croaked.

Chapter Ten

The Commanding Officer of the disbanded 423 Squadron had delivered a very good speech and had done his rounds, chatting amiably to the men, before propping himself up at the bar to get as drunk as he could in the shortest possible time. Now in the smoke-filled room the old squadron members began to relax and talk together of bombing missions, of their absent comrades and of crews who had lost their lives over Germany.

Jim Neal sat down at one of the tables and looked around at the familiar faces, expecting some light-hearted banter, but everyone seemed to be wearing serious expressions as they listened to what Geordie Woodley was saying. 'Well as a matter o' fact I did try the sellin' game, but it wasn't my cup o' tea.'

'That I can understand,' Bill Riley said, nodding his head slowly. 'I did a few weeks on the road selling stationery and it almost sent me round the bloody twist.'

'I got back with the Royal Insurance,' Frank Kenny told the group, 'but I soon realised I'd made a mistake. It wasn't the same somehow. I'm doing a resettlement course at college now. I've always fancied being a draughtsman.'

'What about you, Mack?' Geordie asked a young man

who was sitting slumped in his chair with a blank expression on his badly scarred face.

'I'm in plastics,' Vic McKay told him without taking his eye off the glass of whisky he was holding in his hand.

'There's a good future in plastics,' Bill Riley remarked. 'They'll be making everything out of plastic before long. It's good to get in at the beginning.'

Vic afforded himself a brief smile. 'Yeah, I s'pose so,' he replied, swirling what was left of the whisky around inside the tumbler.

'What exactly does it entail?' Geordie probed. 'Are you on the road a lot?'

'I'll tell you just what it entails,' Vic replied, looking daggers at him. 'I drag myself out of bed every morning to get in the factory by eight o'clock, and for eight hours I stand in front of a machine that presses out plastic trays. I feed that machine all day long. She's insatiable. I call it a she because it somehow reminds me of a woman. As long as I'm there feeding her she'll do the job. Never complains, never plays up, so long as I'm on hand to supply her needs. At five o'clock every evening I put her to bed, so to speak. I'm tempted sometimes to shock her though. One of these days I'm going to put my hand under that press and see if she's got a soul. I doubt if she has. Can you imagine what a human hand would look like pressed into the shape of a dinner tray?'

There was a pregnant silence around the table, and to hide his embarrassment Jim took a large swig from his glass of gin and tonic. What words of sympathy or platitudes that people spout in difficult situations could do any good faced with such bitterness, he thought, sighing to himself.

Vic McKay was once the most sought-after flyer at the station. All the girls wanted to dance with the dashing young man, hoping they would be invited to go for a spin in his open-topped two-seater sports car. Vic's film-star looks and flashing smile had charmed the birds from the trees, and now, thanks to a crash landing in the fens where he was dragged from the blazing wreck, Pilot Officer Victor McKay DFC was employed in a plastics factory operating a power press, having to spend all day with another tangle of metal, numbed with noise and endless repetition. Maybe one day the tragic figure would once more step out into the sunlight, despite his disfigurement, but glancing furtively at him Jim decided it was more likely that sooner or later the poor bastard would sink his head under the press.

'Well, it's about time I did the rounds,' the embarrassed Geordie Woodley announced, getting up quickly.

'I'm gonna prop the bar up fer a spell,' Jim told the rest. 'Anyone care ter join me?'

No one else moved, and as he crossed the room Jim saw Peter Sawbridge beckoning him. That was all he wanted. Ten minutes with Sawbridge would be enough to send him screaming from the gathering. Maybe that wouldn't be so bad after all, he thought. These get-togethers were becoming more doleful than ever and anyone seeing him in conversation with the wearisome Sawbridge would understand if he was carried out in a straitjacket.

'Ye gods, Neal, you look awful. Everything all right, old boy?'

'Yeah, I'm just a little tired,' Jim told the portly officer.

'Plant your arse and let me get you a drink, dear boy. What's your poison?'

'Eh, a gin an' tonic if that's all right,' Jim replied.

Sawbridge was soon back and he leaned forward con-spiratorially over the table. 'Did you hear about Johnny Buckley?' he enquired. 'Got himself in an awful mess. Apparently he's been caught fiddling the books. Bloody fool. Lost a first-class job and banged away for six months into the bargain. Would have got a much stiffer sentence but for his war record.'

Jim acknowledged the news with a nod of his head. 'Are yer workin'?' he asked the ruddy-faced ex-flight lieutenant.

'Between positions, old boy,' Sawbridge told him. 'Tak-ing a short break. I've been offered a post at the Foreign Office. Can't say too much about it you understand. Rather hush-hush. I can tell you though that it involves a lot of travel. Right up my street, what?'

Jim smiled. 'It sounds very good.'

'Good? It's excellent for someone like me,' Sawbridge said quickly. 'Life on the edge, so to speak. Like old times. Christ, I miss those days. Just look around at this motley gathering. There's the station commander getting pissed as a fart, and the exec-officer sitting there looking as though the end of the world was nigh. God's teeth. What's happened to everyone? It's bad news, Neal. You take it from me, this business with the Commies seems to be getting a bit hairy. If they call us reserves up again there'll be a hell of a lot of motivation required to get them all back to operational efficiency.'

Jim looked around the room. The thought of donning a uniform once more was too depressing to contemplate and he drained his glass. 'Can I get you anuvver?' he asked.

'Thought you'd never ask,' Sawbridge replied.

The evening seemed to be dragging past, and as Jim listened to the older man's views on the state of the country and the likely possibility of another conflict he found himself becoming more and more depressed. What was he doing here? It was supposed to be a light-hearted reunion, but instead it seemed more like a wake.

'Did you know old Charlie Marchant bought it?' Sawbridge said suddenly. 'Ran off the road in that Triumph of his. Killed instantly I imagine. Brains all over the dashboard. Oh and Griffin bought it too. Fell in front of the nine forty-five at Fenchurch Street. There was talk of suicide but I don't believe it for a minute. Drunk in charge of a pair of feet more likely. Griff never could take his drink. Remember the time he pranged that kite on a training flight? Landing gear problems, my arse. I happened to know he was shaking like a leaf when he climbed aboard. Did you ever fly with him, old chap?'

Jim shook his head, looking for a suitable excuse to get away. 'No I never did.'

'Good Lord. Is that Jumbo Phillips over there?' Sawbridge said, pointing to the bar. 'Shan't be a moment, old chap. Must have a word with him.'

'It's OK, I'm leavin' now anyway,' Jim told him quickly.

'I say, it's early yet,' Sawbridge replied frowning.

'I need some air,' Jim said weakly.

'Well please yourself,' Sawbridge growled, hurrying away.

Outside the late evening was still balmy as Jim walked along Piccadilly. Theatre crowds were beginning to gather as he strolled into Shaftesbury Avenue and on towards Charing Cross. The sky was darkening, the clouds tinted gold from the setting sun, and the distant rumble of thunder heralded a stormy night.

He had intended to catch a late train to London Bridge but instead he turned towards the Embankment and jumped aboard a number 38 tram. This wasn't a wise move, he told himself, but after wasting the last two hours getting more and more depressed, the prospect of spending a short time in Angela Stapleton's company was something to look forward to.

The tram clattered on towards the Elephant and Castle and Jim stared out of the window, trying to convince himself that it was just an innocent social call, but he remembered the look in Angela's eyes when she invited him to visit her and he knew otherwise. Like his, her marriage had become stale and predictable, and she was looking for some excitement. But what of it? A little mild flirtation was nothing to get worried about. His marriage, unexciting as it had become, was built on solid rock and not in any danger of collapsing at the first signs of fluttering eyelashes and a sensuous smile. Nevertheless, he felt like a fly about to enter the spider's web. This was crazy. Why put himself in a position he might well regret? Better to go straight home and forget it.

As the tram pulled up in New Kent Road Jim stayed in his seat on the upper deck, fighting with his conscience, but as the conductor pulled on the bell-string he suddenly jumped up and dashed down the stairs, leaping from the vehicle as it gathered speed. He hurried into Brant Street and saw the row of neat Victorian houses fronted with railings and short flights of steps up to the front doors. Lace curtains in the windows and polished door knockers served to give the street an air of respectability and Jim smiled to himself as he knocked on number 13. How many intrigues took place behind such veils of respectability, he wondered.

Angela looked surprised when she opened the door to him. 'Well well. So you decided to pay me a visit,' she said, smiling at him. 'Wasn't the reunion all that good?'

Jim shook his head as he smiled back at her. 'It was a disaster.'

'Well, come on in and tell me all about it,' she said, leading the way along the passage in her stockinged feet. She was wearing a light green summer dress with a white knitted cardigan draped over her shoulders, and her red hair was set neatly in soft waves, reaching down to cover her ears. She smiled again as she showed him into the large sitting room.

'You don't mind me callin'?' Jim queried.

'If I had any objection I'd never have invited you, now would I,' she said, the smile never leaving her face. 'Take a seat. No not there. Sit in the armchair so I can have a good look at you. I want to find out if it was just a boring evening and the need of a stiff drink that brought you here, or whether it was because you wanted to see me.'

Jim sat down on the edge of the armchair and watched as she opened the sideboard cupboard and took out a bottle. 'It was both, to be perfectly honest,' he replied.

'I like honesty,' she said, narrowing her eyes as she held out the bottle. 'Do you like whisky? I've got some gin if you'd prefer it but I don't think there's any tonic.

I don't touch gin, it's Laurie's drink, but he never thinks to replace the tonic.'

'That'll do fine,' Jim told her.

'Some soda water?'

'Lovely.'

Angela mixed the drinks and came over to sit facing him, brushing her hands over her dress as she made herself comfortable. 'Nice company and a large whisky and soda. What more could a girl want,' she said with a look of amusement. 'Now tell me all about your evening.'

Jim stared at his full glass for a few moments before replying. 'I don't know why I bovver,' he sighed. 'I've bin goin' ter that reunion fer the past five years an' it gets steadily worse. The first year was good. It was a chance ter meet old friends an' chat about the years in uniform, but since then it's become more like a duty than a pleasure. D'you know I found out this evenin' that one of the lads 'ad fallen under a train at Fenchurch Street an' the burnin' question is, did 'e fall or did 'e jump? I could easily 'ave got blind drunk ternight but I kept finkin' of your invite an' there was no contest.'

'I'm flattered,' Angela said, staring intently at him. 'Was it that bad? If it is why go?'

Jim shook his head. 'I dunno. P'raps it really 'as become a duty, somefing we all feel we've gotta do.'

'A toast to dead friends, is that it?'

'Yeah, I believe it's partly that, an' partly a support fer each ovver,' he went on. 'Everyone seems ter be tryin' ter justify what they're doin'. We always seem ter be makin' excuses fer livin'.'

Angela took a swig from her glass. 'I imagine that's right,

and it's quite understandable,' she replied. 'You survived while others didn't and you feel obliged to justify it. There's no need, Jim. There's a time to live and a time to die. It's the same for all of us. We have no control over our fate. But there I go, prattling on like some philosopher. Drink up and let me get you another.'

Jim drained his glass. 'Tell me about yerself,' he urged her.

Angela smiled as she got up to take his empty glass. 'There's little to tell really. I was born in Croydon and grew up in the area. I was an only child. My father had a grocery shop and he was able to send me to secretarial college after I finished school. I had a happy childhood and I have very little to grouse about.'

'Are yer parents still livin'?' he asked her.

She shook her head. 'My mother was with my dad in the shop when it was hit by a flying bomb. They were both killed outright.'

'I'm very sorry,' Jim said quietly. 'Where did you meet Laurie?'

'We've known each other since we were kids together,' Angela replied. 'We both lived in the same street. It was like a planned marriage. It was expected we'd tie the knot one day. As kids we were inseparable.'

Jim watched as she refilled his glass. 'Yer never 'ad children.'

'I can't have them, which is just as well I suppose,' she remarked. 'I've never been the broody sort. Laurie wanted kids though, but he's resigned to the fact that we can't. He's got his hobby and he's happy doing what he wants to do. At least I think he is.'

Jim got up and walked over to the sideboard. 'Are you 'appy?' he asked.

Angela turned to face him, the drinks forgotten. 'Yes I am, but there are times when I feel a need deep down inside,' she told him. 'It's something that Laurie can't satisfy. I want to know what it feels like to be wicked, to be lecherous and abandon myself. Do you understand what I mean?'

Jim's arms suddenly went around her waist and he pulled her to him. 'I feel the same way,' he said in a husky voice.

She put her arms round his neck and pressed herself to him, wanting him to feel her need, eager to feel his urgency. 'Do you really want to make love to me?' she whispered.

'Can't you tell?' he replied.

She pulled his head down and found his lips, her breath coming faster as she savoured the sharp pleasure. Gasping she pulled away. 'Let's take these drinks upstairs,' she said, smiling excitedly.

Jim followed her up the thick-carpeted stairs and into a large bedroom with a bay window. Small bedside lamps provided a pink glow and there was a distinct smell of lavender. Angela held him at arm's length. 'Don't rush me, Jim. I want us to enjoy this evening,' she said, looking at him eagerly. 'I want to take a bath first. I won't be long. When I call out would you come in and scrub my back?'

Jim nodded, taken aback by her forthrightness, and when the door had closed behind her he went over and peered through the closed curtains at the empty street below. He took out a packet of cigarettes and lit one, inhaling deeply as he sat down on the pink flower-patterned eiderdown and looked round the richly carpeted room. A glass-shaded light hung from the middle of the white ceiling and the walls were decorated in pink and silver striped wallpaper. The bedroom furniture was made of oak; a tall wardrobe was set against the end wall facing the bed, and to the left, beside the bathroom door, the polished surface of the dressing-table was arranged with small bottles of perfume and a large powder box. At the other side of the door on top of the tallboy was a photograph of Laurie standing next to another man and they were smiling broadly. Small bedside cabinets supported the pink-shaded lamps and on the left-hand cabinet beside an alarm clock there was a framed photograph of a couple standing arm in arm on a seaside promenade.

Jim found an ashtray on the tallboy and flicked ash into it just as Angela called out. He went into the bathroom feeling rather uncomfortable but she immediately put him at ease. 'Don't be shy,' she told him. 'I can't reach.'

He smiled as he gazed down at her. She was sitting in frothy suds with her hair piled up on top of her head, her face glowing with the heat of the water. She held a flannel up to her bosom and nodded towards the round cake of soap on the rim of the bath. 'Use that,' she laughed. 'And this.'

Jim's eyes widened as she handed him the flannel, exposing her large breasts. She leaned forward, bringing her arms up and resting her hands on her shoulders. 'Umm, that feels good,' she breathed.

Her back was like satin, and as he moved the soapy flannel down her spine Jim could feel his heart pounding.

This would not be a quick, frantic act performed in a rush, in the heat of the moment. She had made it clear that she wanted more and he wondered if he was capable of restraining himself long enough to satisfy her. She was a beautiful woman, self-assured and in control. She would initiate and direct him, that much he was sure of, and he sought to steady himself as he moved his hands across her back and up on to her shoulders. She leaned back, gazing up at him and he kissed her open lips.

'I won't be long,' she purred. 'You can use the bath after me if you like.'

'Yeah I'd like to,' he answered.

'Hand me the towel,' she said, standing up without any show of coyness. He wanted to avert his eyes as he passed her the large bath towel but he was transfixed by the roundness of her hips, her long shapely thighs, and her large heavy breasts streaked in foam that hid her nipples and navel.

A waxing moon had emerged briefly from behind a storm cloud when Jim came into the bedroom wearing a bathrobe. Angela had left one of the bedside lamps on and she was lying on her back with the bedclothes pulled up around her neck. Jim reached for the lamp switch before disrobing but she stopped him. 'Leave it on, Jim. I want to see your face when you make love to me,' she said seductively.

He slipped into bed quickly and as he reached out for her she rolled over on top of him, her open mouth pressing down on his. He could feel her heart beating and her chest rising and falling rapidly. She moved down, her lips brushing his chest, his stomach, and then lower still. He gritted his teeth in an effort to keep control as her lips found his stiff manhood and her tongue teased him. He wanted to explode but knew that he must not. In desperation he pulled her up on to him and turned her over on to the sheet. She was under him now, his lips exploring her, his hands cupped around her breasts as he caressed her firm nipples. She was groaning, willing him to love her as he moved down on her. Her hands pulled on his hair as she sought to take the utmost pleasure from his darting tongue, and then she suddenly exploded, her whole body tensing as she savoured the exquisite pleasure. She pulled him on to her and he entered her body with confidence, his hips working powerfully and rhythmically, slowly at first and then with an urgency and power that brought them both to a shuddering climax.

The loud roll of thunder from a sky of dark cloud startled Angela and she clung to him, their wet bodies moulding together, her head pressed against his chest. Rain spots hit the windowpane and suddenly a storm was raging. Lightning pierced the curtains and the thunder grew more intense.

'I wish you could stay all night,' Angela whispered as she clung to him. 'I'm terrified of storms.'

'I wish I could,' he said softly. 'I'll stay till it's over.'

Rainwater ran along the kerbside and gurgled down into the drains as Jim Neal finally made his way out of Brant Street. He could still feel the softness of Angela's lips on his body and savour the taste of her as he walked home through the deserted streets. Ruby would be in bed, having left the bolts off, and he hoped he would not disturb her. He needed to wash himself down at the scullery sink first to get rid of Angela's perfume. It had been sheer madness, but along with his strong feelings of guilt were the recollections of a tryst which made him shake with pleasure.

Chapter Eleven

The Saturday evening storm clouds were gathering as Paul Neal walked into the Swan and made his way to the counter. Joey Westlake was already there and he ordered the drinks. Paul mumbled his thanks and took a large gulp. 'I needed that,' he said, wiping his chin.

Joey leaned sideways on the bar counter and looked his friend up and down. 'I bet yer did,' he grinned. 'What a way ter spend Saturday afternoon.'

Paul put his drink down on the polished counter and scratched his neck. 'As a matter o' fact it was very good,' he replied quickly. 'There was this Chinese gel takin' us round the exhibition an' she was somefing again. Talk about beautiful.'

'Did yer chat 'er up?' Joey asked.

'Nah, I never got the chance,' Paul said, sighing.

'Well, it's too late now,' Joey told him with a big smile. 'Still it's just as well. You know the ole sayin'. East is east an' west is west!'

'I dunno about it bein' too late,' Paul replied thoughtfully. 'She comes from round 'ere.'

'The Chinky gel?'

'Yeah, she's Kay's friend.'

'She ain't out o' that Chinky laundry, is she?' Joey asked, frowning.

'Not exactly.'

'She eivver is or she ain't.'

Paul picked up his glass again. 'As a matter o' fact she's stayin' in rooms over the laundry,' he explained. 'Apparently 'er guardian is the bruvver o' the geezer who owns the laundry.'

'Guardian?'

'Yeah. Accordin' ter Kay, this geezer paid fer 'er education over in China an' 'e looks after 'er.'

'Sounds a bit fishy ter me,' Joey remarked, pulling a face.

'It's all above board,' Paul said quickly. 'This gel's really educated an' she works near our Kay. She's an interpreter wiv the Government.'

'It still sounds a bit iffy.'

'What makes yer say that?' Paul queried. 'There's nuffing wrong wiv 'avin' a guardian. It's the way they do fings in China.'

'So now yer an expert on Oriental matters,' Joey teased him.

Paul took another large swig from his glass and then looked closely at his friend. 'I tell yer what, Joey. This gel was stunnin'. I gotta see 'er again.'

'Take a couple o' shirts round the Chinky laundry an' see if she's there, or leave a message,' Joey suggested with a grin.

''Ow can I do that?' Paul growled.

The barrow boy took his friend by the arm and pulled

him towards the counter. 'If yer struck on 'er yer gotta make a play,' he said seriously. 'Just write a little note tellin' 'er 'ow much you enjoyed the show, or whatever it was, an' say yer'd like ter talk more about it. I s'pose you could always get your Kay ter make the introductions. Yer said she knows 'er.'

Paul nodded his head slowly. 'That might be a better idea,' he replied.

Butch Wheeler sauntered into the bar and ran a large hand through his unkempt sandy hair. 'It's gonna piss down before long,' he remarked.

Joey got him a drink. 'What you bin up to, Butch?' he asked.

'Not a lot,' the big man replied, smiling to show the gap in his teeth. 'I saw Sonny this afternoon. 'E got six buckets o' shit knocked out of 'im over in Belfast.'

''E lost the fight then?'

'Yeah, the ref stopped it in the third.'

'The silly git should turn it in,' Joey remarked disgustedly. 'I wouldn't let that trainer of 'is look after my ole moggy. Sonny's bein' used as a punch-bag an' 'e can't see it.'

Butch nodded. 'I make yer right. 'E's comin' in later, at least 'e said 'e was, but yer never know wiv 'im.'

Joey glanced at Paul and saw that he was staring into space, and he nudged the stocky window cleaner. ''E's got fings on 'is mind,' he said.

'What sort o' fings?'

''E's met this Chinky gel.'

'Bloody 'ell, a Chink?'

'Yeah an' 'e's smitten wiv 'er by the looks of 'im.'

'Sorry, I was miles away. What was yer sayin'?' Paul asked quickly.

'It doesn't matter,' Joey said dismissively.

'Tell us about this gel yer met,' Butch prompted him.

Paul glanced quickly from one to the other, and noticing the amused expressions on their faces he realised that he was being set up. 'I ain't in the mood ter talk about it,' he growled.

'Yer courtin' trouble gettin' involved wiv foreign gels, especially Chinkies,' Butch remarked.

'What about that geezer out o' Long Lane who married a German gel while 'e was in the army out there,' Joey went on. 'The people in 'is buildin's wouldn't 'ave anyfink ter do wiv 'er an' 'e 'ad ter move away. It made their lives a misery.'

'Yeah but she was a German,' Butch Wheeler replied. 'The Chinese people were on our side in the war.'

'It's all down ter culture though,' Joey persisted. 'It's two different worlds. I mean ter say, take yer food. They don't eat what we eat. Then there's yer religion. It's totally different.'

'Their standards are different too,' Butch said in support. 'Look at the way they live over in Chinatown. Bloody 'ell, they're all crammed in those little 'ouses, an' I 'eard they sleep ten to a room in most cases. They drink tea wiv no milk in it an' they live on rice. Just imagine bein' married ter one o' them gels an' yer come 'ome in the evenin' after an 'ard day's work to a bowl o' rice.'

'Give it a rest, will yer,' Paul cut in, irritation in his voice.

Joey pulled a face at Butch. 'It don't do ter generalise,'

he said, picking up his drink. 'Some o' those Orientals 'ave got money an' they live the life o' Riley.'

'I 'eard they gamble a lot,' the big window cleaner went on regardless. 'Mah-jong it's called. I was readin' about a case in the paper where a Chinky over in Pennyfields lost a lot o' money gamblin' an' the Tongs cut 'is ear off 'cos 'e couldn't pay up. Fancy that.'

A potential flare-up between the friends was averted by the timely arrival of Sonny Rowland, a short, dark man with the marks of combat starkly evident on his flat face, and as he strolled over to the three compatriots Joey winced. 'Gawd Almighty. You look like yer done fifteen rounds wiv Joe Louis,' he remarked.

'I 'ad a bad night,' Sonny said, shrugging his wide shoulders. 'The geezer I was up against is a good bet ter be the next British middleweight champion. I couldn't seem ter get goin' an' one lucky punch done it.'

'*One* lucky punch?' Butch said grinning. 'Yer look like 'e 'it yer wiv everyfing but the kitchen sink.'

Sonny Rowland touched the plaster over his right eye. 'This was what done it,' he replied. 'I got a bad cut an' the blood was runnin' in me eyes. I couldn't see the punches comin' after that.'

'You wanna ditch that manager o' yours,' Joey told him. 'A few more 'ammerin's like that an' yer'll be punchy.'

Sonny shrugged dismissively. 'So what's bin 'appenin' while I bin away?' he asked Joey.

Paul gave his friend a look of warning and Joey decided to steer the conversation away from the Tongs and mah-jong. 'Tell 'im about that sort in the buildin's, Butch,' he prompted.

The window cleaner grinned smugly, and as he began his story Joey moved a little way along the counter. 'Seriously, Paul, are yer gonna try an' see this gel?' he asked.

'I just got to,' Paul told him earnestly. 'She's a real stunner, an' I can't stop finkin' about 'er.'

Joey shrugged his shoulders. 'If yer meant ter get tergevver yer will,' he said. 'It's like me an' your Kay. Can you honestly tell me she's 'appy wiv that prat Richard Mills? No, course yer can't. She's just wastin' 'er time wiv 'im. I've a good mind ter chin the pompous bastard next time I see 'im . . .' He caught the look on Paul's face. 'I was only sayin' what I'd like ter do,' he added with quick humility.

Paul drained his glass and reached into his trouser pocket. 'Drink up,' he said, calling the barman over. 'I don't fink it'll last much longer wiv Kay an' 'im. Just be patient.'

The bar had started to fill up and the first roll of thunder sounded above the babble of conversation. The pianist took his drink over to the piano and set it down on the top.

'D'you know "Chinese Laundry Blues"?' Butch Wheeler called out to him.

Paul gave Joey a look of despair. 'Remind me ter slip some syrup o' figs in that aggravatin' git's brown ale, will yer,' he growled.

Earlier that evening Richard Mills had arrived at Tanners Alley wearing a pullover over his shirt and carrying a mackintosh on his arm even though the weather was sultry. 'Couldn't take the chance of getting wet,' he announced as they walked out into Grange Road. 'Still got a touch of the sniffles but I'm feeling a lot better. Mother dosed me up with aspirin and cough mixture. She was quite worried about my chest. I am inclined to colds going to my chest, so I suppose it was only natural for her to worry.'

Kay nodded. 'So where are we goin'?' she asked him.

'I thought you might like to see that film on at the Trocadera,' he replied.

'Not really,' she told him.

'Well then, let's take the tram to Southwark Park,' Richard suggested. 'The fresh air will do us both good.'

'Why don't we go ter the Swan fer a drink,' Kay said, guessing just what his reaction would be.

'Kay, I've already told you I don't feel inclined to get in your brother's company, no disrespect to him,' the young man said sharply. 'It's those uncouth friends of his. Besides, I don't want Westlake pestering you. Last time was bad enough. I would have given him a piece of my tongue except that I didn't want to create a scene.'

''E was only bein' polite,' Kay said irritably.

'No. I think the park sounds a better idea,' Richard told her as he gripped her arm.

'Richard, I don't want ter go ter the park,' she said, equally determined.

'You don't want the pictures, you don't want the park. Tell me, Kay, just what do you want to do this evening?' he said puffing loudly.

'I'd like ter go ter the Swan fer a drink,' she replied.

'And I said no.'

'Well, in that case we'd better give this evenin' a miss,' Kay growled.

Richard's temper had risen and beads of perspiration glistened on his forehead. 'If I didn't know you better

131

I'd have said that you wanted to see Joey Westlake,' he declared, eyeing her suspiciously.

'You don't know me at all, Richard,' the young woman said with passion. ''Cos if you did you'd know that I wouldn't be browbeaten inter goin' anywhere I didn't want ter go. As fer walkin' round Southwark Park on Saturday evenin', you can forget it.'

'Don't you start being bossy,' Richard retorted, two pink patches rising on his cheeks. 'Mother said you could be a bit bossy at times, and she was right.'

''Ow would your precious muvver know?'

'She's very perceptive, that's why,' Richard told her indignantly, 'and don't talk about my mother in that tone of voice. She's been very good to you, and don't you forget it.'

'Richard, do me a favour an' go 'ome ter yer muvver,' Kay said in exasperation. 'I can't take any more o' this.'

'Very well, I will, and don't expect me to come running round to you any more,' he spluttered. 'When you've seen sense you can call round to my house.'

'No I won't.'

'What do you mean you won't?'

'What I say. We're finished, Richard.'

The young man dabbed at his hot forehead with his handkerchief. 'Now you're being silly, Kay. You must try to learn that you can't have it all your own way.'

'Richard, do me a favour an' piss off,' she growled.

'Don't you dare talk to me like that.'

'Piss off.'

'I've never been so disgusted in all my life,' the young suitor gasped. 'You sound like a common factory girl.'

Kay swung round on her heel and walked back to the alley, feeling as though a huge weight had been lifted from her shoulders.

'You'll live to regret this,' he shouted after her. 'When you've seen sense don't come running back and expect that we can pick up the pieces. I've had enough too.'

Kay hurried up to her front door, fighting back tears of anger.

'Whatever's wrong?' Ruby said as her daughter stormed along the passage and ran up the stairs two at a time.

'I'm finished wi' that excuse fer a man,' she yelled down from the landing.

'Deary me,' Ruby sighed. 'I 'ope you ain't gonna sit up there in a tizz all evenin'.'

'No I'm not,' Kay told her sharply. 'I'm gonna change me dress, put on some make-up an' then go up the Swan. An' if I'm lucky I'll see Joey Westlake up there.'

'Deary me,' was all Ruby could find to say again as she walked back into the parlour to finish plumping up the cushions.

Chapter Twelve

The Masons lived at number 4 Tanners Alley and they valued their privacy. It was not that either of them was anti-social – in fact Nora Mason often stood at her front door to chat at length with her neighbours, and Jack her husband had a cheery word for everyone – but their home was their castle and there were no invitations for tea and gossip. None of the neighbours had ever crossed Nora's front doorstep but they knew that she was house-proud and guessed that her parlour was as cosy as any of theirs. Every week on Saturday morning the tenant of number 4 shook her mats, whitened her doorstep and changed her net curtains. She swept the front and polished her brass door knocker and letterbox as well as giving the flowerboxes a tidy up. She wore a clean apron to do her chores and her hair was rolled in curlers and contained neatly in a hairnet. She was a slight, nervous woman with mousy hair and eyes that tended to dart about, as though fearful that people were staring at her.

Jack Mason was a dapper man with sleeked-back black hair and he worked as a postman. He had fathered two sons who had married and moved out of the area and he led a simple life, enjoying a drink at the Swan and an occasional flutter on the greyhounds, and tending his small garden, where he grew flowers from seed and tomatoes in a sunny patch. Like his wife Nora Jack enjoyed the quiet life, and Tanners Alley afforded it, except when their next-door neighbour Lizzie Roach played up or when the Thompsons on the other side of them had one of their set-tos.

Nora Mason had been horrified on the occasion when Lizzie found herself trapped under the bed and hammered on the adjoining wall for help, and after raising the alarm she had not dared to follow Ruby Neal and Bel Allenby into Lizzie's house for fear of what she might see. She was very relieved when Bel told her what the problem was and thankful that things could return to normal, but now there was another crisis looming and she fretted anxiously.

'Jack, yer'll 'ave ter go an' talk ter the silly ole mare,' she told her husband as she prepared their Sunday dinner. 'The way she's goin' on she'll burn the 'ole lot of us down.'

Jack Mason knew only too well that Lizzie Roach was a headstrong old lady and nothing he could say would change things. He was worried though. Lizzie had been having a clear-out, and at the bottom of her garden, along with pulled-up weeds and trimmings, she had piled up old newspapers, a three-legged chair and a couple of bulging cardboard boxes.

'I felt a bit energetic when I got up,' she had told Nora over the fence that morning, 'so I decided ter sort me ole junk out.'

'What yer gonna do wiv that lot, put it in sacks fer the dustmen?' Nora enquired.

'Nah, they get shirty when yer stick too much beside yer dustbin,' Lizzie replied.

'So 'ow yer gonna get rid of it?'

'I'm gonna burn it.'

'Burn it?'

''S right,' the old lady told her with a toothless grin. 'See that tin? It's paraffin. That'll get a nice fire goin'.'

Nora looked terrified. 'Lizzie, yer'll set the fence alight, an' the sparks could catch yer curtains.'

'Nah, I'll shut me winders first,' she replied.

'What about *my* curtains?'

'Shut your winders.'

'But yer could set yerself alight wiv that stuff,' Nora said fearfully, eyeing the large silver tin.

'Don't you worry,' Lizzie told her. 'This afternoon I'll soak everyfing in the paraffin then I'll stand back an' chuck a lighted rag over it. That should do it.'

'Gawd Almighty! I don't know what yer finkin' of,' Nora groaned.

'Don't go bringin' 'im into it,' Lizzie said chuckling.

Seeing that she was getting nowhere trying to dissuade the old lady Nora turned to her husband, who was as concerned as she was.

'So what yer gonna do about it?' she asked him. 'We can't let 'er set light to all that stuff.'

'I'll talk to 'er, but I don't see what use it'll be,' Jack replied. 'Yer know 'ow she is. When she gets a bee in 'er bonnet there's no changin' 'er.'

When Jack Mason knocked on Lizzie's front door the old lady was ready for him. 'If yer come about that ole junk in me garden yer wastin' yer time,' she told him. 'The dustmen won't take it so I'll 'ave ter burn it.'

'But Lizzie . . .'

'It's no good you tryin' ter put me off, an' you can tell Nora what I'm tellin' you. After I've 'ad me little nap I'm gonna 'ave a burn-up, an' that's the end of it.'

'It'll be the end of you if yer not careful.'

'So what? I won't be missed.'

'Don't be so silly.'

'Just tell Nora ter shut 'er winders,' Lizzie said as she closed the door on him.

Ruby was deep in thought as she peeled the potatoes in her scullery that Sunday morning. What was happening to them all, she asked herself. Kay had come back home well after the pub had closed last night looking like the cat that got the cream. She had been in the company of that flash barrow boy, that was for sure, although she said she had merely stood chatting for a while to a couple of friends after closing time. Then there was Paul. He came home and went to bed with hardly a word, which was so unlike him. Jim too. What had got into him? It was very rare that he refused her, but last night he was asleep as soon as his head touched the pillow. Normally after a few drinks he was frisky, and yesterday she wanted him. Was he punishing her for not being in the mood earlier that week? Or was it that reunion? Why he went every year was beyond her. He always came home looking miserable and ready for some home comforts. Usually she'd snuggle up close in bed and stroke his neck, which had the desired effect, but last night there had been no response from him. She would have to talk to him. If that was what the reunion did then he would have to think seriously about whether he went to it again.

With the potatoes in the pot all salted ready and the greens sliced Ruby realised that there was little else to do for the moment. The house was looking spick and span and the joint was cooking nicely on a low heat, which only left the beds to be changed. That could wait until the sheets had aired. Bel would welcome her company for a few minutes no doubt.

After going through her usual preparations in front of the mirror Ruby left the house, only to be stopped by Nora Mason.

'Ruby, I'm worried out o' my life,' the nervous woman told her. 'It's Lizzie Roach.'

'Not again,' Ruby groaned. 'What's it now?'

When Nora told her what Lizzie was going to do Ruby patted her arm supportively. 'Don't you worry, I'll talk to 'er after I've 'ad a chat wiv Bel,' she told her.

The warm May sun climbed steadily into the clear blue sky as the two women sat together over a cup of tea in Bel Allenby's parlour.

'I can't see 'er gettin' back wiv Richard, though I 'ope she sees sense,' Ruby was going on.

'P'raps she 'as seen sense,' Bel replied. 'Better they split up than get married an' realise the mistake then.'

'I dunno, what wiv one fing an' anuvver,' Ruby sighed. 'Nuffing runs smoove fer long, does it? Paul's like a bear wiv a sore 'ead, an' Jim came 'ome from that stupid reunion wivout a kiss me arse or anyfink.'

'Are you two all right?' Bel asked, looking over her teacup.

'Course we are,' Ruby said quickly. 'It's just that 'e's bin a bit moody lately.'

'Nuffing wrong wiv 'im is there, physically I mean?' Bel queried.

'Nah, Jim's in 'is prime, but I dunno,' Ruby frowned. 'Anyway I expect 'e'll snap out of it.'

'Yer'll both feel better after yer've 'ad yer 'olidays,' Bel said. 'Is it gonna be Devon?'

Ruby shrugged her shoulders. 'Jim's keen, but I 'aven't made me mind up yet.'

'Why ever not?' Bel said quickly. 'The two of yer on yer own wiv no distractions. It'll be like a second 'oneymoon.'

'Yeah I'm sure,' Ruby said dismissively. 'We seem ter get picky wiv each ovver whenever we're on our own lately.'

'What about the bed bit?' Bel asked. 'Yer've not let that go I would 'ope.'

Ruby pulled a face. 'It doesn't mean as much ter me as it does ter Jim,' she admitted. ''E'd 'ave it all the time if I said yes. They don't realise though, do they? It's more a physical fing wiv men. They can come 'ome an' put their feet up. Wiv us there's always somefing ter do. Cookin', cleanin', runnin' the place. 'Alf the time we get inter bed exhausted. Then they start their tricks.'

Bel smiled and shook her head slowly. 'Ruby, you're never exhausted. You're always on the go, tryin' ter find fings ter do. P'raps if yer let it slip a bit yer'd be ready an' willin'.'

'There's standards ter be kept up,' the younger woman replied firmly. 'There's no way I want my 'ome ter be a tip. Before I was married I . . .'

'Don't go on about that again, Ruby,' her friend cut in.

'If you're not careful yer gonna lose everyfing. One day Kay an' Paul are gonna get married an' then yer find there's nuffing left. I've seen it 'appen to ovver people. Now should be the time fer you an' Jim ter get closer. Before Jack got ill we couldn't leave each ovver alone. I was 'oldin' down a pretty important job at the time as yer know, an' Jack was workin' all the hours God sends, but it didn't stop us. We were like a couple o' love-birds in bed an' I don't mind tellin' yer about it, if it'll make yer see sense. Take my advice. Ferget that 'ousework. Ferget changin' the beds or cleanin' a perfectly tidy room. Get lovey-dovey an' be a bit more adventurous. I'm gonna tell yer somefink. Some o' the best sex me an' Jack enjoyed wasn't in bed!'

'Bel, you are shockin' at times,' Ruby answered quickly. 'I couldn't do it in bed wiv the light on, let alone in the parlour.'

'Well, that's your problem,' Bel said with a shrug of her shoulders. 'You're the loser. Just don't be the big loser. Yer know the ole sayin'. Wet ducks don't fly.'

Ruby put her empty cup and saucer down on the table and sighed deeply. 'I'm not turnin' into an ole prune, am I, Bel?' she asked with concern.

'Course not,' her friend reassured her. 'It's just that yer don't work at it. They say about men that if they don't use it they'll lose it, an' that applies just as much to us.'

'But I'm still dry most times when Jim's ready,' Ruby confessed. 'It makes it very awkward.'

'Yeah, it would do, but a lot o' that is tension,' Bel told her. 'Yer don't let yerself relax enough. You're seein' it as a favour instead of a pleasure ter both of yer. Take my advice an' pick a good day. Tell yerself in the mornin' that yer gonna vamp Jim that night. Send 'im off ter work wiv a big kiss an' whisper somefing wicked in 'is ear. Keep it in yer mind an' dwell on it all day. Try to imagine doin' it, on the edge o' the table, on the stairs, even in the passage. Be a little wicked, an' I promise yer, Ruby luv, it'll work out very nicely, fer both of yer.'

The younger woman looked embarrassed. 'Bel, I never expected you ter talk like that,' she said, her face flushing slightly.

'Why ever not?' Bel replied with a grin. 'You an' me 'ave bin good friends fer a lot o' years now an' if we can't talk openly about sex, who can?'

Ruby stood up. 'Look, I've gotta go. Lizzie Roach is playin' up again an' I'd better see if I can sort it out.'

'What's she bin up to now?' Bel asked.

'She's gonna 'ave a burn-up in 'er garden an' Nora Mason's worried out of 'er life in case the silly ole mare sets us all alight.'

'Well, good luck wiv 'er, an' just remember what I said,' Bel remarked smiling. 'I'll be expectin' you to 'ave a gleam in yer eye before very long.'

Lizzie Roach never ate a Sunday lunch. She had long since dissuaded her neighbours from giving her a cooked meal and they had been made to realise in no uncertain terms that she preferred to cut herself a sandwich or heat up a tin of soup, after which she would usually doze off in her rocking-chair while listening to the wireless. Today though Lizzie could not sleep. She put her renewed energy down to the liver pills she had got Ruby to fetch from the chemist and instead of snoring in the chair the old lady went out into the garden. No time like the present, she told herself as she struggled to take the lid off the tin of paraffin. 'Why do they always do the bloody fings up so tight?' she grumbled aloud. 'Ron, is that you in the garden?'

Her next-door neighbour was busy putting a few marigolds in the ground at Myrtle's behest before going for his usual Sunday drink and he got up to peer over at Lizzie. 'What's wrong, gel?' he asked.

'It's this bloody tin. See if yer can get the lid off,' she urged him.

'What is it?' he asked as he reached over.

'Paraffin.'

'What yer usin' it for?'

'I'm gonna set meself alight wiv it,' Lizzie chuckled.

Ron pulled a face, wishing he hadn't asked. 'There we are,' he said, handing her back the container.

Lizzie set about dowsing the stack of rubbish with paraffin and then when she was satisfied she went back into her scullery to fetch a piece of rag, unaware that she was being watched by Nora Mason who stood at her back bedroom window with a terrified look on her face. She was also unaware that Jack Mason was standing at the ready in his scullery, armed with two buckets filled to the brim with water.

'Right, 'ere we go,' Lizzie said as she struck a match and lit the soaked rag, reaching her arm back to get a good throw. Unfortunately the burning cloth brushed the bottom of her apron which was splashed with the fuel and immediately set ablaze.

'Oh my Gawd!' Nora shouted. 'Jack! Quick!'

Lizzie staggered back as she tried to pat out the flames and was then knocked sideways as a bucket of cold water soaked her from head to foot.

'I told yer what would 'appen didn't I, yer silly ole mare,' Nora called down.

Lizzie's grey hair was dripping with water and hanging down over her face and she parted it with her hands to look up at Nora. 'Who you callin' a silly ole mare?' she growled.

'You, that's who,' Nora raged. 'If it wasn't fer my Jack yer'd 'ave bin burnt alive.'

Lizzie Roach muttered an obscene reply as she went back in the house for a towel, and at that moment Ruby knocked at the front door.

'I'm a silly ole cow,' Lizzie sniffled. 'I can't do anyfing right.'

Jack Mason had meanwhile climbed over into the old lady's garden and dowsed the rubbish with the second bucket. He was making sure with another bucketful passed over by Nora when Ruby came out to see the damage. 'Is she all right?' he asked her.

'Yeah, she's gettin' out of 'er wet clothes,' Ruby told him. 'I dunno what we're gonna do wiv 'er. It's a good job you were on 'and.'

Jack had pulled the cardboard boxes to one side and he looked inside one of them. 'I 'ope she knows what she was doin',' he said. 'There's a load o' papers 'ere.'

Ruby pulled a bundle of envelopes from the box and slowly shook her head. 'The poor ole mare's goin' round the bend, I'm sure of it,' she sighed. 'These are 'er life insurance policies.'

Chapter Thirteen

Ruby stood at the scullery sink on the bright Monday morning watching a wary blackbird that sat on the garden fence. Lizzie Roach's mangy tabby cat would soon be making an appearance and one of these days it was going to catch the bird, she felt sure. There it was, approaching this time from another direction, creeping slyly along the stone path almost like a worm. Inch by inch it closed on the blackbird and soon it would be near enough to make the leap up the fencing. In a way the tabby cat took after its owner, Ruby thought as she quickly filled an enamel jug with water. When Lizzie set her mind on something she usually got her way, often craftily. She knew how to manipulate the situation to suit her needs and that flea-bitten animal of hers was doing the same. It crouched now, its back legs poised for the launch, its back arched ready.

'Myrtle?'

'What now?'

The loud voices sent the bird flying off and the cat scurrying up on to the rear fence where it sat, no doubt disappointed at being denied its breakfast.

''Ow many times 'ave I told yer not ter leave my garden

145

fings out at night?' Ron Thompson raved. 'They'll soon go bloody rusty left out all night.'

'I dunno what yer goin' on about,' Myrtle replied as she stepped into their back garden. 'It wasn't rainin' last night.'

'Yeah but it could 'ave bin.'

'Well it didn't, so stop yer moanin' an' get on wiv what I asked yer ter do,' Myrtle growled at him.

Ruby smiled to herself as she emptied the jug in the stone sink. Whenever Ron Thompson was on late turn at the brewery Myrtle took advantage. She made sure that there was always something for him to do around the house or out in the garden. As she had told Ruby, 'If I leave 'im wiv nuffing ter do 'e'll be noddin' off in the chair an' then straight up the pub as soon as they open. I'd see nuffing of 'im.'

'Myrtle?'

'What?'

'Where exactly d'yer want these plants puttin'?'

'In front o' the marigolds.'

'Nah it's too sunny there. They need the shade. The ovver side's better.'

'There ain't no room on the ovver side,' Myrtle shouted out from the scullery.

'There will be, when I pull these weeds up.'

'Weeds? They're not weeds yer silly git,' she yelled at him. 'They're me asters comin' up.'

'Well I dunno, do I,' Ron said sheepishly.

'You're about as useless as a tailor's dummy,' Myrtle sighed. 'Just leave it, I'll put 'em in later.'

'I fink I'll pop up the shop fer the Grey'ound Express then,' Ron remarked. 'I might pick a few winners.'

'That'll be the day,' Myrtle laughed.

It became quiet next door and Ruby went up to her bedroom to prepare for her spell at the surgery. Normally she would have been eager to get out of the house on a nice sunny morning, but today she felt a little deflated without fully understanding why. Was it something that Bel Allenby had said yesterday? She had certainly been forward, but that was Bel. She never pulled her punches, and for someone of her age it was surprising. 'Whisper something wicked into his ear' indeed. Whatever next. Jim would no doubt be thinking about losing out over the weekend and he would be eager to put things right as soon as possible. Perhaps she should encourage him to be a little loving tonight. It would certainly take him by surprise. Monday nights were never very exciting in that respect, Ruby thought. Maybe it would help lift the feeling of despondency that threatened to take hold of her this morning.

By the time she stepped out of her house into the bright sunlight she was beginning to feel more like her usual self. She had decided to surprise them all this evening. Instead of the normal Monday fare of cold meat, potatoes and pickles she would do a full salad with sardines or pilchards, and to fill a hole she would make a currant pudding and custard.

'Mornin', Ruby,' Connie Wilson called out, leaning against her doorway with her hands tucked inside a clean apron.

'Mornin', Connie. 'Ow's George?' Ruby asked her.

'No better. It'll be a week or two yet,' she replied with a resigned gesture.

'Must fly, I'm late this mornin',' Ruby lied.

'No peace fer the wicked,' Connie said smiling.

Ruby gave her a look of feigned disapproval and hurried out into Grange Road, assailed by the strong sweet smell from the nearby tannery and the acrid fumes as traffic crawled behind a slow-moving, heavily laden horse cart. As she ran up the few steps into the surgery she was confronted by Mrs Childs, who had a problem.

'It's no good, I'll 'ave ter see Dr Ambrose. Last time Dr Phelps mucked me prescription up,' she moaned. 'The cough medicine 'e gave me was useless. I told 'im I wanted the same stuff Dr Ambrose prescribed last time but 'e never took no notice. Gawd knows what's got into 'im lately. 'E used ter be such a good doctor at one time.'

'All right, Mrs Childs, I'll fit you in wiv Dr Ambrose,' Ruby reassured her, 'but you might 'ave ter wait a bit. 'E'll be very busy this mornin'.'

'Suits me, as long as I get the right stuff,' the elderly lady replied, following her through to the waiting room. ''Ere, ain't it about time yer changed these magazines? They've bin 'ere fer weeks.'

Albert Walburton shuffled in behind them and took his usual seat by the door. 'Must be seventy,' he remarked.

'Who?' Mrs Childs asked.

'Why, ole Dr Phelps.'

'I fink it's about time 'e turned it in, ter be honest,' the elderly lady said, clutching her bag to her bosom.

'I prefer 'im to Ambrose,' Albert replied.

'Ambrose is a good doctor,' Mrs Childs said defiantly.

'Yeah that's as it may be, but 'e rushes yer off out before yer've caught yer breath,' Albert went on. 'I come in 'ere a couple o' weeks ago wiv a pain in me bladder.

Couldn't pass water. Well I could, but it took me ages ter get anyfing out, an' then it was just a dribble. Anyway 'e asked me ter give 'im a sample. I was in that karsey fer quite a while, an' yer know what it's like tryin' ter piss in those silly little bottles they give yer.'

'D'you mind,' Mrs Childs said abruptly.

'I'm only tellin' yer,' Albert said, looking aggrieved.

'Well, I'd prefer not to 'ear about it, if yer don't mind,' she told him sharply.

'Please yerself.'

The surgery began to fill up fast and Ruby was kept very busy. Mrs Caulfield was back with Billy and the Harringtons came in, followed by the portly Mrs Young, who found it difficult to make herself comfortable wedged between Albert and Mrs Childs.

''Ave yer got enough room, luv?' Albert asked her sarcastically as he felt himself being squashed between her bulk and the wall.

Mrs Young nodded, wiping her watery eyes on a large handkerchief.

'What's that fat lady cryin' for, Mum?' Billy asked.

'Shh. Don't be nosy.'

'Yeah, but why's she cryin'?'

'She's not cryin'. Now shut up.'

'Mum?'

'Now what?'

'Mum, will it 'urt bein' circumscribed?'

Mrs Caulfield pulled a face at her inquisitive son to cover her embarrassment. 'The doctor's only gonna take a look at it,' she growled under her breath.

Very slowly the waiting room emptied as one by one

the patients' various problems were dealt with by the two overworked doctors, and just as Ruby finished replacing the stack of case notes in the filing cabinet Pam Mills walked into the surgery.

'I'm sorry, the doctors 'ave just left,' Ruby told her.

'It's not them I came ter see,' Pam answered. 'I wondered if I could 'ave a word wiv yer.'

'Is it about Kay an' Richard?'

Pam nodded. 'I was shocked when Richard came 'ome the ovver evenin' an' told me they'd finished. I thought it was all goin' so well between 'em.'

'Yeah, so did I,' Ruby replied. 'I don't know what's got inter that gel o' mine.'

'I do,' Pam said haughtily. 'It's that barrer boy Westlake. 'E's the one who's come between 'em. Turned Kay's 'ead 'e 'as. An' there was me finkin' 'ow level-'eaded she was. I don't mind tellin' yer, Richard's really taken it badly.'

'What can I say?' Ruby sighed, shrugging her shoulders. 'Kay's not a child.'

'Well, I'd 'ave some fings ter say,' Pam retorted sharply. 'She'll 'ave ter go a long way ter find anyone as good as my Richard. She could 'ave 'ad a good life wiv 'im. 'E's very 'ard-workin', an' 'e's got good prospects fer the future. She wouldn't 'ave wanted fer a fing. Put that against what that spiv Westlake can offer 'er.'

Ruby took a deep breath. She had started the day a little glum and had tried to lift her spirits, despite the niggling of the patients and the undefined worries that were trying to surface inside her mind. Now, just as she was beginning to feel more like her usual bubbling self, Pam Mills had to appear on the scene. 'Look, Pam, I've tried ter make that gel o' mine see sense,' she said quietly. 'I've spelt it all out to 'er but at the end o' the day it's not down ter me, nor you. It's up ter Kay an' Richard ter sort it out between themselves.'

'Richard told me 'e was very shocked the way Kay swore at 'im that evenin',' Pam went on. ''E won't put up wiv that sort o' fing.'

'Well, all I can say is, if my Kay swore at your boy then 'e deserved it,' Ruby said quickly. 'Now if yer don't mind I've gotta close up.'

'Well, if you're gonna side in wiv 'er there's nuffing more ter be said, is there?'

'No I fink not,' Ruby replied.

Pam Mills left the surgery without another word, and as Ruby walked home she felt as though one small care had suddenly fallen away. As she had pointed out to the Mills woman, Kay was not a child and she would have to make her own decisions. It was crystal clear now. She had been wrong in trying to act as marriage broker and it had caused her daughter, and Richard, quite some pain. What was more, she would sit down this evening with Kay and tell her that she had been wrong. Perhaps it would go some way in healing the rift that had been growing between them.

Jim Neal changed into his overalls and sat down on the bench in the maintenance room to roll a cigarette before starting work. The wall clock showed ten minutes to eight o'clock and he was grateful for the short respite before the busy day began. He pulled his tool-bag towards him and checked that all the equipment was there to finish the job in Angela's office. The pipes round the ceiling still had to be dismantled which would take a couple of hours and she would be in by nine. Seeing her again after what had happened would be a little embarrassing for both of them, he imagined. He had not stopped thinking about Saturday night and he had caught Ruby giving him some searching looks throughout Sunday. She couldn't know anything, unless he had been talking in his sleep. No, his guilt had made him nervous. Ruby would have been wondering why he didn't respond to her when he got into bed in the early hours of Sunday and she would have been searching for a reason.

'Jim, yer'll 'ave ter leave that office till later,' Percy Bradley told him as he put his head round the door. 'We've gotta strip that wrappin' machine down.'

Jim picked up his tool-bag and followed the maintenance foreman to the work floor, starting nervously as the factory hooter sounded. It was alarming how rattled he had become and he realised he had to pull himself together. It had been a purely physical thing, they both understood that, so why should he feel like a lovesick schoolboy, desperate to see her again?

'Jim, are you gonna stand there starin' over at Mary all day? We've gotta get this bastard machine sorted out.'

'Sorry, Percy,' Jim said quickly. 'I was miles away. 'Ere, let me do that, I got a longer reach.'

The older man sat back on his haunches and wiped his greasy hands on some cotton waste. 'Can yer get to it?' he asked.

'Yeah just about,' Jim answered, grunting with the effort.

Within a few minutes he had succeeded in loosening all the nuts securing the machine cover, and with Percy's help the retaining bolts were removed.

'It should be straightforward now,' Percy said looking pleased.

'I can manage, if yer've got ovver fings ter do,' Jim told him.

'Right-o, son. I'll leave yer to it,' the older man replied, getting up with a grunt. 'By the way, I got me retirement date. I leave in August.'

'Good fer you, Percy, yer've earned it,' Jim said smiling.

'Yer do know you're down ter replace me,' the foreman said, throwing the cotton waste under the machine and grinning at him. 'I put a good word or two in for yer but at the end o' the day it's Norris's decision. Len Moody'll be in the frame too. 'E's got the years in, but the tools don't sit in 'is 'ands like they do in yours. That much I told Norris. Anyway, son, keep yer fingers crossed, an' in the meantime get this bastard stripped down quick as yer can.'

Jim was still smiling as he set to work. Percy Bradley was of the old school, a first-class engineer who also knew how to get the best out of his workers. He was going to miss him.

In the meantime though, a factory change-around meant that this rather ancient machine was being consigned to the first floor to be replaced by a multi-wrapper, a fast-wrapping contraption which was expected to double the daily output of Cellophane-packaged individual pork pies. The new machine was due to be delivered and set up the following day and the space had to be made ready. Mindful of the urgency Jim immersed himself in the job and did not hear Angela's footsteps until she was standing over him.

'Good morning, Jim. I can see you're busy,' she said smiling down at him.

He slid out from under the rollers and looked up at her, noticing the twinkle in her eyes. 'Yeah, this is goin' upstairs.'

'Yes I know,' she replied, looking amused. 'I'm on my way to see Percy. I had to come and say hello.'

Jim stood up facing her, wiping his oily hands on a piece of rag. 'Are you OK?' he asked.

'I feel just fine,' she said, her smile lingering at the corners of her small mouth. 'I thought about you all day Sunday.'

'I thought about you too.'

'Can I see you at lunchtime?' she asked.

Jim hesitated for a few moments. 'Eh, yeah, OK. Where?'

'The Galleon?'

'OK.'

'One o'clock?'

Jim nodded as he saw the factory foreman coming along the alleyway.

'The dates are confirmed, Mr Neal. Two weeks in August,' Angela said as the foreman passed them.

'Much obliged,' Jim replied.

'Don't be late,' she said winsomely as soon as the foreman was out of earshot.

Chapter Fourteen

Across the Thames and eastwards, three young men gathered in the small back room of a dilapidated house in Pennyfields. They were dressed in suits and open-necked shirts, in contrast with the elderly owner of the house who wore traditional Chinese dress: an indigo-dyed jacket folded over to the right breast, adorned with gold-coloured embroidery, and black silk trousers that reached to just above his ankles. The old man wore a round flat hat and his feet were encased in slippers with a thick white sole as he shuffled in to light the joss-sticks spaced in tiny vases around the tatty room. According to the arrangement a meal was to be provided, and satisfied that the sticks were all smoking Wu Sung shuffled out to prepare rice and chicken.

Various premises were used in rotation by the notorious 'Sons of Heaven', a Tong gang that struck terror into the local Chinese community, frustrating every effort by Chief Inspector Kennedy of Limehouse police to hunt down the perpetrators of a series of violent crimes in the neighbourhood. The killer of Charlie Wo went unpunished, although almost everyone knew his identity. So too did the person responsible for chopping off two of Su Dung's fingers. It was common knowledge in the little backstreets around the Chinese quarter of Limehouse that both men had lost heavily at the mah-jong tables and had not been able to honour their debts. It was said that Charlie Wo had refused to give dues to the Tong and had paid the ultimate penalty.

As they waited for their appointed leader to arrive, Billy Chou held court. He and the three other young men were the sons of Chinese seamen who had remained ashore and settled in the area back in the twenties, and they spoke in staccato English, Cantonese being their second language.

'Tommy Lo is too familiar with Kennedy for my liking,' Billy Chou was saying. 'Stroking the tiger is a bad thing.'

'Tommy knows what he's doing,' Danny Ling told him confidently. 'We're strong through having trust and it's a bad thing to talk that way.'

'It's a bad thing to fester like a boil,' Billy growled. 'I'm speaking openly. Would you deny me that?'

'Billy's right,' the third member of the group cut in. 'The police raid last week on the Chungking foodstore must have been due to a tip-off. They found cases of tinned fruit that Sou Chi could not account for.'

Danny Ling looked unimpressed. 'We all know that Sou Chi deals in opium. Did the police find opium there? No of course not. Sou Chi was pre-warned of the raid, and I tell you that when he comes to court he'll have the necessary permits for the tinned fruit.'

Victor Sen, the third member, chuckled. 'Tommy Lo does not stroke the tiger, he feeds it scraps. The red meat remains ours to devour.'

They heard the front door open and close and then footsteps on the stairs. Tommy Lo came in the room with a wide grin. 'I was pulled in this morning,' he announced.

'The police?'

'Chief Inspector Kennedy was in a bad mood,' the Tong leader told them. 'Sou Chi went into Limehouse police station yesterday with permits. It seems that he found them after all.'

'Not even a scrap of meat for the inspector,' Danny Ling said, looking over at Billy Chou.

Tommy Lo beckoned them to the table. Like the rest he was slightly built. He wore a smart navy blue suit, white shirt and neatly knotted striped tie. His white teeth flashed a smile as he ran a slender hand lightly over his sleek raven hair that was parted down the middle, but his long dark eyes glinted with seriousness as he addressed them. 'A visit will have to be paid to Cater Street in Bermondsey as soon as possible,' he said, looking at each of the members in turn. 'Ho Chang who runs a laundry over there is in debt at the Peking Club. His promissory note has now expired and there's been no word from him.'

'Would that be the one who had the laundry in Solomon Street?' Danny queried.

'The same.'

'How much does he owe?' Billy asked.

'Seventy pounds and the interest.'

'Do we go in force?'

Tommy Lo looked across the table at Billy Chou and shook his head. 'Remember, Bermondsey is south of the river,' he told him. 'Barbarian country. We have no Tong brothers there and we'll be treading on strange ground. I'll make the initial visit alone, and a new time for payment will be set. If Ho Chang continues to disregard his debt then it will be time for us to demonstrate to him that the Sons of Heaven have many and varied means of extracting payment.'

Wu Sung shuffled into the room and spoke in Chinese. Tommy nodded to him and then loosened his tie. 'We'll eat first and deal with the candlemaker afterwards,' he declared.

Victor Sen nodded. 'Another hour in the cellar among the rats will help him think about his children, if not his wife.'

'The candlemaker is going to spend the rest of his life wishing he'd been more careful with that hot wax,' Billy Chou said with venom as he unwrapped a machete and tested the blade with his thumb.

Wu Sung brought in bowls of hot clear soup heavily spiced with chillies and a large dish each of rice and chicken covered in curried sauce from which the young men helped themselves. The meal was eaten in silence and then Billy Chou produced a bottle of spirits. Tommy Lo stopped him with a quick shake of his head. 'It's getting late. We should finish our business,' he told them.

Billy Chou picked up the bundle from a chair and followed the rest of the Tong members downstairs to the dark passageway. Under the stairs was a door that led down into the cellar and Tommy pulled a face as he smelt the stench. 'What does Wu Sung keep in this cellar, apart from candlemakers?' he growled.

Victor Sen felt for the switch at the bottom of the stairs, and as light flooded the small, evil-smelling room the young gangsters saw the pathetic-looking man huddled in a corner against the slimy wall. He was tethered by a chain which stretched from ankle fetters to a metal ring in the wall. Tommy Lo unlocked the clasps and Billy Chou kicked the man viciously. 'Sit in that chair,' he ordered.

The candlemaker appeared to be resigned to his fate and he dragged himself into the chair and looked up at the Tong members who gathered around him. 'It was an accident,' he said in a low voice. 'I meant to throw the wax against the wall in my temper but the young child ran in front of me. All day long I'd been listening to my wife telling me that I was a bad husband. She can't understand that a man who works hard for long hours every day without rest needs to take succour from the pipe once in a while.'

'Your youngest child will quite possibly carry her scars for life,' Tommy Lo told him.

Billy Chou unwrapped the weapon and leaned over the slumped figure who was now sweating heavily. 'Chi San will never be allowed to forget the day you scalded her and neither will you. Tie his right hand to the arm of the chair, Victor.'

'I beg you,' the candlemaker screamed out. 'Don't take away the only means I have of earning a living for my family! What good is a candlemaker without both his hands? Maim me and you punish my family too.'

Victor Sen ignored the man's pleading as he strapped his forearm to the chair. 'Who's going to do him?' he asked.

'I'll do it,' Billy Chou said. 'This blade isn't as sharp as it could be though, I might have to saw him a bit.'

'I'll do it,' Tommy Lo announced.

'Let me,' Billy said, gripping the machete tightly in his fist.

'Give it to me,' Tommy told him.

Billy Chou reluctantly handed over the weapon and Tommy moved to stand over the shaking figure in the chair. 'Better for you to close your eyes,' he said as he raised the knife over his head.

The candlemaker started to whine, his head lowered on to his heaving chest as he shook with fear. Suddenly Tommy Lo brought the machete down sharply and it cut into the arm of the chair half an inch from the tips of the captive's fingers.

'We've shown you mercy today,' he said, his dark eyes widening, 'but it's only because of your family. Now go home to them and make your peace. Just remember if you come before us again we'll cut your throat out.'

Outside in the shade of a large plane tree the three young men lounged.

'I tell you, Victor, Tommy Lo's lost his appetite for proper retribution,' Billy declared. 'His roots are not as strong as ours. His Chinese blood's diluted and runs thin in his veins. We should consider very carefully whether it's appropriate to use the special vote.'

'I think it's too drastic a step to even consider at this time,' Victor Sen told them. 'Better to wait and see how he handles the urgent business in Bermondsey.'

Danny Ling nodded in agreement. 'If he fails then maybe it will be time,' he said.

Freda Lo dragged her heavy frame into the old church

gardens and sat down wearily on the hard bench facing the west wall of St Barnabas. As she rested in the shade, watching the pigeons strutting to and fro, she thought about many things. Would that she could have had her life over again. No way would she have chosen the same stony path. As it was, she had been disowned by her own kith and kin, and was barely suffered by the local Chinese population. For a start she would never have married Sammy Lo. Not that Sammy had been anything but a good man; he had always treated her well and had loved her in his own way, and she had loved him too. She missed him now and his photograph still stared down at her from the mantelshelf in the tiny kitchen of her flat in Pennyfields. His remains were resting on the bottom of the North Atlantic along with many of his shipmates, and Freda had been left to bring up Tommy on her own.

Freda cast her mind back to the day when she first came into London's East End. It had frightened her. Oriental figures in foreign clothes moved like ghosts through the foggy streets of Chinatown and the noise of traffic going in and out the docks seemed never-ending. Born and brought up in Norfolk, she had found work as a housemaid to the Mainwarings, a Yarmouth family who had connections with the sea. John Mainwaring like his father before him was a ship's captain, and when he took charge of the Oriental Lines flagship he moved his family to London.

Eunice Mainwaring was never able to settle in the large, cold Victorian house in Limehouse and she became very difficult to please. Freda felt that the woman was slowly losing her mind, and she became convinced of it when Eunice accused her of stealing a necklace, a comparatively cheap piece of marcasite which was later found under a cushion. Freda decided that she had no choice but to leave the Mainwarings' employment and, desperate for money and shelter, she took a job at a seamen's hotel in Wapping. Her wages were only a few shillings a week but food and a bed were provided.

It was while working in the kitchen that Freda first got to know Sammy Lo. A ship's cook, he spoke good English and had a ready smile for everyone. Sammy's dream was to leave the sea and open his own eating house in Chinatown. Freda smiled at the recollection. 'You are a good cook, young missy,' he had said. 'You must come and work for me when I open my place. I will treat you very well.'

Alone and without friends, Freda formed an attachment to the likeable Chinese character which bridged their differences of culture and upbringing, and when Sammy finally realised his dream he was as good as his word. Still a comparatively young man, he made a good living from the 'China Sea' and Freda was able to share in his success. As she sat in the shade of the large plane tree she remembered Sammy's sweaty face peering at her through the steam and announcing that they should get married. 'The business will then be half yours,' he told her with his customary grin.

Although shunned by her own family for her choice of partner and referred to by many people as 'Chinese meat', Freda was happy, and when Tommy was born her contentment was complete. The lad grew strong, learned Cantonese from his father and did very well at a local school which had many Chinese amongst its pupils. The family business did not interest him, however, and craving travel and adventure Tommy joined the merchant service.

Came the war and Sammy Lo went back to sea, driven by patriotism for the land of his birth and for the country which had adopted him, leaving Freda to run the business. During his last shore leave he lived in hope of meeting up with his son but it was not to be. Tommy's ship docked in Gibraltar on its way home with storm damage the day Sammy sailed away to meet his death.

The 'China Sea' was destroyed during the Blitz and with it went all Freda's motivation. With Tommy back home and in bad company, it was as much as the widow could do to struggle on and provide a home for her son as long as she could, knowing that in so doing she was able to assert some influence and authority over him.

He was coming towards her now, his shoulders hunched and his hands deep in his trouser pockets. He often met her here in the peace and serenity of St Barnabas churchyard but he did not have his father's ready smile. He was always troubled lately and Freda feared for him. She had learned long ago through close association that families and ancestry played a prominent role in the lives of the Chinese community, and she knew only too well that her son Tommy Lo was walking a thin, perilous line. His blood was mixed and his thinking influenced by his upbringing in a Western society. The Tongs were unforgiving, and one wrong move could spell the end.

'Good boy, you can carry my bag home,' she told him as he reached her.

'I saw you come in,' Tommy said quietly. 'I was with the others under the tree.'

They walked out of the churchyard together and Freda

looked at her son with concern. 'There's talk that you're going to punish the candlemaker,' she said.

'It's done with, Ma,' he replied. 'We just frightened him.'

'We should leave this place,' Freda sighed. 'I can see nothing but bad things coming.'

'Where would we go?' Tommy asked.

'I could go back to Norfolk and you could go back to sea,' she told him. 'I'd miss you of course but I'd see you after your trips and the dangers wouldn't be as bad as they are right now.'

'Maybe we will leave this place,' Tommy said, smiling at her. 'One day.'

They walked into Pennyfields and one or two Chinese shopkeepers gave them furtive glances as they stood outside in the afternoon sunlight.

'I loved this place once,' Freda remarked with a distant look in her eyes. 'But it means nothing to me now, not any more. There's talk of pulling this area down and relocating the people. Where will they go?'

'Certainly not back to China,' Tommy said grinning.

They had reached the entrance to their block and they climbed the flight of wooden steps to the first-floor flat. Inside the front door on the hessian mat was a sealed envelope. Tommy picked it up and tore it open. 'It's just a message from Billy Chou,' he said lightly.

'I'll make some soup,' Freda said.

'Not for me, Ma,' Tommy told her. 'I'm going over to Bermondsey tonight.'

'Think on what we talked about, Tommy,' she said with sadness in her voice.

Tommy Lo left the flat and stepped out into the cool evening. Resting in his coat pocket was the revised bill for the urgent attention of Ho Chang the Bermondsey laundryman. With interest it had now trebled and Tommy knew that Billy Chou and the others would be impatient to see how he fared in recovering the money.

Starlings were chattering in the leafy trees above the empty churchyard of St Barnabas as the sky changed colour and the sun sank down towards the west, and in a nearby street, in the secrecy of his workshop, the candlemaker slowly recovered, helped in no small way by the euphoriant he kept in a locked drawer beneath his wax-spattered bench.

Chapter Fifteen

Kay Neal hurried round the corner to Waterloo Bridge a few minutes after five o'clock and was delighted to see Mei Li boarding a waiting bus. She jumped aboard just as the vehicle moved away from the stop and climbed to the upper deck. Mei Li had just slipped into a vacant seat. She looked up as Kay sat down beside her and her face broke into a happy smile. 'I thought about you at the weekend, Kay,' she told her. 'I was very sorry I didn't have time to talk to you and your brother. Did you both like the exhibition?'

'It was really good,' Kay said enthusiastically. 'Paul liked it too. 'E finks you're very pretty by the way.'

Mei Li brought her hand up to her mouth and stifled a giggle. 'He was just being nice,' she replied.

Kay smiled at her. 'Paul kept on about it all weekend. An' that story yer told us.'

'The Chinese Lantern?'

'Yeah. What a lovely story.'

'It's a very old legend,' Mei Li explained. 'But here in the West there are many stories that are very old. I remember Snow White, and the girl with the long hair, Rapunzel isn't it? Then there's Romeo and Juliet.'

'I still like your story best,' Kay told her.

The conductor came along the aisle humming grandiloquently to himself and he gave the young women a curious glance as he put two tickets into the machine hanging round his neck and punched a hole in them. 'Two ter Grange Road,' he said in a tired voice.

'I'm so glad I met yer this evenin',' Kay said. 'Paul was askin' me so many questions about what we saw an' I 'ad ter tell 'im I knew as little as 'e did. 'E's become really interested in those old pieces o' pottery an' 'e told me 'e's gonna get a book from the library ter learn as much as 'e can.'

'I have some books that he might like to borrow,' Mei Li told her.

'Could 'e call round for 'em?' Kay asked, feeling that she was making progress on Paul's behalf.

Mei Li bit on her bottom lip thoughtfully. 'It could be difficult,' she said. 'It would be rude to meet your brother at the door without inviting him in, but you see it's my guardian's home and he would have to make the invitation.'

'Do you drink?' Kay asked her, not wanting to let the chance slip.

'Drink?'

'Do you drink beer or spirits?'

'I like light ale, and port and lemon,' Mei Li said with a grin.

'Do you go to pubs?' Kay pressed.

'Only if I'm escorted,' Mei Li said quickly. 'I understand it's not right for a woman to go in a public house alone.'

'Will yer let Paul escort us both ter the Swan?' Kay

asked. 'It's a respectable pub in Dock'ead an' we can 'ave a nice long chat tergevver.'

'I'd be very pleased, but I'd have to get permission, and my guardian would expect to meet you first,' Mei Li said, looking a little awkward.

'We'd be only too glad ter meet 'im first,' Kay told her.

'I'll, erm . . .' Mei Li thought hard. 'I'll cross my fingers!' she said smiling.

''Ere what d'yer fink o' this?' Kay asked her, taking a folded fashion magazine from her handbag. 'D'yer fink that jumper would suit my colourin'?'

Jim Neal walked home from work through the backstreets in a very confused frame of mind. That lunchtime he had met up with Angela in the Galleon, a riverside pub not far from the factory, and they had sat on a veranda overlooking the busy River Thames watching a Danish freighter docking a little way downstream. Angela had seemed very relaxed and comfortable with the situation. 'You look troubled, Jim,' she had said. 'Are you?'

He recalled his quick reply. 'Ter be honest I am.'

She reached across the wooden table and gently laid her hand on his. 'There's no need to be,' she told him. 'We're both adults, in control of our own lives. What we did happens to lots of people in similar circumstances. We were attracted to each other and it just happened. It doesn't mean to say that both our marriages are ruined as a result. On the contrary. We can both take strength from it and get on with our lives as though it never happened.'

'What about the guilt feelin's?' Jim replied. 'Don't you 'ave any?'

'Of course I do,' Angela said quickly. 'Laurie's a lovely man and I'm sure you feel the same way about Ruby, but as I said, these things happen sometimes and as long as we're sensible no one gets hurt. That's the important thing.'

Jim took a sip from his glass. 'I've never bin unfaithful before, but I 'ave no regrets. In fact I couldn't stop finkin' about yer all day Sunday.'

'That's the way it was for me too,' Angela replied. 'I saw us as two lonely souls comforting each other and bringing that special something that's missing in each of our lives.'

He nodded his head slowly. 'I feel like that as well, but you describe it much better than I could,' he told her.

Angela toyed with her glass for a few moments then she looked up at him. 'I don't want this to be a one-off thing, Jim,' she said with feeling. 'I'd like us to see each other when we can. I couldn't bear it for you to say it can never happen again.'

'I never set out ter take advantage of yer,' Jim replied.

'Of course you didn't,' she said, her smile gently mocking him. 'I wanted you every bit as much as you wanted me and we were just grabbing that special pleasure. Just tell me. Do you want it to carry on?'

'It could be very dangerous,' he said quietly.

'You haven't answered my question, Jim.'

'Yes, yes. I've thought of nuffing else.'

'I'm so glad.'

'Bein' seen tergevver like this could start tongues waggin' though,' he reminded her.

Angela smiled at his serious expression. 'This pub is a meeting-place for people like us,' she told him. 'Just look over there at that young couple holding hands. The young man looks quite ill at ease and I've noticed him glancing around nervously. Look at the young woman. She's wearing a wedding ring. Would you say they were husband and wife?'

He smiled back at her. 'I just 'ope no one from Madeley's spots us 'ere tergevver,' he replied.

'I think it's pretty safe here,' she reassured him. 'And in any case, we could be having an innocent meeting to discuss world events, or even your holiday arrangements come to that.'

'I wish I 'ad your style,' he laughed. 'I feel as nervous as a kitten.'

Angela became serious. 'Don't get me wrong, Jim,' she said earnestly. 'I do care very much about protecting my marriage and I do care about the consequences for you if anything got back to Ruby, but I dearly want us to grab some of the happiness and passion that we both seem to be lacking and both need so much. We can do it, Jim, and we can gain from it. Don't let feelings of guilt prevent us from being together whenever we can. Saturday night for me was the most wonderful experience. I hope it was for you too.'

'Yes it was,' Jim said sincerely.

Angela's hand brushed his and her green eyes flashed. 'We can make time for each other, Jim. We must,' she whispered.

Jim was still deep in thought as he turned into Grange Road. That morning as he busied himself stripping the wrapping machine he had agonised over what had happened and had steeled himself for the task of telling Angela that it had been a mistake on his part to take up her offer and visit her on Saturday night. The whole thing had been folly and to continue seeing each other would only bring unhappiness to both of them. It made good sense to end it before things got out of hand. The words were all there in his head that lunchtime, but when he looked at Angela, felt her hand on his and saw the desire in her eyes the words stuck in his throat.

'Is that you, Jim?' Ruby called out as he entered the house and kicked off his shoes in the passage. 'Kay's just come in an' Paul's 'ome early fer a change. Wash yer 'ands an' I'll serve up.'

Jim came into the scullery and stood behind her, leaning over her shoulder to kiss her cheek, and she moved her head back to let his lips brush her neck.

'What's that stuff you've got on?' he asked. 'It's different.'

'Do yer like it?' Ruby asked. 'I'd used the last o' that perfume you bought me an' I saw this nice-shaped bottle in the chemist. "Forbidden Desire" it's called. The man in the shop let me try some on me wrist an' I really liked it. Do yer fink I'm bein' extravagant?'

'No of course not,' Jim replied quickly, wincing inwardly at the name of the product. 'I like yer ter smell nice.'

Ruby gave him a warm smile. 'I've got somefing different fer tea ternight.'

'Oh?'

'Yeah well, it'll make a change,' she said casually.

'Now go an' give the kids a shout. Tell 'em I'm servin' up right away.'

'Are we out o' pickles?' Paul remarked as Ruby placed a plate of salad in front of him.

'No we're not, but I thought this would be a change,' she told him.

Paul pulled a face at Kay and set about the food. ''Ave you ever took any laundry ter that Chinese place in Cater Street, Ma?' he asked her.

'No. Why?'

'I just wondered,' he replied.

'Paul's got a fing about the Chinese gel who's stayin' there,' Kay cut in, 'the one who invited us ter the exhibition.'

Ruby frowned at her son. 'I wouldn't get too involved if I were you,' she said quickly. 'They're different to us. They've got different standards. We're worlds apart.'

'I dunno,' Paul said as he reached for another slice of bread. 'People are people wherever they come from. Besides, I never said I was gonna get involved. I just fink she's a very nice gel.'

Ruby held her feelings in check, remembering the confrontation she had had with Pam Mills that day. 'Don't get me wrong,' she replied quickly. 'I was just makin' a point about the difficulties involved.'

Kay had already told her brother about meeting her new-found friend on the way home from work and she thought it a good idea to clarify things. 'Mei Li's a very educated gel an' she's got a good job wi' the Government,' she said. 'As a matter o' fact she's invited us ter meet 'er guardian.'

173

'Guardian?' Ruby queried.

'Yeah. This old man saved 'er life when she was a baby an' 'e paid fer 'er education,' Kay explained. 'Mei Li told me all about 'im. Apparently 'e's got a business in Singapore an' she managed ter get 'im a permit ter stay 'ere fer a while.'

'It all sounds very mysterious,' Jim remarked.

'Yer can say that again,' Ruby added, giving him a questioning look.

'There's nuffing mysterious about it,' Kay said defensively. 'Mei Li explained that the man who owns the Chinese laundry is 'er guardian's bruvver an' when she was offered the job wiv the British Government she got 'er guardian a permit so 'e could meet 'im again. Apparently they 'adn't seen each ovver fer years an' years.'

'So you two are gonna meet this guardian of 'ers,' Jim said.

Kay nodded. 'As a matter o' fact I asked Mei Li ter come out fer a drink one night an' she said she'd 'ave ter get 'er guardian's permission first. That's why we're gonna go an' meet 'im as soon as it can be arranged.'

'Sounds very interestin',' Jim remarked. 'Just be careful yer don't let 'im talk the pair of yer inter tryin' the opium pipe.'

Kay smiled at the intended humour but Ruby looked very serious. 'It's s'posed ter be rife over in Lime'ouse,' she said.

'What is?' Kay asked her.

'Opium smokin'.'

'Yer not suggestin' me an' Paul's gonna be drugged an' end up in some Chinese opium den are yer, Mum?'

'No of course not, but just be careful, that's all I'm sayin'.'

Jim pushed his empty plate back and stretched. 'That was very nice,' he declared.

Ruby looked around the table. 'Now who fancies some currant puddin' an' custard?'

The evening had become sultry and distant flashes in the sky warned of a storm brewing as Jim went out into the small back garden. The wireless was playing next door at the Thompsons' and the orchestral music made him feel melancholy. He stood leaning against the shed rolling a cigarette, his mind in a turmoil. Ruby had gone out of her way that evening to provide a good meal and she had made it clear in her own inimitable way that she wanted him. The signs were all there and she knew that he would pick them up. A dash of perfume, the ready smile and her unusual reticence were hints he would not misunderstand, but tonight he felt unable to respond. To pretend would in itself be a betrayal, and with guilt nagging at his insides he found he could not summon the desire to make love to her.

Ruby walked out into the garden and blew through her pursed lips. 'Phew, it's very close,' she said.

'It looks like a storm comin' up,' Jim remarked as he exhaled a cloud of tobacco smoke.

'Paul's gone ter the Swan an' Kay's gone out too,' Ruby told him.

'Where's she gone?'

'She said 'er an' Joey are goin' ter the pictures.'

'She'll be OK, Ruby,' Jim told her kindly. 'Let 'er lead 'er own life an' make 'er own mistakes. It's the only way.'

Ruby nodded. 'We've just 'ad a chat,' she said. 'I told 'er more or less the same. I said I wouldn't interfere any more, an' as long as she was certain that Joey Westlake was what she wanted I wouldn't stand in 'er way.'

Jim caught the pain in Ruby's eyes and suddenly his heart ached. He reached out and gently pulled her to him. 'You know your problem, luv,' he said softly. 'You try ter be all fings to everybody an' you can't be. Just stand back an' draw breath.'

She nestled close to him, aware of the romantic music drifting into the garden. 'Are yer gettin' fed up wiv me, Jim?' she asked.

'Don't be so silly,' he chided her gently.

'I needed you over the weekend but you ignored me,' she told him. 'I reached out fer yer last night but you just grunted an' took my arm away. Yer've never done that before.'

'It was that reunion I expect,' he answered. 'I've decided not ter go any more.'

'I'm glad,' she whispered.

He held her close to him, feeling the shape of her body, the smell of her hair and he closed his eyes. He could not deny her tonight. She needed him and deep down inside him he realised that he needed her too. She was his and his alone. She had always been his, and at that moment as she hugged him tightly he despised himself, and his deep love for her knew no bounds.

Chapter Sixteen

Ho Chang the Bermondsey laundryman and his wife Su lived in the rooms above his business. He owned the house next door and had made plans to extend his activities by installing a couple of sewing machines in the ground-floor space and branching out into clothing alterations and repairs. Su was a very proficient seamstress and as far as he was aware there was little if any competition in the immediate area. The bank had shown some interest in helping to finance him and the prospects looked good, or rather they had done, until Ho Chang decided to chance his luck once again at the mah-jong tables. He had learned his lesson before and this time he would be more cautious, by playing within his means instead of riding his luck.

Ho's dutiful and hardworking wife was not a party to his decision. It was she who had persuaded him to move away from Limehouse and start afresh in Bermondsey when she realised that he had become addicted to gambling. As far as she knew Ho was visiting his relatives in the East End, though she began to suspect that he had an ulterior motive when the visits to Limehouse became more frequent over the weeks. She knew that Ho and his relatives were not that close, and distant cousins were not that important, especially after working hard all day in the steamy atmosphere of the laundry.

For a time Su Chang suffered in silence, but one night when her husband came home later than usual looking as white as bedsheets fresh from the boiler she confronted him. 'Are you seeing another woman?' she asked him, using small fish as bait to catch a larger one.

'We have been married more than twenty-five years now,' Ho replied with a frown. 'If I had sought the company of another woman it would have been in the years when I was young and virile, not now. Toiling all day in the laundry drains me dry.'

'Yet you find the energy to visit your many cousins very often,' she reminded him.

Ho remained secretive and Su decided to call his bluff. 'I want to get started with the dressmaking and alterations,' she informed him, 'so I think we should buy the sewing machines now, especially with the summer months ahead.'

Ho hunched his shoulders and sighed deeply. 'I haven't got the money,' he told her, his eyes fixed on the floor.

'But it was put aside,' she said incredulously.

Ho Chang knew then that he would have to tell her everything, and the lights above the laundry burned late into the night as they talked.

Li Fong had been very pleased when his ward Mei Li managed to get him a permit to stay in the country for an extended visit, enabling him to spend some time with his only surviving brother. Li was also very happy to be offered the first-floor rooms next door to the laundry, for which he insisted on paying a small rent. Ho Chang had made the rooms comfortable by installing some of his own furniture and he had covered the walls with paper hangings adorned with scenes of ancient China. Knowing that his brother Li was a religious man he erected a small shrine of sandalwood with a statue of Kuan Yin the Goddess of Mercy, and some scented candles, to create an atmosphere that would be pleasing and relaxing.

With rain beating against the windows and loud thunder rolling, the atmosphere was far removed from what Ho Chang had intended as he and his older brother discussed the imminent crisis.

'Dishonour weighs heavily on me, Li, and I don't know what to do,' he sighed. 'Su took it all very well, better than I had expected, but after tonight she is terrified of what will happen.'

Li Fong stared searchingly at his brother and felt for him. Ho was bowed and thin, ageing prematurely from the long hours spent in the laundry, and his sunken eyes reflected terror. 'In Singapore I have a thriving business, as you know,' he told him, 'but I was not allowed to bring much money into the country, certainly not the sum you need to clear up your debts.'

'Don't worry on that score,' Ho replied quickly. 'I couldn't take your money anyway. It would be shameful.'

'How much time do you have?' Li asked him.

'One week.'

Li stroked his chin. 'I was expecting you to say a day or two,' he remarked. 'They don't usually give that amount of time.'

'I'm known to the Tong and I think it helped me,' Ho

explained. 'Their leader Tommy Lo said that the interest was being doubled daily now and if the money was not available by the end of the week I must expect the worst. I fear for you too, Li. When they come they'll kill me and destroy my business. It'll go up in flames and this house will burn too. You must leave before the week is out.'

'That's out of the question,' Li told him firmly. 'Perhaps I can speak with this Tommy Lo and ask him for more time. Tell me about him, and what you know of his Tong.'

Ho picked up the small bowl of green tea in front of him on the low table and took a sip. 'Tommy Lo is half English,' he replied. 'His mother married a merchant seaman and the young man was sent to an English school. He is very intelligent and is respected by the Tong as a whole, though they do not like him.'

'It's very unusual for a Tong leader to be of mixed blood,' Li reminded him.

'True, but in Tommy Lo's case he has a certain influence outside of his people and he uses it to help them. Without that he would not have survived in his position for so long. He would have been subjected to the special vote and executed long ago.'

'Special vote?' Li queried, frowning at his brother. 'Are you telling me that the Tong we are talking about are the Sons of Heaven?'

'Yes.'

'Then you are very fortunate to have been given a week to find the money,' Li said quickly. 'In China you would have already died the death of a thousand cuts. What about this influence of Tommy Lo's you mentioned?'

Ho Chang took another sip of his tea. 'Before Tommy

Lo was promoted into the inner circle he was arrested by the police for assault and damage to property. Word had it that he was released without charge on condition that he became the eyes and ears of the Limehouse CID. They wanted someone from the area to liaise with. Tommy Lo went back to the Tong and told them everything, knowing that he could have been killed for even agreeing to such an arrangement. The inner circle were impressed by his courage and they decided to use him for their purposes, and to his credit he used them. Crime was contained within the area and the police raids on opium houses became less frequent. Undesirables were offered up to the police like sacrificial goats and everyone was happy. The policeman involved in the arrangement was an Inspector Kennedy and he has now been promoted to Chief Inspector and put in charge at Limehouse.'

'And Tommy Lo walks a dangerous path,' Li commented.

'The arrangement was beneficial to the Tong and the reason why Tommy Lo was voted into the inner circle. It also keeps him alive.'

Li Fong's stern face relaxed momentarily into a smile. 'It could also be the reason why you have been given more grace than you had the right to expect,' he said quietly. 'Tell me, Ho. How do you know so much about the Tong and its working?'

'To my eternal shame I spent many many hours at the mah-jong tables before my good wife pressed me to leave Limehouse,' Ho told him, 'and during that time I listened and learnt many things. When the pipe was passed round tongues became relaxed and things were said that could have got us all killed.'

Li Fong reached forward and took up the teapot, filling both bowls. 'So how are you going to repay the money?' he asked.

'It will mean going to the bank for a loan,' Ho declared. 'They've said that they would help finance me in extending my business.'

Li Fong shook his head. 'It won't work, Ho,' he replied. 'As soon as they realise there will be no extension they'll foreclose the loan.'

The laundryman smiled cynically. 'Then at least the worst I can suffer is losing my business, not my life.'

Li Fong leaned back against a cushion and folded his arms. 'If I wired Singapore and was successful in getting money sent over somehow, would you accept it as a loan?' he asked.

Ho Chang looked sad. 'I appreciate the thought, but we both know that there isn't enough time. I have only one week.'

'It might be possible for me to liaise on your behalf,' Li suggested. 'Can you arrange for me to meet this Tommy Lo?'

'I can get a message to him, but I doubt that you will have any luck, brother.'

'We must try,' Li urged him. 'Remember the saying of Confucius. "He who never strives never conquers."'

Ho Chang nodded. 'I have troubled you and I am sorry,' he said rising up from his cushion.

'What about Su?' Li asked him. 'It would be better if she left the area for the time being.'

'I've pleaded with her but she will not listen,' Ho sighed sadly. 'She said that the laundry will not run itself and I can't cope alone. I'm just happy that we have no children to worry over. The Tong does not discriminate.'

'You must try to get Su to change her mind,' Li told him. 'We'll talk again tomorrow.'

A bright flash followed by a heavy roll of thunder broke menacingly as Ho Chang hurried next door and let himself into the shop. His brother was right. He must try to persuade Su to go away until this thing was resolved, for better or for worse.

The lights were burning late in Chief Inspector Kennedy's office at Limehouse and the senior policeman's face was etched with tiredness as he listened to the young detective.

'It was a single blow to the neck that killed him,' Sergeant Murray was saying. 'Most likely a machete or a sword.'

'Who found him?' Kennedy asked.

'His wife.'

The inspector eased his heavy bulk in the leather-padded chair and ran a hand over his stubbled chin. 'We knew that the Tong had taken Kano and they were out to extract some vengeance but this is puzzling. If it was down to them why take him and then kill him in his own workshop?'

'To shift the blame is the only thing I can think of, sir,' Murray offered.

Kennedy shook his head. 'The Oriental mind in my experience is very methodical. The Tong would have killed him in the cellar of one of the houses they use and then moved the body after dark. After all, there are very few people walking the streets of Limehouse at night, especially a night like this. There's something strange about this business.'

'Could it be family who were responsible?' Murray queried. 'A relation, or even his wife?'

'It's a possibility,' Kennedy replied. 'There would have been plenty of them angry enough to kill him. That child was lucky the wax wasn't boiling or she would have been terribly scarred. As it is she'll carry some scars for the rest of her life.'

'Is there any news on Tommy Lo, sir?' Murray asked.

'He didn't get the message I left at the corner shop and no one's seen him about this evening,' the inspector said with a frown.

Sergeant Murray leaned back in his chair. 'Talk about the inscrutable Chinese,' he sighed. 'The dead man's wife showed no expression whatsoever when I was taking the statement. There was no look of guilt, remorse or anything else you might expect.'

'You might expect, not me,' Kennedy corrected him. 'Remember, sergeant, I cut my teeth with the Hong Kong police before the war and I've been working in Limehouse for five years now. Trying to gauge guilt from their expressions is an impossible task. So is trying to fathom the Chinese mind. Strangely enough, they regard us as the most inscrutable people of all.'

'Have the Tong been getting ready to give us a scapegoat do you think?' Murray asked.

'Like some drug-crazed character who had chanced to fall out with Kano,' Kennedy suggested. Murray nodded and the police chief smiled cynically. 'It would have been a standard way for the Tong to kill two birds with one stone, if they had not already taken the candlemaker in beforehand. Since the man had all his fingers when someone tried to hack his head off it figures that the Tong had merely frightened him into behaving himself in future. If they had wanted him dead they would have done the job, dumped him in some alley and sent in the fall guy, as our American cousins say.'

Murray looked puzzled. 'Why didn't the Tong cut his fingers off?' he asked. 'That would have been their usual way of doing things.'

'Tommy Lo,' Kennedy informed him. 'Tommy knows that we're taking a battering from the top brass about the blood-letting that's been going on lately. Every time the Tong start chopping bits off of people the local hospital has to do the patching up, and they're obliged to report it to us as you well know. There are six outstanding cases on file and the pen pushers at headquarters are not amused.'

'So the Chinese are starting to play ball,' Murray said scratching his chin.

'Only in as much as it suits them,' Kennedy replied. 'My gut feeling is that someone is already lined up for a visit from the Tong and they want the pressure taken off them till they get their job done. There is another factor, and this is confidential. Hong Kong Police have given Scotland Yard details of an unusually large opium shipment bound for London. The port authorities have already been advised and arrangements have been made at top level to intercept it at the point of delivery.'

Murray whistled through his teeth. 'With that in the offing I can see why the Tong would want it all sweetness and light.'

Kennedy ran his fingers through his thick grey hair and

leaned back in the chair with his hands clasped behind his head. 'It's been a long day, sergeant,' he said. 'You'd better get off home.'

Murray hesitated. 'I was going to ... Never mind it'll keep.'

Kennedy looked at his subordinate with some irritation. 'What is it, Murray? Spit it out then.'

'I was going to ask you about these Sons of Heaven,' the sergeant replied. 'Last time we talked at length you mentioned that Tommy Lo needed to watch his step. You said something about the special vote. I was going to ask you about it then but we got bogged down with other matters.'

Kennedy's eyes narrowed. 'The special vote is a sick ritual peculiar to the Sons of Heaven Tong,' he remarked with distaste. 'There are four other branches of this Tong operating in the country, one in each of the large ports, namely Liverpool, Glasgow, Bristol and Southampton. Two months ago the special vote was taken at the Tong meeting in Glasgow and it developed into a very nasty business. What happens is this. If a member of the inner circle abuses his oath of allegiance in any way he is challenged at a special hearing that can be called by a minimum of two members. The accused has an allotted time to account for his actions, behaviour or whatever, after which the members of the inner circle leave the room to take a vote. They use mah-jong blocks which are dropped into a black bag, and when they return the contents of the bag are emptied on a table in front of the accused. He hopes and prays that all the pieces are of the west wind, which will absolve him, but one piece of the east wind placed in the bag would be his death sentence. If this is the case then the condemned man is allowed ten minutes' grace to make his getaway. Eyes of the Tong follow his every move and when ten minutes is up the execution squad come looking for him. Usually it's drawn from the junior members, all of whom are eager to prove their worthiness to be elected into the inner circle. All that the victim can hope for is a quick death, since it's virtually impossible for him to escape. If he battles hard enough he's killed with a single thrust of a blade, but if he cowers and pleads for mercy he dies slowly of a thousand cuts.'

Murray looked horrified. 'Is Tommy Lo in that sort of danger?'

Kennedy nodded. 'All Tong leaders walk the thin line. One mistake is all that's needed for some crazed pretender to seek his removal.'

'That's a chilling account to sleep on,' Sergeant Murray said as he got up to leave.

'If you've ever felt that I handle Tommy Lo with kid gloves then what I've just told you should make it plain enough why,' Kennedy said quietly.

Billy Chou finished cleaning his razor-sharp machete and then wrapped it carefully in the cloth before putting it back in its hiding-place under the stairs. The others might suspect him of being responsible for the candlemaker's death but they would need proof before they could accuse him of conduct liable to bring the Tong into disrepute. To that end he had been very careful to provide himself with a respectable alibi. Husi Kang, the owner of the Peking Club, would be prepared to state under oath that Billy

Chou had been in the club all evening. In exchange Billy had promised to ensure that the business of Ho Chang's expired promissory note would be brought to a speedy and satisfactory conclusion.

Chapter Seventeen

The morning streets were fresh after the night rain and the sun rose brightly in a clear blue sky as workers hurried to and fro. Laden horse carts trundled by and the early traffic built up steadily in Grange Road. Connie Wilson left the alley to get the morning paper and her husband tested his suspect back by turning over in bed. Myrtle Thompson swept the front and promised to water the tubs that day, and Nora Mason enjoyed a leisurely cup of tea after her husband Jack had left the house to do his early post round.

At number 2 Tanners Alley Ruby fussed over the cushions, pulled the net curtains into even pleats and tried to find a reason to clean the windows for the second time in a week. There was nothing else to do, she thought, unless she turned the scullery cupboard out. No, that could wait until she got back from the surgery, and it would fill in her time nicely before starting on the tea.

Ruby sat down at the table and looked around the immaculate parlour, adjusting the tablecloth and brushing off imaginary crumbs before she got up and went back into the scullery. There was still an hour before she had to leave but she could not relax. It felt as though she was wound up like a clock spring, charged full of energy with nothing to expend it on. What was happening to her, she wondered? Last night was the first Monday night in ages that she had made love with Jim, and after he had fallen asleep she had lain awake, wanting him even more. It might be due to her time of life, she thought, or just one of those things that sometimes happens to a woman leading too orderly an existence. But then Jim had been unusually daring and he had responded to her need with a performance of uncharacteristic emotion, which had both excited and puzzled her. He had been nervous and apprehensive to begin with and it was a side of him she had never seen before.

The letterbox sounded. 'Ruby, are you about?'

Ruby smiled to herself. Anyone else would have knocked but Bel invariably called through the letterbox. 'Come in, luv,' she told her as she pulled back the front door.

Bel stepped inside and made her way into the parlour. 'So what's bin 'appenin'?' she asked.

'Kay's dumped Richard an' our Paul's moonin' around over this Chinese gel that Kay knows,' Ruby told her.

Bel sat down with a sigh. 'Is she back wiv Joey?'

Ruby nodded. 'I'm not all that keen on 'er goin' back wiv 'im but it's 'er life,' she replied.

'That's just what I said,' Bel reminded her. 'An' what about you? You look like a cat on 'ot bricks. Sit down fer a minute.'

Ruby sat on the edge of the armchair facing her old friend. 'We're goin' ter Devon in August,' she announced.

'So yer finally made yer mind up.'

'I'm not all that fussy really but Jim's keen ter go.'

'It'll do the both of yer good.'

'Are you goin' anywhere?'

Bel shook her head. 'I was finkin' o' goin' ter see our Lucille but I ain't decided yet,' she answered. 'It's that feller of 'ers that puts me off. I can't stand the bloke.'

Ruby got up and went over to the sideboard to adjust the runner. 'Did I tell yer Jim's in line fer the foreman's job?'

Bel gave her a questioning look. 'Yeah yer did. What's wrong, Ruby? Yer can't keep still.'

'I'm fine,' Ruby told her.

'D'yer feel fit enough ter put the kettle on?'

'I'm sorry,' she said, smiling.

Bel got up and followed her out into the scullery. 'Are you an' Jim OK?' she asked quickly.

'Yeah, course we are.'

'Well, somefing ain't quite right,' Bel persisted. 'I can always tell when somefing's worryin' yer.'

'There's nuffing worryin' me,' Ruby said, her voice rising slightly.

Bel watched as she filled the kettle and put it on the iron gas stove. 'Wouldn't it boil quicker if yer lit the gas?' she said, grinning.

Ruby brought her hand up to press her temples with thumb and forefinger. 'I'm at sixes and sevens this mornin',' she replied. 'You're not 'elpin' eivver wiv yer stupid questions.'

'Sorry fer breavvin',' Bel said mockingly.

Ruby spooned tea-leaves into the china pot and set it down on the table. ''Aven't you ever 'ad one o' those days when yer feel all troubled inside but yer can't put yer finger on it?' she asked.

'Yeah, it 'appens ter me all the time,' Bel told her. 'Seriously though, are fings as they should be wiv you an' Jim? All right, tell me ter mind me own business, but you two are my business, Ruby, an' ter be honest I can't fink of anyfing else that should be worryin' yer. Yer all workin', an' you look very well I might add.'

Ruby sat down at the table facing her friend. 'Do you fink Jim's goin' off me?' she asked.

'Certainly not.'

''E could do.'

'Yeah, if yer gave 'im enough reason.'

'Which I don't.'

'Well what yer worryin' about then?'

Ruby shrugged her shoulders. 'You make everyfing black an' white, Bel, but it's not always the case.'

The older woman brushed a strand of grey hair away from her forehead and leaned forward on the table. 'Now listen ter me, Ruby,' she said firmly. 'You an' Jim 'ave bin married fer twenty-three years now by my reckonin', an' fings can get a bit stale, a bit predictable, but that 'appens to every couple an' yer gotta accept it. It's knowin' the signs an' doin' somefink about it that matters. All right, yer not spring chickens any more, but yer still young enough to enjoy yer life tergevver. In fact it can get better if yer work at it, I know from me an' my feller. The way yer gotta look at it is, if yer still active in bed fings are OK. It's when 'e turns 'is back on yer yer gotta start worryin'. Nearly every man needs it regularly, an' yer can bet yer life if they're not gettin' it at 'ome they're gettin' it somewhere else.'

Ruby got up to turn the gas out under the boiling kettle. 'We're OK in that way,' she replied.

'Yer not bickerin'?'

'We don't bicker,' Ruby told her as she filled the teapot.

'Then all I can say is yer worryin' over Kay or Paul, or both of 'em, wivout realisin' it,' Bel said with conviction.

'I 'ave ter say I'm a bit worried about this Chinese gel,' Ruby admitted. 'I've never laid eyes on 'er ter tell yer the trufe, but Kay said she's a very pretty gel. The trouble is there's so many problems come up when people meet from different upbringin's.'

'Paul's a sensible lad,' Bel replied. ''E'll know the score. An' take a close look at Kay. Ask yerself if she's lookin' more 'appy now she's back wiv Joey.'

Ruby poured out the tea. 'Were you an' Jack always 'appy, Bel?' she asked. 'I mean, wasn't there ever a time when yer felt 'e might be gettin' fed up wiv yer?'

'Once or twice,' Bel confessed, 'but I worked at makin' fings better, just like I told you ter do.'

'No one ever tried ter come between yer, did they?' Ruby pressed.

Bel lowered her head to study her fingernails for a few moments, and when she raised her head again there was a faraway look in her eyes. 'I shouldn't be tellin' yer this, not in the mood you're in, but yes, there was one occasion.'

Ruby sipped her tea expectantly. 'Go on, Bel.'

'Do you remember when Jack went up ter Leeds ter do that buildin' job?' she began. 'Two months 'e was away an' I only saw 'im every ovver weekend. I was very lonely an' I got all screwed up inside. I was sure that Jack 'ad found someone. Why did 'e only come 'ome every ovver weekend? What was 'e doin' on the weekends when 'e wasn't wiv me? I daren't ask 'im in case 'e felt I didn't trust 'im, but it kept eatin' away at me an' I even got a picture of this woman in me mind. It was stupid, but I was younger then an' lackin' in confidence. Jack was a good-lookin' feller an' I got to imagine all sorts o' fings. But d'you know the worst of it, Ruby? I became spiteful. What was good fer the gander was good fer the goose I told meself. So one night I took up the offer of a night out wiv the gels I worked wiv. We went ter this pub in Woolwich an' there were some fellers there that one or two o' the gels knew. Ter cut a long story short I got chattin' wiv this good-lookin' bloke an' 'e invited me to a party at 'is place. Needless ter say there was no party, but I was past carin' by then. We ended up in bed an' next mornin' 'e was gone. Worst of all 'e'd left a pound note beside me 'andbag.'

Ruby looked shocked. 'Did Jack ever find out?' she asked.

Bel smiled bitterly. 'A few months later when Jack was back 'ome we went to a weddin'. 'E 'ad too much ter drink an' a couple o' fellers 'elped bring 'im 'ome. While I was gettin' 'is trousers off 'is wallet fell out on the floor. I'd never seen the inside o' that wallet before. It was lyin' open at me feet an' there was a dog-eared photograph pokin' out of it. The woman in that photo was a big, busty blonde. She looked just like the picture I'd planted in me mind of the gel Jack was 'avin' it off wiv.'

'What did yer do?' Ruby asked in a hushed voice.

'I put it back an' tucked the wallet back in his trousers.'

'An' yer never asked 'im what it was doin' there?'

'Never.'

'An' did Jack never find out about you an' this feller?'

Bel shook her head slowly. 'The next time I looked inside that wallet was after Jack died an' I was goin' frew 'is fings. The photo 'ad gone, an' I felt strangely elated. The way I saw it was, Jack 'ad bin every bit as lonely as I was an' the woman 'ad meant nuffink to 'im, just as the man I slept wiv meant nuffink ter me. It was all in the past an' it was too late fer recriminations anyway. I've never told anyone about this, Ruby.'

'I won't let it 'appen ter me, ever,' the younger woman said, her eyes misting.

'Please God it never will,' Bel replied.

Mei Li had always treated her guardian with respect, and ever since she was old enough to know of his importance in her life she had remained a little in awe of him. Their relationship was inclined to be formal, lacking in the closeness between a father and daughter, but sincere and relaxed enough for the young woman to open her heart to him on certain occasions. Li Fong was now a successful businessman trading from Singapore and he was currently spending much of his time building up contacts in Great Britain. He wrote letters in Mandarin and Cantonese and got his young ward to write in English as a means of promoting his business. He also travelled about London meeting people and with firm orders for his varied products Li Fong was now in the process of negotiating with the Government for import licences.

Now in his late sixties and feeling the ravages of time, the trader was looking forward to going home and spending the rest of his days in comfortable retirement. Much had been done to make sure that his company would be left in safe hands, and the young man Li Fong had appointed to head it was Lin Chen, a refugee from war-torn China, an exceptionally clever businessman who had progressed through the company in record time to become an executive director before he reached his fortieth birthday. Lin Chen was the man Li Fong had selected to be Mei Li's husband and the old man was looking forward to seeing the union consummated. He could then die a happy man, knowing that his ward would never want for anything.

Mei Li had accepted the situation with resignation. Lin was short, bordering on obese, but he had a sharp wit and a personality that made people take to him instantly. The planned union was dear to her guardian's heart and in traditional fashion Mei Li had taken the lotus blossom with a bow of her head and a coy smile. The arrangement meant little to her at the time. A lot of travelling lay ahead, and a job with the American Government. In four or five years hence it would be time enough to concern herself with marriage.

Mei Li thought her guardian looked very pensive as she went into the sitting room they shared. 'I wanted to talk to you last night, Li, but you and your brother were very busy discussing things till very late,' she told him.

The trader shook his head slowly. 'It would seem that my esteemed brother has made himself some very dangerous enemies by his lack of discipline and common sense,' he replied.

'Gambling?'

Li Fong nodded. 'He can't pay and the interest charges rise by the day.'

'What will happen to him?'

'He will lose his business and possibly his life.'

Mei Li's hand came up to her mouth in anguish. 'Is there anything you can do, we can do to help him?' she asked.

'Apart from offering him a loan from funds I don't have in this country there's nothing either of us can do,' the trader sighed.

'I have some money put away,' Mei reminded him.

'I can't let you lose all your savings, since Ho Chang would never be able to repay you,' he said. 'Besides, my brother would rather suffer death before any further dishonour.'

'But it's avoidable,' the young woman replied firmly. 'Surely there's some way of making him accept it.'

Li Fong smiled briefly, with a glint in his eyes like an old dragon. 'I think you're starting to become corrupt, young lady,' he said, waving his bony finger at her. 'I hope we'll be able to get back to Singapore before your mind has been completely taken over.'

'I am looking forward to returning,' Mei Li replied, 'although I have a few reservations. It will be an anxious time to begin with.'

'You and Lin can be married within two weeks and then you will have all the time in the world to adjust,' Li Fong told her. 'You will be happy with him, I promise you.'

'If it is what you want,' Mei Li sighed.

'It is, and it should be what you want,' her guardian said, frowning as he studied her downturned face. 'There must be thousands of young women on the island who would gladly change places with you.'

'I know,' Mei replied. 'I will learn to love him and be a credit to him, for your sake if nothing else.'

Li Fong nodded his head slowly. 'You will be a credit to both of us,' he said. 'And now we should get away from all this seriousness before it makes me older than I already am. Would you like to go to the Peking Club in Limehouse this evening? The food's good and I'd like to discuss an urgent matter with the proprietor.'

'That would be very nice, Li,' the young woman told him, 'but first I have a request. I want you to meet two friends of mine, a brother and sister who live nearby. They both came to the cultural exhibition and wish to return the compliment. I told them I would need your permission and you would have to meet them first.'

'Yes, certainly I'll meet them,' Li Fong replied, 'but let's not delay any further. We can make the arrangements while we travel to Limehouse in the taxi.'

Next door in the rooms above the laundry Ho Chang sat despondent. 'At least I tried,' he said. 'The bank made things impossible.'

'You knew it wouldn't be easy,' Su reminded him.

'The possibilities for raising the money are not exhausted yet,' Ho said, trying to ease the apprehension he saw reflected in his dutiful wife's large dark eyes.

Su smiled to reassure him but inside she felt numb with fear. Her usually timid husband had taken to arming himself, and beneath the counter he had concealed a razor-sharp, wide-bladed knife.

Chapter Eighteen

The young man from Canton who walked into Tanners Alley on Thursday morning clutching a sealed envelope still felt very sad, but he understood the situation. Ho Chang and his wife Su had been good to him and had given him work and a shelter over his head at a crucial time in his life, but now they had dispensed with his services for reasons which he appreciated were very serious. He was also aware that with no papers, no passport or permit of residence, he would be deported back to China if he were picked up by the authorities.

Ti San was twenty-seven years old and had spent five years as a stoker on the Oriental Shipping Lines, sweating in the boiler room in temperatures that sometimes reached one hundred and twenty degrees while the ship was travelling through the Indian Ocean. The hard toil in atrocious conditions was just about bearable, but the chief engineer's bullying had become so bad that the young man was left with no choice but to jump ship when it docked in London. He ended up in Limehouse and was found by Ho Chang sheltering in the doorway of his laundry one morning when he arrived to open up. The kindly laundryman found him work lighting and fuelling the boilers, and when Ho Chang moved his business to Bermondsey Ti San was happy to go with him.

Now, as he went along to number 2 and slipped the envelope through the letterbox, the young man from Canton realised that it was the last task he would ever do for Ho Chang. His future now was uncertain, but for the Changs their fate was in the hands of one of the most ruthless of the Tongs and he would not have changed places with them for all the treasures in all the palaces of China.

'George, come 'ere quick,' Connie Wilson called out. 'There's that Chinky bloke puttin' somefing frew Ruby's letterbox.'

The convalescent docker hobbled painfully to the front door. 'Where is 'e?' he asked.

'Yer too late, 'e's just walked out o' the alley,' Connie told him. ''E looked really scary. It's their eyes what frighten me.'

George looked puzzled as he scratched his head. 'I wonder what that's all about,' he remarked.

'Gawd knows,' Connie said stroking her chin. 'That's the second time 'e's come 'ere.'

'I shouldn't take no notice,' George told her as he shuffled back to his comfortable chair in the parlour. 'It could be somefing ter do wiv the doctor's.'

'What d'yer mean?'

'Well it could be ter do wiv that Chinese laundry. Maybe the Chinky's a patient o' Dr Ambrose an' 'e's sent somefing round fer Ruby ter take in.'

'It could be,' Connie admitted, still not looking convinced. 'Nah, it's somefing else. I wish I knew what it was.'

'It's nuffing ter do wiv us anyway,' George said irritably. 'Now are yer gonna put that kettle on or am I gonna 'ave ter do it meself?'

Connie went out to do her husband's bidding, still puzzling over what she had seen, and after she and George had finished drinking their tea she took her coat down from behind the door.

'Where are you off to?' George asked.

'I fergot ter get somefing when I done me shoppin',' she replied. 'I won't be long.'

Mrs Mason answered the knock and looked surprised to see Connie standing there. ''Ello, Connie,' she said, blocking the opening in case her neighbour decided to step inside.

'Sorry ter trouble yer, Nora,' Connie said, 'but I wondered if yer saw that Chinese bloke come in the alley?'

'No I never, luv,' Nora told her. 'I was upstairs turnin' the beds as a matter o' fact.'

''E came in the alley bold as brass an' slipped somefing frew Ruby Neal's letterbox,' Connie informed her. 'It just seemed strange ter me. I was wonderin' if you knew what it was all about.'

'Search me,' Nora replied, shrugging her shoulders. 'Seems a bit queer.'

'That's what I thought,' Connie went on. 'I mean ter say, we're out the way stuck down 'ere, an' we gotta look out fer each ovver.'

'You're quite right,' Nora said, nodding her head vigorously.

'Yer can't trust them people,' Connie remarked. 'I mean, 'e could 'ave gone in there an' slit 'er froat or somefing.'

'But yer said 'e just delivered somefing.'

'Be that as it may, but s'posin' the door was open.'

'Good Gawd, it don't bear finkin' about.'

'That's why I knocked. At least it puts you on yer guard.'

'I never leave my front door open,' Nora Mason said quickly. 'If I was you I'd do the same, now them people are strollin' in an' out the alley. I'm worried about ole Lizzie. She sits out the front dozin' off 'alf the time wiv 'er front door wide open.'

At that instant the old lady appeared as if on cue, dragging a chair behind her with one hand and holding a cushion in the other.

'Mornin', gels. Nice day again,' she remarked.

The two women watched as Lizzie thumped the cushion and placed it on the chair. 'I prefer me rocker but it's too 'eavy fer me ter bring out,' she said with a pitiful look on her face. ''Ere you wouldn't oblige me, would yer?'

'I don't fink it's a good idea sittin' out 'ere on yer own,' Connie warned her. 'There's bin some very dodgy people in an' out of 'ere lately.'

'I ain't seen any,' Lizzie replied. 'What sort o' dodgy people?'

'Connie was just tellin' me she saw this Chinky feller come in the alley,' Nora said.

'What was 'e sellin'?' Lizzie asked.

''E wasn't sellin' anyfink,' Connie said quickly. ''E was deliverin' a letter ter Ruby Neal by the look of it.'

'Well, that's a turn-up fer the book,' Lizzie chuckled. 'A Chinese postman.'

'It's no laughin' matter,' Nora said sharply. 'We're

finkin' o' you. You could be attacked sittin' out 'ere on yer own.'

'Cobblers,' Lizzie growled. 'Who'd wanna attack me?'

'Well, don't say we didn't warn yer,' Connie told her, looking hurt.

'Now are you two gonna get me my rocker out or not?' the old lady said, looking from one to the other.

Myrtle Thompson had been standing inside her front door trying to hear what Connie Wilson and Nora Mason were chatting about, and when she found out she decided that it was only right for her opinion to be heard. Picking up the coconut mat she opened the front door, humming loudly to herself. 'Mornin', gels,' she said, trying to look surprised as she set about flapping the mat against the wall under the window.

'Don't go in fer a minute, gel, I wanna 'ave a word wiv yer,' Nora told her. 'We're just gonna get that silly ole mare's rocker out for 'er.'

Once Lizzie was settled Nora Mason explained about the visitor to the alley that morning.

'I fink yer both right,' Myrtle said nodding. 'Yer can't be too careful these days.'

'Yer certainly can't,' Nora said righteously. 'Yer read it all the time in the papers. Only last week there was a bloke found wiv 'is froat cut over in Lime'ouse. Can't trust 'em yer can't.'

Lizzie started chuckling to herself, which elicited a clicking of tongues.

'It's not funny, Lizzie,' Connie said crossly.

'I wasn't laughin' at you,' the old lady replied. 'I was finkin' about ole Sweeney Todd. The demon barber o' Fleet

Street 'e was known as. 'E used ter cut people's froats while 'e shaved 'em an' then 'e pulled a lever an' they dropped in the cellar. 'E used to 'ave an assistant who cut 'em up an' gave the bits ter the local butcher who made pies out of 'em.'

'Would you believe 'er,' Nora mumbled. 'Yeah, all right, Lizzie, we've 'eard the story, but this ain't a laughin' matter.'

'Nor was Sweeney Todd,' Lizzie countered. ''Ow would you like to end up in a pie?'

'Just ignore 'er,' Connie said puffing.

'I fink I'll go an' 'ave a word wiv Ruby later,' Nora declared. 'It might set our minds at rest if we know what's goin' on.'

'They never ever caught 'im,' Lizzie went on. 'It was only after some ovver barber took the place over that they found out about what 'ad bin goin' on. They caught the butcher though. 'E got strung up. They said 'is last meal was a pie. Makes yer wonder.'

'You just be careful, that's all,' Myrtle told her. 'That Chinky bloke could come in an' ransack your place while yer asleep.'

'Well, if 'e comes in my place I'll tell 'im 'e can 'ave a nice shufty round providin' we go 'alf each on anyfing 'e finds,' the old lady said, folding her arms as she prepared for her morning nap.

Jim Neal had seen very little of Angela during the last few days. She had come down to the factory floor on one occasion accompanied by her boss and another well-dressed individual whom Jim did not recognise. She had been taking notes and apart from one brief glance in his direction she appeared to ignore him. Jim felt glad as he got on with his work replacing a worn belt. He needed time to pull himself together. He was determined that the affair should end before it really began, but he was also very much aware that he was putty where she was concerned. The only answer was to avoid meeting up with her and let the ardour cool. At least he had been spared the job of finishing the removal of the pipework from Angela's office. Percy the foreman had sent Len Moody up to complete the job while Jim was busy working on the faulty machines.

As he left the factory and stepped out into Dockhead Angela called out to him. 'Jim. Just a minute.'

He turned to see her hurrying up to him with a smile on her face, her red hair dancing on her shoulders.

'I've hardly seen anything of you,' she said breathlessly as she drew level.

'I've bin very busy,' he told her.

'Too busy to put your head in my office and say hello?' she replied with a winning smile.

'I need a reason ter go up ter the offices,' he reminded her.

'I'm sure you could invent one,' she went on. 'If anyone asked you what you were doing, which they wouldn't, just say you were coming to see me.'

They walked in step along the busy pavement and Jim tried to avoid making full eye contact with her. Angela's smile remained on her face as she moved a fraction nearer to him, and he felt the light brush of her arm on his.

'Are you working this Saturday?' she asked after a while.

'No.'

'You could be.'

'I don't fink so.'

'You could tell Ruby you were working the whole of Saturday on some emergency job and we could go out for the day,' Angela said, glancing at him.

Jim grinned, shaking his head. 'We've got a little ritual. Any overtime I earn goes away for our 'olidays. Ruby knows 'ow much is there.'

'Poor Jim,' she mocked. 'Never mind, it was just a thought.'

They reached the bus stop and Angela joined the back of the queue. 'I've got a good idea, Jim,' she said, giving him a seductive wink. 'I'll tell you about it tomorrow. Don't worry, I'll come looking for you.'

Jim waited till Angela was safely aboard the bus, and as it pulled away from the stop he carried on home. What devious plan had she concocted, he wondered? More to the point, would he be able to extricate himself from this dangerous liaison before he was found out?

Ruby was not one to encourage conversation around the dinner table, but after the meal was over she was keen to tell everyone what had happened that afternoon. 'I was surprised ter tell yer the trufe,' she remarked. 'I opened the door and there was Connie Wilson, Nora Mason an' Myrtle standin' there. They all looked really bovvered. Apparently they were all worried over me, would you believe.'

'Silly bitches,' Kay said smiling at Paul.

'Connie told me 'ow she saw this Chinese bloke puttin' somefing frew our door an' alerted the alley,' Ruby went on.

'I told 'em it was an invitation to an opium-smokin' party at the laundry an' they'd be gettin' their invites soon.'

'You never!' Kay said laughing aloud.

'Well, I was so disgusted wiv 'em,' Ruby told her. 'They've bin seein' too many Charlie Chan pictures. Connie was certain I was in some sort o' danger.'

'Did yer put 'em straight?' Paul asked.

'Course I did,' Ruby replied, a smile forming at the corner of her mouth. 'I told 'em it was a letter fer you from your Chinese friend acceptin' the invitation ter the party you was givin' an' sayin' that there'd be ten of 'em comin' in all.'

Jim shook his head slowly. 'Ruby, yer a scream,' he declared.

'Yer didn't leave it at that, did yer, Mum?' Kay said grinning.

'Yeah. It'll give 'em somefing ter worry about now.'

'Wait till I tell the lads I've got a date wiv Mei Li,' Paul said.

Jim leaned back in his chair. 'Don't get too excited about it,' he warned. 'It won't be the same datin' an Oriental gel.'

'You're not gonna start talkin' like the three witches o' the alley, are yer, Pop?' Paul asked him.

Jim leaned forward over the table. 'Now listen, son,' he began. 'I don't know 'ow much yer've bovvered ter find out about the Chinese way o' life, but from what I know it's a common occurrence fer Oriental women ter be promised ter someone from child'ood. You could get serious wiv this young lady an' then discover she's engaged ter some rich merchant back 'ome.'

'Yeah, I did take that on board,' Paul replied, 'but after listenin' to 'er speakin' at that exhibition I could tell she's very educated. Besides, she's bin workin' over 'ere fer a few years an' I'm sure she'd 'ave somefing ter say about bein' promised ter someone she 'ardly knew, if at all.'

'It might be out of 'er 'ands,' Jim reminded him. 'It could all depend on 'ow much of an 'old that guardian's got over 'er. Just play it very careful, that's all I'm sayin'. Me an' yer muvver wouldn't like ter see yer get 'urt.'

'Yer farvver's right,' Ruby cut in. 'From what Kay told us the gel's got a work permit an' a visitor's permit fer that guardian of 'ers. What 'appens if the Government decides they won't renew 'em?'

Paul shrugged his shoulders. 'It's all up in the air, ain't it? It's best ter take fings a day at a time. Anyway, I'm goin' up ter get ready, there's a darts match at the Swan ternight.'

Jim got up from the table and took down his tobacco tin from the mantelshelf. 'I'm off ter the garden fer a smoke,' he announced.

Ruby was of a mind to relax her rule about smoking in the house but she held back. She had made enough concessions for the time being, and it was important not to forget that rules were rules, and had to be observed if the home was to be run efficiently.

Chapter Nineteen

It was late night service at the barber shop in Abbey Street, and as Paul slipped into the chair and ordered an easy trim he was feeling anxious. The wall clock showed six-thirty and he and Kay were due to present themselves in one hour. It was always the same when he had planned something, the young man groaned to himself. Friday evenings were virtually always early finishes but today there had been a jam-up on the lines and it had taken some time to sort the problem out.

'Would yer like a friction?' Norman the barber asked him as he snipped away round the back of Paul's neck. 'I got some new stuff. Lovely smell an' it does yer scalp good.'

'No, I'm pushed fer time, Norm,' the young man told him. 'I got a date.'

'Oh yeah, anyone I know?' the barber asked.

'I don't fink so,' Paul replied, looking up at the clock once more.

'Keep yer 'ead still.'

'Is that clock right?'

'Yeah, give or take a few minutes.'

Norman ran the comb through Paul's thick hair and stood

holding a clump between his fingers. 'It needs a bit off the top,' he said.

'Nah, leave it,' Paul said quickly. 'Just so's it looks tidy round the neck.'

Norman sighed in resignation. 'Butch Wheeler was in this mornin',' he remarked. ''E wanted a short back an' sides. 'E still wasn't satisfied when I finished. Got me ter run the clippers over 'is barnet. Disgusted I was. 'E looked like a convict. Still, there's no accountin' fer taste.'

Paul nodded, not wishing to get involved in a drawn-out conversation, and as the cloth was whipped away from him he jumped out of the chair. ''Ere y'are, Norm, keep the change.'

'Anyfing else yer want?' the barber asked, motioning towards the side shelf where the toiletries were stacked.

Paul shook his head as he slipped on his coat. 'See yer, Norm.'

Ruby greeted him with a look of irritation as he hurried into the house. 'Yer never late on Fridays,' she moaned. 'If yer tea's all dried up it ain't my fault.'

'Where's Kay?' the young man asked as he scoffed his food.

'Gettin' ready,' Ruby told him as she watched him eat. 'That's the quickest way ter get an ulcer.'

'It couldn't be 'elped,' Paul protested with a mouthful. 'The lines were down an' it was an emergency.'

'All right I fergive yer, now stop talkin' an' get on wiv it,' she answered.

Twenty minutes later the two young people hurried from the alley and crossed the quiet Grange Road. 'Are yer sure I look all right?' Paul asked with concern.

'Course yer do,' Kay replied, brushing a piece of fluff from his shoulder. 'Just relax, an' don't go over the top.'

'What d'yer mean?' Paul asked, giving her a questioning look.

'Ease up on that charm. Just be yerself.'

'Don't I always?'

'I've seen yer perform in the Swan when there's young women about,' Kay said smiling.

'Leave it ter me,' Paul grinned back. 'I'll be discretion itself.'

Cater Street comprised two twin rows of terraced houses, bisected in the middle by Heron Street, and the Chinese laundry was situated on a corner of the junction. Kay knocked at the side door and heard footsteps on the stairs. When Mei Li opened the door with a sweet smile Paul drew a quick breath. She looked stunning, he thought. Her olive green, calf-length dress was figure-hugging, with a split at the side running to just above the knee. She was stockingless, her feet encased in tiny high-heeled shoes, and her glistening raven hair was parted in the middle and brushed forward either side of her head.

'Exactly on time,' she remarked. 'Please come up.'

The flight of stairs led on to a narrow landing and the young Chinese woman opened the far door facing the stairs. 'Li, these are my friends,' she announced and, turning back to them, 'this is Li Fong my guardian.'

The elderly man was seated on a low chair which was totally concealed by a huge, flower-patterned cushion. He was wearing a flat black hat on the top of his head and a long traditional multi-coloured dress coat with very wide sleeves under which his hands were concealed. Paul noticed that his black trousers were made of silk and his slippers were adorned with gold-coloured thread. 'Take a seat,' he said, removing one hand from the voluminous folds and waving towards the low table in front of him.

Paul sat down with no trouble but Kay slid down sideways, holding on to the bottom of her dress to prevent it riding up. Mei Li sat to one side, her tiny hands clasped on her lap as she waited to speak.

'It was nice of you to invite us,' Kay said slowly for his benefit.

'I am very pleased to see you,' the Chinese trader replied with a smile that creased the side of his eyes. 'Mei Li tells me that you went to the cultural exhibition. Did you like it?'

'It was lovely,' Kay told him with a friendly smile.

'Yeah, it was very good,' Paul added, glancing shyly at Mei Li.

'The mysterious Orient,' Li Fong said, slowly nodding his head. 'You will have seen many treasures.'

'We were told the story of the Chinese lantern,' Kay said. 'It was lovely, 'specially the way Mei Li told it.'

Li Fong smiled as he nodded again. 'The lantern of the soul. Fuelled by the three essences. Yes, I know it well.'

'Do yer like livin' over 'ere?' Paul asked him.

'It's very interesting,' Li Fong replied. 'I have been fortunate to see some of your beautiful country but not as much as I would like.'

Paul glanced briefly at Mei Li once more and she lowered her eyes coyly. 'We would very much like to return the 'ospitality an' take Mei Li out fer a drink,' he said.

The elderly trader nodded. 'I am sure Mei Li would like

that,' he replied, turning to her. 'I think it is time we drank some tea.'

Mei Li got up and went outside and Paul gazed at the hangings and the ornaments that were placed around the room.

'My ward tells me that you are interested in Chinese culture,' Li Fong remarked.

Paul nodded. 'I want ter find out as much as I can,' he answered, hoping that he sounded sincere.

'It is commendable,' Li Fong told him. 'Lack of knowledge and understanding of different cultures breeds mistrust and fear of the unknown. Unfortunately China itself has fallen prey to such folly now. The land of my birth has built another great wall around itself, but this time the barbarians are within. I myself cannot go back, yet, but I live happily enough in Singapore, in hope of one day returning to the hills I knew as a child.'

Mei Li came back into the room carrying a wooden tray laden with a tall teapot and a set of wide-brimmed bowls which she laid out on the table. 'My guardian would like you to try some of our traditional green tea,' she said. 'It's strongly flavoured and slightly bitter to the taste but very beneficial. It's said to be good for preventing diseases of the stomach.'

Kay and Paul watched as Li Fong picked up his filled bowl with both hands and they did likewise, following his lead as he took a sip then set it down on the table again. It tasted bitter and Paul was reminded of the time his mother tried to get him to drink some cabbage water when he was younger.

'Is it to your liking?' Li Fong enquired.

'Yeah, it's very nice,' the young man lied.

The trader drained his bowl. 'Mei Li has told me of your kindness to her,' he said to Kay. 'It is very appreciated.'

'It was nothing,' Kay replied with a smile.

'One small kind act is preferable to a large amount of sympathy,' Li Fong quoted.

'More tea, Li?' Mei asked, picking up the pot.

He nodded, and when she had refilled his bowl she turned to the visitors with a smile. 'If you want some more just ask,' she said, noticing that both Kay and her brother had some tea left in their bowls.

'No, this is fine,' Kay answered quickly, reluctantly picking up her bowl. Paul left his sitting in front of him.

'Kay tells me you 'ave some books I might be able ter borrer,' Paul said to Mei Li.

'I'll be happy to let you have them,' she replied.

The elderly trader leaned back in his seat. 'I think I am taking up too much of your time,' he said smiling. 'I will be happy for you to escort Mei Li to the public house. The Swan you call it?'

Paul nodded. 'It's quite respectable,' he replied. 'We go there a lot. Mei Li'll be quite safe.'

'I have no doubt,' Li Fong told him. 'I'm sure it will be preferable to sitting here talking to an old man.'

'It's bin a pleasure,' Kay replied.

'Yeah it's bin very nice,' Paul added.

'I'll get my coat,' Mei Li said, looking happy. 'We can make some arrangements later for getting the books to you.'

Kay slipped her arm through Mei's as they walked out of Cater Street into Grange Road in the balmy evening air.

'I 'ave to admit I was a little scared,' she confessed as they made their way along Abbey Street towards Dockhead.

Mei Li giggled. 'My guardian isn't a tyrant,' she said. 'In fact I can, how do you say it, twist him round my fingers.'

Paul walked beside them with his hands in his trouser pockets, wondering what reception they would encounter at the Swan. Joey Westlake would be there, and Butch Wheeler too, sporting his recent crop.

They crossed Jamaica Road into Dockhead and Paul took a deep breath as he led the way into the pub.

Joey Westlake was leaning on the counter talking to Butch and he waved them over. 'So this is Mei Li,' he said smiling. 'Pleased ter meet yer I'm sure.'

The big man held out a huge hand. ''Ello, luv. I'm Butch.'

Joey slipped his arm around Kay's waist. 'Well, what'll it be? I'm in the chair.'

While the drinks were being ordered Kay leaned towards Mei Li. 'I need ter powder me nose,' she whispered in her ear.

As the two young women walked away Joey raised his eyebrows in an approving gesture. 'She's really tasty, Paul,' he said.

'Yeah, she's a cracker,' Butch added, rubbing his hand over what was left of his hair.

'Do us a favour, lads,' Paul said. 'Give us a bit o' space. I've gotta make some 'eadway 'ere.'

'All right, all right, we know when we're not wanted,' Joey replied with a quick look at the big man. 'We're not good enough now ter be in 'is lordship's company, Butch.

215

It's all your fault. That bloody 'aircut makes yer look like a real scruff. Yer've frightened the bleedin' life out o' the poor gel.'

Butch took the ribbing in good humour but Paul looked concerned. 'No disrespect, lads,' he said, 'but yer know 'ow it is.'

Joey nodded. 'Only jossin' yer, pal. Good luck ter yer. She's a real doll. I'll come over an' take Kay off yer 'ands later an' then it's up ter you.'

The pub was beginning to fill up and the pianist started to tinkle on the ivories. Paul left the money for a drink with Joey and steered the two women over to a vacant table.

'Butch is a funny man,' Mei Li giggled.

'Yer can say that again,' Paul told her. ''E's as strong as an ox but 'e's got an' 'eart o' gold.'

'I like him,' Mei replied. 'It's very nice in here. People seem friendly.'

Kay began to point out a few characters to the young Chinese girl and occasionally whispered into Mei Li's ear. Paul sat back and sipped his pint of beer, his eyes constantly returning to the young woman by his side.

'Joey Westlake's my boyfriend,' Kay was going on. ''E works in the market. 'E's a barrer boy.'

'Down the Blue,' Mei Li quoted, which brought a smile to Paul's face.

'No, in Tower Bridge Road,' he told her.

'Are you engaged to him?' Mei asked Kay.

'No, but we are goin' steady,' she replied.

Paul excused himself from the table and sauntered over to Joey and Butch. ''Ere, are you gonna come over an' get Kay?' he said quickly. 'She's bloody well monopolisin' 'er.'

'Say no more,' Joey grinned, turning to Butch. 'I dunno, a bloke can't do right fer doin' wrong. There's Kay tellin' me ter back off fer a while an' I've got this berk on me back now.'

A few minutes later Joey ambled over. 'Kay, I need ter talk ter yer,' he said. 'Can you come an' sort this argument out between Butch an' me?'

Kay got up and glanced at Paul. 'Look after 'er,' she told him, turning quickly to give Mei Li a large wink.

'Your sister's very nice,' Mei said with a smile once they were alone at the table.

'Yeah she is,' Paul replied. 'She finks you're very nice too. So do I as a matter o' fact.'

Mei Li flushed slightly at the compliment. 'I've fooled you both then,' she joked.

Paul grinned. 'It must 'ave bin very strange fer you at first, all this travellin' I mean,' he said, clasping his hands on the table.

'I soon adapted,' Mei Li told him. 'In America I stayed with a Chinese family whose children had grown up there and they always accompanied me when I went out for an evening. I like it here very much. It is very different to America.'

'Are you plannin' on stayin' long?' Paul asked.

'I hope so but it all depends on my guardian,' she replied. 'Li's getting old and he wants to return once his permit has expired. He misses the business, although it's in very safe hands.'

Paul noticed the sudden faraway look in Mei Li's eyes and his heart beat faster. 'Will you 'ave ter go 'ome too?' he asked.

'It will be expected,' she replied, her eyes matching his and sending a shiver through him.

'When does the permit expire?'

'In three months.'

'Can it be renewed?'

'Possibly, but it's not certain.'

'I 'ope it can,' Paul said quietly.

Mei Li smiled and his heart leapt again. 'It's all in the lap of the gods,' she said, running her small fingers over the rim of the glass.

'Let me get you a refill,' he offered.

It did not take him long to get served, and as he came back and sat down he caught that faraway look in her eyes again. 'Are you OK?' he asked with concern.

'Yes, it's very nice talking to you,' she told him.

'It's very nice talkin' ter you,' he replied. 'I couldn't wait ter see yer again after that day at the exhibition. You did the talk so well.'

'Thank you,' she said coyly.

'Is there anyone special in yer life?' he heard himself asking her.

Mei Li shook her head. 'My work takes up much of my time and I know very few people socially.'

Paul was rapidly gaining in confidence now. ''Ave yer seen much of London since yer've bin 'ere?' he asked her.

Mei smiled. 'I've seen Buckingham Palace, Parliament, and Trafalgar Square,' she replied, counting off on her fingers.

'Is there any place yer'd like ter see?'

'Petticoat Lane,' she said quickly.

Paul laughed aloud. 'Petticoat Lane? That's strange.'

'Why?' she asked, frowning at his amusement.

'I dunno, I was expectin' you ter say Oxford Street or Piccadilly Circus, or even a trip down the river.'

'I've seen those places, though I've never been on the river,' Mei Li replied. 'It's just that Petticoat Lane is supposed to be the biggest market in the world. I wondered how it compares to places in China and Singapore, and America too.'

'Would you let me take yer ter Petticoat Lane?' Paul asked.

The young woman met his gaze and was taken by his boyish enthusiasm. 'I'd like that, though I'd have to . . .'

'Get permission.' Paul finished the sentence for her with a broad smile. 'I understand.'

Mei Li studied his face. His smile was open and warm and she felt safe in his company. His eyes too were frank and honest, and he had a pride in himself that she liked. 'My guardian feels a great responsibility for me,' she said quietly, her closed hand going up to her chest, 'and I have to respect his wishes. He only wants for me to be safe and happy, and for my part it's my life that I'm indebted to him for.'

Paul reached out and touched her hand gently. 'Believe me, I do understand,' he replied.

Mei Li allowed her hand to remain under his for a few moments then she gently withdrew it. 'Will you come for me?' she asked.

'Can you be ready by ten o'clock on Sunday mornin'?'

'Yes I can.'

'An' will yer guardian not mind?'

Mei smiled, her eyes sparkling as she looked at him. 'I see no problems,' she said.

The clear night sky was full of stars as the two young people walked back to Grange Road chatting easily, and when they turned into Cater Street Mei Li rested her hand on his arm. 'I've really enjoyed talking to you and your sister,' she said in a soft voice. 'Thank you for showing me your public house. And Butch,' she added with a muffled giggle.

'I was just about ter say 'ow much I enjoyed this evenin',' Paul replied. 'I'm really lookin' forward ter Sunday mornin'.'

'And so am I,' she told him.

The young man reached out and felt her cool, tiny hand slip into his for a fleeting moment. 'Goodnight, Mei Li,' he said, deliberately keeping his distance.

'Goodnight, Paul, and thank you,' she replied.

He waited until she had let herself into the house next to the laundry then he turned away, feeling elated. He could see her still, her smile that turned him to jelly, and the softness of her tiny hand enclosed in his. There was no use denying it. She had stolen his heart.

Chapter Twenty

On Saturday morning Mei Li walked through the Tower Bridge Road market in search of a small gift for Su Chang. It might help to cheer her up, the young woman thought, as she stopped at a clothes stall to look at the racks of blouses and tops. Poor Su worked hard all day at the laundry, sweating in the hot, steamy atmosphere with little reward save the knowledge that the business was managing to survive at least. Now her husband's very life was in jeopardy and her fear of what might happen showed in her thin lined face.

The clothes were bright and fashionable, Mei Li thought, but Ho Chang's dutiful wife did not have a social life, and anything too vivid and expensive-looking would remain in her bedroom drawer for ever.

'These few are reduced, luv,' the stall owner told her. 'I'm knockin' 'em out cheap 'cos they're the last o' the range. Take a gander, yer won't find better anywhere, not fer that price.'

Mei Li took a mauve blouse from the rack and held it up in front of her. It had a wide collar, with a line of silver-coloured buttons running down the length of it. It was nice, and not too fancy. Su might be persuaded to wear it, she decided.

Armed with the present, and a multi-coloured chiffon scarf that she had bought to wear on Sunday morning, Mei Li made her way home to Cater Street. The prospect of going to the Sunday market at Brick Lane with a young man excited her. Paul was nice and he had been very gentlemanly when he escorted her home last night. He had not tried to kiss her, which might well have proved to be a pleasant experience under different circumstances, but she had realised that her guardian would be lingering near the window listening for their footsteps and she was sure that he had been peeping through the curtains. He had in fact been a little peeved that it was late and the young man's sister was not with them. He had reminded her that it would be unwise to form an attachment to the young man, considering the future that was planned for her.

Mei Li smiled to herself as she walked along Grange Road in the bright morning sunshine. Li Fong's eyes had widened in alarm when she told him that she would be going to the famous Petticoat Lane on Sunday morning and the young man would be her escort. He had puffed in exasperation and mumbled under his breath as he went off to bed, leaving her feeling pleased with herself for not being cowed by him. Although she was young, she was more worldly-wise than he in some respects. Li Fong had grown up in the old China and his roots ran deep in the clay, but the ways of the West had pulled at her, moulded her to a large extent, and she possessed few of the fears her guardian harboured.

Su Chang was in the backyard chopping wood for the laundry coppers when Mei Li arrived and it was her very worried-looking husband who showed the young woman in. 'I have to leave now,' he told her. 'There's much I have to do and so little time.'

'I'm so worried about him,' Su confessed as she embedded the sharp chopper in the stout block with a heavy blow. 'He's going to see a money lender this morning but he'll need some security for a large loan and what has he got to offer? These business premises and the house next door are ours only while we can pay the mortgage.'

Mei Li watched sadly as Su Chang wearily sat down on a rickety chair. 'Did you know that Li Fong has spoken with the man who owns the Peking Club?' she asked.

Su nodded. 'The man who came to see us about the debt is meeting with Li this evening,' she replied. 'His name is Tommy Lo and I understand he is the Tong leader. I am not hopeful. The Tongs do not wait for payment and I fear that Li Fong is not in a position to bargain with them.'

Mei Li put her hand on the older woman's shoulder. 'My guardian is a good man who loves his brother,' she said quietly. 'He'll do all he can to get them to wait. You do know he has sent off to Singapore for money?'

Su sighed. 'We're both very grateful, but I fear the money will not arrive in time. Li has explained that there are many restrictions on money coming into the country.'

Mei squatted down beside her. 'Look, I have some money put away. You can borrow it to pay off the debt until the money arrives from Singapore.'

Su shook her head vigorously. 'It's not for me to make decisions. It would be for Ho to decide, and I know that he would refuse your kind offer, whatever the consequences for us. There is too much dishonour already.'

'But it doesn't make sense,' Mei Li said coaxingly.

'Surely Ho will see that it's only a temporary loan. Where is the dishonour in that?'

Su lowered her head, fighting back tears of frustration and despair. 'Every day more interest is added on,' she said, her voice quavering. 'We could not hope to repay you in full for years, and that money you have ensures a future for you. At least Li Fong is Ho's brother, but you are not of our family.'

'Maybe not in blood, but I am in every other respect,' Mei Li replied with feeling. 'I see Li Fong as my father and I love him as a father, and he loves me as a daughter.'

Su looked up slowly, her almond eyes bright with anxiety. 'Ho wants me to leave this place, but where could I go? And how could I leave him to fire the boilers, and do all the washing and ironing and everything else that's needed to run the business? He could never manage.'

'He is concerned for your safety,' Mei Li said weakly.

'He should have considered that before he sat down at the mah-jong tables,' Su replied bitterly.

The young woman handed her the paper bag she was still holding. 'I've bought you a little gift,' she said smiling. 'I hope you like it.'

Su opened the bag and her eyes widened as she took out the blouse. 'It's lovely,' she said.

'You must wear it,' Mei told her firmly.

Su got up and put her arms around her. 'I'll wear it this evening,' she replied, suddenly overcome with emotion.

Mei Li held her tightly, gently patting her back. 'It'll all turn out fine, you'll see,' she said sighing. 'Li Fong is a good businessman and he's also very wise. He won't let anything happen to you and Ho.'

Su ran the back of her hand over her eyes. 'I've made you unhappy with my problems,' she said bravely. 'Come into the house and tell me all about this young man you've met.'

'How did you know?' Mei Li asked, looking surprised.

Su smiled slyly. 'Those messages you asked Ti San to deliver, and then your guardian's concern for you when he called on us last night while you were out,' she explained. 'He told us you were visiting a pub with your English friend and her brother. I was curious, so I peeped out of the window when I heard footsteps stop outside. He looks a very nice young man.'

'He is,' Mei Li said smiling. 'In fact he's taking me to Petticoat Lane tomorrow morning.'

'Do you like him?' Su asked with a cheeky smile, giving her a searching look.

The younger woman flushed slightly. 'We're just friends,' she sighed. 'I couldn't allow it to be any more than that. My future is already set out like the painted pictures on a set of ginger pots. I'll soon return to Singapore and marry the man whom my guardian has chosen for me. I'll want for nothing and I'll be very productive. There'll be many children if my husband so wishes and I'll make him happy.'

'And will you be happy, Mei Li?'

'I'll be happy to repay Li Fong for all his love and caring.'

'It's not the same,' Su said pointedly. 'I asked you if you'll be happy. Will you not be lonely?'

'I'll work hard at my marriage and I hope to find happiness,' Mei Li replied with a fatalistic expression.

Su looked up at the ornamental clock on the mantelshelf.

'There are still a few minutes left before I have to open the shop again,' she said. 'Tell me more about this young Englishman.'

Winston Norris was the general manager of Madeley's Food Factory, and he prided himself on his efficiency. The firm's owners very rarely visited their London depot, knowing that it was in good hands, which was more than could be said for their three provincial factories. Norris ran a tight ship but he was not afraid to delegate responsibility where needed. He regarded himself as lucky in that he had a good team around him. His secretary Angela Stapleton he considered to be a gem. She kept the books, organised the day-to-day running of the firm and generally made his life very comfortable and trouble-free, a blithe state of affairs which his counterparts in the other depots had not enjoyed for quite some time.

Winston was a fatherly figure, and his paternal instincts were roused on Friday afternoon when he returned to the office after a leisurely lunch and drinks at a nearby pub and noticed that Angela was dabbing at her eyes.

'Are you all right, Angela?' he asked as he settled himself behind his desk.

'I'm sorry, Mr Norris, but I just feel a bit low,' she replied, smiling weakly.

'We can't have this,' Norris told her firmly. 'As soon as those yearly accounts are finalised and the shareholders' meeting is over and done with we must see about allowing you a day or two off. You'll have earned it.'

'No really, I'm fine, Mr Norris. It's just that everything's got on top of me,' she answered, blowing into her lace handkerchief.

There was little for Winston Norris to do in the way of work that afternoon and he leaned back in his leather-bound chair, joining the tips of his fingers together in his distinctive pose. 'Now out with it,' he said in a firm voice. 'Mustn't bottle things up, it's not good for anyone.'

Angela smiled bravely. 'Laurie broke his ankle last weekend and he's in plaster,' she sighed. 'I was hoping he'd fix that tank in our loft but he can't manage the ladder.'

'Oh dear, I am sorry,' Winston replied. 'Give him my condolences won't you.'

'Thank you, Mr Norris. It's very kind of you,' Angela told him.

'I shouldn't worry too much,' the general manager advised her. 'I broke my ankle some years ago but it's fine now.'

'It's not just Laurie,' she replied. 'Last night we had a flood. Apparently the ball-cock in the loft tank got stuck and the water just ran over. It brought our bedroom ceiling down and you can imagine the mess. Poor Laurie had to hobble down into the street to turn the main stop-cock off. Until the job's done we've got to rely on next door for water. It's become so embarrassing.'

'When are they going to fix it?' Winston asked.

'Not till next week unfortunately,' Angela said with a deep sigh. 'Tuesday was the earliest I could get. The plumbing firms are all so busy at the moment by all accounts.'

'Disgraceful,' Winston declared with passion. 'I've an idea. Why don't you have a word with Percy Bradley? He might be able to spare one of his lads to call round and take a look at it for you.'

'That's very sweet of you, Mr Norris,' Angela said smiling, 'but they're all very busy stripping and moving the machines around. I wouldn't dream of asking him. Saturday would be the earliest, and it would mean paying overtime. Thanks anyway for your thoughtfulness.'

'Now just a minute. What are we talking about? A couple of hours?' Winston went on. 'We're well down on our overtime expense anyway.'

'Yes but you know how unseen problems come up,' Angela reminded him. 'It often happens that a two-hour job ends up taking six hours.'

Winston Norris had never before been told he was a sweet person, and very rarely described as being thoughtful, and it felt very gratifying. 'Goodness gracious me, woman,' he exclaimed. 'Two hours, four hours, six hours. It's not going to break the bank, is it?'

'If you're really sure,' Angela replied with a captivating smile. 'I'll be so relieved to get it fixed. The worry of it all has been making me feel really ill, to tell you the truth.'

All the passion and emotion had made Winston Norris feel quite tired. 'You go and see Percy right away,' he told her. 'I'm off now to a meeting. Can you hold the fort?'

'Of course I can,' she assured him. 'And thank you very much for your kindness.'

Winston Norris was feeling very pious as he caught the early train to Maidstone, unaware that he had been used in a sticky web of intrigue.

Chapter Twenty-One

Tommy Lo was taken completely by surprise and he rubbed the side of his head ruefully as he straightened himself on the rear seat of the police car. 'What's all the rush?' he growled as Chief Inspector Kennedy climbed in beside him and motioned to the police driver to set off.

'Sorry about that, but we had to make it look good. We wouldn't want to put you on the spot, now would we?' Kennedy said smiling.

'What's this all about?' Tommy Lo asked as he ran his fingers through his dishevelled dark hair.

'Kano San, the candlemaker,' Kennedy replied, his expression becoming serious. 'He's been murdered.'

'That's bad news,' Tommy said without emotion. 'But why drag me in this car just to tell me that?'

'Don't get lippy with me, son, or I might forget our little arrangement,' the inspector rounded on him. 'We've been combing the streets for you. You took Kano and locked him up in one of your safe houses. The Tong were the last to see the candlemaker alive, so that puts you in the frame, wouldn't you say? I want a name. Now.'

Tommy Lo shrugged his shoulders. 'If it had been the

Tong's wishes that Kano San should die you would've dragged his body from the river.'

'I never said where we found him,' Kennedy replied quickly.

'No but everyone's talking about it,' the Tong leader answered. 'Kano was found in his workshop with his head almost cut off. Word on the street says it was a family thing.'

'I don't think so,' Kennedy said coldly. 'A name, Tommy. Give me a name.'

'You know I couldn't do that, even if I knew who did it,' Tommy replied quickly. 'I'd be cut down in the street.'

The chief inspector leaned towards him menacingly. 'Now you listen to me,' he grated. 'When I was serving in the Hong Kong police I saw what happened when a renegade Tong member went against the rest. It ended up in a bloodbath. You've got a renegade, Tommy, and I believe you know who it is.'

The young man shook his head. 'None of my members would act on their own.'

Kennedy leaned back in the seat as the car sped along West India Dock Road towards Canning Town. 'I'm disappointed in you, son,' he remarked. 'As a matter of fact I've been given a name and I was hoping you'd verify it. It's one of your Tong, and for your sake it'd be better having him locked away in a cell than running wild. You don't want me to remind you that it'll only be a matter of time before he invokes the vote. I've no desire to see you stretched out in the morgue.'

Tommy Lo looked down at his clenched hands for a few moments. 'Tell me the name,' he said.

'Billy Chou,' the policeman replied.

The young man nodded slowly. 'If you pulled him in you'd be wasting your time,' he said quietly. 'Billy Chou would have made sure he had a good alibi.'

Kennedy looked out of the window at the grimy factories and then he turned back towards the troubled Tong leader. 'I take it you'd vouch for him as well?'

'I'd have to.'

'If you did you'd end up perjuring yourself, Tommy,' the inspector told him. 'Last night about the time the candlemaker was topped you were over the river. You were seen getting on a number eighty-two bus and you were still on it when it went through the tunnel.'

'You're having me followed?' Tommy said in surprise.

'Let's just say we're keeping an eagle eye on you boys,' the policeman replied with a smile. 'You've been overstepping the mark lately and your own people are beginning to take umbrage. Your Tong's been bleeding them dry. Where they once saw us as the enemy they now look to us for some form of protection. They're running scared.'

Tommy Lo took a deep breath and puffed out noisily. 'We took the candlemaker as you say, and it was for a good reason,' he insisted. 'We held him for some time and then we scared the shit out of him. He thought he was going home without some of his fingers, but we let him off with a warning. That's the truth. The Tong were not responsible for his murder.'

'One of your members was though.'

'If it was Billy Chou who killed him then he was acting on his own.'

'Why would he do that?'

Tommy Lo shrugged his shoulders. 'It might have been a personal vendetta,' he suggested. 'Or else the first move in challenging my authority.'

Kennedy leaned forward and whispered something in the driver's ear. The man nodded, swung the car into a sidestreet and threaded his way back out on to the main thoroughfare, heading back towards Limehouse.

'Have you still got your maritime ticket?' the inspector asked.

'Yeah, I thought I might need it again one day,' Tommy replied.

'I'd make use of it, if I were you,' Kennedy told him. 'It's obvious your authority's being undermined, and I can see history repeating itself before long.'

'Blood on the streets?' Tommy Lo said with a cynical smile.

'Your blood, as sure as God made little apples,' the policeman warned him. 'Go back to sea. Do yourself a favour.'

'It's a possible option,' the young man replied. 'First though I've got some important business to take care of.'

Kennedy said something to the driver and the car ground to a halt.

'You'd better get out here.'

Tommy Lo stepped out on to the pavement, then he leaned his head back inside. 'Billy Chou keeps a machete at Wu Sung's house, wrapped in a cloth under the stairs,' he said. 'Don't go straight to it or he'll put two and two together.'

'What do you take us for?' Kennedy growled as the car drew away from the kerb.

Tommy Lo watched it disappear into the distance then he walked along to the bus stop. Husi Kang, the owner of the Peking Club, had set up the Saturday evening meeting with Li Fong, trader and brother of Ho Chang, and the young Tong leader knew that Billy Chou and the other members were eagerly awaiting results. Tomorrow, Sunday, was the seventh day, and if the money was not forthcoming by then they would expect to go in force to Bermondsey. Ho Chang would pay the ultimate price. His business would be totally destroyed, and the mark of the Tong put on his brother Li Fong.

The young man's mind was troubled as he boarded the bus that would take him south of the river. Kennedy had had him followed and he would know where to point the finger if a Chinese national in Bermondsey became a victim of Tong justice. The only safe way out for everyone concerned would be for the laundryman to pay his debt by Sunday, and considering the added interest that had built up day by day this solution did not look very likely.

Li Fong was wearing his traditional Cantonese robe of embroidered silk and a tight-fitting black cap and slippers as he prepared himself for the meeting. Mei Li had tidied the room, set out the tea bowls and lit joss-sticks and a scented candle to encourage a serene atmosphere. Now, as she watched her guardian take his place on the low seat facing the door, she felt very nervous. Li clasped his hands in his lap and began rolling his thumbs, a sure sign that he too was feeling uneasy.

Mei Li had confronted her guardian earlier that day, after her talk with Ho Chang's wife Su, and she had insisted on being present at the meeting. Li reacted just as she had predicted: women must know their place and not interfere in the important business of men. She had rounded on him angrily, reminding him that if the Tong struck it would be indiscriminately and both she and Su would be in just as much danger. She also made it clear that she and Su were not prepared to leave for a place of safety. This was England not China, she had told him, and she was a part of the modern world now, not bound by ancient customs and the dictates of village elders. To his credit Li Fong had understood her reasoning, though he did remind her that her roots held her to her Chinese lineage and she must never abandon them totally. He had also reminded her of his wishes for her future, and for the first time Mei Li experienced a sense of dread.

The streets were cool and the sky above banded with copper when Tommy Lo arrived at Cater Street and was shown up to the first-floor room by Mei Li.

Li Fong loosed his hand from the wide sleeve of his robe and waved the Tong leader into a seat facing him, then nodded for Mei Li to fill the tea bowls. 'I welcome you to my humble home,' he said. 'It is right that we talk, you in your capacity as enforcer and I as Ho Chang's agent.'

Tommy Lo was eyeing the young woman closely as she poured the tea and he turned to Li Fong with a sardonic smile. 'Agent?' he queried. 'Ho Chang can employ an agent but cannot honour his debt. He should be here to speak for himself.'

Li Fong nodded. 'I do not wish to argue the rights and

wrongs,' he replied calmly. 'It is on my insistence that my brother has allowed me to talk to you privately.'

'You are aware that tomorrow is the last day for payment in full,' Tommy Lo reminded him.

Li Fong picked up his filled bowl and motioned for his guest to do the same. 'Let us drink first,' he said simply.

The young man's dark eyes returned to Mei Li as she carried the teapot out of the room. 'Husi Kang told me that the young woman is your ward,' he remarked.

Li Fong nodded. 'Husi and I had a civilised discussion when I visited his club. I asked him for an extension to give my brother time to arrange a loan from the bank but he told me that it was out of his hands now.'

It was Tommy Lo's turn to nod. 'The Peking Club is under the Tong's protection,' he replied. 'All debts that are not honoured become our responsibility. We have our ways of ensuring that payment is made and the club survives.'

'Ho Chang has tried everywhere to raise the money he owes but it was not possible in the time allowed him,' Li Fong told him. 'I have managed to persuade him to accept a loan from me but it will be money transferred from my business in Singapore and it will take two weeks to arrive.'

The young man shook his head. 'Time has run out,' he answered with a note of menace in his voice. 'For me to go back to the Tong without the payment and then allow yet another extension would be unthinkable. Either the money is paid by tomorrow, or Ho Chang will have to face the consequences, and you do not need me to remind you what that means.'

'But you are the Tong leader. Surely your voice carries

respect and obedience,' Li Fong said astutely, his deep eyes unwavering.

Mei Li had come back into the room and was listening intently, desperate to add her voice to the argument, but she had been made to promise her guardian she would not interfere in any way. Here a man's life was at stake and a sensible solution was possible, if only Li Fong would allow her to make her savings available. Instead she had been lectured on honour, dishonour and ancestral respect, and it angered her.

'You as Chinese know that the will of the Tong is all-powerful,' Tommy Lo said in a rising voice. 'There is no bargaining possible after the deadline. It would be unprecedented weakness, and I would not be fit to consider myself leader.'

Mei Li could bear it no longer and she stood up and coughed to attract the men's attention. 'Would you like some more tea?' she asked, her eyes fixed on Tommy Lo.

'Yes, child,' Li Fong said, irritated by her interruption as he was about to argue his corner.

The young woman picked up the figured teapot. 'If you will permit me a question,' she began, addressing herself to the young man. 'Why did you become involved with the Tong?'

A silence seemed to thicken the room and Li Fong looked at her with angry eyes, but she was not to be swayed. 'You are young and obviously intelligent. Husi Kang told us that you have an English mother, grew up in this country and were educated at an English school, yet you follow the ancient law of the Tong.'

'You find it surprising?' Tommy Lo said with some amusement.

'Yes I do,' Mei Li told him. 'There is so much to do to improve the lot of the Chinese people in Limehouse, but you and your members rule by fear and violence.'

The young man smiled at her, his eyes moving approvingly over her shapely body. 'It's hard for outsiders to understand,' he replied, growing serious again. 'You live here in Bermondsey, away from your own people, and you embrace the style, culture and thinking of the West. In Limehouse the Chinese community can barely get a foothold in this world. For many of them old China is more real than England, and the customs and traditions of the homeland still hold sway. Remember, many cannot even speak English and they feel excluded and isolated. That's why the Tongs rule in Chinatown.'

'That doesn't necessarily follow,' Mei Li said undaunted.

'It's easy for you to say that,' the young Tong leader remarked. 'If you had grown up in Pennyfields, without the privilege you have obviously enjoyed, you would understand. Where does the average Chinese person go for redress? Not to the police. Where does he go for justice and protection? Neither to the police nor the courts. He comes to us, and we punish the wrongdoer and protect the innocent and the weak. Our code is ruthless, yes, but it has to be. Fear and obedience go hand in hand.'

'Tell me,' Mei Li said, her eyes widening. 'What can be gained from maiming and killing? A dead person cannot make recompense or pay a debt. And do you really protect the innocent and the weak, or just bleed them dry?'

Li Fong clapped his hands together loudly. 'That will be enough,' he declared angrily.

Tommy Lo held up a hand. 'It's good that your ward is trying to understand,' he said quietly, turning back to Mei Li. 'Without the Tongs the people of Chinatown would be at the mercy of anyone strong enough and ruthless enough to exploit their vulnerability. As it stands we keep order and mete out justice and punishment in time-honoured fashion. We are not the worst arbiters they could have.'

'And tomorrow, when Ho Chang's debt has still not been paid, you will come in force and mete out justice here,' Mei Li said in a coolly mocking voice.

'The Tong will meet to decide the laundryman's fate and the punishment will be carried out. There is no other way,' Tommy Lo replied.

Li Fong beckoned for Mei Li to come closer and he whispered in her ear. Her reaction was to stare unbelievingly at him for a few moments before he waved her away to do his bidding. 'I think there is a middle path and we must explore it,' he said.

'Do not waste my time, Li Fong,' the Tong leader replied quickly.

'That I will not do. I only want you to hear me out.'

'Only the debt paid in full will satisfy,' Tommy Lo reminded him.

Mei Li came back into the room carrying a dusty parcel wrapped in brown paper and tied with string. She looked at her guardian appealingly and he smiled at her as he took the parcel, touched by the expression in her eyes. 'What price can be put on a life?' he asked her. 'Would a blind man begrudge parting with a fortune to see again, to watch one sunset or to look just one time upon the face of his newborn child?'

Mei Li wiped a tear from her eye as she took her place by the door and Tommy Lo frowned in puzzlement as the older man set the parcel down on the table and untied the string. The scented candle sputtered and its flame died as he reached into the box and carefully placed the contents one by one on the table in front of him. Tommy Lo leaned forward in his seat and Mei Li touched her lips with the tips of her fingers.

'What you are looking at is a very rare set of ginger pots,' the trader began. 'I have spent my whole life searching throughout China to complete this set. In all the world there are only six known sets and they are priceless. Museums and art galleries anywhere would pay a vast sum of money to acquire these. Take them as security for two weeks, and if by then Ho Chang's debt has still not been paid, these priceless pots will become the property of the Tong.'

Tommy Lo looked closely at the figuring. 'The legend of the lantern,' he said quietly.

Li Fong nodded. 'If you doubt the genuineness of these pots, then seek the truth in Chinatown. It will not be at all difficult to substantiate.'

Tommy Lo nodded in return. 'I will come back tomorrow evening after the Tong has met to consider your request. But tell me. How can you trust us to return these pots? What if the Tong's decision is to take them as payment in lieu?'

'That is the risk I will have to take,' Li Fong replied. 'But I would not have been prepared to risk parting company with such a priceless asset had you not explained just a few minutes ago that the Tong metes out justice as well as punishment in time-honoured fashion. I believe that I have acted honourably on behalf of my brother and I feel sure that you will do likewise.'

Mei Li left the room, unable to contain her emotions, and she did not return until she had heard the front door close behind Tommy Lo. 'I'm sorry to have disobeyed you and made you angry, Li,' she said, lowering her head, 'but I could not keep my promise to you when I felt there was some chance of helping the Changs.'

Li Fong laid his bony hand on her arm. 'Confucius said, "Make only the promise you can keep", but in his teachings there are also allowances for human frailty, and selfless generosity too. Let's sleep on what's transpired this night and hope that tomorrow will bring a better day.'

Mei Li leaned forward and kissed her guardian on his forehead. 'Ho Chang is very lucky to have you as his brother,' she replied.

Chapter Twenty-Two

Jim Neal walked down the garden path to the small shed and went inside. There was barely room to turn around, what with the rickety shelves piled with flowerpots of all sizes and the narrow floor space littered with garden tools and a rolled-up hosepipe. He heard laughter coming from the open door of the scullery and the aroma of bacon frying mixed with the sour smell of earth inside the shed. Next door the Thompsons were listening to 'Two-Way Family Favourites', and he could hear clearly the message from a serviceman in Germany to his loved ones in England.

It was a warm Sunday morning, a time to laze and enjoy, but as Jim searched for two pots of seedlings Ruby had asked him to fetch he was feeling nervous and ill at ease. He could see her now, welcoming him into her home with that sultry smile that made his heart race, and he could still feel her as she came close and told him how clever she had been. Damn the woman, he thought. She was going to ruin his life and his family too. He could feel the tension building between him and Ruby, yet he was too weak to put a stop to it. He couldn't go on like this, being manipulated and having to lie and cheat at every twist and turn. Coming home after six o'clock yesterday and pretending that the overtime had jaded him was bad enough, but worst of all was having to disregard Ruby's barely disguised hints that after all it was Saturday night, and she felt like making love.

Jim took a tobacco tin from his shirt pocket and rolled a cigarette, aware that his hands were none too steady. Ruby had not made much of it last night but he knew that she would be wondering what had happened to his sexual feelings towards her.

'Can't you find 'em?' Ruby called to him down the garden.

Jim exhaled a stream of tobacco smoke. 'Yeah, I can see 'em,' he called back.

'Come on then, yer breakfast's ready.'

He stubbed his cigarette under his foot and took the two pots down from the shelf. As he walked into the scullery Ruby gave him a critical look. 'Couldn't you leave those pots outside?' she puffed. 'No, leave 'em on the table now, an' take this in wiv yer.'

Jim sat himself at the parlour table where Paul was wiping the remains of a fried egg from his plate with a hunk of bread. 'You're up early this mornin',' he remarked.

The young man grinned. 'I'm goin' ter Petticoat Lane, would yer believe,' he replied.

'Petticoat Lane?' Jim queried. 'It'll be packed solid.'

'I'm takin' Mei Li,' Paul told him. 'She's never bin there.'

'Does yer muvver know?' Jim asked, nodding his head towards the scullery.

'Yeah, an' I got a bit of a lecture,' the young man frowned, pushing his empty plate back.

'It's only that she's worried,' Jim said cutting into his bacon.

'Yeah, I know the problems involved,' Paul replied quickly, 'but I like the gel a lot, an' I'd much sooner be wiv 'er than some o' the gels I've gone out wiv in the past.'

'Just as long as yer realise.'

'Yeah I do, Farvver,' Paul replied in an end-of-conversation tone of voice as he got up from the table.

Kay passed him in the doorway and sat down facing her father. 'Dad? Did Jim tell yer 'e's takin' Mei Li out this mornin'?' she asked.

Jim nodded. 'Yer mum's not too 'appy about it, so I understand.'

'She's a bit worried.'

'Paul's old enough ter make 'is own mind up about who 'e goes out wiv the same as you but it don't stop us worryin', nonetheless,' Jim remarked. 'We wouldn't wanna see eivver of yer get 'urt.'

Kay leaned back in her chair and folded her arms. 'I've never known Paul get so excited about a gel,' she said. ''E's not stopped talkin' about 'er.'

'Yeah 'e seems smitten. And what about you?'

She smiled at him. 'Me an' Joey are gettin' on really well.'

'No regrets about endin' it wiv Richard?'

'Definitely not.'

''Ave yer seen anyfing of 'im since yer split?'

'No.'

Jim finished the last of his breakfast and reached for another slice of bread. 'Me an' yer mum 'ave decided ter go down ter Devon fer a week,' he told her.

243

'That'll be nice,' she replied. 'You've bin workin' 'ard lately an' it's beginnin' ter show. It'll do Mum good too ter get away fer a week.'

Jim sighed deeply. 'Yeah, I reckon it will.'

Kay studied her hands for a few moments then she looked up at her father. 'Joey wants us ter get engaged,' she announced.

'It's a bit soon ain't it?' Jim said quickly.

Kay shrugged her shoulders. 'We wouldn't get married this year, Dad, but me an' Joey 'ave decided it's what we want,' she said keenly. 'Honestly, yer wouldn't credit 'ow different 'e is. 'E's nowhere near as flash as 'e used ter be, an' 'e's so attentive. 'E's got plans to open anuvver stall down the Blue. 'E works really 'ard an' I know we'll be 'appy tergevver.'

'You 'aven't said anyfing about this ter yer muvver, 'ave yer?' Jim queried.

Kay shook her head. 'Joey wants ter come round an' see yer both first, just ter do it properly. I told you so yer can be on yer guard if Mum creates.'

'When does 'e want ter see us?'

''E was finkin' some time next week, if yer reckon it'll be all right.'

Jim pulled a face. 'I dunno. Better let me try an' break the ice first.' Seeing his daughter's reaction he added, 'Don't worry, I won't say anyfing about what yer've got planned. I'll just say 'ow 'appy yer look since yer've bin back wiv Joey.'

Kay smiled gratefully. 'Fanks fer bein' so understandin', Dad. I really am 'appy.'

Jim rose from the table. 'Well, I'd better get ter work,'

he sighed. 'Yer muvver wants that patch dug over. She's got some seeds ter put in.'

Tommy Lo sat with the rest of the Tong leaders in the public bar of the Cutter, a pub near the Millwall Dock gates which was frequented by the local Chinese community. It was run by an old merchant seaman known to everyone as Kipper Joe, a large, gregarious character who had been torpedoed twice while serving on the transatlantic convoys during the war. Joe stood no nonsense from anyone, and even the Tong treated him with grudging respect. If there was any form of trouble in his pub Kipper Joe was able to call not only on his old seafaring pals but also on his many docker friends who were in the habit of frequenting the saloon bar.

'I see the Chinks are 'ere in force,' an old seaman remarked to the landlord.

'As long as they be'ave themselves I couldn't care less,' Joe told him.

'What d'yer fink about the candlemaker business?' the sea dog said, picking up his pint.

'Rum affair,' Joe replied. 'They say it was family.'

'Some family.'

A few feet away the Tong members huddled over a table as they discussed the killing, and Victor Sen was offering his opinion. 'It'll be seen as Tong business even though we've put the word out that it was a family matter.'

Tommy Lo caught Billy Chou's eye. 'It's understandable. The method bore the mark of the Tong,' he said pointedly.

'We've got nothing to fear,' Billy Chou remarked dismissively. 'Now what about Ho Chang?'

Tommy Lo looked around at the gathering. 'So we're in agreement to grant the two weeks.'

'Subject to Vu Ping inspecting the pots,' Victor Sen said quickly.

'Can we trust his judgement?' Billy Chou asked.

'Vu Ping is very reliable, one of the most knowledgeable authorities in his field,' Tommy Lo replied. 'He lectures on ancient Chinese works of art and dynastic tradition. Who better than he to assess the value?'

Billy Chou seemed convinced and Tommy Lo leaned back in his chair and folded his arms. 'Putting the pots up as security tells me that the money will be forthcoming within two weeks. Would he take such a risk with his priceless possessions if he felt otherwise?'

Billy Chou made a face. 'If they are what he says.'

The Tong leader looked at each one in turn. 'I don't like the idea of the pots remaining at the house. As soon as Vu Ping has seen them we must find a secure hiding-place.'

'We could ask Husi Kang to put them in his safe at the Peking Club,' Victor Sen suggested. 'I'm sure it's big enough to take the parcel.'

Tommy Lo nodded. 'We'll speak to Husi. And now if we're finished here we should go and see Vu Ping.'

'There is another matter I'd like to discuss,' Billy Chou declared. 'Assuming the pots are as valuable as you describe, and the two weeks' extension is given, you'll then be giving our decision to Li Fong, is that correct?'

The Tong leader frowned. 'That's correct.'

'I think we should handle it differently,' Billy Chou replied.

'Well, go on. We're all interested in what you have to say,' Tommy Lo remarked sarcastically.

'Tonight we all go to Bermondsey in the van. We'll call on Ho Chang first, and then when we've left him quaking with fear we visit Li Fong with our decision.'

'It's not the way of the Tong to act in such a manner,' Tommy Lo said angrily. 'What you're saying is that we grant the extension with one hand and take retribution with the other.'

Billy Chou had a sly grin on his face as he looked around him. 'I didn't say that we should harm Ho Chang. We would just go prepared, with the usual fighters armed and ready for action. It would be enough to show the laundryman that the Tong is allpowerful and its will cannot be disregarded.'

'Ho Chang is very much aware that the threat of death hangs over him like a swinging sword,' Tommy Lo pointed out. 'Behaving like mad dogs will serve nothing.'

Danny Ling had remained silent, growing worried over the constant challenge to Tommy Lo's authority posed by Billy Chou, and he knew that it would not be long before the leader-in-waiting felt strong enough to show his hand. In the meantime he considered it vital to prevent a head-to-head confrontation. 'I think I speak for all of us when I say that we're happy for you to meet with Li Fong tonight,' he began, 'but Billy Chou has a point. It will be good for the junior members to see that the Tong still has its teeth, and the visit to the laundryman will not only spur Li Fong into redoubling his efforts to get the money in time, it will remind him that should he fail he would lose not only a fortune but his dishonoured brother as well.'

Billy Chou seemed pleased with Danny Ling's contribution and he smiled evilly as he nodded his head. 'That's something that I've been pondering,' he said. 'Should the Tong accept that a payment in lieu is honour satisfied, or should we punish the laundryman for hiding beneath the cloak of his generous brother?'

'That will be for the Tong to decide in two weeks,' Tommy Lo replied. 'If the money from overseas is forthcoming Ho Chang will receive it as a loan and pay his debt in full. That will be the end of the matter as far as we are concerned.'

'But if not?' Billy Chou pressed.

'I won't repeat myself,' Tommy Lo said sharply. 'I've just told you what will happen.'

'Shall we go to see Vu Ping now?' Victor Sen asked, beginning to feel irritated by the tone of the discussion.

Billy Chou looked at him briefly and then turned to Tommy Lo. 'I would still like an answer,' he said quickly. 'Do we go to Bermondsey tonight as a proud Tong, or is it to be another social call?'

The leader met the malcontent's eyes and held them in his hard gaze. 'Prepare the van and summon the men to be ready,' he said, 'but remember, no harm is to be done to Ho Chang, nor his property at this time. Now if there's no other business to discuss I suggest we go to see Vu Ping right away.'

In Tanners Alley the neighbours were at their front doors in the sunshine and Lizzie Roach rocked contentedly to and fro as she listened to the church bells. 'It's lovely to 'ear 'em,' she remarked to Nora Mason who was watering her flower tubs. 'Different in the war though. If you 'eard the bells then it meant the Germans were comin'.'

Nora nodded. 'That was one fing that terrified me, the thought of 'earin' those bells,' she replied. 'We got used ter the sirens but I'd 'ave died if those bells 'ad started ringin'.'

'No yer wouldn't,' Lizzie said chuckling. 'You'd 'ave done the same as me. Tied yer carvin' knife on the end o' yer broomstick an' jabbed the bastards while they were still comin' down in their parachutes.'

Nora leaned against the doorpost. 'Ruby's daughter's 'avin' a bit of a party then,' she said.

'Ruby ain't said nuffing ter me about it,' Lizzie replied quickly.

'They're Kay's Chinese friends by all accounts,' Nora went on. 'She's a funny gel that Kay. She 'ad that nice chap Richard an' she chucked 'im in fer a barrer boy. I can't understand 'er. I was speakin' ter Mrs Mills only yesterday an' she's really upset about it. As a matter o' fact she said that Kay effed and blinded at 'er boy when they split up an' 'e was shocked. I wouldn't 'ave thought it of Kay, but I'm sure Mrs Mills ain't a liar.'

Lizzie pulled her cap down further over her forehead. 'At least it shows the gel's got spirit,' she remarked. 'I used ter give my ole bastard what for when 'e come 'ome pissed.'

'I don't like to 'ear a woman swear,' Nora replied. 'It makes 'em sound so common.'

'Well, in that case I'm as common as muck then,' Lizzie told her.

'I just don't fink it's right 'avin' those Chinkies in the alley,' Nora declared.

'I dunno,' Lizzie retorted. 'I wouldn't mind a nice Chinky bloke makin' eyes at me.'

'You'd be sorry,' Nora replied. 'From what I've 'eard they treat their women like slaves.'

'Yer don't wanna believe all you 'ear,' Lizzie said scornfully. 'That bloke in the Chinky laundry seems ter get a good report from people. Mrs Charles over the road takes 'er ole man's collars to 'is place an' they come back like new. Ida Brown takes 'er washin' there too. She said what a nice man 'e is, an' 'is wife.'

'Well, I'm still not 'appy about 'em comin' 'ere fer a party,' Nora persisted.

Lizzie's rocker had slowed down, which told Nora that the old lady was dropping off to sleep, and she glanced over to see her other next-door neighbour at her door. ''Ere, Myrtle. Did you know the Neals are 'avin' a party?' she enquired.

Myrtle looked blank-faced. 'No. What's it in aid of?'

'It's Kay. She's invited some of 'er Chinese friends by all accounts.'

'That'll be nice for 'er.'

Nora realised that she was going to make no headway with Myrtle and she went in to speak to Jack who was cleaning his best boots at the scullery door. 'Did you get that bolt from the ironmonger's?' she asked.

'Nah, I fergot,' he told her.

'Well, yer better get it soon as yer can,' she growled.

'Anyone would only 'ave ter lean on our front door an' they'd get in. I don't fancy bein' done in while I'm asleep.'

'Well, at least yer wouldn't know much about it, would yer?' Jack Mason chuckled.

The church bells had stopped ringing and Lizzie Roach slumbered peacefully in the warm sun, dreaming of a ball where all the men were Chinese and all the women wore crinoline dresses. She was dancing in the arms of a huge man with a pigtail down to his waist, and then she spotted Nora on the edge of the floor making signs with her finger across her throat.

Bel Allenby had come to her door to take the air and she glanced over at the old lady who was starting to mumble in her sleep. 'She's 'avin' a go at somebody,' she called out to Myrtle. 'It sounded like she said, "Shut up yer silly bitch."'

Chapter Twenty-Three

Paul smiled at Mei Li as she stepped out into the street wearing a long tight-fitting dress of olive green. 'You look very nice,' he said shyly.

'Thank you,' she replied. 'You look very smart too.'

The young man felt the collar of his white shirt and pulled the wing from under his grey checkered sports coat. 'If we walk ter the Trocette we can pick up the number forty-two bus to Aldgate,' he told her. 'Petticoat Lane's just a short walk away from there.'

'It is a very nice day,' Mei Li remarked.

'Yeah, but it's gonna be warm in that crowd,' he reminded her.

'I don't mind, as long as you don't,' she smiled. 'I've heard so much about the market I had to see it.'

'I bet there's some big markets in China,' he said.

'They tend to be small but very busy,' Mei Li replied, 'though I don't really know about now. It's a long time since I left China.'

The smell of the tanneries hung in the air as the two young people strolled along Grange Road. Further along the smell of aniseed became predominant as they passed the fur factory and then the sweet, fruity aroma coming from Hartley's jam factory greeted them as they crossed the Tower Bridge Road.

'These smells are always around, even on Sundays,' Paul remarked.

'It was one of the first things I noticed,' Mei Li replied. 'Do you like living in Bermondsey?'

'I wouldn't live anywhere else, well, not out o' choice,' Paul enthused. 'This is an exciting place ter live. There's the river an' its traffic, the tanneries and the skin factories, an' the people o' course. All right, it might not be everyone's cup o' tea but fer me the place is alive an' vibrant, even on Sundays.'

'You describe it well,' Mei Li told him.

They reached the bus stop and Paul leaned against the post. 'Normally the forty-two isn't very frequent, but we might be lucky,' he said smiling.

Just then a bus came into sight and they looked at each other and laughed. They found seats on the upper deck and Mei Li felt a shiver of pleasure as the bus swayed and the young man involuntarily leant against her.

'Look, there's Traitor's Gate,' Paul told her, pointing along the river. 'Very few who went in there ever came out. They usually ended up on Tower 'Ill wiv their 'ead on a block.'

Mei Li looked suddenly frightened and he cursed himself for being flippant. 'I'm sorry if I scared yer,' he said quickly.

She smiled, a warm smile that made his heart leap. 'No, it's nice to learn about things that are part of your history, but it reminded me of something else, something I'm trying to forget.'

Paul looked concerned and he laid his hand gently on hers for a moment. 'I understand,' he said quietly. 'Kay told me about you an' yer guardian 'avin' ter flee right across China when the Japs invaded your country.'

'That was in the past and I don't let it upset me now,' she replied. 'No, the bad things that trouble me are here now, around us.'

She paused, but Paul's look of puzzled sympathy encouraged her to go on. 'The Chinese community in Limehouse suffer a lot of violence and abuse. They live in fear of the Tongs and because of language and cultural differences they have no way to escape them.'

Paul nodded his head grimly. 'I've read about it an' talked ter people who know the area,' he said. 'I've 'eard it's a lot ter do wiv those gamblin' dens.'

'Partly, but it goes much deeper,' Mei Li explained. 'The Tongs rule like the gangsters in American films. They extort money in protection rackets, as you call them, and exploit the problem of gambling addiction. Lots of people see a chance to win on the mah-jong tables but they usually end up losing heavily, and then they find themselves at the mercy of the Tong who are recruited to collect the outstanding debts. They can be very cruel. My guardian's brother has gambled heavily on the tables and he's in debt himself.'

'I can understand you bein' worried,' Paul said quietly.

Mei Li forced a smile. 'I'm trying to put it at the back of my mind for the time being at least,' she replied.

Paul returned her smile. 'Do you like seafood?' he asked her. 'Shellfish I mean.'

She frowned. 'When I was growing up in China we were

hundreds of miles from the sea but there were streams flowing through the hills and we caught catfish,' she explained. 'I never knew about lobsters until I travelled to America and then I couldn't bring myself to try them. It was the thought of them being boiled alive.'

Paul laughed aloud. 'No I meant cockles and whelks. There's a stall by Petticoat Lane that sells the best cockles you could wish for. Would you like to try some?'

'Cockles and whelks aren't boiled alive, are they?' she asked fearfully.

'Definitely not,' he laughed.

Mei Li smiled, her eyes flashing. 'Yes, why not,' she said.

They stepped down from the bus in Aldgate and Mei Li slipped her arm through Paul's as they made their way into the busy market. He could feel the pressure of her hand as the crowd became more dense and it gradually became almost impossible to walk side by side. He took her by the shoulders and eased her in front of him then he held her waist to reassure her as they walked further into the Lane. On either side stall owners called out loudly, each trying to outdo the next one. Everything from miracle cough cures, unbelievable metal polish and unmatchable dresses straight from Paris to crockery as used by the kings and queens of Europe was there to buy and at ridiculous prices, so the traders shouted. 'I'm gonna go skint at this rate,' one called out. 'It cost me more ter buy these than I'm chargin' yer, missus,' another told an elderly customer. 'No, yer can't buy one plate. They come in sets. Well, there's no need ter be like that, missus. Well, sod you an' all. Come on, gels, take yer pick.'

Paul felt hot as the crowds pressed in on them and he was aware of Mei Li's tenseness in the crush of bodies. He stared at her long raven hair tied neatly with a green ribbon at the neck and was taken by the way she eased her way through the throng, deftly turning her slim shoulders. Everything about her was delicious. He gently rubbed her arm to get her attention. ''Ave you 'ad enough o' this crowd?' he asked.

She nodded and he steered her on to the pavement and led her into a sidestreet that was filled with clothes stalls. The crowds here were less dense and they managed to work their way back on to the main thoroughfare.

'I never realised it would be so busy,' Mei Li said dabbing at her face with a handkerchief.

Paul smiled. 'Petticoat Lane's a better idea in winter,' he told her.

'Is that the shellfish stall?' she asked as they neared a gaily decorated stand which had a striped canopy supported by ornate brass poles.

'That's it,' Paul replied. 'Tubby Isaacs' stall no less.'

Mei Li stood back while the young man ordered two plates of cockles and she looked a little apprehensive as he handed one to her.

'Look, this is what yer 'ave ter do,' he said grinning as he reached for a large bottle of spiced vinegar. 'Yer swamp 'em wiv this till they're swimmin', then yer add a touch o' pepper like so, then yer eat 'em wiv yer fingers. 'Ere, take this plate.'

Mei Li was still hesitating when Paul finished flavouring his portion and she timorously put a single cockle into her mouth. The young man wolfed his plateful down and then glanced at her enquiringly.

'They're very nice,' she said in answer to his raised eyebrows.

'Yer don't 'ave to eat 'em all, honestly,' he said.

'No I like them, and I'm hungry too,' she replied.

'Actually no one'll mind if yer pick up more than one cockle at a time,' he told her grinning.

Mei Li saw the comic look on his face and became more adventurous. 'They really are nice,' she remarked.

When she had cleared her plate they left the stall and crossed the busy road, making for the bus station.

'Could we walk some of the way home?' Mei Li asked. 'It's a lovely morning.'

They turned into the Minories and strolled down towards the Tower Bridge approach, gazing up as they passed the white stone Tower of London which looked even whiter than normal in the bright sun. Mei Li gave out a deep sigh as they stepped on to the bridge. 'It's so peaceful on Sundays,' she remarked.

Paul nodded as they stopped to look down at the eddying Thames. 'This is nice,' he said simply.

'I've enjoyed our little visit, even though it was very busy at the market,' Mei Li replied.

Paul looked into her eyes. 'I want to see you again, Mei Li,' he said quietly.

She looked away, her sad gaze fixed on where the river turned, and for a few moments that seemed like an eternity she was silent. 'I like you, Paul. I like you very much, but I don't think it's a very good idea for us to see each other again,' she said in a quiet voice.

'Why ever not?' he asked anxiously.

'My life, my future, is already planned.'

'I don't understand.'

'I'll be going back to Singapore soon.'

'Do you 'ave ter go?'

'Yes, it's the wish of my guardian.'

'But you 'ave rights, surely?'

Mei Li turned to face him, her eyes misting. 'It's probably hard for you to understand,' she sighed. 'In China marriages are very often planned by families, and I'm to be married when I go home to Singapore.'

Paul shook his head slowly, trying to take in what she was saying. 'Yer mean ter say that yer goin' back ter marry a man yer guardian picked for yer?'

'Li Fong is very dear to me and I can't go against his wishes,' Mei replied. 'He only has my best interests at heart. The man he has picked for me is a successful businessman and I'll have a good life.'

''Ave yer met this man?'

'Yes I have.'

'More ter the point. Do yer love 'im?'

'What is love?' Mei Li asked him, averting her eyes to gaze down at the swirling river. 'Love is caring, and I'll learn to care for my husband. Love is being obedient and dutiful, and I'll learn to do the things he wants me to do. Love will grow, like a sapling into a tree, and be strong against the winds of fate.'

Paul suddenly took her by the shoulders and turned her to face him. 'When I first saw you I listened fascinated when yer told the story of the lantern,' he said eagerly. 'An' I understood what you were sayin'. Yeah, OK, love is all those fings yer mentioned, but it's more than that. Love is somefing that just 'appens between two people. It's about needing someone, about the feelin' that flows between two people an' wantin' ter spend every minute in each ovver's company. No, don't look away, Mei Li. I felt somefing in me 'eart when I first saw yer. I saw the light in your eyes. Tell me truthfully that you don't feel anyfing an' I'll say no more.'

'I hardly know you, Paul,' she said, struggling with herself, 'but I liked you quickly, I like being with you. Believe me I want to follow my heart, but I can't, I must follow my head. I must return home with Li Fong. It's my duty.'

Paul sighed deeply, his heart aching like a heavy weight in his chest. 'You won't be goin' 'ome yet awhile, will yer?' he asked her.

'Not for a few weeks,' she replied.

'Well, let me see you again. Let me 'ave some memories ter cherish of our friendship. Say yer'll see me again, Mei Li. Please.'

'It's probably not a wise thing to do, but I don't want to refuse you that. I'll cherish our friendship too, and the friendship of your sister as well.'

'Let me see you tonight,' he asked earnestly.

'I can't. Not tonight,' she told him. 'Li Fong is receiving a visitor and I have to be there. It's important, very important.'

'Tomorrow then?'

'I can see you on Tuesday evening.'

'I'll come callin'. Seven sharp?'

She smiled. 'Yes, Paul. Seven sharp.'

They moved away from the centre of the bridge, walking slowly, and it seemed to Paul that the pressure of her hand on his arm had increased, as if she were clinging on to stop herself falling. His heart pounded in his chest and he hardly dared to look at her. There was time for him to woo her with all the intensity he could muster. He would kindle the caged love in her soul and make the light burn fiercely and proudly in her eyes. It had to be. She was for him, and he would never give her up to some obscure trader from the other side of the world without a desperate struggle.

They were walking under a railway arch and for a moment it seemed as though the whole world had stopped. They were completely alone. They stopped as though an invisible hand had stayed them, and Mei Li turned to face him. 'Hold me tight, Paul,' she said in a quiet voice edged with anxiety.

He took her slim body in his arms, holding her gently but firmly and she moulded herself to him. He could smell the fragrance of her raven hair and he brushed her cheek with a gentle kiss. No words were spoken, but in the darkness of another world a lantern flared.

Chapter Twenty-Four

On Sunday afternoons Ruby usually found time to put her feet up for an hour or so, and after reading the newspaper she invariably dozed off to sleep. Jim would be nodding off too in the chair facing her and Ruby would be content, feeling that they had both earned the short respite. Today however she could not find anything to interest her in the *News of the World* and she leaned back in her armchair with a worried sigh. What was happening to the family, she wondered? Jim seemed as restless as she was and he had gone out into the garden to potter around in the shed, not his normal practice on a Sunday afternoon. Paul seemed unsettled too. He had eaten his Sunday dinner without a word of conversation and it had been left to Kay to make the small talk. Were they all suffering from some malaise? It was so unlike Paul to be silent round the table, and as for Jim, God knows what was troubling him. He looked worried and preoccupied and had snapped at her when she asked him if there was anything wrong. Kay was of the opinion that Paul was suffering the pangs of a young man in love and her father's moodiness was due to overwork. 'You both need the 'oliday,' she had remarked as they washed up after the meal.

Ruby wished she could agree with her daughter's point of

view, but she was becoming more and more convinced that Jim's attitude and strange behaviour were due to something more sinister than overwork. He had never been this way before. It seemed a while now since they had made love and her little overtures in that direction were not getting through or were simply being ignored. Physically he looked well, and he would have been quick to let her know if he was worrying over his health. No, there was some other reason, and the niggling fear that he was no longer happy with her left her feeling sick inside. Another woman? No, not Jim. He couldn't. He wouldn't. He was a family man through and through and she was being silly even to consider it. Nevertheless the seed in her mind was germinating, and try as she might to banish it its tendrils lingered at the back of her thoughts.

Jim finished tidying the shelf and realised that he had been wasting his time. He had not made any space at all and the stack of flowerpots still remained leaning against the shed. He rolled a cigarette and lit it, watching the first exhalation of blue smoke wafting up to the timbered roof. It was stupid, he realised. He should have weighed up the pros and cons before embarking on such a senseless affair. It was idiotic. He had a wife who adored him, two grown-up children who looked up to him, and he was in the process of throwing it all away. And for what? Was he starved of love? Was he so henpecked and trodden-down that he needed the company of another woman with whom he could assert himself and be a whole man? He certainly wasn't starved of love, that was for sure. Ruby had been making all the running in that department lately. Maybe she was house-proud, and had set strict house rules, but he could have baulked her. Having to change into his slippers before going into the parlour and being required not to smoke indoors were things he should have stamped on right from the start.

Ruby stepped out into the garden and shielded her eyes from the dipping sun. 'Jim? Are you gonna spend all afternoon in there?' she called out.

He came out of the shed and jerked his thumb towards the flowerpots. 'I was tryin' ter make room fer 'em,' he replied.

Ruby walked down the path. 'I've read the paper an' I couldn't sleep,' she said. 'I wish yer'd come in an' relax. That can wait.'

'You was moanin' about 'em bein' left there yesterday,' Jim reminded her.

'Yeah but I didn't expect yer ter do it terday.'

''Ave the kids gone out?' he asked as he put his foot on the stub of his cigarette.

Ruby nodded. 'Kay's gone up West wiv Joey an' Paul's gone somewhere wiv Butch Wheeler. Butch called for 'im ten minutes ago.'

Jim closed the door of the shed. 'It gets warm in there when the sun's on it,' he said puffing.

'Come in an' I'll make yer a cuppa,' Ruby told him. 'Then yer could 'ave a lie-down fer a while. We both could.'

Jim caught the suggestion in her eyes. 'I 'aven't read the paper yet,' he replied.

'Read it ternight.'

'It's very warm.'

'So am I. Let's go upstairs.'

Jim followed her into the scullery. 'What was that about tea?'

'You go up now an' I'll bring it wiv me,' she told him. 'I've bin missin' yer, Jim.'

He saw an almost pleading look in her eyes and he felt disgusted with himself. 'Yeah, all right,' he said, giving her a weak smile.

As he walked into the front bedroom Jim realised that Ruby had planned the afternoon. The net curtains had been pulled against the sun and there was a distinct smell of lavender. The bed had been changed and the blue china jug resting in the matching basin on the marble-topped washstand had been refilled with water. He sat down on the edge of the bed and tried desperately to cast the image of Angela from his mind. Unless he could he was going to be no use to Ruby, and he rubbed a hand over his hot forehead. He could hear her stirring the tea and he got up quickly and peeled off his shirt before pouring some water into the basin.

Ruby came into the bedroom carrying two mugs of tea and she set them down on the bedside cabinet nearest the door. 'I love Sunday afternoons,' she said, smiling at him. 'We should do this more often.'

Jim finished drying himself and reached for his tea. 'It's bin a busy time lately,' he said casually.

'You know what they say about all work an' no play,' Ruby replied, still smiling as she sat down beside him on the bed.

He put the mug down on the cabinet and stood up to draw the drapes over the net curtains.

'Leave 'em, Jim,' she bade him.

'It's a bit light.'

'Will it worry yer?'

'No but I thought . . .'

Ruby stood up and came over, pressing herself against him. 'It's bin a while since we did it an' I need yer ter love me, Jim,' she said in a soft voice. 'Just leave the curtains.'

His arms went round her and as she snuggled closer he shut his eyes tightly, fighting to summon up the passion she was demanding of him. Her hands were moving slowly down to his hips and he responded by searching for the zip of her light cotton dress.

'Yer've gotta love me, darlin',' she whispered. 'I can't wait no longer.'

She stepped out of her dress and began to fondle him. 'Yer do love me, don't yer, Jim?' she breathed as his hands went round to unclip her brassiere.

'Of course I do,' he said quickly.

'Then show me. Make love ter me now,' she gasped, passion possessing her. She was leading him away from the bed towards the back of the door, initiating. 'Remember that night when we were courtin' an' you got all sexy at the dance?' she whispered. 'We nearly did it in the doorway o' that ware'ouse down by the river. We would 'ave done too, if that copper 'adn't shone 'is torch on us. Come on, let's pretend.'

Jim spun her round against the door, feeling her firm breasts pressed against his chest as she reached up to kiss him with her mouth open in expectation. His hands followed the contours of her round hips and as he slid her knickers down her thighs she groaned. 'Tell me yer want me. Say what yer said that night.'

He was sweating now, beads of perspiration breaking out on his forehead and trickling down the side of his face as he pressed himself against her nude body. She brought her leg up, arching her foot as she rubbed it along his calf and he began to panic. This was unreal. She was vamping him, unashamedly and with a lust that frightened him. This wasn't the dutiful wife who usually lay docile beneath him and let him work his will upon her.

'Talk ter me. Say fings,' she gasped. 'Tell me yer must 'ave me, like that night by the river.'

He was struggling desperately to summon strength and he mumbled the words she wanted to hear.

'Take me now,' she groaned.

'I can't,' he almost shouted.

She kissed him breathlessly and he could feel her heart pounding.

'You can! Please, Jim!'

'I can't!' he gasped.

'Yer've gotta love me,' she cried, pushing him back towards the bed.

He fell backwards across the covers and she was kneeling astride him naked, her head arched back as she lowered herself down on to him. He was trembling now, shocked by her unbridled lust. In all of their years together she had never taken control, never adopted a dominant role and he saw above him not Ruby but the woman who had come between them. This was Angela, leading, coaxing and taking her pleasure as she willed, and at that very instant his passion died.

Ruby let out a long shuddering groan as she slumped down on top of him and he could feel her tense body slowly go limp. 'Yer don't love me any more,' she sobbed.

He moved his hands slowly up and down her back as he

struggled to find words that might excuse his failure. 'I do love yer, Ruby,' he said, 'but I can't turn it on, no more than you can. Yer've often told me that.'

She rolled over and reached for her dress, draping it over the front of her body. 'There's someone else, an' don't lie ter me, Jim. Don't compound yer deceit.'

'There's no one else,' he replied, averting his eyes.

'Look at me!' she screamed out. 'Look me in the eye an' tell me there's nobody else. Swear on my life, swear on the children's lives.'

'Don't ask me ter do that,' he said angrily.

'Do it! Swear on our lives there's no one else.'

He rose up into a sitting position on the edge of the bed, his shoulders hunched in abject misery. 'All right, I can't bear ter lie ter yer,' he said, his voice faltering. 'There is somebody else, but she means nuffing ter me. It's a physical fing. I don't love 'er. Love was never on the cards. I was gonna end it anyway. The guilt's bin drivin' me mad.'

'Who is it? Someone at work?' Ruby croaked, hardly recognising her own voice. ''Ow long's it bin goin' on?'

'It doesn't matter. It's not important,' he replied. 'What is important is that this doesn't destroy us. All right, I know yer'll never be able ter trust me any more, an' I understand that. I also realise yer'll never want me ter touch yer again, an' that's no more than I could expect, but we must try to 'old on ter somefing, if it's only the ability ter live under the same roof wivout making each ovver's life a misery.'

Ruby had slipped on her dress and she stood over him, her hands clenched into hard fists at her side. 'You bastard!' she spat out. 'You go wiv this whore wivout any thought fer what it would do ter me an' the kids an' then yer've got the bloody nerve ter preach ter me. What can she supply that I can't? Does she flatter yer by tellin' yer what a stud you are?'

'It's not like that, Ruby,' he sighed. 'She was just there when I was feelin' low an' she picked me up, made me feel good again. It was all innocent at first, but then it got out of 'and. It 'appened so fast.'

'I bet it did,' Ruby snarled. 'An' where was I? Couldn't you come ter me, confide in me?'

'I tried but yer shut me out, turned yer back on me.'

'So yer cried on 'er shoulder.'

'We talked, yeah.'

'She talked you right into 'er bed an' you were too stupid ter realise,' Ruby grated. 'It's the oldest trick in the book. The sympathetic ear, the shoulder ter cry on an' the cuddles ter make yer feel safe an' secure. Christ! I gave yer more credit, but I was obviously foolin' meself. You're pathetic, an' I'll never be able ter fergive yer fer what yer've done.'

'I don't expect yer to,' he said quietly, 'but while we're both bleedin' just take a good 'ard look at yerself. Yer've turned this place into a show room fer a domestic science class at school. "Get yer shoes off, Jim. Wash yer 'ands, Jim. Stop messin' about, Jim, an' go ter sleep, it's not Saturday." God Almighty, I must be the only bloke in Bermon'sey who 'as ter go in the garden fer a smoke. Yer can't stand the smell, but me an' the kids 'ave gotta put up wiv the constant stink o' polish, air wicks an' carbolic. Do yer wonder I got sick an' tired of it all?'

'Don't bring the kids inter this argument,' she raved. 'They appreciate a good tidy 'ome even if you don't.'

'They suffer it, Ruby, just like me.'

'Don't give me that,' she snarled. 'Maybe yer'd like it

better if I let this place become a shit-tip. I was brought up in a good clean 'ome an' my parents were particular about such fings. There was always a meal waitin' fer me dad when 'e got in from work an' the place was like a new pin. I was brought up ter believe that was what men liked an' expected in a wife, but it seems I've bin wrong all along.'

Jim lowered his head, feeling too utterly drained to argue any more. 'Do yer want me ter go?' he asked.

'An' leave me to explain it ter Kay an' Paul?' she spat out at him. 'No, we'll continue ter live under the same roof, an' I'll continue ter cook yer meals an' do yer washin' an' ironin', but me an' you are finished as 'usband an' wife. I couldn't bear yer ter touch me ever again. I don't want yer near me in bed an' yer can smoke the place out fer all I care. Come in the parlour wiv yer work boots on an' sit down ter yer tea wiv filfy 'ands. I don't care. Do what yer like, but just keep yer distance.'

Jim stared at her as she sat down on the bed sobbing loudly. There was nothing more to say. Trying to ease her pain with words of comfort and sympathy would be like twisting the knife. He stood up. 'I need ter go out fer a while,' he said.

As he reached the door and glanced back her eyes came up to meet his, and he knew that never in a million years would he be able to forget the utter misery that filled them.

Chapter Twenty-Five

Tommy Lo led the way into the back room of Vu Ping's house in Pennyfields carrying the ginger pots in their original packing, and as he nodded to the old man he was waved into a seat beside a low, intricately carved table. All around the room there were reminders of China. Watercolours in cheap frames covered the walls, and facing the drawn curtains a large hessian mat hanging from the ceiling displayed a group of peasants toiling in the rice fields against the background of a distant snow-covered mountain range, tinted gold by the setting sun. It was an impressive piece of work and it attracted some attention as the young men positioned themselves behind their leader.

Vu Ping was dressed in formal clothes and his long bony fingers tapped nervously against the sleeves of his silk coat as he sat with arms folded. 'If you will be so kind,' he said in a voice that sounded as old as some of the paintings around the room.

Tommy Lo untied the string and reverently opened the cardboard box. 'We have to be sure that these are genuine works of art, Mr Ping,' he said.

The old man stroked his wispy beard as his young guest placed the pots down in a line on the table. His eyes were puffy and heavy-lidded and gave no indication of surprise or pleasure as he looked down at the items. For a couple of minutes he merely stared, his eyes moving from the larger pieces to the smallest of the six, then he reached down inside the folds of his robe and took out a snap case, removing a pair of metal-framed glasses. 'Please pass me the largest one,' he asked.

The young man did as he was bid and stood watching as Vu Ping ran his fingertips over the indentations and around the rim and the base. The old man started to nod slowly and his hoary features seemed to mellow, reflecting the pleasure he was feeling holding such a valuable item in his hands. 'Only once have I ever seen the like,' he said without lifting his eyes from the pot. 'It was in the Grand Palace in Chungking, many many years ago.'

'They are very valuable then?' Tommy Lo said, glancing quickly around the group.

The old man nodded. 'Yes, it's undoubtedly the work of Cho Tsung. There can be no mistaking it. This set of pots is over one hundred and sixty years old, and in all the world very few sets remain.'

'How much could be raised on them?' Billy Chou asked him.

'Who can say?' Vu Ping replied. 'Museums and art galleries throughout the world which specialise in works of art from the Ming dynasty would pay vast sums to acquire such treasures, and there are a few private collectors in the West who would also be prepared to part with enormous sums of money. You see, it's acknowledged by many who have studied Ming dynasty porcelain that these Cho Tsung ginger pots are equal, if not superior, to the original items that were produced over two hundred years earlier. That was why the craftsman who made them was forced to flee China. His whereabouts were never discovered, but it's said that he died in poverty without ever producing the like again.'

'We are indebted to you, Vu Ping,' Tommy Lo told him.

The ancient one stroked his stringy beard once more as he looked up at the young man. 'It's not for me to enquire where you got these,' he said, his eyes narrowing, 'but I would advise you to take extreme care in the handling of them and keep them in a secure place.'

'It has been arranged,' Tommy replied.

Vu Ping clapped his hands and a young woman came into the room carrying a tray.

'Now if you and your friends will join me in taking tea I will tell you a little more of what I know about the life and works of Cho Tsung,' he said.

On the edge of Chinatown by the waterside stood a derelict warehouse that had once been used to store tobacco, and it was there that the junior members of the Sons of Heaven Tong gathered to make the van ready. They chatted excitedly amongst themselves as they worked, eager for the opportunity to prove their worth and further their ambitions of enrolment into the prestigious inner circle, and they suspected that the coming evening might well present the chance to demonstrate their loyalty and ruthlessness.

The van parked in the yard was a pre-war Commer, its paint peeling and oil leaking from the engine sump, but it was very soon to become unrecognisable. On each of its sides the young men attached tarpaulin sheets, lashed together over the roof. The small windows of the rear doors were quickly covered with cardboard squares and over the front of the bonnet a false cooling grill was fixed with stout wire. Finally false number plates were attached and the men stood back to admire their work. The Commer van had now become a Ford belonging to a Mr Charlie Wong, knife grinder and hardware merchant from East Ham. Inside the vehicle two benches had been placed, and when Billy Chou arrived he smiled with satisfaction. If the police or any other inquisitive person took notice and made notes the trail would not lead back to Chinatown.

'You've done well,' he remarked. 'Be ready to leave at seven o'clock.'

For a while Billy Chou chatted to the young men and then he returned to Vu Ping's house. The other Tong members had gone but Tommy Lo was waiting for him, and together they took their leave of the old man and went on to the Peking Club, where they watched as Husi Kang placed the cardboard box containing the ginger pots in his large safe.

'I'm not interested in what this parcel contains,' he told them, 'but I can assure you it will be as secure here as in the Bank of England.'

Tommy Lo smiled. 'There is one proviso,' he said, looking briefly at Billy Chou as he took a pound note from his pocket and tore it into three pieces. 'Take this piece of the note, and under no circumstances surrender the box to either of us, or to any other Tong member, unless you're given both matching pieces by whoever asks for the box. Is that clearly understood?'

Husi Kang nodded dutifully. He considered it an honour to be taken into the confidence of the most powerful Tong in Chinatown, and he was sure that his standing would grow accordingly. 'It's understood and you have my word that your instructions will be carried out to the letter,' he replied.

Tommy Lo handed the second piece of the note to Billy Chou. 'We are relying on you, Husi,' he said with emphasis, 'and if you do not comply it will be under pain of death.'

The afternoon sun had disappeared, leaving dark shadows in the parlour, and Ruby got up to turn off the wireless as the chimer on the mantelshelf struck six. The intense romantic sound of gypsy violins was aggravating her pain and she slumped back down in the armchair, burying her head in her hands. What had happened just a short time ago was still almost too shocking to believe. 'God in Heaven, tell me it was all a bad dream,' she groaned aloud. Thoughts and questions tormented her mercilessly as she sought to make sense of it. Why? Have I been so impossible to live with over the last twenty-two years? What's going to happen now? How can I get through it?

For a while she sat staring down at a tiny piece of cotton on the mat by her feet, then abruptly she got up. Jim would be back soon and she could not bear to face him. She could go to see her sister Amy. It had been a long time since she had visited her. No, Amy would only compound her misery by fussing over her. Better to go and talk to Bel, her old and trusted friend. She would be a crutch, a comfort, and she'd offer good advice. Dear Bel. She was always there in times of need.

Outside in the alley long shadows had climbed up the

brickwork and Lizzie Roach was stirring in her rocking-chair as Ruby passed by.

'It's gettin' a bit chilly, gel,' the old lady said, scratching her ear and yawning widely. 'D'you fink it's chilly?'

'Yeah, it is a bit,' Ruby replied as she walked up to Bel's front door.

'Young Freddie Wilson's bin kickin' a bloody ball up the wall an' 'e woke me up,' Lizzie moaned. 'Some people ain't got no consideration fer us old 'uns.'

Bel had her hair in curlers and looked surprised when she answered the knock. 'Are you all right?' she asked. 'Yer look white as a sheet.'

Ruby bit on her lip to hold back a flood of tears as she walked into Bel's untidy parlour. 'I 'ad ter come an' see yer,' she gulped. 'I was right. Jim's got anuvver woman.'

'Yer jokin',' Bel said incredulously.

'I wish I was,' Ruby replied. ''E confessed 'e was seein' someone.'

''E told yer?'

'Yeah, this afternoon.'

'I can't believe it.'

'I can't believe it eivver. It's a nightmare, Bel, a wakin', livin' nightmare that's never gonna end.'

'Did 'e say who it was?'

''E wouldn't say.'

'You poor fing. Come 'ere.'

Ruby collapsed into Bel's open arms and sobbed pitifully. 'What am I gonna do?' she moaned. ''Ow can I carry on? I wish I was dead.'

Bel patted her back tenderly. 'Look, you sit down an' I'll

put the kettle on. A good strong cuppa's what you could do wiv right now.'

While she waited for the kettle to boil Bel sat forward in her chair holding Ruby's hands in hers. 'I'd never 'a' believed it, not Jim. Yer've always seemed so 'appy tergevver,' she said shaking her head.

''E told me 'e was sick an' tired o' the way I treated 'im,' Ruby went on. ''E said I was more interested in keepin' the place clean an' tidy than in 'im an' the children. 'E was fed up wiv not bein' able ter smoke in the 'ouse an' 'avin' ter put 'is slippers on before comin' in.'

'That sounds a feeble excuse ter make,' Bel replied. 'What was stoppin' 'im tellin' yer at the beginnin' instead o' lettin' it fester all those years?'

'Am I that bad a wife, Bel? Am I such a dragon?'

Bel got up as she heard the water boil over and quickly made a pot of tea. 'I'll just let it brew fer a while,' she said sitting down again.

Ruby chewed on her thumbnail. ''Ow am I gonna tell the kids, Bel?'

'Fer a start they're not kids any more,' Bel reminded her. 'Yer'll just 'ave ter sit down an' tell 'em the trufe. Where is 'e now, Ruby?'

''E went out. 'E said 'e'll be back later. I should've chucked 'im out fer good, but I couldn't.'

'Well, there's 'ope fer the two of yer yet.'

'We're finished fer good,' Ruby spat out, her eyes flaring. 'I couldn't bear ter let 'im touch me ever again.'

Bel got up and went into the scullery to pour out the tea and when she came back into the room carrying two brimming mugs there was a determined look on her face.

She knew the truth about Ruby and it was time to speak her mind, please or offend. 'Ruby, I want yer ter listen ter me,' she told her. 'You know you're my best friend an' I wouldn't 'ave you 'urt fer anyfing, but sometimes fings 'ave ter be said. The trufe 'as ter be brought out inter the open, whatever the cost.'

Ruby frowned. 'What are yer tryin' ter say, Bel?'

'I met yer sister Amy down the market the ovver day an' we went fer a cuppa in Joe's café,' Bel began. 'I 'adn't seen 'er fer such a long time an' she was pleased ter bump inter me. She said she was gonna pop round ter see yer soon.'

'So?'

'We got talkin' about yer. She was askin' me a lot o' questions about you an' Jim, an' the kids. You an' 'er should keep closer, Ruby, she finks the world of yer.'

'What are yer tryin' ter tell me?'

Bel took a deep breath and looked directly into her friend's sad, red-rimmed eyes. 'Ever since I've known yer yer've bin very 'ouse-proud. Yer've told me yerself that yer set standards an' Jim an' the kids 'ad to abide by 'em. Don't yer fink yer've bin some way ter blame fer Jim goin' off the rails?'

Ruby shook her head quickly. 'No I don't. Yer just said yerself it was a feeble excuse fer 'im ter come out wiv it now.'

'Yes I know I did, but while I was makin' that tea I remembered what yer said last week,' Bel went on. 'You asked me then if I thought Jim was goin' off yer. Well, there must 'ave bin a good reason fer you to ask me such a question. It came over as Jim not bein' interested in yer as a woman, an' if yer remember I gave yer a bit of advice.

OK, you thought I was goin' over the top, but it was the way I saw it. You set standards, an' I'd be willin' ter bet it includes yer love life. Yer can't organise passion an' want. It's eivver there or it isn't.'

'Yeah, an' I'm not a playfing eivver,' Ruby said sharply. 'I can't turn it on every time 'e needs it.'

'No, but yer might be a little more responsive if you 'adn't spent all yer time scrubbin' an' polishin'.'

'That's the way I am, an' Jim knew that when 'e married me,' Ruby countered.

'Yeah, but it must grate after a while,' Bel replied.

'An' I s'pose Amy agreed wiv yer when you two were discussin' my business,' Ruby said quickly.

'What I'm tryin' ter say is, don't go on livin' a lie,' Bel told her. 'Don't make Jim an' the kids suffer frew it.'

'I don't know what yer talkin' about,' Ruby said, glaring at her.

'Standards, that's what. You set the standards yer own mother set, right?'

'Yeah that's right.'

'Don't pretend any more, luv,' Bel said kindly. 'Amy told me everyfing. Yer farvver an' muvver spent every penny in the pub an' the place was a pigsty. There was never enough food in the 'ouse an' then after yer farvver died yer muvver brought men 'ome. Amy told me that you two 'ad at least five uncles on the go at one time. Feet 'angin' out yer shoes an' dresses darned an' patched by the neighbours. Sent out in all weavvers wiv a crust o' bread an' marge while yer muvver entertained 'er men friends. That's the trufe of it. Amy also told me about what finally 'appened. Yer muvver ended 'er days in Deptford Infirmary, 'er mind crazed from syphilis. She talked about Aunt Polly too, 'ow she took yer both in even though she was poor as Lazarus. She said it was the only time you two were 'appy as children, an' she told me 'ow fankful she was that both of yer found good men as 'usbands. There's no shame in it fer you an' Amy. You were the victims. She understands that, an' so should you. Don't live the lie, there's really no need. A few newspapers lyin' around an' a mat that needs a good shakin' isn't a crime. Put an ashtray in the parlour an' 'ide Jim's slippers. Do it, Ruby, an' fight fer yer man. Don't give 'im up ter some tart who'll ditch 'im in 'er own good time, as surely as God made little apples.'

'I do still love 'im, Bel, but I can't fergive 'im,' Ruby sobbed. 'What am I gonna do?'

'If yer still love 'im yer'll 'ave ter fergive 'im, even though yer can never ferget,' Bel told her quietly. 'Start at the beginnin', wiv yerself. Start ter live fer yerself, an' don't be scared o' the past. As I just said, there's no shame ter bear, an' when yer finally realise that an' put it inter practice yer'll find that all the pieces of yer life'll fall back inter place. I just 'ope an' pray yer don't take too long.'

The alley was empty when Ruby made her way back to her house at fifteen minutes after seven. Lizzie Roach had forsaken the old rocker for her rickety armchair beside the unlit grate and the sound of the wireless drifted out from the Thompsons' house. A van rumbled past out in Grange Road, too quick for Ruby to read the wording on its side, and it turned into Cater Street with its engine backfiring, much to the amusement of Butch Wheeler who happened to be passing at the time.

Chapter Twenty-Six

Paul Neal had spent Sunday afternoon helping his friend Butch move from his parents' place in Abbey Street to a more suitable location in Dockhead. They had transported the bits and pieces on a barrow, which Butch had borrowed from one of the market men, and when the job was done they sat chatting over cups of tea until six o'clock. They arranged to meet at the Swan later and when Paul arrived back home to get washed and changed he immediately sensed the tension. His mother was noisily busying herself in the scullery and his father was sitting in the parlour, staring into the grate with his chin resting on his hand. It was obvious that words had been said, and he lost no time in getting out of the house. Perhaps it would be better to find himself some digs like Butch, he considered. His friend's life had been made almost unbearable until he upped and left and now he was settled in two upstairs rooms in the house of one of his customers. Things were nowhere near as bad as far as Paul was concerned, but he was feeling more and more stifled lately, and his friendship with Mei Li seemed to be creating tension in the home.

As Butch had said, 'There comes a time ter make the move. Yer tend ter get under their feet, an' they need their privacy just like we do. It's different when yer a kid, but at our age yer take up too much space.'

Butch was right, he thought. His friend was not the most articulate of men but when he did have an opinion he tended to hit the nail on the head.

'You're out early ternight,' the barman remarked as Paul ordered his drink.

'Sorry. I can always come back later, Reg,' he joked.

'Yer might as well stay now yer 'ere.'

'Fanks, I will.'

'Are the lads comin' in?'

'Butch'll be 'ere in a minute,' Paul told him.

''Ow did the move go?'

'There wasn't much ter move really. It didn't take us all that long.'

Reg held the glass he was polishing up to the light. 'Nice lad, Butch. A bit dozy at times but a nice lad none the less fer that.'

Paul gave him an old-fashioned look. ''E's far from dozy. 'E's just inclined to undersell 'imself at times.'

'No offence meant,' the barman said quickly.

'None taken.'

'What's 'e doin' now? Still winder cleanin'?'

Paul nodded. 'It suits 'im. Better than road sweepin'.'

''E's better orf in digs,' Reg went on. 'Sonny Rowland was tellin' me Butch's muvver used ter take almost every penny off 'im. Bloody shame really. Still, there yer go.'

Paul was glad when the barman went off to serve a customer who had just walked in. He wanted time to think, to go over in his mind what Mei Li had told him. Was she really needed at home that evening, or was it a ploy to avoid going out with him? She had said she would be going back to Singapore within three months and it figured that she would not want to get too close to him, especially when there was a suitor waiting to marry her. Maybe she would change her mind if he persisted. Perhaps she would tell her guardian that she had found someone she liked and did not want to marry a man she hardly knew, even though it was custom.

The young man sipped his drink, recalling with pleasure the touch of Mei Li's soft body against his that morning. It had been a spontaneous embrace and her deep sigh as she nestled in his arms told him that she did feel something for him.

Butch Wheeler came into the bar grinning widely. 'This is my shout,' he said as he banged a ten-shilling note down on the counter. 'Yer've earned a pint, Paul me ole son.'

As the glass was being filled Butch chuckled and Reg looked up quickly. 'What's so funny about me pullin' a pint?' he asked.

'Nah I was finkin',' Butch replied. 'The fings yer see round 'ere lately.'

'What's 'e on about?' the barman appealed to Paul.

'Search me.'

'They're gettin' everywhere, no disrespect ter Mei Li,' Butch said, still grinning.

'Who are?'

Butch ignored the barman and turned to Paul. 'I've just seen Charlie Wong's van pull inter Cater Street,' he told him.

'Who the bloody 'ell's Charlie Wong?' the barman asked as he put the drinks down on the counter.

'Charlie Wong, Knife Grinder, it said on the van,' Butch went on. 'I can just see it. A little Chink in pigtails treadlin' away over that stone, then testin' the sharpness of a knife wiv an evil grin on 'is face. It's enough ter frighten the ole gels away.'

Paul looked at him with a frown. 'The van was pullin' inter Cater Street, yer say?'

'Yeah that's right.'

The young man felt a sudden twinge of anxiety in the pit of his stomach. Mei Li had told him that morning about Ho Chang's gambling debts and that the Tong would be sure to pressure him for payment. 'I'll be back soon,' he said quickly.

Butch and the barman stared in confusion as Paul hurried out.

'Where's 'e orf to I wonder?' Reg said scratching his bald head.

'Gawd knows,' Butch answered. 'It must 'ave bin somefing I said.'

As was the custom the junior Tong members had drawn straws, and those holding the shorter ones made themselves ready. Now as the disguised van trundled into Bermondsey the four sat impassive. They wore black shirts and trousers, each with a red bandanna wrapped round his head like the shadow warriors of old. They carried razor-sharp long knives and each wore the insignia of the Sons of Heaven Tong, on a figured cotton band knotted around his waist. Billy Chou sat with them along with Victor Sen, and Tommy Lo sat in the passenger seat next to Danny Ling who was driving.

'Now remember what I said,' Tommy Lo told them as they reached their destination.

Inside the locked laundry Su Chang was busy raking out a firepan beneath a large copper. Under normal circumstances it would have been the hired hand's job, but he was no longer working with them and Su Chang wanted to save time on Monday morning. It was irksome that most of the extra work had fallen on her shoulders, but that was the way it was. Ho Chang had been weak, there was no denying that. He had all but ruined them and had brought dishonour on the family, but she was his wife and it was the wife's duty to support her erring husband, fool that he was.

Ho Chang came down from the flat above and stood watching his wife for a while without speaking. The takings during the week had not been good and he knew that unless the bagwash, ironed shirts and starched collars were ready on time the customers would go elsewhere. At least on Monday the coppers would be fired more quickly. He and his wife would both have to start an hour earlier too if the work was to be finished on time. A potential buyer would want to see the books, know that the business was a going concern before he committed himself. Two people were interested at the moment, businessmen who were keen to get away from the more closed world of Chinatown, and Ho Chang prayed that one would make him an offer. Part of the money would pay off his debt and the remainder would tide them over until he could think of some other means of making a living.

Su Chang looked up quickly at the sound of the knock and Ho went over to peer through the blind. He opened the door a few inches to speak to the man standing there but was knocked back violently as Billy Chou threw himself through the doorway. Su screamed as the Tong members rushed in and grabbed her husband by the arms. He shook in terror as the fearsome-looking young men took up their positions around the shop, each holding a cruel-looking knife down at his side.

'Husi Kang is running out of patience,' Tommy Lo said as he strolled up to the quaking laundryman. 'Every day the interest builds up and soon it will be an impossible figure to repay.'

'We have an arrangement,' Ho Chang gulped. 'The money will be forthcoming within two weeks as promised.'

'There is no arrangement until we sanction it,' Billy Chou cut in. 'And how can we be sure that your brother will honour your debt?'

'Because he gave you his word. He's an honourable man,' Ho whispered.

'But there's already dishonour within your family,' Tommy Lo reminded him. 'A stain will spread.'

'The money will be available on time. I swear on the life of my wife and myself,' the laundryman said, holding out his hands pleadingly.

Tommy Lo nodded peremptorily to one of the junior members who was standing beside a row of shelves. The young man shouted out loudly as he twirled his knife above his head in a blur of movement, then with a deft flick he speared a bag of clean washing and slit it open. Clothes spilled on to the floor and Tommy smiled at the laundryman. 'What a sharp knife. It sliced that bag open easily enough, didn't it?'

Ho Chang was shaking visibly and his wife cowered

against his heaving chest. 'Please don't harm us,' she begged. 'You will be paid.'

'Yes, we will be paid,' Billy Chou said, strutting towards them.

The terrified laundryman looked around at the young men who all wore evil grins. 'Kill me if you must, but spare my wife,' he pleaded. 'She has no part in this.'

Tommy Lo sat down on a stool by the counter. 'Bring him here,' he ordered Billy Chou.

Ho Chang was dragged forward protesting, sure that he was about to lose some of his fingers. 'Speak to my brother Li Fong. He'll tell you that the money's on its way,' he whined.

The junior members in the room waited, standing with their legs splayed and their chests pushed out in an aggressive pose, all of them sure that they would be the one selected to perform the ritual chop.

Tommy Lo's eyes moved slowly from one to another of the young men and they came to rest on the one who had sliced the washing bag. 'Step forward,' he ordered.

The apprentice grinned as he came over to the counter, tapping his long knife against his thigh. 'My blade is honed to perfection, as quick as the wind,' he bragged.

The leader looked past him at the two members standing by the door and with a flick of his head he summoned them over. 'Secure him,' he said quickly.

Ho Chang was pressed forward over the counter with his left hand pulled out away from his body. His fingers moved frantically like the legs of a fly trying to extricate itself from a sticky web. 'No, I beg you,' he screamed out.

'Please don't harm him,' Su Chang pleaded in a voice that shook with terror.

It took Paul Neal less than five minutes to reach Cater Street, and when he ran into the turning his heart sank. He could see the van parked outside the laundry and two young Chinese men standing together on the pavement beside the vehicle, and as he reached it they moved towards him.

'What's goin' on?' he asked them.

'This is none of your business,' Victor Sen told him sharply. 'Go away.'

Paul looked at each of them in turn then his eyes moved up to the first-floor window of the house next door. 'I've got business wiv Li Fong,' he replied.

'Later. Not now,' Danny Ling told him.

'No. Right now,' Paul said, moving towards the door.

Suddenly he was grabbed by the arms and though he struggled violently he could not break their grip on him as he found himself being dragged through into the laundry.

'We have a visitor,' Victor Sen announced. 'He wishes to see Li Fong.'

'What's your business with Li Fong?' Tommy Lo asked him.

Paul took a deep breath. 'My business is with his ward, Mei Li,' he replied boldly.

'Are you the boyfriend of Mei Li?'

'Yeah I am.'

'What's your name?'

'Paul Neal.'

'Then you shall also be a witness to the power of the Tong, Paul Neal,' the leader told him with a ghost of a smile on his flat face.

'What yer gonna do?' Paul asked, shocked by the sheer terror that contorted the laundryman's white face.

'You'll see,' Tommy Lo replied. Then he turned to face the young member he had selected. 'When I give the signal make your knife dance like the wind, but don't take your eyes from my face. When I blink it will be the signal for you to cut off the hand of the laundry-man.'

'Have mercy! I beg you!' Su Chang screamed.

Ho Chang began to mumble incoherently, his whole body shaking violently.

'You can't do it! It's barbaric!' Paul shouted.

'The Tong is all-powerful,' Billy Chou said in a voice edged with the pleasure of sadistic excitement.

'Yer won't get away wiv this. Yer'll all be caught,' Paul shouted as he struggled to free his arms.

Tommy Lo ignored him. He walked slowly over to the junior member nearest the door and took the knife from him, then he walked back and stood by the counter, looking into the chosen apprentice's eyes. 'When I lift the knife you will begin,' he said in a calm voice, 'and when you see my eyes blink you will remove Ho Chang's hand. Is that understood?'

The young man nodded and stood with his legs wide apart, the tip of the knife held against his forehead. 'I am ready, leader,' he declared.

Paul struggled gamely but another of the members ran over to help hold him in check. Suddenly Tommy Lo raised his knife and the acolyte began his ritual. The sharp metal flashed as the young man twisted and sliced the air, cutting out a figure of eight at frightening speed, and at the instant his leader blinked he brought the blade down with a shout of exultation, shattering the awesome silence with the sound of steel sparking on steel. Tommy Lo's knife had made a diagonal bridge over Ho Chang's hand in a movement almost too quick to follow.

'Nothing is certain, and not always as it seems,' Tommy said quietly as he reached across to take the blunted knife from the young man. 'It will be a good lesson for you to remember. I was moving as I blinked, and you after I blinked, so I had the advantage. But you were fast, very fast.'

The young member's face relaxed somewhat as he took the plaudit. 'Thank you,' he said humbly.

Billy Chou was shocked by Tommy Lo's skilful use of the knife and he remained silent as he glanced around at the young members. They all looked in awe of their leader and the exercise had done no harm to his cause.

'You're mad. Stark ravin' bloody mad,' Paul growled at Tommy Lo. 'That poor sod could 'ave bin missin' an 'and by now.'

The Tong leader smiled and waved for the members to release him. 'Go back to the van,' he ordered them, then he turned to Billy Chou. 'Take the van home and we'll meet at ten o'clock tonight at the house.'

The malcontent was expecting to go with Tommy Lo to meet with Li Fong, but he knew it was the wrong time for the junior members to see him challenge an order and he nodded in compliance.

As soon as Billy Chou had left Su Chang ran over to kiss Tommy Lo's hand. 'You will not be sorry for the mercy you've shown,' she said tearfully.

The young leader waved her away. 'See to that dishonourable husband of yours,' he told her, 'and impress on him that the two weeks is all he'll be granted. Next time the Tong calls there will be no mercy at all, believe me.'

Paul had been standing watching and he warily walked up to Tommy Lo. 'Are you the visitor Li Fong's expectin'?' he asked.

Tommy Lo nodded with a grin. 'And is Mei Li expecting you tonight?' he enquired.

'No, but I intend ter see 'er anyway,' Paul replied forcefully.

'Then we'll go together,' Tommy told him.

The curtains were drawn in Li Fong's room and scented candles burned in small china bowls, casting a pink glow on the ceiling. The old man sat with his hands hidden beneath the wide folds of his robe and his eyes appeared to be almost closed as Tommy Lo spoke.

'Neither Ho Chang nor his wife has been harmed, but he has been given a lesson in the power of the Tong,' the leader explained. 'I think Paul Neal may have learnt something too. He had to be restrained from interfering.'

Li Fong looked over at Mei Li as she sat to one side next to Paul and saw her briefly touch his hand. 'I am indebted to you for your attempt to help my brother,' he told him. 'Brave as it was, a foolish gesture nevertheless. The Tong is all-powerful.'

Tommy Lo bowed his head at the compliment. 'Two

weeks has been granted,' he said curtly. 'The value of the pots you have put up as security was verified. I can only hope for your sake that they will be back in your possession soon.'

'I am confident,' Li Fong replied.

Paul glanced at Mei Li and saw the fear in her eyes. He surreptitiously squeezed her hand and she turned her head and smiled at him. Her small, even teeth shone pure white and Paul was aware of the delicious scent coming from her body. His eyes wandered from her long raven hair and slender neck to the slope of her shoulders and the fullness of her firm breasts and he wanted desperately to take her in his arms, reassure her and kiss her rosebud lips until she was breathless. As if to control his runaway thoughts he turned to Tommy Lo. 'So there'll be no repeat o' this evenin'?' he queried.

'For two weeks the laundryman will be left in peace, if there is any peace in his soul,' Tommy Lo replied.

Gunpowder green tea was served and drunk in silence, but Mei Li smiled at Paul as he struggled to finish his.

'It's time I should go,' Tommy Lo announced. 'I would like a few words with Paul Neal first though.'

Mei Li led the way down the stairs and showed them out. 'I'll keep the door ajar,' she whispered to Paul.

Outside it was dusk, with a cool breeze getting up. Further along the street a few women were chatting on their doorsteps and a young lad pedalled past the laundry on his homemade scooter.

'It was nice to meet you, Paul Neal,' the Tong leader said, 'although I wish it had been under more amiable circumstances.'

'I wish I could say the same meself,' Paul replied contemptuously. 'That poor ole sod was terrified. What if that stunt of yours 'ad gone wrong?'

'It wasn't going to,' Tommy Lo said smiling.

'But it could 'ave.'

'I wasn't playing games,' the young man said quickly, his face becoming deadly serious. 'You don't understand my reasons for such a stunt, as you call it. Suffice to say that it was necessary, for my benefit as well as Ho Chang's.'

Paul shook his head slowly, his eyes searching Tommy Lo's. 'I'm very fond o' Mei Li an' it's my intention ter marry 'er one day,' he told him. 'I don't want 'er hurt, nor Li Fong fer that matter.'

'You have my word,' Tommy Lo replied, matching his stare. 'We're not savages, despite what you saw tonight. We're foreigners in your country, living like strangers in a land of mirrors. We do what we have to. The Tongs have always been there, in one form or another, and they always will be. Human nature. Your people are not exactly unfamiliar with gangs, are they, Paul? It's only the methods of control that vary, and we could talk for many hours about that. I could teach you something, and maybe you could teach me something.'

Paul had to concede a grudging admiration for the young Chinese man. 'That might be rewardin',' he said.

Tommy Lo made to leave then turned back. 'I understand Li Fong favours the Peking Club in Limehouse,' he said. 'Maybe you should join him next time. It might be a good opportunity to continue our conversation.'

Paul nodded. 'I might just do that,' he replied.

Mei Li was standing inside the door and she reached out

to him as he stepped into the dark passageway. Her body moulded against his and she raised her head to look at him. Her red lips looked irresistible and he brushed them with his, but her response took him by surprise. She kissed him with an open mouth in a way he had never been kissed before and he shuddered at the deliciousness.

'You were very brave,' she whispered after a while.

'Someone told me that the laundry 'ad visitors an' after what yer told me this mornin' I was worried,' Paul said breathlessly. 'I thought of you an' Li Fong. As a matter o' fact I can't stop finkin' about yer, Mei Li.'

'It's the same for me, but it's a bad thing for both of us,' she sighed. 'Our lives and destinies are planned the minute we're born. I know my destiny and I can't change it. I know it's hard for you to understand, but you must try, Paul.'

'I only know I've fallen in love wiv yer, Mei Li, an' I won't give you up wivout a fight,' he said hoarsely. 'I'll foller you ter the ends o' the earth if I 'ave to.'

'But you hardly know me. It's madness.'

'I fell in love wiv yer the first time I saw yer,' he confessed helplessly.

'Please, Paul, don't make it harder for me,' she almost pleaded.

'Listen,' he said, taking her by the shoulders and stepping back to look into her eyes. 'I'm comin' callin' termorrer evenin'. We'll go ter the pictures, the park, whatever, just as long as we're tergevver.'

'I – I can't,' she wavered.

'I'm not takin' no fer an answer,' he said stoutly. 'If yer refuse I'll stand under yer winder an' sing love songs till yer change yer mind.'

'You are a funny man, Paul Neal,' she giggled.

They heard Li Fong shuffling out of his upstairs room and Mei Li moved back from the young man. 'I'll be ready by seven,' she said quietly.

Paul left the house and strolled back to the Swan, feeling as if he were walking on air. Butch Wheeler'll be full of questions, he thought, but I'd bet a pound to a pinch of shit he won't believe me.

Chapter Twenty-Seven

Kay was disappointed on Friday night at not seeing Mei Li on the bus going home from work but she breathed a huge sigh of relief that her working week was over. Normally a proficient typist, she had struggled every day to produce documents that were up to standard, but after a series of typing errors the supervisor had felt the need to call her into the office.

'These are important Government documents and there can be no margin for error,' the hawk-faced woman told her. 'It's so unlike you to be sloppy in your work, which leads me to believe you're either not well or there's something on your mind, worrying you. Now come on, out with it.'

Kay felt very well, physically, but all week she had pondered and fretted over several serious matters concerning her family and her, and she knew full well that was why she found herself in Marjorie Coombes' office. The problem was, how could she tell Hawk-face that things like that had been preoccupying her? The typing pool supervisor would want to know all the intricate details and Kay had no intention of giving her the pleasure.

'Well it's like this, Miss Coombes. My mother and father are going through a very bad patch in their marriage for some reason and they're not speaking to each other at the moment. My brother has fallen madly in love with a Chinese girl who probably loves him too, but she's going back to Singapore before long to marry someone else. And as if that wasn't enough for the poor sod to be getting on with, he came close to getting slashed by a Chinese Tong last Sunday evening. Oh and by the way, my boyfriend wants me to sleep with him and he's being very demanding at the moment. No I don't think there's anything else, apart from a few neighbours who feel that I'm encouraging foreigners into our street and putting them in dire peril of their lives.'

Kay smiled to herself as she glanced out of the bus window. Her excuse that she had been feeling under the weather that week but had not wanted to lose time was grudgingly accepted by Marjorie Coombes, who gave her a sharp lecture on the importance of Government typists being ultra-efficient. Kay had nodded and looked serious and it seemed to satisfy the supervisor, who dismissed her with a reluctant smile.

The bus pulled up at Waterloo Station and the young woman glanced down at the man working the fruit stall by the entrance. He always reminded her of Joey and images of her boyfriend rose up in her mind. She had seen a lot of him lately and it was so nice being with him. How different he was from Richard. They had become very close, and on one or two occasions that week she had had to use all of her guile and willpower to prevent things getting out of control. She was in love with him and wanted him, but for the moment there was too much going on within her family for her to add to the worries by putting herself at risk. Getting pregnant at this stage would be the last straw.

The bus trundled on through the evening rush-hour traffic and Kay's thoughts turned to Mei Li. They had met on the bus going home on Wednesday evening and had a long chat. Mei had been reluctant to say anything about what was going on between her and Paul, but Kay had managed to glean a few things from her and it soon became obvious that her friend was going through an emotional turmoil. Kay found it hard to understand the value Mei Li placed on family respect and honour. Here she was, schooled in the ways of the West, educated and highly intelligent, but still clinging to the old mores of her native land even though she had not set foot in China since fleeing the country with her guardian while still a child. If she could only bring herself to discuss her dilemma with Li Fong, Kay sighed, she might manage to make him understand that her future happiness was here in England with Paul, not thousands of miles away in Singapore with a comparative stranger.

Traffic was dense at the Elephant and Castle, and for a while the bus remained stationary at the huge junction. What was going on with her parents, Kay wondered? Her brother was of the opinion that their father was having an affair, which Kay dismissed as being preposterous. Their mother was certainly acting strangely and doing things totally out of character though. She had forgotten to leave their father's slippers by the stairs on two occasions at least that week, and she had even placed an ashtray in the parlour. Whether they were acts of atonement or merely conciliatory gestures was anyone's guess, but their father was having none of it. He found his slippers before going into the parlour and still went out into the garden for a cigarette.

The neighbours had been offhand too lately, which made

a bad situation worse. Since Nora Mason had called on her mother to ask whether it was a good idea to hold a party for Kay's Chinese friends they had hardly spoken to her, and Ruby's refusal to tell them it was all a joke had not exactly helped matters.

'I've been there for 'em all at one time or anuvver,' Ruby had moaned, 'an' that's the fanks I get. It was only meant as a bit of a laugh but that silly cow couldn't see a joke if it got up an' strangled 'er. She's got 'em all fired up an' even Lizzie Roach is on their side. Fank God fer Bel Allenby. At least she wasn't 'avin' any of it.'

Kay finally stepped from the bus in Grange Road feeling jaded. Joey was calling later and she wanted to be at her best. He was going to speak to her parents about them getting engaged and it couldn't have come at a worse time, she sighed.

'They've took Lizzie away terday, luv,' Connie Wilson called out as Kay stepped into the alley.

'Who did?'

'She's in St Olave's 'Ospital,' Connie told her. 'She 'ad a fall. Yer mum found 'er when she looked in on 'er way ter work.'

Myrtle Thompson was standing at her front door. 'Shame about poor Lizzie,' she said. 'The ambulance men strapped 'er legs tergevver. I fink she's broke 'er 'ip.'

'Dear oh dear,' Kay said sadly. 'Poor ole Lizzie.'

'It's times like these when yer really appreciate good neighbours, ain't it, luv?' Myrtle went on. 'After all, we all 'ave ter live tergevver.'

Kay forced a smile as she went into the house and she found her father sitting on an upturned tub by the shed, smoking a cigarette. 'Mrs Thompson just told me about Lizzie Roach,' she said. 'Is that where Mum's gone?'

'Yeah, she's gone in wiv a few o' Lizzie's fings.'

'Why don't yer smoke in the 'ouse?' Kay asked him.

'I'm used ter smokin' outside.'

'Mum puts an ashtray out for yer now.'

'Yeah I know, an' she's stopped naggin' me about wearin' me slippers too,' Jim remarked sarcastically.

'I fink it's nice she's stopped bein' so particular,' Kay said defensively. 'It shows she cares about yer.'

'Yeah, I expect so,' Jim replied unconvincingly.

Kay wanted to confront him about the strained atmosphere in the house but she held back, dreading what her father might tell her. If there was another woman in his life as Paul suspected then he might not be staying with them much longer. Things would have to come to a head sooner or later.

'Well, I fink I'd better start the tea,' she told him.

Ho Chang let his brother into the laundry then slid the heavy bolts across the door before taking him up to the flat above. Su was preparing a meal for them all and she listened from the kitchen while they talked.

'It's not good news,' Li Fong said with a slow shake of his head. 'I was at the Bank of China this afternoon and they told me that there would be a delay in getting three hundred pounds transferred from a Singapore dollar account,' he explained. 'It's a bad time. For one thing there are many Government restrictions on private transfers and then there are further controls in operation due to the international situation. The manager was decent enough when I saw him. He told me that businesses with Far Eastern links were finding it difficult at the moment to get funds transferred, and for private clients it was worse.'

'But you're a businessman with such links,' Ho Chang said in a worried voice.

'Yes, but you must understand that I have no business actually operating in England,' Li Fong replied. 'My permit was issued with many restrictions and I doubt whether I would have been granted one at all if it hadn't been for Mei Li working here. It complicates matters that I'm registered as a Chinese national even though I live and work in Singapore.'

Ho Chang slumped down in his seat. 'You don't feel there'll be enough time?'

'I remain hopeful until the last possible moment,' Li Fong told him, 'but we must have another plan ready should the money not arrive in time.'

Ho Chang's forehead creased into a deep frown. 'What are you saying?'

'If the money has not arrived by next Friday when the bank closes for the weekend we will know we have only one day left. On Sunday the Tong will come back to Bermondsey and you must be gone.'

'There's nowhere we can go,' Ho Chang replied despondently.

'Now listen to me carefully,' Li Fong said, his eyes widening. 'I've tried to protect you and Su by putting up a valuable possession of mine as surety for payment. Unfortunately the Tong might still come for you, even though they have in their hands something that will bring them money far in excess of the debt owed. I've been suspecting that since last Sunday when they paid you a visit. We have to anticipate the maliciousness of their minds and try to imagine how they might twist things. They might claim that Husi Kang will not accept anything in lieu of the money, in which case you will still be in default.'

'If that happens and they keep what you have given them I will never rest until I have repaid you for your loss,' Ho Chang answered gravely.

Li Fong stroked his wispy beard thoughtfully. 'I recently had to remind my ward Mei Li of the teachings of Confucius,' he said. '"Make only the promise you can keep." If you lived to be a very old man you would still not be able to pay for it, Ho Chang. The possession I gave to the Tong is priceless. All my life has been spent acquiring it.'

Ho bowed his head for a few moments and when he looked up there were tears in his eyes. 'Why, brother? Why have you risked what should one day be Mei Li's inheritance?'

'Because we are brothers.'

'But we are only half-brothers. We don't share the blood of one father.'

'But we were born of the same mother, we lived as children in the shadow of the large mountain and we hunted and fished together,' Li replied quietly. 'Did we ever question or make comparisons? Did we ever not share each other's happiness when as children we watched the harvest celebrations and when the fish took our bait? Did we not share the sadness in our lives and cry together? As men we went our different ways, but we carried the love of each other in our hearts. Who can say that our roles could not have been reversed? In the West they have a saw: "There but for the grace of God go I." I am pleased to be able to help my brother.'

'And I am humbled by your goodness and kindness.'

'Enough of that,' Li Fong said quickly, giving him a brief smile. 'Now you must listen carefully. On Monday you will go to this address. The company will act as agents in selling your business. You will sign the necessary papers, which will be held in abeyance until you give the word to proceed. You will then take care of any outstanding business and pack ready. On Friday evening if my bid for the money fails you and your wife will catch the night train to Liverpool. There is a large Chinese community living near the docks and I have friends among them who will look after you until it's safe to return to London. Take this name and address and keep it with you.'

Ho Chang nodded his head quickly as he pocketed the slip of paper. 'I fear I shall never be able to return,' he said sadly.

'Never is a long time,' Li Fong replied. 'Young men become old men. Wild animals are tamed and the law of the Tong is not eternal. I do fear though that it is unlikely we will ever meet again in this lifetime. I am an old man now and I am tired. Daily the urge to return to the East becomes stronger and I will not be seeking to renew my visitor's permit.'

'I will do as you say, brother,' Ho Chang answered with a break in his voice, 'and I will always remember the mountain that wore a hat of snow each winter and the ice-cold streams we drank from and fished together in the spring of our lives. When we are dust our souls will be united there in the shade of the mountain and we will soar beyond the peak together as brothers of one spirit.'

Li Fong blinked once or twice to clear his misting eyes and he stood up as Su Chang entered the room to announce that the meal was ready. 'You are just in time,' he joked. 'Your husband is beginning to make me feel quite sad.'

Across the river in Limehouse Billy Chou sat together with Danny Ling and Victor Sen in the public bar of the Cutter.

'My patience is running short with Tommy Lo and I think it's time for us to seriously consider our options,' the malcontent said forcibly. 'Look at what's happened lately. The police have raided the house and Wu Sung said that they paid careful attention to the cupboard under the stairs, the place where I keep my knife. It was fortunate that I had recently instructed Wu Sung to find a more secure hiding-place for it. As it happened it was under the clothes that were boiling in the copper at the time of the raid, but I have to ask the question, were the police acting on information given?'

'Surely not,' Victor Sen said quickly.

'You're too trusting,' Billy Chou rounded on him. 'Think about the little game Tommy Lo devised at the laundry. We've seen his dexterity and acuteness before but it was very impressive nevertheless, a demonstration of his skills for the benefit of the junior members and at the same time an effective means of asserting his leadership. Think on it though. On two occasions now we have seen him spare a transgressor. Why?'

'In fairness he did instruct us not to harm the laundryman,' Victor Sen remarked.

Billy Chou scowled across the table. 'His behaviour worries me. At one time it was to our advantage for Tommy Lo to have an arrangement with the local police chief, but things have altered. Who's in whose pocket now I ask you?'

'What are you saying?' Danny Ling asked.

Billy Chou looked from one to the other. 'The newspapers report increasing violence in Chinatown and the publicity is sure to make people in high places take notice. They will demand action. The local police chief finds himself in the firing line and he's forced to come down hard on Tommy Lo. Names are required, houses are raided in consequence, and our leader is given an ultimatum. Deliver or else. He's walking a thin line and he has to think hard. One of us could be offered up as a sacrifice, with enough evidence manufactured to secure a conviction. Who would be the scapegoat, I'm tempted to ask? You, Danny Ling, who concurs with just about every decision made? Or you, Victor Sen, who spends much time on the fence wondering which way to jump? Or will it be me? After all, I am the one who challenges decisions and argues the point.'

The two men remained silent as Billy Chou looked at each of them in turn. 'What worries me more than anything at the moment is the fact that very soon the *Honi Maru* will arrive at the King George Dock and we'll be receiving the biggest opium consignment ever. What if something goes wrong?'

'Are you saying that Tommy Lo's warned the police chief of its imminent arrival?' Danny Ling queried.

Billy Chou smiled bitterly. 'I ask you to think hard. Let's suppose that the police will be lying in wait. We'll all end up behind bars serving long sentences and Tommy Lo walks free, safe from us and able to dispose of the ginger pots for a fortune. The police chief gets his share of the proceeds and most probably a promotion into the bargain.'

Victor Sen shook his head. 'I find it hard to believe that Tommy Lo would ever betray us. And you forget too that the pots are in the safe at the Peking Club and they can't be removed without the two pieces of the banknote being presented.'

'I haven't forgotten,' Billy Chou replied with a sly grin. 'Husi Kang's to be trusted, and he'll act honourably. He has to, because he's afraid of us. What is likely, however, is that he's only looking after a worthless pile of crockery.'

'I don't understand,' Victor Sen said quickly.

'I'm totally lost too,' Danny Ling added.

'Yesterday I was talking with Wu Sung,' Billy Chou went on. 'He's a very wise old man, and during our conversation he said that it was foolish only to consider the obvious and ignore any other possibility, however unlikely. It got me thinking, and last night I remembered something important. On Sunday after we left Vu Ping's house I went to supervise getting the van ready, then I went back to Vu Ping's as arranged with Tommy Lo and together we went to the Peking Club. Tommy Lo had been alone with Vu Ping for just over half an hour, time enough for them to remove the pots and replace them with some cups or plates or whatever. We're fooled into believing that the pots are locked in Husi Kang's safe and meanwhile Vu Ping makes preparations to sell them.'

'It's all supposition,' Victor Sen replied. 'And in any case Vu Ping would be too frightened to face the consequences.'

'Let's call on Vu Ping,' Danny Ling suggested. 'If he is being dishonest he might well give himself away, and in any case we can remind him of what will happen should he be trying to cross us.'

The evening street was quiet when the three young men arrived at the lodgings of Vu Ping. Their knock was answered by an elderly Cantonese woman. 'You're too late,' she told them with a toothless chuckle. 'Vu Ping left on Wednesday evening.'

'Do you know where he went?' Billy Chou asked her.

'The Royal Albert Dock,' she replied. 'The ship left for the East on the midnight tide.'

Chapter Twenty-Eight

Just before the working week ended at Madeley's Food Factory the main wrapping machine developed a fault. The initial inspection revealed that the bearings had seized up and Winston Norris had no alternative but to sanction overtime for the maintenance team. Jim Neal was pleased when asked to work through Saturday, for he was not looking forward to a full weekend spent at home. He and Ruby were only speaking when they had to, and both Kay and Paul would be out most of the time. He knew that the awful atmosphere at home was entirely his fault, and he knew he had to suffer the consequences, but at least this Saturday he could take some respite while he tried to think about the future. Angela didn't know that their little secret was out of the bag, but she would have to be told.

Len Moody threw a large spanner down into the canvas tool-bag and arched his back. 'It's gonna be a long day,' he moaned. 'It'll take us ages ter strip this fing down.'

'Well, we've got all day,' Percy Bradley replied, winking quickly at Jim.

There was no love lost between Percy and the man who seemed most likely to succeed him as maintenance foreman, and it had become an obsession for each of them to score points off the other.

'We could save time by removin' the bearin's from underneath,' Len said authoritatively.

Percy shook his head. 'Nah, that way yer'll 'ave ter drop the mountin's. Do it the easy way an' take them side-plates off. The spindles need ter be slid out from the sides anyway.'

Len Moody searched his bag for the appropriate box spanner while Jim began to remove the nuts on the opposite side-plate.

As soon as Percy Bradley walked away Len looked across the machine. 'Yer don't need ter take that side lot off,' he said. 'We can pull the spindles frew this side.'

'Not the main one yer can't,' Jim told him. 'It's too long. There's not enough room between the machine an' the wall.'

'Yeah there is. I did it this way before,' Len replied.

Jim was in no mood to provoke another sulking session from his childish workmate and he shrugged his shoulders. 'All right, I'll come round that side an' give you an 'and.'

'That's the trouble wiv ole Bradley,' Len Moody remarked as they set to work on the double row of retaining nuts. ''E's gettin' too old fer the job. These new machines are far more complicated than the ones 'e's bin used to. It needs a younger 'ead ter tackle these bleeders, someone who knows what it's all about.'

Jim worked with a will, trying to ignore the asinine remarks Moody was making, and twenty minutes later the last of the side-plates were removed. The foreman-in-waiting scratched his balding head with a greasy hand. 'We could 'ave saved all this time, but there yer go.'

The bearings proved difficult to free and when the first of them was pulled out Len Moody smiled with satisfaction. 'I told yer didn't I?' he said triumphantly. 'There's inches ter spare.'

'There won't be wiv the main bearin',' Jim warned him.

'Nah, yer wrong,' Moody persisted. 'It'll come out easy. There's tons o' room.'

Percy Bradley came back to inspect their progress. 'What about the opposite side-plates?' he queried.

'I told Jim we don't need ter take 'em off,' Moody declared. 'There's room enough this side.'

Percy and Jim exchanged quick glances. 'Right then, if yer sure,' the foreman said. 'It's comin' up fer ten o'clock so yer'd better take a ten-minute break. That main bearin's gonna be a cow ter get off.'

'It won't be no trouble,' Moody said confidently.

'Well go on then, off yer go fer ten minutes,' Percy told them.

Jim collected a mug of tea from Nobby Smith the storeman and walked out into the firm's loading area. He sat in the bright morning sun with his back propped against a stack of wooden pallets, far enough away from the rest of the team to be out of earshot. The last thing he wanted was to listen to Len Moody bragging to Fred Williams the other maintenance man and Billy Thornton the apprentice.

'What a mess I've got myself into,' Jim sighed to himself. Things couldn't go on the way they were. He would have to move out and the kids would have to be told the reason why. He owed them that much.

'What's the matter wiv you this mornin', Jimbo?'

He looked round to see Percy Bradley standing there. 'Nuffink. Why?'

The older man grunted as he sat down beside him. 'I thought Silly Balls might 'ave upset yer,' he remarked, nodding in Len Moody's direction.

Jim shook his head and forced a smile. 'Nah. 'E's a pain in the arse at times but I don't let 'im get ter me.'

Percy took out his briar and tobacco pouch from his overall pocket. 'The trouble wiv know-alls is they can't admit it when they're wrong,' he said.

Jim watched as the foreman packed his pipe with dark stringy tobacco. 'When will yer be leavin', Percy?' he asked.

'I got two months yet till I'm sixty-five, but they might decide ter let me finish a bit earlier,' the foreman told him. 'I got a lot o' time owin'.'

'I'll be sorry ter see yer go,' Jim said, putting his mug down between his feet.

Percy studied his pipe for a moment or two. 'I'm gonna be gettin' under my ole woman's feet an' she won't be none too 'appy,' he sighed. 'I dunno why they don't let us sixty-fives work on if we're still fit enough an' want to. The trouble wiv retirement is the idleness. Yer work all yer life an' then yer find yerself gettin' up every mornin' an' realisin' that there's nuffink ter do. The woman gets used ter that pay packet on the table every Friday an' then it ain't there any more. Yer down ter livin' on a pittance. I ain't bin able ter put much aside towards me retirement. Who can? Still, it'll be nice ter turn over in bed on a frosty mornin' wivout 'avin' ter worry about what might go wrong at the factory that day.'

'At least you'll 'ave earned yer rest,' Jim remarked, not knowing what to say.

'Take my advice, Jim boy,' the foreman said, sucking on his briar. 'Get yerself some insurance fer yer old age. There's endowments yer can take out these days. I wish I'd 'ave bin able to when I was a younger bloke.'

Jim nodded. 'Yeah, I'll 'ave ter consider it,' he replied.

'You an' Ruby are young yet,' Percy went on, 'but time flies so quickly. Before yer know where you are yer starin' retirement in the face. It's frightenin', believe me.'

Jim took out his tobacco tin and rolled a cigarette, and as he looked up he saw Angela crossing the yard. She was coming towards him and Percy had spotted her too. 'Well, I'd better go an' see Nobby,' the foreman said, getting up on to his feet with some difficulty.

Jim gave Percy a quick glance. He knows what's going on, he thought, and he's making himself scarce.

'So this is what you do on overtime,' Angela said smiling as she reached him. Jim made to stand up but she held up her hand. 'Stay there, I'll come up on the bank.'

'What are you doin' in this mornin'?' Jim asked her as she reached the top of the stone steps.

'I need to get some papers I forgot yesterday,' she told him. 'I must have all the figures ready for the auditor by Monday.'

Jim saw that Len Moody and the others were going back into the factory and he turned back to Angela. 'I've gotta go,' he said quickly. 'Will you be around at lunchtime?'

She smiled. 'If you want me to,' she replied. 'I've felt that you've been avoiding me all week.'

'I've been very busy,' Jim told her. 'I'll see you in the usual place, OK?'

'I'll be waiting,' Angela said seductively as she turned and walked into the building.

'I saw yer chattin' that Angela up,' Len Moody remarked to Jim as they set to work once more. 'What a tasty sort. I'd like ter give 'er one.'

'Pass me that wrench, this nut's burred,' Jim said in an effort to shut Moody up.

'You an' 'er are pretty friendly,' Moody went on. 'I've seen yer talkin' to 'er on quite a few occasions.'

'So what?' Jim responded crossly.

'Some o' the gels on the belt were talkin' the ovver day. They fink you an' 'er are at it.'

'Look, I'm not interested in what anyone finks,' Jim rounded on him. 'Now let's 'ave that wrench or we'll never get this job finished.'

Soon the main bearing was freed from its housing and Len Moody grunted with satisfaction. Together the two men eased the thick steel spindle sideways from the machine and then Moody cursed aloud. The end of the rod was pressing against the wall with the other end still not free from its seating. 'I'd 'ave swore I took it out this way last time,' he growled.

'Well yer couldn't 'ave done,' Jim told him sharply. 'I warned yer it wouldn't come out this way but you wouldn't 'ave it.'

'P'raps we could dismantle the mountin' an' drop it,' Moody suggested.

Jim shook his head. 'There's only one way an' that's ter take the ovver side-plates off an' pull it frew that way.'

Len Moody's face was dark as thunder as he set to work loosening the nuts from the large panel. Jim Neal can hardly wait to tell Percy Bradley, and the two of them will be having a good laugh at my expense, he fumed. If Bradley had his way Neal would be the next foreman, but there was time yet. What would Mr Norris's reaction be if he found out that his secretary was having an affair with Neal? It was common knowledge that he was a regular churchgoer and he would be certain to frown on adultery, especially when it concerned his secretary and one of the workers. Perhaps it was time Mr Norris learned what was going on under his nose.

Jim moved his forefinger round the rim of his glass as he sat facing Angela in the small riverside pub. 'I just couldn't lie to 'er,' he said sighing.

'Would it have been that hard, Jim?' she replied. 'At least you would have been protecting her.'

'I only wish I 'ad your gall,' he told her. 'But then it's different fer you.'

'How is it different for me?' Angela asked, her green eyes widening in anger.

'Because you're the woman you are, but I can't make love wiv Ruby, I've not bin able to properly since you an' I 'ave . . . you know.'

'You could, if you weren't so obsessed with the truth,' Angela snapped. 'What is the truth? Have you stopped loving your wife just because you and I are having an affair? No of course you haven't. You're allowing your guilt to tear the two of you apart. Try and see it the way I do. Laurie's not exactly a monk. He does get amorous at

317

times, but when he's making love to me I imagine it's you and that's my way of coping. As for guilt, I don't dwell on it, or I might end up feeling the way you do.'

'It's just a game wiv you,' Jim said angrily, 'but it's not that way wiv me. I can't play games.'

'What are you trying to say, that we should run off together and set up house somewhere?'

'Of course not.'

'Then what are you saying?'

'I dunno, I'm totally confused.'

Angela's expression softened and she leaned across the table to lay her hand on his. 'Look, Jim, you've told Ruby that you've been unfaithful and she's reacted as any wife would. Tell her you're sorry, that it was a mistake you made, and tell her you've put it all behind you. Convince her that you want to try again to rebuild your marriage. It won't be easy and it'll take time, but she'll come round eventually, you'll see.'

'And where would that leave us?'

'Nothing would change for us.'

'I couldn't do it, Angela. I couldn't be that two-faced.'

'So are you telling me it's over, that you don't want to see me any more?'

Jim stared down at his glass for a few moments then he raised his eyes to hers. 'When I'm not wiv yer it's easy. I feel strong. I can get the right words tergevver in me mind, but as soon as I come face ter face wiv yer they're all gone. I just wanna take yer in me arms an' love yer madly. You're like a drug that I can't do wivout. You're dangerous, infuriatin', an' I can't resist yer.'

Angela squeezed his hand. 'It's time we made a move,'

she said. 'Come round tonight. Laurie's away bird-watching as usual. I honestly think he's got another woman hidden away somewhere.'

'Would it 'urt you that much if 'e 'as?'

'Yes it would. Does that surprise you?'

'No. I know you love 'im.'

'I love him dearly.'

'I love Ruby too.'

'I know you do.'

Jim felt his insides churn as he walked out on to the path by the river. Angela was mocking him and reassuring him together, as a mother would her child. Short of strangling her he could see no way of ending the affair. She was playing havoc with his emotions and he was too cowardly to do anything about it.

Billy Chou led the way into the Peking Club and was greeted obsequiously by Husi Kang. 'This is an unusual hour of the day for you to grace me with your presence,' he said.

'This is strictly business,' the young man replied. 'Can we go to your office?'

The rotund club owner turned to a young man who was polishing the cutlery nearby. 'Bring some tea to my office,' he ordered before leading the way up a steep flight of thickly carpeted stairs to his comfortable domain, where he motioned for the Tong members to make themselves at ease. 'What can I do for you?' he asked, a slight frown creasing his flat forehead.

'We would like to see the contents of that parcel you have in your safe,' Billy Chou told him.

Husi Kang looked frightened. 'You know I can't let you

have that parcel unless you possess the two pieces of the note,' he reminded him.

Billy Chou held up his hands in a calming gesture. 'We don't want to take it away from you, Husi. We only want to have a look at the contents. There's nothing that prevents you from letting us see.'

'Very well, but does Tommy Lo know of your visit?' the club owner asked.

'Just show us the parcel,' Billy Chou said testily.

Husi Kang went to his large safe and stood blocking his visitors' view as he twirled the knob left and right. 'I'll be interested to see for myself what treasure I'm guarding,' he said as he swung back the heavy steel door and removed the parcel, placing it carefully down on his desk.

Billy Chou got up and stood over it, staring down for a moment or two before he untied the string. He held his breath as he removed the top layer of packing and then expelled air with a loud hiss. 'Just as I suspected,' he growled at the other Tong members. 'Worthless tea mugs!'

Husi Kang stared down into the parcel. 'I don't understand,' he said. 'I've been guarding these with my life. What foolishness is this, Billy Chou?'

'We've all been tricked,' the young man replied. 'The real treasure's somewhere on the high seas by now, on its way back East.'

'I don't understand,' Husi repeated frowning.

'This parcel should have contained a very valuable set of ginger pots,' Billy Chou explained. 'The pots were given to us as security until the money owing to you was paid in full. It seems that Tommy Lo has replaced them with this junk.'

'But why?'

'I should have thought it was obvious. Our noble leader's seeking to become rich at our expense.'

'But he dare not go against the Tong,' Husi replied. 'He would never live long enough to enjoy his wealth.'

Billy Chou smiled malevolently. 'Make no mistake about it, Husi. Tommy Lo is a very clever operator. His plan was for us to be permanently removed from the scene, leaving him with a free hand. Unfortunately for Tommy he made the fatal mistake of underestimating us. He didn't expect any of us to look inside that parcel. His reward now will be the same as for all those who disgrace themselves. He will be subjected to the special vote.'

'And I'll be a loser too,' Husi Kang groaned. 'Now I'll never see the colour of the money owed to me by that dishonourable laundryman Ho Chang.'

There was a knock on the office door and the young waiter came in carrying a tray laden with bowls of steaming jasmine tea which he set down on the desk.

'Don't worry about your money, Husi,' Billy Chou told him as the waiter left. 'The Tong will recover the debt. Someone will be made to pay, and Ho Chang will receive the full punishment.'

Chapter Twenty-Nine

Saturday morning had started bright and sunny but by late afternoon the sky was full of rain clouds and thunder rolled in the distance.

'We're in fer a right ole storm,' Bel Allenby remarked as she handed Ruby a mug of tea and sat down facing her. 'Excuse the mugs. I should've got the cups an' saucers out but I'm just a slob lately.'

Ruby forced a smile. 'Mugs 'old more anyway.'

Bel sipped her tea. 'So go on, tell me about Lizzie.'

'Talk about cantankerous,' Ruby sighed, pulling a face. 'As soon as she knew there was nuffing broken she asked fer 'er clothes. She started moanin' as soon as I got to 'er bed this afternoon. She was goin' on about the food, then about the woman in the bed next to 'er, an' she reckons the matron's a man in disguise. She said she's gonna discharge 'erself if they won't let 'er come 'ome, an' she made me promise ter take 'er clothes in ternight. I'll take 'em in, but I'm gonna try an' persuade 'er ter stay, at least till Monday. I mean, she 'ad trouble gettin' around before the fall. Anuvver one would just about put the kibosh on it. I told 'er she was very lucky she didn't break 'er 'ip.'

Bel shook her head slowly. 'You know Lizzie. She'll 'ave 'er way if it kills 'er.'

'Yeah, an' it will one day,' Ruby puffed.

'So 'ow about you?' Bel enquired. ''Ow's fings indoors?'

'Don't ask,' Ruby said with another sigh. 'Last night Kay brought Joey round. She said 'e wanted to 'ave a quiet word wiv me an' Jim. 'E asked if we'd mind 'em gettin' engaged.'

'An' what did you say?'

'I said it seemed a bit sudden, an' Joey said they wasn't plannin' ter get married till next summer but they needed ter know if it was all right so they could get their names down on the Council waitin' list fer a place.'

'That's sensible,' Bel remarked. 'Joey seems a nice lad, Rube. 'E's always very pleasant when yer go to 'im at the market. I'm sure 'im an' Kay'll be 'appy tergevver.'

'Yeah, 'e 'as changed,' Ruby conceded. ''E's nowhere near as flash.'

'Did Jim 'ave anyfing ter say about it?' Bel asked.

''E just said it was OK an' they should get their names down on the housin' estate lists as well as the Council.'

'It makes sense,' Bel said nodding. 'An' what about Paul? 'Ow's 'e gettin' on wiv that Chinese gelfriend of 'is?'

''E's bin out wiv 'er every night this week 'cept Wednesday. 'E's absolutely besotted wiv 'er.'

'An' 'ow's she feel about 'im? D'yer know?'

Ruby shook her head. 'Paul brought 'er round on Tuesday evenin' but they didn't stop long. It was only to introduce 'er. They were off ter the pictures as a matter o' fact. I 'ave ter say she seems a very nice gel. She's very pretty, an' she's got a nice personality. I can see why Paul fell fer 'er.'

'So yer not so worried now?'

'I wouldn't be if she was plannin' on stayin' 'ere,' Ruby said sighing, 'but apparently she an' 'er guardian are goin' back ter Singapore soon.'

'Did she tell yer that?'

'No, but I over'eard Paul talkin' to our Kay about it. Somefing ter do wiv the ole man's permit runnin' out.'

'She could stay though, couldn't she?' Bel queried. 'After all, she works 'ere.'

'I dunno, it all seems up in the air,' Ruby replied with a frown. 'Trust our Paul ter get involved wiv someone like Mei Li. 'E never does fings by 'alf.'

Bel leaned back in her armchair and crossed her legs. 'Are yer copin' all right, luv?'

'Just about,' Ruby said, her eyes suddenly filling with tears. 'It's all very civilised. We don't speak about it. In fact we don't speak about anyfing. Jim comes in from work an' 'e sits readin' the paper till tea's ready, then 'e says the meal was nice, an' back 'e goes in the chair. Bedtime's the worst. 'E goes up before me an' 'e's asleep, or pretends ter be, when I get inter bed. Can you imagine what it's like, Bel? We sleep in the same bed an' we're both careful not ter touch each ovver. I can't stand much more of it, it's killin' me slowly.'

Bel leaned forward and took Ruby's hands in hers as the tears fell. 'That's it luv, let it all out,' she said softly. 'Yer'll feel better for it.'

'I don't wanna lose 'im, Bel, despite what 'e's done,' Ruby sobbed. 'I will do though, I know I will. That woman'll take 'im from me. It's only a matter o' time before 'e moves out.'

'That's enough o' that sort o' talk,' Bel urged her staunchly. 'Remember what we said. Yer don't 'ave ter live a lie any more. Yer've made a start, an' now yer can fight. Yer've got to. Speak to 'im. Make 'im talk about it. Pick the right moment an' 'ave it out wiv 'im. Demand ter know who this woman is an' go an' confront 'er. Yer don't 'ave ter rant an' rave. Just let 'er see that yer not givin' yer 'usband up wivout one bloody 'ell of a struggle. An' don't make it easy fer Jim by givin' 'im options. Let 'im see yer gonna fight this fing. An' above all, fer goodness sake make 'im aware o' what it was really like fer you an' yer sister Amy as kids. It might 'elp 'im understand what's motivated yer all these years. Ter be honest, I fink Jim's a decent feller at 'eart. You two'll make a go of it, you'll see. Fings'll work out for yer I feel certain.'

Ruby blew her nose loudly. 'I bet yer fink I'm a right wiltin' lily, but I'm not, Bel. I am gonna fight ter win 'im back, so get ready ter see the sparks fly.'

'That's my gel,' Bel said with gusto. 'Now, 'ow about anuvver mug o' tea?'

On Saturday evening the Swan was busy as usual. The pianist was getting into his stride, laughter rang out, and in the far corner Gert Ransome almost choked on her stout as her old friend Maggie Watson recounted her wedding night. 'Fifty years ago terday it was,' she was going on. 'There was I, innocent as the driven snow, an' there was 'im, pissed out of 'is brains. When I fink back I dunno 'ow I didn't die o' shame when we came out o' the church. That ole bastard o' mine was workin' at Pace's at the time an' 'is pals brought us back ter my street on an 'orse an' cart. They 'ad trestle tables out in the turnin' an' they got a bloke ter play the accordion. Bert's bruvver Alf was always trouble in drink an' Bert told 'im 'e wasn't welcome at the party, but it didn't make any difference, 'e turned up anyway. Before long 'im an' my Bert got at it an' some ovver blokes joined in an' it was like the Battle o' Waterloo. Anyway when fings quietened down we left the reception an' went 'ome ter the two rooms we'd rented in Weston Street. It was dark by that time an' Bert was well sozzled, so I went up ter get ready fer bed. I remember as though it was yesterday. I 'ad this lovely lace nightie, all pink an' crinkly, an' Mrs Sampson 'ad given me a bottle o' lavender water. So I puts me nightie on, splashes meself all over wiv the stuff an' I waits fer Bert's footsteps on the stairs. Like I said, I was young an' innocent an' me 'eart was goin' nineteen ter the dozen. I remember there was a nightlight burnin' in the saucer an' I wasn't too 'appy about it. I didn't want Bert oglin' me when 'e come up so I blew it out. I tell yer, Gert, I must 'a' laid there in the pitch black waitin' fer what seemed hours. Unbeknown ter me 'e was as scared as I was an' 'e was still knockin' the drink back. Anyway, ter cut a long story short I must 'ave fell off ter sleep 'cos I never 'eard 'im come inter the room. Next mornin' I woke up an' felt 'is arm over me, an' I ses ter meself, well, my gel, it must 'ave 'appened while yer've bin asleep. So I turns round an' snuggles up close an' I give 'im a little kiss. Now yer gotta remember I'm still 'alf asleep, but Bert's moustache tickled me face an' it made me sneeze. Then all of a sudden I was wide awake. Bert didn't 'ave a moustache. I shot up in bed an' saw it was Bert's bruvver Alf lyin' there beside me.'

'My good Gawd!' Gert exclaimed.

'True as I'm sittin' 'ere,' Maggie went on. 'Apparently Alf 'ad come round ter say 'e was sorry an' 'im an' Bert got back on the turps. My ole bastard ended up kippin' in the armchair an' Alf must 'ave thought the bed would be more comfortable.'

'An' did 'e?'

'An' did 'e what?'

'You know. Did 'e interfere wiv yer?'

'What d'yer fink?'

'I dunno. That's why I'm askin' yer.'

'Well, put it this way,' Maggie said grinning. 'Nine months later I 'ad our Percy. Me an' Bert always wanted a football team but we never 'ad any more kids after 'im. 'E was a real right carrot-top when 'e was a kid was Percy, an' Bert was dark-'aired. It never bovvered 'im though. 'E said Percy must favour 'is side o' the family. Apparently Bert's farvver was ginger, an' so was Alf.'

'Say no more,' Gert replied, sipping her stout.

Maggie picked up her glass. 'When Bert run off wiv Alf's wife people expected me an' Alf ter get tergevver but it wasn't ter be.'

'That's a shame,' Gert remarked.

'We might 'ave got tergevver eventually, if the poor sod 'adn't gone an' got 'imself killed in France a few days before the armistice. Still, never mind, that's 'ow life is. Same again, luv?'

On a nearby table Butch Wheeler and Sonny Rowland sat together looking gloomy as they sipped their beer.

'It used ter be a right laugh when we all got tergevver on Saturday nights,' Butch was saying, 'but since Paul got in tow wiv Mei Li I don't see much of 'im at all.

It's the same wiv Joey. Since 'e got back wiv Kay 'e's a different bloke.'

Sonny felt his bruised cheekbone. 'Yeah it's sad really. I was 'opin' ter 'ave a couple o' bevvies wiv 'em. I wanted ter let Paul know I've got a fight comin' up at the Manor Place Baths in case 'e wants a ticket. This geezer I'm fightin's an up-an'-comin' kid, but my trainer finks we got a chance ter make a few bob on the side. Apparently this bloke's a sucker fer a left 'ook an' 'is chin's suspect.'

'I thought yer said 'e was up-an'-comin',' Butch remarked. 'It sounds more like 'e's down an' goin'.'

'Yeah but 'e ain't bin stretched yet an' they reckon I'm the bloke ter do it,' Sonny went on. 'The bookies are makin' 'im five ter four on. We can get six ter one on me. I'll ponce around fer a few rounds then wham. The ole left 'ook'll draw 'is curtains fer the night.'

'I remember yer sayin' somefing o' the sort last time,' Butch reminded him, 'an' after the fight you walked in 'ere lookin' like yer'd 'ad an argument wiv a bus.'

The boxer shrugged his broad shoulders. 'That was last time,' he replied. 'This time it'll be different.'

Butch sipped his drink. It would never be any different where Sonny Rowland was concerned, he thought sadly. The man was as tough as they came, but when they were giving out brains he wasn't exactly at the front of the queue. He would continue to be over-matched and used until one day he ended up a shuffling wreck, sweeping the gym and relying on handouts from those who once stood in the ring against him and helped batter him stupid. 'I 'ope so, pal, I really do,' he said sincerely.

Sonny swigged his beer and looked thoughtful. 'Do yer

fink it's serious wiv Paul an' that Chinese gel?' he asked after a while.

Butch nodded. ''E's crazy about 'er, but there's problems.'

'What d'yer mean?'

'She could be goin' back ter Singapore soon.'

'Bloody 'ell. That's a shame.'

'She might decide ter stay, but it's unlikely by the look o' fings.'

'I bet Paul's gutted.'

'Yeah 'e is. An' there's ovver fings goin' on too.'

'Like what?' Sonny asked.

'There was a bit of a rumpus at the laundry in Cater Street last Sunday,' Butch explained. 'I saw this van drive in the turnin' when I was on me way 'ere an' it 'ad "Charlie Wong, Knife Grinder" written on the side. I mentioned it ter Paul 'cos it tickled me, an' you should 'a' seen 'is face. 'E shot out of 'ere like a bullet. Apparently this bloke Chang who owns the laundry is the bruvver of Mei Li's guardian. That van was full o' Chinks from Lime'ouse. They'd come over the water ter put the fright'ners on 'im.'

'Who, Mei Li's guardian?'

'Nah, the laundryman,' Butch said quickly. 'Accordin' ter Paul this Chang bloke owes a lot o' money an' the bloke 'e owes it to sent this Tong over ter collect.'

'Tong? What's a tong?' Sonny asked, frowning.

'Don't you know nuffink?' Butch sighed irritably. 'A Tong is like a gang but they're Chinese. They do the same as our gangs, like beatin' people up who cross 'em, an' they're inter the protection racket. I read in the paper only last week about the goin's-on over in Lime'ouse recently. People 'ave 'ad their fingers chopped off an' there's bin a few murders over there as well. I tell yer, Sonny, those Tongs make our local gangs seem like powder puffs. They all carry these long knives, more like swords, an' they're razor sharp so the bastards can slash yer up. Believe me, they're a right evil load o' gits.'

Sonny Rowland did not look impressed. 'I don't care 'ow evil they are an' 'ow sharp those knives are,' he replied. 'The local mob's tooled up, an' nobody argues wiv a shotgun.'

'Well all I know is, Paul went round Cater Street last Sunday ter make sure Mei Li was all right an' this Tong mob collared 'im.'

'Bloody 'ell,' Sonny exclaimed. 'What 'appened?'

'They never touched Paul but they made 'im watch while they pretended ter chop the laundryman's 'and off. 'E said the bloke was like a gibberin' idiot. They scared the shit out of 'im.'

'I bet 'e'll pay up now,' Sonny remarked.

'Yeah, I would,' Butch replied.

Sonny took another sip of his drink. 'Paul should be careful gettin' involved wiv that lot,' he said. 'Anyway, if they do 'ave a go at 'im we'll 'ave ter steam into 'em. We're ole mates an' we gotta stick tergevver.'

'I s'pose we could go over ter Chinatown an' give 'em a bit o' stick,' Butch joked. 'We could borrer a few shotguns from the Kerrigans.'

'I'm bein' serious,' Sonny said crossly. 'We should 'ave a chat wiv Joey as soon as poss. If that Tong come over 'ere again chuckin' their weight about we can be ready. I can get a few lads from the gym an' Joey knows some 'ard nuts who wouldn't take kindly to outsiders tryin' ter muscle in on Bermon'sey.'

Butch smiled and shook his head slowly. 'You're a scream, Sonny. Do yer seriously fink that Tong's gonna advertise the fact that they're comin' over the water? They'll be in an' gone before yer know it.'

The boxer looked hurt. 'I mean if Paul gets the word before'and,' he said sheepishly.

'Yeah, well that's a different matter,' Butch replied, feeling sorry for being so short with his old friend. 'Come on, let's buy yer a drink. Who knows, we might be graced wiv Paul's company later, an' Joey's.'

Large rainspots hit the pavement as Ruby stepped down from the tram in Rotherhithe and walked through the hospital gates. She was carrying a bag containing Lizzie's clothes, and a bunch of flowers to soften the blow if the old lady was forced to stay there in the hospital until Monday.

The ward sister was waiting. 'I'm sorry, Mrs Neal, but the doctor has told Mrs Roach that she must stay here for a few more days. She was very lucky you know. Most people of her age break bones when they fall, especially hips, but in Mrs Roach's case she only suffered severe bruising. Nevertheless it is vital that we keep an eye on her for a few more days.'

Ruby walked up to the old lady's bed and saw the stern look on her face as she lay propped up with pillows, arms folded. ''Ello, luv, an' 'ow yer feelin'?' she asked smiling.

'Bloody terrible,' Lizzie growled.

'Well, yer bound ter be fer a few days. You 'ad a nasty fall.'

'It's nuffink ter do wiv the fall. It's 'er.'

'Who?'

'Why that dopey mare who's runnin' this ward,' Lizzie told her. 'Got right up my nose she 'as. "No yer can't go out ter the toilet, Mrs Roach." "No yer can't 'ave a Guinness, Mrs Roach.' I said she could call me Lizzie but she looked all mean an' 'orrible. Dopey prat.'

'Well, anyway I brought yer some flowers, luv,' Ruby said smiling. 'I'll get one o' the nurses ter put 'em in water when I go.'

'Mmm, they're nice,' Lizzie said without enthusiasm, 'but yer shouldn't 'ave bovvered. I'm comin' 'ome this evenin', if yer remembered ter bring me clothes. Yer did remember, didn't yer?'

'Yeah I brought 'em, but the sister said that the doctor wants you ter stay 'ere till Monday.'

'Well 'e can say what 'e likes. I'm still comin' 'ome.'

'You 'ave ter take notice o' the doctor, luv.'

'Balls. Gimme me clothes an' draw them screens.'

'Yer'll 'ave ter sign ter say yer discharged yerself.'

'Well don't just sit there. Go an' get the form.'

Ruby leaned forward on the bed and took Lizzie's hand in hers. 'Now listen, gel,' she said. 'The medical staff 'ere are only interested in your welfare. That doctor wants you ter walk out of 'ere feelin' well. If you come 'ome too soon yer might 'ave a relapse. What then? Could you expect the staff ter take care of yer after you dischargin' yerself?'

'That's what they're 'ere for, so you said,' Lizzie scowled back at her.

'Lizzie, I've gotta say it. You can be a cantankerous ole cow when yer like an' it don't become yer. Why can't yer

333

see sense? Two more days won't make that much difference. Me an' Bel can go frew yer 'ouse in the meantime an' it'll be all nice an' tidy when yer do come 'ome. I'll get Jack Mason ter fix that rocker for yer an' we'll blacklead yer grate an' change yer bed. It'll be nice.'

'Two more days 'ere, listenin' ter that scatty tart goin' on about 'er bladder,' Lizzie growled, jerking her thumb towards the next bed. 'I'd go round the bloody twist.'

The old lady next to Lizzie smiled over. 'Is that yer daughter, luv?'

'No she bloody ain't.'

'Yer can see the resemblance.'

'Shut yer silly row up.'

'I bin in 'ere fer goin' on two weeks,' the old lady said in a croaky voice. 'They can't find out what's wrong wiv me.'

'I could tell 'em,' Lizzie said, rolling her eyes.

'I'm a bit deaf,' the old lady went on. 'It was the war. I ain't bin able to 'ear since that bomb dropped on the flats.'

'Shut up an' go back ter sleep, yer gormless ole mare,' Lizzie growled.

'I 'ave ter read lips. Can't 'ear a word at times.'

'Well, all I can say is you ain't much good at it.'

'Lizzie, be'ave yerself,' Ruby chided her. 'The poor ole dear's only tryin' ter be friendly.'

'Well, I can do wivout 'er friendship. Now are you gonna draw those poxy screens or do I 'ave ter do it meself?'

'If yer won't listen ter reason I'll wash me 'ands of yer,' Ruby said sharply.

'Stop naggin' an' go an' get that form fer me ter sign,' Lizzie demanded.

Ruby shook her head in exasperation as she got up and Lizzie chuckled. 'Oi, deafy. I'm goin' 'ome.'

'That'll be nice,' the old lady said closing her eyes.

Ruby was soon back, accompanied by the ward sister who looked darkly at Lizzie Roach. 'I won't have it, do you hear, Mrs Roach? No one has ever discharged themselves on my ward.'

'There's a first time fer everyfing,' Lizzie told her grinning. 'Now where's that paper I gotta sign?'

'I won't permit it.'

'Oh yer won't, won't yer? Well try an' stop me.'

'Lizzie, be sensible,' Ruby implored her.

The old lady slipped her feet over the side of the bed. 'Now are you gonna draw those screens or am I gonna show all the visitors me bare arse?'

The sister pulled the plastic curtains around the bed with a look of disgust on her angular face. 'I'm going to ask you for the last time to reconsider your actions,' she said sternly.

'Gimme that form ter sign.'

'I haven't got it with me.'

'Well go an' get it.'

The sister looked at Ruby appealingly. 'Can't you talk some sense into her?' she said sighing.

'I've bin tryin' fer years,' Ruby replied.

'Just remember that Mrs Roach could aggravate that injury going home tonight on the bus or tram,' the sister warned her before leaving the old lady's bedside.

'She's right, yer know,' Ruby said in a last attempt to make Lizzie change her mind. 'It'll be awkward gettin' on the tram, an' it might be full downstairs. You couldn't climb up those steep stairs.'

Lizzie rewarded her with a wide, toothless grin as she reached into the bedside locker for her purse. 'We ain't goin' 'ome on no bus or tram. We're takin' a taxi, an' I'm payin'. Now tell Pratty Lill ter bring me that form ter sign, an' while yer at it tell 'er ter phone fer a cab.'

Chapter Thirty

Freda Lo left her first-floor flat and walked out of the buildings into the Sunday morning sunshine, and as she made her way to St Barnabas church she was feeling very worried. Tommy had not been home for two days. That in itself was not so unusual since his involvement with the Tong often meant that she did not see him for days at a time, but this morning Freda had had a note pushed under her door telling her that her son wanted to meet her at the church at eleven o'clock. It was an alarming way of contacting her and she could only think that his life must be in danger and he was hiding from someone.

It was a good time to meet, Freda told herself. There was a morning service at eleven o'clock and she and her son would be less conspicuous with people milling around. It was also the last place the Tong would be expected to visit, and in any case they would most likely be sleeping off the after-effects of a night spent at the Peking Club. Nevertheless Freda was wary as she joined the worshippers who were entering the churchyard.

The elderly vicar was standing at the top of the stone steps beneath the portico with a beaming smile on his ruddy face and a Bible clutched to his snow-white cassock, and he did not notice Freda veer off and make her way to the rear of the gardens. Ten minutes later the first of the morning hymns rang out and as Freda listened to 'All Things Bright and Beautiful' she became anxious. Tommy had still not shown up. Normally he could be relied on where time was concerned and she hoped and prayed that nothing bad had happened to him.

Five minutes later she saw him coming towards her with a smile on his handsome face and she wanted to shake him. 'I was gettin' worried,' she growled at him. 'You said eleven. It must be twenty past at least.'

'I'm sorry, Ma, but I had to take a roundabout route.'

'What is it? What trouble are you in?' Freda asked quickly.

Tommy Lo sat down on the wooden bench next to his mother and looked around cautiously. 'Do you remember the last time we talked here?' he asked.

She nodded. 'I told yer then that you should go back ter sea an' I 'aven't changed my opinion, fer what it's worth.'

'Well I've been to Liverpool,' Tommy said smiling.

'Liverpool?'

'Yeah. I've signed on as a cook with a Liverpool shipping line,' he told her. 'They have ships going back and forth to the Far East and Australia. There'll be a place for me soon and I've got to keep in touch with their London office in Canning Town.'

Freda looked at him with concern. 'It's the right move, but why the change o' mind? You're in some bad trouble, I can tell.'

The young man sighed and hunched his shoulders. 'It seems I've upset the Tong and they're not too pleased.'

Freda looked aghast. 'Does that mean . . .'

'The special vote,' Tommy completed it for her.

'What 'ave yer done?'

'It's a long story, Ma,' he said heavily. 'There's no time to go all through it now, but I'm being pulled in two directions at once and I can't go on that way.'

'Is Kennedy getting rough on yer?' she asked.

He nodded. 'The killing of the candlemaker was the last straw. People in high places have been demanding a clean-up in Limehouse and Kennedy wants names. The killing wasn't sanctioned by the Tong but I'm pretty certain that Billy Chou was responsible. On top of that there's a big consignment of opium due very soon and I've got a gut feeling that Kennedy's been tipped off. That's the only reason he's holding fire. Under normal circumstances the Tong members would have all been pulled in for questioning.'

Freda nodded. 'In ovver words 'e's givin' yer just enough rope to 'ang yerselves.'

Tommy smiled wryly. 'The consignment's bound for the Peking Club and when the Tong take delivery they'll all be picked up along with Husi Kang. The police know he's in the centre of the opium trade locally but they've never been able to prove it. Husi's always been one step ahead of them, but this time, if I'm right, the police will know just when to swoop and the Tong and the opium dealers will all end up behind bars for a very long time.'

'And that means you too.'

'No, Ma,' he said reassuringly. 'I've been planning my survival for some time now. You know the ways of the Tong. Any leader has to watch his back and I'm no exception. I'm tired of the violence, tired of witnessing the terror and the pain inflicted in the name of honour and blind obedience. I want out. I want to travel the world and find a little peace and happiness. I want to put all this behind me.'

Freda took a deep breath. 'It's good that you feel as yer do,' she told him with a fond look in her eyes. 'I could never understand the reason why yer joined the Tong, but I won't waste time now with recriminations. I'm just so 'appy that yer gettin' out of it. Your farvver was a good man and there's a lot of 'im in you. 'E loved the sea an' 'ad a cravin' ter see the world an' all those different countries. We spent many 'appy years tergevver, an' now that 'e's gone you're all I 'ave left. This place isn't what it was an' most of me friends 'ave gone, but I still carry the memories inside me.'

Tommy Lo nodded slowly. 'Knowing that makes it easier for me, Ma,' he said. 'I want you to leave this place. It could be dangerous for you to stay now. When the Tong come looking and they can't find me they might well use you as a lever to force me into giving myself up.'

'But where could I go?' Freda asked quickly.

'Last time we spoke you mentioned about going to live in Norfolk,' he replied. 'It's far enough away from London for you to be safe and I'd rest easier.'

Freda stroked the side of her face thoughtfully. 'I do 'ave some cousins in Newmarket an' there's a niece livin' near Yarmouth. I s'pose I could pay 'em a visit an' see if one of 'em could put me up fer a few days while I look fer a place.'

'Do it, Ma,' Tommy appealed to her. 'When you're settled you can give the shipping office your address and they'll get it to me. We can meet up when my ship docks in Liverpool. I could come to see you when I'm between ships.'

'All right, son, I'll do it,' Freda said positively.

'Do it soon, Ma. Don't waste any time. It's important for both of us.'

She forced a smile as he stood up to leave. 'I'll go termorrer.'

Tommy smiled back at her, then his face became serious. 'Before I leave, I want to ask you one thing. Don't believe the stories you'll hear about me, however plausible they sound. I tell you now on my life that what I've done to upset the Tong was honourable and done for a very good reason. I won't get the chance to see you again before you leave London, so make sure when you get to Norfolk that you send a forwarding address to the Canning Town office of the shipping line. Here's their address.'

Freda took the slip of paper and glanced down at it, and the letters began to swim as tears filled her tired eyes. 'Don't let the Tong take yer, Tommy,' she implored him. 'I know enough about what goes on when a special vote's called. They'll 'unt yer down like an animal an' they'll show no mercy.'

Tommy smiled. 'They won't take me, Ma,' he replied. 'I've got the advantage of knowing their intentions beforehand.'

''Ow did yer find out what they were up to?' Freda asked.

'A young man called Ti San used to work for Ho Chang the laundryman whose business is over the river in Bermondsey . . .'

'I remember Ho Chang,' Freda cut in. ''E used ter be in Pennyfields.'

Tommy nodded. 'Anyway, when he got into trouble with

the Tong he decided to let Ti San go for his safety. I'm known to Ti San and he asked me if I knew of any jobs he could apply for. I spoke to Husi Kang who took him on to serve on the tables and it was Ti San who warned me about what's developing. Apparently he was taking some refreshment to Husi's office and he overheard Ho Chang's name being mentioned, and mine in the same breath. He said he listened from outside the door and heard enough to realise that both our lives were in danger.'

'Where will yer go while yer waitin' fer yer ship?' Freda asked with concern. 'Couldn't you wait up in Liverpool? It'll be much safer than 'ere.'

'There are things I have to do here first,' he replied, 'but I promise you that once I've finished I'll go straight to Liverpool. Just think, I'll be able to send you cards and letters from all parts of the world.'

'Just stay safe, that's all I ask,' Freda said tearfully.

'And you promise me you'll leave Limehouse as soon as you possibly can,' Tommy Lo said as he took her by the shoulders. 'Now come on. No tears, Ma,' he said softly. 'I want to remember a happy face wearing a big smile when I'm far out at sea.'

She sniffed loudly and gave him a wide smile. 'There, now off yer go, an' may the good Lord sit on yer shoulder always.'

'He will, Ma,' the young man said as he kissed her on the cheek, then he turned away and walked quickly from the church gardens.

Freda sat for a while alone with her sad thoughts, then as the congregation began to leave the church she got up and walked towards the steps. It had been many years since she had set foot inside St Barnabas, but today she hoped that she might be forgiven her long lapse, and that whoever reigned in Heaven might listen to her prayer, and take heed.

Kay turned over on to her back in the bed and opened her eyes. She could hear church bells in the distance and the sounds of domesticity coming from the tiny kitchen across the landing. Her nakedness and the fact that she was not in her own bed did not trouble her, but she pulled the bedclothes up around her chin and had a big yawn. As if to reassure herself she eased her arm from under the sheets and glanced at the solitaire diamond ring on her third finger. It was real enough, and so was the delicious feeling of being fulfilled. Joey had been very gentle and understanding; he had had to be, she recalled. She wanted him so much and let him know it, but her body had tensed up at the crucial moment leaving her in despair. He had understood and caressed her tenderly as he whispered sweet words of love, slowly dispelling her fears and anxiety until she was shaking with desire. He had taken her out of herself and she finally responded in the way she wanted to, giving herself to him unashamedly.

Joey's hair was still a mess when he came back into the bedroom carrying two large mugs of tea. 'I'm sorry about this,' he said grinning. 'In all the films I've seen the lover brings the tea in a china cup an' saucer wiv a silver spoon, but I can't remember where I've put the best china.'

'Not even a biscuit,' Kay remarked disdainfully as she sat up with the sheets still held around her neck.

Joey's face dropped. 'I knew there was somefing I fergot when I went shoppin',' he replied.

'I'm only teasin' yer,' Kay said quickly. 'This tea's like the nectar o' the gods.'

'As a matter o' fact I've only got these two mugs, one large dinner plate an' a couple o' smaller plates,' Joey confessed as he sat down on the edge of the bed. 'I got plenty o' knives an' forks though.'

She smiled at him and he suddenly became embarrassed. 'Was it good last night?' he asked, a sudden anxiety in his eyes.

Kay put the mug down on the bedside cabinet and let the sheets drop as she held out her arms to him. ''Old me, Joey, an' I'll tell yer,' she said softly.

He took her in his arms and stroked her back gently. 'When I woke up this mornin' I felt terribly guilty,' he admitted. 'I'd given yer the ring an' we'd enjoyed a lovely evenin' tergevver. On top o' that we both 'ad quite a lot ter drink an' I 'ad this terrible feelin' when I woke up that I'd taken advantage of yer.'

'You were wonderful, Joey, an' I feel like I wanna shout it out ter the world.'

'Don't, fer Gawd's sake,' the young man said, making big eyes at her. 'My landlady warned me about bringin' women back when I first moved in 'ere, an' I told 'er she needn't worry 'cos I was a confirmed bachelor.'

Kay brought her hand up to her mouth. 'What will she say now?'

Joey shrugged his shoulders. 'I'll just tell 'er we're engaged. Don't worry, ole Clarrie ain't the dragon people make out. She won't give me no grief, well not much.'

'I still can't believe it,' Kay said, holding her hand up to the light. 'See 'ow the light catches the diamond.'

'There's just one fing, Kay,' Joey remarked as he stood up. 'Could yer keep that ring out o' sight while it's still 'ot?'

Kay threw a pillow at him. 'Go an' wash those mugs up while I get dressed,' she told him.

Joey had still not come back into the room by the time Kay had made herself presentable to the world and she sighed with sheer happiness as she sat on the side of the bed facing the window. Down below she could see two young children sitting at the kerbside watching another youngster spinning a top and an old couple walking along arm in arm. They would be on their way to church, she thought, or the Sunday market. Come on, Joey, leave what you're doing and take me in your arms. Whisper the words I want to hear and make my day complete. This was true love and it always had been with her and Joey. She had never stopped loving him, even after they split up. He was the only man she could ever truly love, the man who had taken her virginity on a cold wet night in a warehouse doorway, the man who had won her back and given her so much happiness these last few weeks. She was aching for him again but she sighed in resignation. She should really be getting off home. Her parents would be worried even though she had told them she was going to a party and would be staying over.

There were footsteps on the stairs and she heard Joey talking to his landlady in a low voice. A few minutes later he came into the bedroom with a smile on his handsome face and took her in his arms.

'What did she 'ave ter say?' Kay asked fearfully.

Joey laughed. 'She told me I was a naughty boy an' I told 'er I've just got engaged. Then she said she 'oped I wouldn't make an 'abit of it, to which I replied, of course not, Mrs Groombridge. Then I give 'er a peck on the cheek an' she gave me a big smile. I bet it's bin years since anyone gave the poor ole cow a kiss, judgin' by the way she reacted.'

'Joey, you're a charmer,' Kay said as she nestled close to him.

'Yeah I know,' he replied with a straight face.

'I'd better be goin',' she told him.

'Yeah, OK,' he said. 'I'll walk yer 'ome. I gotta see your bruvver about that trouble at the Chinky laundry.'

'I don't want you two gettin' involved any furvver,' Kay said firmly. 'From what Paul told me the laundryman's run up a big gamblin' debt an' this Chinese gang from Lime'ouse came over the water after 'im.'

'They're called Tongs,' Joey corrected her.

'Gangs, tongs, I don't care what they call 'em, you just stay clear,' she insisted. 'It's not your fight.'

'It's not as easy as that, Kay,' he said with a frown. 'Me an' Paul go back a long way. 'Is trouble's my trouble. Anyway I just wanted ter tell 'im I've got some backin' amongst the market men. If that Tong comes over this side o' the water causin' trouble they'll be met wiv more than they can 'andle.'

The sun had gone in behind a bank of cloud and suddenly Kay felt a cold shiver run the length of her spine. Euphoria was such a fleeting state, she sighed to herself.

Chapter Thirty-One

Ruby Neal had always enjoyed Sunday mornings. A panful of sizzling bacon, toast on the go under the grill and eggs spattering in the small frying-pan were things that helped to set it aside from the weekday morning rush. The sound of church bells coming through the open scullery door made the day seem special, and the earthy smell from the garden after the night rain was something she could enjoy at leisure too. Her daughter Kay would invariably be helping her get the breakfast ready, with Paul popping his tousled head round the door to check on their progress, a famished look on his unshaven face as the eggs were carefully scooped from the hot fat on to a plate.

On this Sunday morning, however, Ruby looked sad and worried as she prepared the food. Kay had stayed out all night and was still not home, and Paul had got up and rushed out after making do with toast and marmalade for his breakfast. Jim had been wearing a sorrowful expression when he looked into the scullery to declare that he wasn't hungry and a bacon sandwich would do, which made her want to fling the frying-pan at him. He was making her feel as though she was to blame for the upset and the bad atmosphere in the home. How was she supposed to react?

347

He had gone out last night after putting in a full day's overtime at the factory and come home late, expecting her to believe that he had spent the evening in a pub. He had been with her, that trollop, it was obvious.

Ruby scooped a fried egg on to the plate beside slices of streaky bacon and took it into the parlour. 'This is what you always 'ave on Sundays,' she said coldly as she put the plate down on the table.

He did not reply as he picked up his knife and fork and she went back into the scullery. It was all right for Bel to give her advice on bringing things out into the open, she sighed, but it wasn't happening to her. Where could she start, and did she want to, even though she had told Bel that she did? Maybe she should just tell him to go. It seemed as though that was what he really wanted, but was too cowardly to say so. Perhaps she should tell Kay and Paul that their father was seeing someone else. They both knew that something was wrong.

Ruby transferred a panful of boiling water from the copper into the sink and proceeded to wash up. There was a lot she could do to keep out of Jim's way. There were the beds to change and the usual household chores to take care of, but she could raise no enthusiasm. It didn't seem to matter now if the chores got left. Jim was welcome to smoke in the house if he wanted to and he could walk all over the clean mats with his work boots for all she cared, which would no doubt please Bel Allenby. 'Don't live a lie any more,' she had told her, which was a nice way of saying let the house go to pot. It was like locking the stable door after the horse had bolted, she thought.

As she worked away at the frying-pan with a pot scourer

Ruby began to dwell on the other woman in Jim's life. What was she like? Was she more enthusiastic in bed? Was she married? How was this woman able to lure him away?

'That was nice, fank you,' Jim said as he came into the scullery and put his empty plate down on the draining-board.

'What's she like?' Ruby said mechanically, fixing him with her eyes.

'Don't quiz me, Ruby, it's over an' done wiv,' he replied.

'I need ter know.'

'What good will it do?'

'Is she prettier than me?'

'No.'

'Is she younger?'

'I can't stand this,' he grunted.

'Well yer'd better get used to it, 'cos I wanna know what it is that made yer go for 'er in the first place,' Ruby said forcibly.

'I dunno,' he sighed. 'It was just a brief affair. It's over an' done wiv.'

'I don't believe yer. That's where yer were last night, isn't it?'

'I've already told yer,' he answered. 'I went fer a couple o' pints ter give me time ter fink fings over.'

'Don't lie ter me, Jim, you're a bad liar. It shows in yer face.'

'I told yer, I went fer a drink.'

'I wanna know who it is,' Ruby said, her eyes burning into his.

'What good would it do?'

'I'd go an' see 'er, an' warn 'er off.'

'It wouldn't serve no purpose,' he replied. 'I keep tellin' yer, it's over an' done wiv.'

'I don't believe yer, Jim,' she said, shaking her head.

He sat down heavily at the small table. 'Look, it was wrong what I did, an' I don't expect you ter fergive or ferget,' he said quietly, 'but if we're gonna live under the same roof we've gotta stop torturin' each ovver.'

''Ow do we do that?' Ruby asked.

'By acceptin' the fact that none of us are perfect,' Jim replied. 'You've always made demands on us. Don't smoke in the 'ouse, take yer boots off before yer come in, an' everyfing done on a rota. It's like bein' back in the services.'

'OK, so I've bin obsessive in the 'ome,' Ruby conceded angrily, 'but like you just said, none of us are perfect. Anyway I s'pose it's missed your notice that there's an ashtray in the parlour, an' I don't go on about yer slippers when yer get 'ome at night.'

'It's not missed me notice,' he replied. 'But the dos an' don'ts 'ave gone on fer so long I feel guilty about lightin' up a fag in the 'ouse, an' I still look fer me slippers. OK, it's partly my fault fings are the way they are. I should 'ave done what a lot o' men would 'ave done an' defied yer at the beginnin', but I didn't. I knew what it meant to yer, an' me an' the kids went along wiv it.'

Ruby took a deep breath, feeling that now was the time. 'You're right, it did mean a lot ter me,' she began. 'In my stupid way I saw it as no more than was expected from a wife. I wanted you ter be proud o' me an' the way I managed the 'ome. I told yer often enough that it was the way I was brought up. But what you didn't know was, the 'ouse I lived in as a kid wasn't the place I made it out ter be. It was a filfy rotten 'ole, wiv bugs breedin' in the bedsprings an' chamber-pots under the bed spillin' over wiv piss. My parents were past carin', wiv me farvver drunk most o' the time. That was the child'ood I remember, an' I could never bring meself ter talk about it, to anybody, so I tried ter bury it. I promised meself early on that when I got married my place would always be immaculate. I invented this nice little story an' I almost got ter believin' it meself. It was Bel Allenby who made me realise where I was goin' wrong. It was 'er who said I was livin' a lie, an' until I came ter terms wiv it I was on a loser. Well, I've come ter terms wiv it, so when yer look at that ashtray an' yer can't find yer slippers yer'll know why.'

Jim was silent for a few moments, letting it all sink in, and then he looked up into Ruby's eyes. 'I wish you'd 'ave told me at the start,' he said with a sigh.

'I just couldn't,' she said shaking her head slowly. 'I was too ashamed.'

Jim clasped his hands together and studied his thumbnails for a few moments. ''Ave the kids guessed about me?' he asked.

'I've not said anyfing, but they know somefink's wrong,' Ruby replied.

'Maybe it'd be better if I left,' he remarked.

'That's the easy way out,' she said bitterly.

'I wasn't finkin' o' me, I was finkin' o' you an' the kids,' Jim answered.

'I'm not gonna tell yer what ter do,' Ruby said resolutely. 'That's fer you ter decide.'

He got up and left the scullery, returning with his tobacco tin and the ashtray. 'Fanks fer tellin' me about what it was like for yer as a kid,' he said as he sat down at the table once more. 'It makes me understand a lot o' fings.'

Ruby sat down facing him and watched as he rolled a cigarette. 'Am I so unattractive?' she asked quietly.

'It'd be easier fer me if yer were,' he replied. 'There's bin so many times I've wanted us ter make love, but it didn't 'appen, Ruby. There was always excuses. I got ter finkin' that when it did 'appen yer did it out o' duty, not 'cos yer needed me.'

'So yer sought the company of a woman who made yer feel special,' Ruby said bitterly. 'Yer wanted a woman who was ready an' willin', who told yer the fings yer wanted to 'ear, fings yer never 'eard from me.'

'No, I've always wanted you, but I fell inter the trap,' Jim confessed. 'I dunno, call it feelin' sorry fer meself, bein' bloody stupid, whatever. All I know is that love didn't enter into it. It was purely physical.'

'If there's gonna be any way back fer us yer've gotta finish wiv this woman,' Ruby told him firmly.

'I've already said it's over,' he replied.

'Don't compound fings by lyin' ter me, Jim,' she said. 'Yer've never bin able ter lie ter me. I can see it in yer face. Eivver finish wiv 'er or finish wiv me. I won't play second fiddle to anuvver woman. I just couldn't.'

He lit his cigarette and then met the steady gaze of her eyes. Her pain cut into him like a knife and he hated himself. That Saturday night spent with Angela had been unbelievably passionate. She had sought to make him forget his strong feelings of guilt and had almost succeeded, but deep down he knew that somehow he must find the strength to finish the affair before it destroyed him. 'You say I can't lie ter yer, Ruby,' he said quietly, 'so when I tell yer that you're the only woman I've loved, or will ever love, you'll know that I'm bein' sincere.'

'If you still love me as yer say yer do then it should be easy ter get 'er out of yer life,' Ruby told him as tears filled her eyes. 'Do it now.'

He stubbed out his cigarette and watched as she walked out of the scullery. It should be easy, he thought, but it wasn't. Angela had a hold on him that he couldn't find the strength to tear himself away from. Out of sight she wasn't daunting. He could tell himself, go over in his mind, the things he would say to her which would put an end to the madness. He understood why he had to do it and she would not be able to dispute what he said to her. When he came face to face with her, however, his resolve evaporated and he was hers, a plaything that satisfied her needs and kept her happy and amused.

Jim got up and paced heavily through the scullery doorway into the midday sun. The garden looked immaculate, with the bedding plants beginning to show patches of colour. Some empty flowerpots were piled up neatly by the shed and he walked up to them. He had intended to find a space for them inside the shed, but instead he stretched out his foot and kicked them over.

The loop of the Thames looked like a wide band of quicksilver from the promenade high above in Greenwich Park, where the two young people strolled hand in hand near the meridian that divided the world.

'I can't let yer go, Mei Li,' he said with passion in his voice. 'It's like I've known yer fer ever.'

She sighed deeply as she gazed down at the tramp steamer making its way slowly towards the Pool of London. 'Our lives began on the same day, Paul, and perhaps we were destined to meet,' she said softly, 'but I can't stay here in London for always. My guardian is getting old and he's very tired. He's anxious to go home once things have been resolved with his brother.'

'But yer don't 'ave ter go wiv 'im,' Paul argued. 'Yer've lived an' worked 'ere fer some time now an' this is yer 'ome.'

'My roots are Chinese, Paul,' she replied, 'but I can't return to China now that there's a Communist government, nor would I want to. My happy memories are of growing up in Singapore. That's my home now and I must go back there soon.'

Paul stopped beside a wooden bench and turned to face her. 'I know the real reason why yer goin' back an' it's killin' me. I can't bear ter fink of yer bein' wiv anyone else, bein' married to a man you 'ardly know.'

Mei Li sat down on the bench, still clutching his hand and he moved closer to her. 'This last few weeks 'ave bin the best I've ever known,' he said with feeling. 'I live fer every minute we're tergevver. I love yer smile an' the way yer 'ave of makin' me feel ten feet tall. I know I could make yer really 'appy. Stay, Mei Li. Stay wiv me. Li Fong is an old man in the autumn of 'is life. 'E'll understand. 'E wants the best for yer an' I'll make 'im see that your 'appiness is all that's important to me. I'd take good care of yer, an' one day we could visit Singapore. You wouldn't be lost to 'im fer ever.'

Mei Li placed her other hand over his and squeezed hard. 'I've never been so happy as this last few weeks, and I will never let the memories die, Paul. They'll be all I need to sustain me. When I feel sad I'll close my eyes and see your smile. When I feel the cool breeze on my face I'll remember the rose garden you showed me. I'll smell the scent of the flowers and feel the touch of your hand.'

He sat down beside her, his eyes pleading. 'I could never be wiv anyone else, Mei Li,' he said hoarsely. 'Would you want me ter spend the rest o' me life alone, dyin' a little every day, tortured in the knowledge that you were bein' 'eld in anuvver man's arms?'

'Please, Paul, don't make it any more difficult than it is already,' she replied with a sob. 'I have to do what's expected of me. I owe my life to Li Fong and I could never desert him. He wants only for me to be happy and secure, and in his mind the answer lies back in Singapore.'

The young man lifted his head and saw a scurrying cloud, a clipper ship in full sail on a bottomless blue sea. It was carrying her away, far away, and he closed his eyes tightly, searching for the words that would make her stay. It was hopeless. She was a child of the Orient, her future planned for her by an old man who would never live long enough to see her wither in the cage he had made for her. 'Look at me, Mei Li,' he told her. 'I can see the lantern flame in your eyes. Will it flicker an' die when you an' Li Fong sail away?'

'The lantern you have lit will always burn brightly, Paul,' she whispered.

'Will your future 'usband see it when 'e looks into your eyes?' he asked her.

'The flame was kindled by you, and only you will be able to see it,' she replied.

'I wanna make love to yer, Mei Li,' he said, hardly recognising his own voice.

'I want you to,' she murmured, her cheeks flushing.

'I wanna wrap you up in me arms an' let the feelin' burn inter me, like a brand that'll mark me fer life,' he said in a cracked voice.

A large cloud obscured the sun, and the glittering silver below them changed to grey. The tramp steamer had disappeared, and as the rising breeze sent a chestnut leaf tumbling by their feet Mei Li shivered. Paul stood up and pulled her to him. His arms went round her tiny waist and he leaned down to kiss her rosebud lips. The feeling was delicious and he shivered too.

'I must get back,' she said. 'Li Fong will be expecting me. Su Chang is cooking a meal for us.'

They walked down the steep hill, beneath the high, wide chestnut trees and out through the wrought-iron gates. On the tram they sat close, their bodies touching, and Mei Li slipped her hand in his. 'Smile, Paul,' she said quietly. 'Your smile makes me happy.'

He forced a smile, his eyes clouded with sadness, and Mei Li leaned her head on his shoulder. 'I have never made love, Paul,' she said suddenly.

Paul felt his heart leap and he gently kissed the top of her head. The cloud passed from the face of the sun and it shone brightly again, reflecting blindingly from shopfronts in the street. The young man looked up at the sky through the dusty window of the tram and sighed deeply. Today was for savouring. Tomorrow was another day.

Chapter Thirty-Two

On Monday morning after her family had left for work Ruby washed up the breakfast things, and instead of drying them with a tea towel she left them piled up on the draining-board. It was something she would normally not do, but this morning she felt different. The blackbird was back on the fence, preening itself in the warmth of the sun, and it suddenly flew down to search for likely titbits amongst the strewn flowerpots beside the shed. They could stay where they were too, she thought as she glanced at the alarm clock on the dresser. If she got ready now there would be more time for her to check on Lizzie Roach and have a cup of tea with Bel before dashing off to the surgery.

Ruby hurried up the stairs and into her bedroom. This hair looks a mess, she sighed to herself as she sat down at the dressing-table. She gathered it up in her hand and turned sideways to see the effect. It was a bit daring for work, but never mind, it would make a change.

'Mornin', Ruby,' Connie Wilson called out as she saw her next-door neighbour stepping out into the sunlight. 'Anuvver lovely day.'

'Yeah it is,' Ruby replied. 'By the way, 'ow's George?'

'Much better fanks, luv. 'E went back ter work this mornin'.'

'Glad to 'ear it,' Ruby said smiling as she walked along to Lizzie's house.

Myrtle Thompson at number 3 was watering her flower tubs. 'Mornin', Ruby. Nice day.'

'Yes it is,' Ruby replied. 'Is Ron on earlies?'

'Nah 'e's still snorin',' Myrtle told her. 'I let 'im sleep in when 'e's on lates. I don't like 'im under me feet when I've got fings ter do.'

Nora Mason at number 4 was busy adjusting the net curtains in the parlour and when she saw Ruby talking to Myrtle, she hurried to the front door and stood arms akimbo as she viewed her efforts with the curtains. 'Oh 'ello, Ruby,' she said casually. 'I've just put these new nets up. D'yer fink they look all right? I got 'em down the Blue on Saturday. They 'ave some good stuff on that stall.'

'Are they starched?' Myrtle asked her.

'Course they're starched.'

'They look very nice,' Ruby told her.

''Ave you 'ad yer 'air done?' Nora enquired.

'Nah, I just done it different,' Ruby said with a smile.

'It looks very nice pulled round the back like that. It makes yer look younger,' Nora remarked.

'Fanks. I did it fer a change.'

'Are yer goin' in ter see Lizzie?' Myrtle asked.

'Yeah I'm just gonna look in.'

'Don't worry, if she wants 'er rocker pulled out my Ron'll do it, soon as 'e gets up.'

'Fanks, I'll tell 'er,' Ruby replied.

Lizzie Roach was sitting by the hearth when Ruby let

herself in. 'I was 'opin' yer'd look in, gel,' she said. 'I need some more o' those pills yer got fer me. You know the ones.'

'Yeah I know,' Ruby said, looking anxiously at her. 'Is yer back playin' yer up again?'

'Nah, it's me leg.'

'Well what d'yer want liver pills for?' Ruby asked.

Lizzie looked up with a sorrowful expression on her lined face. 'Fer the pain. This bloody leg's bin givin' me gyp all night long. Those pills yer got me took the pain away from me back an' I fink they'll do me leg good too.'

'I doubt it, luv, but I'll get yer some anyway,' Ruby sighed. 'Now d'yer want me ter do anyfing before I leave fer work?'

'Nah, I've just 'ad a cuppa an' a slice o' toast.'

'Ron Thompson'll be in later ter take yer rocker outside,' Ruby told her.

Lizzie nodded and reached down by her side. 'I found this ole walkin' stick,' she announced. 'It belonged ter that ole bastard o' mine. 'E cracked me round the bonce wiv it one night when 'e come in pissed. Did I go fer 'im. 'E run out in the karsey an' locked 'imself in. I'd 'ave swung fer 'im that night if I could 'a' got 'old of 'im.'

'Never mind, Lizzie, yer all right now,' Ruby said kindly, 'an' yer can sit out yer front an' dream away all day, as long as yer remember yer cap.'

'Yeah, better than sittin' in that bloody ward,' the old lady remarked. 'Bed-pans indeed. I nearly 'it the roof when that scatty, jumped-up prat told me I mustn't get out o' bed.'

'Let me shake yer cushion up be'ind yer back, it's all screwed up,' Ruby said as she went over to her.

361

'Nah, leave it,' Lizzie replied. 'You get off ter work, an' don't ferget me pills.'

Ruby left her and knocked at Bel's front door. 'Got the kettle on?' she asked when her friend answered.

'Come in, luv, it won't take long,' she said smiling. 'What yer done ter yer 'air? It looks different.'

'Are yer sure it looks all right?' Ruby asked.

'Yeah, it makes yer look younger.'

'That's what Nora Mason just said.'

'Well she's right, fer once.'

Ruby made herself comfortable in the armchair by the hearth. 'I've left the washin' up on the drainin'-board an' I ain't even opened the curtains in the bedroom,' she declared.

'Slovenly cow,' Bel told her as she went out to the scullery.

Soon the two friends were enjoying mugs of tea and sharing a plateful of broken biscuits and Bel smiled as she searched for another bourbon. 'Nora gave me these,' she said. 'She got 'em down the Blue. There's a stall down there that sells rejects from Peek Frean's. A tanner fer a great big bagful.'

Ruby smiled as she dunked half a ginger snap. 'I've not even shook the mats this mornin'.'

'Good fer you.'

'The funny fing is, I couldn't care less.'

'Nor should yer.'

'I'd never let the place go ter rack an' ruin though.'

'Nah, course yer wouldn't.'

'I'm gonna do a stew fer a change terday.'

'That'll be nice.'

Ruby saw the twitch in the corner of Bel's mouth and she pouted her lips. 'You're mockin' me.'

Bel leaned forward and touched her hand in a spontaneous gesture. 'Nah, I'm not, luv,' she said quietly. 'I'm just so pleased that yer seein' sense. Plan a day at a time, not yer 'ole life. All right if the place gets a bit scruffy, yer can always 'ave a day goin' all frew it. That's what I do.'

Ruby nodded. 'Me an' Jim got talkin' yesterday,' she remarked.

'That's good,' Bel replied. 'Did it 'elp clear the air?'

'Well, I dunno about that, but at least 'e knows the trufe now.'

'Yer told 'im?'

'Yeah I did.'

'Was 'e surprised?'

''E certainly looked it.'

Bel squeezed Ruby's hand in hers. 'Well, at least it'll make 'im fink.'

'Yesterday was the first time since we've bin married that 'e smoked in the 'ouse,' Ruby went on. 'I asked 'im about this woman 'e's seein' an' 'e told me 'e'd finished wiv 'er.'

'An' do yer believe 'im?'

Ruby shook her head. 'Jim could never lie ter me,' she said sadly. 'That's 'ow it all came out in the first place. I honestly believe 'e's tryin' ter finish it though.'

Bel leaned back in her chair. 'I'd give 'im some time, luv,' she advised. ''E's already cursin' the day 'e got involved wiv this bitch. 'E's got too much ter lose if 'e carries on seein' 'er. All right, I know it ain't gonna be easy, but try ter be patient. Anuvver fing. Don't allow yerself ter mope. Yer've started right. When Jim comes 'ome ternight the first fing 'e's gonna notice is that yer've done yer 'air differently. Then 'e's gonna smell the stew. They're only little fings but they're enough ter be goin' on wiv. Don't empty the ashtray neivver, an' fer Gawd's sake don't stick them slippers of 'is in the passage. Stick 'em somewhere out the way an' if 'e asks for 'em tell 'im yer don't know where they are. Like I said the ovver day, yer gotta stop lyin' ter yerself, an' you 'ave, more ter yer credit. Fings can move on now, an' I bet yer before long that feller o' yours is gonna be all round yer. That's when the crunch'll come. Will yer feel yer can let 'im touch yer again or will yer be repulsed by 'im? Only you can decide. Whatever 'appens, gel, don't let yer 'ead drop.'

'What would I do wivout yer, Bel,' Ruby said with feeling. 'Yer've always bin there fer me.'

'Maybe I'm just an interferin' ole cow,' Bel replied smiling, 'but sometimes yer gotta get involved when yer see fings ain't right wiv yer nearest an' dearest. I ain't got no family ter fret over yer see so I can indulge meself.'

'Yer got me,' Ruby said quietly. 'I treat you like me older sister. I always 'ave.'

Bel gave her another pat on the hand then looked up at the chimer on the mantelshelf. ''Ere, look at the time.'

'Sod me, I'm gonna be late,' Ruby exclaimed with a horrified look as she jumped out of the chair, but Bel's raised eyebrows made her pause. 'What the bloody 'ell am I panickin' for? Me bein' five minutes late won't 'urt 'em.'

'Yer doin' OK, luv,' Bel said, grinning widely. 'Now off yer go, an' walk, don't run.'

*   *   *

Tommy Lo spent Sunday night at the seamen's hostel in Rotherhithe and on Monday morning he decided to pay Li Fong a visit.

'What business brings you back so soon?' Mei Li's guardian asked anxiously.

'We need to talk,' the young man told him.

Li Fong led the way up to his rooms and waved Tommy Lo into a seat. 'You look very troubled. Tell me, what is it?'

The younger man hunched his shoulders. 'My days as the Tong leader are virtually over,' he said quietly. 'Plans to replace me have already been hatched.'

'Will it mean . . . ?'

Tommy Lo's nod answered the unfinished question and Li Fong stroked his thin beard thoughtfully. 'Why are you telling me this? If you do not lead the Tong then what happens to my family doesn't concern you any more. Surely your thoughts should be centred on staying alive.'

The young man ignored his remarks. 'I don't know what's going to happen now that another Tong member seeks to take my place,' he replied. 'I can only guess that the Tong will come for Ho Chang before the week's out.'

'But why?' Li Fong asked anxiously. 'The Tong has my valuable possession in their hands, and if the money owed by my brother is not forthcoming on time then they will be very rich, and I that much poorer.'

Tommy Lo looked down at his clenched hands for a few moments. 'The man who seeks to replace me is called Billy Chou. He is unpredictable. His brains are often scrambled by the amount of drugs he uses, and to him the Tong is everything. I know the man very well and I can tell you that his principal ambition is to become the famed and feared leader of the most powerful Tong outside of China. Killing Ho Chang, and quite possibly his wife too, will not serve to recover the money owed to Husi Kang but it will be enough to strike fear into everyone in Limehouse when the news gets back. That was the reason for my visit. You must tell Ho Chang and his wife to leave Bermondsey, and you and your ward should leave too.'

'But I have not done anything to anger the Tong,' Li Fong said quickly.

Tommy Lo gazed intently into the old man's eyes. 'Listen to me. My mother is the only family I have, and yesterday I warned her too. I told her to leave Limehouse. Billy Chou could use her to get to me just as he could force you to tell him the whereabouts of your brother.'

'How much time do we have?' Li Fong asked.

Tommy Lo stroked his stubbled chin. 'They won't move until they conduct the special vote. Once I am finished Billy Chou will rule supreme.'

'And if you cannot be found?'

'Then he will allow two days at the most before assuming leadership, as laid down in the rules. It's my guess that the Tong will come on Wednesday, and late in the evening when the streets are quiet.'

'Will you leave London too, or will you face them?' Li Fong asked him.

'I'll go back and defend my actions. That at least I'm allowed to do.'

'And if you fail?'

'I'll be hunted down like a wild animal and killed out of

hand, quickly with a sharp thrust, or slowly by a thousand cuts, depending on what kind of fight I put up.'

'Is there no one who you can turn to for help?'

Tommy Lo smiled sardonically. 'Already word is out that the Tong intends to invoke the special vote. When the day is set Limehouse will hold its breath. People will close their doors and shutter their windows. To aid the victim of the vote means certain death. The junior members will be like coiled springs as order turns upside down and mercy is forbidden. To be the executioner, to cut off the dragon's head, will be the one and only desire maddening their minds. The successful one is guaranteed entry into the senior level. If I'm found guilty of betrayal I'll be given ten minutes to make my escape and then the hunt starts. The junior members will be everywhere and it won't be difficult for them to find me. The most a victim can hope for is to battle bravely and die quickly.'

'Then why go back?' Li Fong asked, frowning with confusion. 'Surely you must leave London now.'

'I can't tell you why. It's something I have to do.'

'Forget your notions of honour and bravery. Life itself is more important,' Li Fong said solicitously.

Tommy Lo had been expecting him to bemoan the likely loss of his prized collection of ginger pots, but instead the old man seemed more concerned about the safety of his visitor. 'I'm surprised by your calmness, Li Fong,' he replied. 'Those pots are priceless and there is a very good chance that you'll never lay eyes on them again.'

Li Fong smiled. 'Never is like the blink of an eye, from the perspective of eternity. I am an old man and age brings serenity. I am sad at the thought of losing such a possession, naturally, but my sadness is for Mei Li. The ginger pots were to be given to her on her wedding to Lin Chen once we got back to Singapore.'

'She is spoken for then?' Tommy Lo said in surprise. 'I thought she and the Englishman Paul Neal were . . .'

'He is just a good friend,' Li Fong told him, 'though I feel their friendship threatens to influence her thinking, given the amount of time Mei Li and the young man spend together.'

Tommy Lo chuckled quietly. 'I think that age has not only brought serenity to you, Li Fong, it has clouded your eyes and dulled your perception.'

'How so?'

'I have spent very little time in their company,' Tommy explained, 'but even I have seen the look that passes between them. They're in love.'

'Love?' the old man said sharply. 'It's not love you saw, it's the excitement that bedevils the young before they leave their childhood behind. Love takes time to grow, like a tree spreading its roots deeply and firmly down into the ground. Lin Chen is the man she is to marry, the man who will nurture in her the adult love that sustains this world.'

Tommy Lo shrugged his shoulders. There were too many years between them for him to argue. 'I hope your ward will be happy in Singapore,' he said solemnly. 'Now I must leave. There's much I have to do. Remember what I've told you. Lose no time in persuading your brother and his wife to leave Bermondsey, and do not be tempted to stay behind. It would be very foolish.' He stood up to go. 'There is one thing I want you to do for me. Here's a message for Paul Neal. Can you see that he gets it by this evening?'

Li Fong nodded as he took the sealed envelope. 'Yes, I can do that,' he replied. Then as Tommy Lo reached the door he called him back. 'There is one other course of action you should consider,' he said.

'And what's that?'

'Go to the police. Tell them everything about the Tong in exchange for protection and immunity from prosecution,' Li Fong advised him. 'I'm given to understand that it's possible to make a deal of that sort, which will be honoured.'

'Yes you're right, Li Fong. It is possible to do a deal of that sort,' the young man replied, 'but there would be many of the junior members remaining free. Any one of them with ambition enough could kill me from behind one night in a dark alley. I could never really escape the revenge of the Tong. My way is the only way.'

'And you will die anyway.'

'Only time will tell,' Tommy Lo said with a sly smile. 'There are many things to do and many places to see before I die. I have no intention of giving up my life that easily.'

The old man watched from his window until the fugitive had finally disappeared from view and then he stroked his beard thoughtfully as he sat down again. He had turned out to be quite an enigma, this Tommy Lo. Why should he risk going back to face the Tong when he could quite easily leave the area? Why did he want to contact Paul Neal? What card did he hold that made him seem so confident of defeating the vote against him? It seemed that, as the young man had said himself, only time would tell.

Li Fong looked around the quiet room which had been his home for the past few months. It was time to leave now, leave England for his adopted home in Singapore. It was the time for Mei Li to leave too. The young Englishman was playing much more of a part in her life than was good for her. The parting would be sorrowful, but to delay any further would add to the pain. Mei Li was sensible. She would understand.

Chapter Thirty-Three

On Monday morning Paul Neal was busy wiring up a telephone system in a renovated factory at Dockhead, and during the lunch break he declined his workmates' encouragements to join them at a nearby pub, preferring to eat his sandwiches up on the roof of the building. It was quiet and cool there, and a pleasant relief from the dusty atmosphere inside. It gave him time to think about the future too. He had learned enough to know that time was running short for Ho Chang, and from what Mei Li had told him there seemed little chance of her guardian being able to get the money in time to satisfy the Tong. The old man would lose everything and quite likely decide to return home. Mei Li had hinted as much.

He wondered how long he had to try to persuade her that her future was with him, not with a fat businessman thousands of miles away who would treat her like a chattel. It was wrong of Li Fong to map out her life for her, but Mei Li had simply shrugged her shoulders when he told her so. It was the custom in China, and done for the best reasons, she had said. He tried to impress on her the fact that she was a modern woman living her own life in the West and never likely to return to her country of birth and

371

its old traditions, but it was like hitting his head against a brick wall. Chinese families were beholden to their parents and ancestors, she stressed, and people would hardly ever disregard their parents' wishes. Li Fong was her only family and he had taken it upon himself to provide for her. She owed him much, she owed him her very life, and she could never go against his wishes for her future.

Paul finished the last of his sandwiches and unscrewed the Thermos flask. He was going to lose her, he sighed. Even if they became lovers she would go, content to take the memories with her, leaving him desolate and alone. What could he possibly do to persuade her to stay?

He sipped the hot sweet tea, watching a drifting cloud high up in the deep blue sky as he felt the soft stirrings of the breeze on his face. Maybe he should go to see Li Fong and try to persuade him where Mei Li's happiness lay. He seemed genuine and approachable. Tonight might be the best time, he thought. Mei Li was working late that evening with a party of Chinese businessmen from Hong Kong and Li Fong would be alone.

As he went back to work Paul felt a little better. A new switchboard was being set up in the factory office and the complicated wiring diagrams took up all of his concentration. The afternoon seemed to flash past and that evening as he made his way home he picked up the thread of his thoughts and began to go over in his mind what he would say to Li Fong.

Nora Mason was at her front door talking to Myrtle Thompson as the young man strolled into Tanners Alley and they nodded a little stiffly to him as he walked along to his house.

'I don't know what it's comin' to round 'ere,' Nora was going on. 'I mean ter say, it's frightenin'.'

'Yer right, luv,' Myrtle sided with her. 'I got nuffink against 'em, mind you, but it ain't right to encourage 'em, is it? If we ain't careful this alley's gonna be like bloody Chinatown. When that Chinky woman come down 'ere this afternoon I was gettin' a bit of air at the front door an' I said ter meself, 'old tight, what's goin' on 'ere? I didn't wanna look like I was bein' nosy so I went indoors an' peeped frew me curtains. I saw 'er put this letter frew Ruby's door. What is goin' on there I'd like ter know?'

'It could be that gel's muvver.'

'What gel's muvver?'

'The Chinese gel Paul Neal's cartin' out.'

'I didn't know 'e was goin' out wiv a Chinese gel.'

'It's bin goin' on fer a few weeks now.'

'Well you do surprise me.'

''E brought 'er round 'ere the ovver night.'

'Is that right?'

'I saw 'em walk in the alley. Laughin' an' jokin' they was.'

'What's she like?'

'Very pretty I 'ave ter say.'

'Mind you, they age very quick. It's the life they lead.'

Nora slipped her hands inside her clean apron and crossed her ankles as she leaned against her doorpost. 'I've always believed in live an' let live, but it does worry yer when they start movin' in the area. Before long there'll be aunts an' uncles in tow an' all the ovver relatives an' friends. The place'll be worse than Lime'ouse. My Jack said it's terrible over there, what wiv one fing an' anuvver.'

Lizzie Roach had been taking a nap in her rocking-chair, and although her eyes were still closed she had been awake long enough to get the drift of what her neighbours were talking about. 'I reckon they'll all be chucked out before long,' she remarked from under her tilted cap.

'What makes yer say that, Lizzie?' Nora asked.

'Don't you two ever read the papers?' the old lady said mockingly.

'I don't get much time,' Nora replied.

'Nor do I,' Myrtle added.

'Well, if yer'd take a bit more notice o' what's goin' on in the world yer'd know that China an' Russia signed a pact this year,' Lizzie informed them. 'If Russia starts on us China's gonna come in too.'

'Dear oh dear,' Myrtle said, looking worried.

'I couldn't stand anuvver war,' Nora groaned.

Lizzie chuckled. 'If they drop that there atomic bomb yer won't 'ave time ter worry. Yer'll end up lookin' like a bit o' burnt toast.'

Myrtle looked even more distressed. 'So yer reckon they're gonna chuck 'em all out?'

Lizzie pushed her cap back on her head and nodded. 'Spies, that's what they're worried about. Those Chinkies livin' over 'ere could tell their Government lots o' fings that'd be useful in a war. My daughter took me ter see a film once. It was about German spies. This German butcher 'ad bin livin' in London fer donkey's years an' when the war started 'e sent messages ter Berlin from the back of 'is butcher's shop. People used ter come in 'is shop an' say fings like, "Could I 'ave a bit of extra meat, Fritz?" That was 'is name, Fritz. "I got me son 'ome on leave from the navy an' 'e's goin' back later ternight. As a matter o' fact 'e's sailin' termorrer." So Fritz obliged, an' then 'e went straight ter the transmitter an' reported that there was a convoy leavin' the next day. It transpired the U-boats were waitin' an' we lost 'alf our ships.'

'An' those Chinkies could be doin' the same.'

'Presactly. That's why they're finkin' o' chuckin' 'em all out before it's too late,' Lizzie told them authoritatively.

'I wouldn't be at all surprised if that laundry bloke's got a transmitter in the back of 'is shop,' Myrtle said fearfully.

'Ruby Neal should be more careful, encouragin' such people,' Nora remarked.

'So should young Paul,' Myrtle added. 'They could lock 'im up as well fer bein' a collaborator if war did break out again.'

Paul read the message that had been delivered that afternoon and stroked his chin thoughtfully. 'I wonder what this is all about?' he said.

Ruby read the piece of paper he passed to her and frowned. 'Who's Tommy Lo?' she asked.

'Someone who came ter see Mei Li's guardian when I was there,' Paul told her, not wishing to go into details.

'What's 'e want wiv you?'

'Gawd knows.'

'You be careful,' Ruby warned him. 'I don't like the sound o' this at all.'

Paul grinned. 'Don't worry, Ma. They ain't likely ter whisk me off ter some opium den. 'E just wants me ter meet 'im fer a drink this evenin', that's all.'

Jim Neal picked up the message. 'The Windjammer.

That's a bit of a rough pub as I remember. It's right next door ter the seamen's 'ostel down in Rovver'ithe an' they get all sorts in there.'

'Don't worry, I'll be careful,' Paul assured them.

Kay looked up with concern as she slipped off her shoes. 'It might be a good idea fer me ter let Joey know,' she suggested. ''E could come wiv yer.'

'I don't need a chaperon, Kay,' the young man said quickly.

'Well, you just be careful then,' Ruby said sternly.

At eight o'clock that evening Paul stepped down from a tram outside the Windjammer and walked into the saloon bar. He saw Tommy Lo sitting alone at the far end of the bar and the young Chinese man got up and raised his hand. 'Can I get you a drink?' he asked.

Paul studied him as he came over to the counter. He was short and stocky, muscular rather than fat, with a confident air about him, but he drummed nervously with his fingers on the polished surface while the drink was being pulled and Paul sensed that something serious was on his mind.

'Thanks for coming, Paul Neal,' he said as they carried the drinks back to his table.

'It's no trouble,' Paul replied. 'I'm curious though.'

'I'm not on the best of terms with my workmates any more,' Tommy Lo told him with a self-deprecating grin. 'It seems I'm being replaced, and with Tongs it's not always an amicable business.'

'Yer mean they're out ter get yer?'

'You could put it that way.'

'From what I've seen they're a vicious crowd,' Paul remarked a little archly.

Tommy Lo leaned forward on the iron table. 'I know that you and Mei Li are very close and for that reason I'm going to trust you,' he began. 'Both she and Li Fong are in danger as well as the laundryman. I saw Li Fong today and warned him to leave Bermondsey as soon as possible. Obviously this will affect you, considering your feelings towards Mei Li, but it's for the best. She may tell you where she and her guardian will be going to, but I suspect not. Li Fong will forbid it, considering that they'll be leaving for Singapore very soon.'

''E told you this?'

'Not in as many words but I could tell he intends to return very soon,' Tommy replied. 'He's an old man and his concern is for Mei Li's happiness. He wants to see her settled in marriage before he dies.'

'Fanks fer the information,' Paul said, suddenly looking very glum. 'I don't know what I can do ter make Mei Li stay.'

'Nothing, I fear,' Tommy said quietly. 'I thought you should know, but to be honest there's another reason why I wanted to see you.'

Paul looked mystified. 'Go on.'

Tommy Lo drew breath and expelled it through his clenched teeth. 'The Tong member who's out to finish me is called Billy Chou, and Chou was responsible for the murder of Kano San the candlemaker in Limehouse, though I haven't got any firm proof yet. Another thing. You remember that van we used to visit the laundryman?'

Paul nodded. 'Charlie Wong, knife grinder.'

Tommy Lo smiled. 'It was disguised with tarpaulins carrying those adverts. In fact it's an old Commer belonging to Danny Ling, one of the Tong. It's kept at a warehouse at Canton Street in Limehouse, near the Millwall Dock gates.'

Paul held up his hands in protest. 'Just a second, Tommy. Why are yer tellin' me all this?'

'Because you're the only one I feel I can trust. If anything happens to me in the next twenty-four hours I want you to give this information to the police at Limehouse. It'll have to be on Wednesday morning. Ask to see Chief Inspector Kennedy. Can you remember all this?'

Paul nodded, still looking puzzled. 'But 'ow will I know if anyfing's 'appened ter yer?' he asked.

Tommy Lo thought for a second or two. 'Is there anywhere I can contact you by phone?'

'The Swan pub in Dock'ead,' Paul told him. 'Ask fer Reg Donaldson. 'E'll be sure ter get the message ter me.'

Tommy nodded. 'If you don't hear from me by closing time tomorrow you'll know that I've joined my ancestors, and you'll know what to do.'

Paul studied his face for a moment or two. 'Are yer workin' wiv the police?' he asked.

Tommy Lo smiled cryptically. 'Yes but not out of choice. Now one thing more.'

''Ang on a second,' Paul interrupted, 'let's see if I've got it straight. Billy Chou killed – what was 'is name – the candlemaker?'

'Kano San.'

'Sorry, Kano San the candlemaker. And Charlie Wong the knife grinder's van is a Commer belongin' ter Danny Ling, a Tong member. It's kept at a ware'ouse in – what's the name o' the street again?'

'Canton Street.'

'Canton Street, by the Millwall Dock gates,' Paul reiterated.

Tommy Lo nodded his head seriously. 'Now this is the most important bit of all, and the reason why you must take the information I've given you to the police on Wednesday morning unless you hear from me. A large consignment of opium is due to arrive at King George the Fifth Docks on the *Honi Maru* from Shanghai on Wednesday evening. It's bound for the Peking Club in Pennyfields. If I'm still alive by then I'll deal with it, but if not it'll be up to the police.'

Paul puffed loudly. 'I should really write all this down.'

'Don't,' Tommy said quickly. 'Commit it all to memory, it'll be much safer for you, and for me.'

Paul drained his glass. 'Let me get you a drink,' he offered.

'I could do with a brandy, if that's all right,' the young Chinese man said.

'Sure fing.'

As he went to the counter Paul looked across to the public bar and was a bit taken aback to see Joey Westlake and Butch Wheeler sitting together. They looked up and Joey gave him a large wink and a reassuring smile.

Paul sighed contentedly as he walked back to the table. It was nice to have such friends to count on, he thought to himself.

Tommy Lo took a swig from his glass and pulled a face. 'I'll be going back to Limehouse tomorrow,' he said matter-of-factly. 'By tomorrow night it'll be settled, one way or the other.'

'Why do you 'ave ter go?' Paul asked quickly. 'Surely it'll be best if yer give all this information ter the police an' then disappear. You could stay at our 'ouse. Me muvver would gladly put you up fer a while till yer sorted yerself out.'

'It's very kind of you, but I must go back to face the Tong,' Tommy replied. 'There are important reasons, reasons that I won't trouble you with.'

Paul took a large gulp of beer from his glass. 'I feel sorry fer Li Fong,' he said sadly. 'I don't s'pose 'e'll ever see those ginger pots again.'

Tommy Lo drained his glass. 'Yes, it's a big loss for him. Now I must go. Remember everything I've told you, Paul Neal.'

They shook hands, and after the fugitive had left, the young man went to get his friends.

'Wassa matter wi' you?' Butch asked. 'Yer got a face as long as an 'orse.'

'Nah I'm just finkin',' Paul replied, forcing a grin.

'Finkin'?' Butch said, smirking at Joey. 'I bet that 'urts. You need a decent drink at the Swan by the look o' fings. It's your shout by the way.'

Chapter Thirty-Four

On Tuesday morning Li Fong called into the laundry with bad news. 'The transfer has been held up and I'm afraid there's nothing more I can do, brother,' he said sadly.

Su Chang lowered her head to hide her tears and Ho Chang patted her back gently. 'You have lost everything through my stupidity, Li Fong,' he replied in a humble voice.

'It's not the time to dwell on human weakness. You prepare to leave now. Tomorrow might be too late,' the older brother warned him.

'Are you sure the Tong won't accept the security you put up and leave us in peace?' Ho Chang asked.

'I wasn't sure a couple of days ago but now I'm certain,' Li Fong replied. 'The Tong leader has been to see me. He told me that he's being deposed and the man who'll succeed him is ruthless and cunning. They'll be sure to come in strength.'

'Then the decision is made for us,' Ho Chang sighed. 'We'll get ready to leave tonight. I've already made the arrangements you advised when we last spoke.'

'That's good. You have the chance to settle in Liverpool amongst our countrymen,' Li Fong said nodding. 'And maybe when you prosper you'll decide to visit Singapore. I'll be waiting for the day when we can see each other again.'

'What about you and Mei Li?' Ho Chang asked. 'You won't stay here surely.'

'No, we'll leave this evening. I've found us a nice hotel at King's Cross, and we can stay there till I manage to book passage to Singapore. It should only be a week at the most.'

Su Chang looked up at Li Fong. 'I think it'll be hard for Mei Li to leave England, and at such short notice,' she remarked. 'She's made friends here, and the young man is special to her.'

Li Fong shrugged his shoulders. 'She's young and young friendships very often evaporate like strange dreams in the light of morning. The memories will fade once she's back home and married. Her life will be a busy one there.'

Su Chang knew otherwise. Mei Li had blossomed this last few weeks and it was obvious why. She had fallen in love with the young Englishman. The parting would be very painful, despite what her guardian thought. How could the old man be so blind? But he was a man, and men could not begin to understand the depth and all-consuming fire of a woman's love. From unlikely circumstances and strange seed it could grow without regard, slow and steady like the germ of life that she would one day hold within her belly and feel growing inside her. For men love is a passion that rises and falls like a running tide, but for a woman love burns an even flame inside her soul.

'You look very thoughtful, Su,' Li Fong remarked.

'I'm just thinking about this place,' she replied. 'The

people of Bermondsey have been kind to us. I'll miss them.'

'You and Ho Chang will make new friends in Liverpool and the people there are friendly too,' Li Fong said supportively. 'Now I should go. There are a lot of things I have to do. We'll meet later to say our goodbyes.'

Winston Norris read the printed note once more and shook his head sadly. 'What possesses people to act so cowardly?' he sighed. Why couldn't they just get on with their own lives and leave others to do the same?

'Have you signed the letters, Mr Norris?' Angela asked as she looked in the manager's office. 'If so I can get them in the midday post.'

'Yes, here they are,' he replied. 'Oh, Angela, can you spare me a minute or two?'

She seated herself beside his desk expecting him to dictate a letter, but instead he sat there pulling on his chin and looking a little troubled. 'I wasn't going to bother you with this, Angela,' he began, 'but it has happened once before and I'm concerned.'

'Another anonymous letter,' she said quickly as he reached for the note in front of him.

'Yes I'm afraid so.'

'And who is it this time?' she asked with a sharp edge to her voice.

'James Neal.'

'It's contemptible,' she declared with passion.

'I agree entirely,' Norris said quietly, 'but it is worrying. Someone has obviously noted something quite innocent and put the wrong connotations to it. We are dealing with a sick person who is harbouring a grudge against you, or possibly Mr Neal. I suspect it is you though, considering it's happened once before.'

'Can I see the note?' Angela asked.

'Yes of course.'

She picked it up and stared at the crude lettering scrawled in black crayon.

To Mr Norris.
You should watch your secretary and Jim Neal.
They are comitting adultery under your nose.
A friend.

'Whoever's responsible for this is certainly sick,' Angela said disgustedly. 'The only time I've had a conversation with Mr Neal in the factory was two weeks ago when we were trying to sort out his annual holiday requirements.'

Norris puckered his lips thoughtfully. 'Did you happen to mention to anyone about Mr Neal fixing your water tank?'

'Definitely not,' she replied quickly. 'I treated it as a confidential matter, realising that it could cause you problems if it was known about.'

Winston Norris picked up the note and studied it for a few moments, then he reached into a drawer and took out the previous note. 'Yes, this is one and the same sad individual,' he said. 'Compare the two. Although the first one was made up of letters cut from newspapers the wording is similar, and look at the way the word committing is spelt. In both notes there is only one letter M.'

'Will you be calling in the police?' Angela asked.

'I'm tempted,' Norris replied, 'but we have to ask ourselves, does an anonymous message of this sort constitute a crime? It could be seen as defamation, but the recourse would be a civil action, once the sender has been identified. No, I think I'll put these notes away and hope that I can discover who's responsible. I would like to have a few words with Mr Neal, however. He might be able to throw some light on whoever's doing this.'

Ruby walked home from the surgery with her head buzzing. It had been a morning to forget. Dr Phelps was off sick and the locum, a large female with short cropped hair and a brusque manner, had succeeded in upsetting almost everyone she saw that morning. Mrs Caulfield had been enraged by the suggestion that if her son Billy washed properly he would be less inclined to get ear infections. Mrs Childs had taken it badly too when she was told that cough medicine was prescribed for a cough, not to promote sleep and a sense of well-being. Her argument that it was all linked left the locum unimpressed. If there was no cough then there was to be no cough mixture.

Mrs Childs swore she would go to the market in future and have a word with the man who sold patent cough cures. ''E might not be so bloody awkward,' she fumed.

Only Albert Walburton had had anything nice to say about the stand-in. 'She's a bit of all right,' he remarked. 'An' she wasn't 'eavy-'anded when she felt me waterworks.'

Normally she would hurry home to fuss around the house, but Ruby was now, by her own admission, a changed woman. There was plenty of time before the family came home for tea. She had all afternoon in fact.

Maybe it would buck her up if she took a trip down the Blue. Yes, why not. She might even buy herself a new blouse, or a summer dress.

The early afternoon sun felt warm on her back as she strolled along the line of stalls. The fishmonger was expertly slicing and gutting a large plaice and next to him a stallholder was demonstrating the best way to clean brass and silver, with his patent metal polish that was guaranteed to make anything shine. A few stalls along Ruby saw the most becoming dress and she stopped to examine it. It was her size, a creation in silver grey, with a low cross-over front and lined below the nipped-in waist.

'Nice ain't it,' the stallholder said smiling. 'It's just meant fer you, if yer'll pardon the cheek. But I gotta say it, yer'll look a dream in that. Try it on.'

'What 'ere?' Ruby said in horror.

'Nah, in the shop. Go on, do yerself a favour.'

Ruby thought for a few moments then nodded. 'All right I will,' she told him.

Twenty minutes later she walked into the small café at the end of the market and ordered a milky coffee. She felt she had been a bit extravagant but the dress fitted her perfectly and the stockings she had bought on the next stall were exactly the right shade. It seemed ages since she had bought anything for herself, but things were different now.

'Why 'ello. I didn't recognise you at first.'

Ruby looked up to see Pam Mills standing there holding a cup of tea. ''Ello, Pam. Take a seat,' she said.

''Ow's the family?'

'They're all very well.'

'An' Kay?'

'Yeah she's fine. 'Ow's Richard?'

'Doin' very well,' Pam told her. ''E's bin promoted again. I can see 'im goin' right ter the top. They fink the world of 'im.'

'Is 'e courtin'?' Ruby enquired.

'Yes 'e is as a matter o' fact.'

'That's nice for 'im.'

'Lovely gel she is. So proper.'

'Is she from round 'ere?'

'Goodness no. She lives in Streatham. 'Er farvver's someone in the City.'

'That's nice,' Ruby mumbled as she sipped her coffee.

'I've got a photo of 'er. Would yer like ter see?'

'Yeah why not?'

Pam produced a dog-eared snap from her handbag and passed it over. 'There we are, that's Prudence.'

Ruby studied the fat-faced young girl in spectacles and nodded. 'She looks very nice.'

'They make a lovely couple,' Pam remarked. 'Richard brings 'er round every Sunday evenin' an' while 'e gets on wiv 'is stamp collection me an' Pru work on a woollen rug I'm doin'. It'll be a present fer Richard an' Pru when they get married.'

'Will that be very soon?' Ruby asked, stifling a yawn.

'Goodness me no, not fer two years. They've both agreed ter wait. In two years Richard should be chief draughtsman an' Prudence will 'ave done 'er exams.'

'Oh, an' what's she doin'?'

'She works in a library an' she's 'opin' ter be a librarian, once she passes the exams.'

'I'll tell Kay that I saw yer,' Ruby said finishing her coffee.

'Is Kay back wiv that barrer boy?' Pam asked with a funny note in her voice.

'Joey Westlake yer mean? Yeah she's very 'appy wiv 'im, an' 'e's a nice lad, despite what people fink,' Ruby replied defensively.

'There's not much prospects I would 'ave thought. Still it wouldn't do fer us all ter be alike.'

'Nah, yer right, Pam. Richard likes messin' about wiv stamps an' Joey likes ter get pissed,' Ruby said cuttingly. 'Prudence is content ter sit makin' rugs an' Kay likes ter go dancin'. They're all different.'

Pam looked disgusted. 'It's a good job they are,' she said quickly.

'Well, I must be off,' Ruby told her.

Outside the sun was shining and the noise of the market was music to her ears as Ruby made her way home. How nice it had been, she thought, apart from the tedious meeting with Pam Mills. God! What had she been thinking about when she tried to pair her daughter off with Richard? Kay was happy now and it showed. It was her life and she had to live it the way she wanted to. Paul too. His courting of Mei Li was likely to bring him pain and misery, but it was his choice and he would live and learn by it. One thing was for certain: he would have the family behind him. He and his sister were very close, and Ruby vowed that she would be there for him too, come what may. As for Jim, he would play his part, once he got that woman out of his life.

Ruby walked into the alley and noticed that Lizzie was

dozing in her rocking-chair. She let herself into the house and hung the dress behind the parlour door. Was she doing the right thing, she asked herself as she put the kettle over the gas flame? Should she have been more aggressive? No, it was not her way. As she had told silly Pam, people were different. Some women would have reacted violently at finding out that their husband was cheating on them and taken a carving knife to him. Others would have wept and wilted, or shouted and screamed. Whatever the initial reaction, what followed was all-important. In the cold light of day decisions had to be taken and Ruby prided herself on having made the right ones, thanks largely to Bel's words of wisdom. She was going to fight for her man, not allow some lax tart to come into his life and destroy a family in the process.

Ruby looked up at the dress. She would wear it this weekend, and tonight she would make a treacle tart for afters. That would surprise them all. She might even go some way towards being pleasant to Jim, as long as he didn't wear that hangdog look. One thing was for certain. She was going to fight this intrusion into their lives with all the will, guile and cunning she could muster.

Winston Norris motioned Jim Neal into a chair. 'You'll be wondering what this is all about so I'll get straight to the point,' he began. 'I want you to look at this note.'

Jim read the message and shook his head slowly. 'This is ridiculous,' he said quickly.

'Mrs Stapleton feels exactly the same,' Norris replied. 'I'm afraid we have a disturbed individual on our payroll and it's very worrying.'

'There's no truth in this whatsoever,' Jim told him.

'No, of course not,' Norris said. 'Whoever wrote this is harbouring some grudge against Mrs Stapleton in particular. I say that because this isn't the first note I've received. There was one before, accusing my secretary of having an affair with a clerk by the name of Crawley who used to work here. In fact it upset Mr Crawley so much he left soon after. He was married with a baby on the way and he couldn't cope with it.'

'Do you believe that the two notes were written by the same person, Mr Norris?' Jim asked.

'Yes I do,' the manager replied. 'As I pointed out to Mrs Stapleton, there's a spelling error that's repeated on the second note. She asked me if I was going to bring in the police but I told her no. After all, what crime has been committed? I want you to think hard, Mr Neal. Can you recall anyone watching you closely when you and Mrs Stapleton were discussing your holiday dates in the factory area?'

Jim drew breath. The last time he was engaged in a conversation with her on the factory floor his holidays were not an issue. There were quite a few factory hands who would have seen them talking, and on Saturday the rest of the maintenance team saw him chatting to Angela on the loading bank. 'No, I'm sorry but I don't recall anyone watching us that closely,' he replied. 'If I remember rightly the conversation was very brief anyway.'

'Thank you, Mr Neal,' the manager said. 'Try not to worry over this. I shall get to the bottom of it before long.'

As he left the inner sanctum Angela was waiting. 'There's

no need to worry, Jim,' she said smiling. 'Whoever's doing this is just sick.'

'Whoever it is seems to 'ave a down on you,' Jim remarked, 'an' if Norris doesn't respond in the way they expect 'im to then it might get even nastier.'

'You mean our spouses might get similar letters?' Angela replied arching her eyebrows.

Jim nodded. 'Look, I've got a machine 'alf fixed. Can we talk later?'

'I could see you after work,' Angela suggested.

Jim shook his head. 'No I can't. I can find an excuse ter get out later this evenin'.'

'Sorry, Jim, Laurie'll be home early tonight.'

'We'll fix somefing up later then,' he told her before hurrying off.

Winston Norris came out of his office carrying his brief-case. 'I don't think I'll be back today, Angela,' he said. 'Try not to worry.'

She smiled her best smile, then as soon as the door closed behind the manager she picked up the phone. 'Hello, could I speak to Mr William Crawley please? Hello, Bill. Yes it's Angela. Who did you think it was? No of course not. Yes I trust you, you know I do. Bill, the reason I'm phoning is, it's happened again. Mr Norris got another anonymous note this morning. No of course there's nothing going on. Would I have bothered to phone you if I was up to no good? The poor man involved is devastated. He's a devoted husband with two children. Yes, tonight. Come round as soon as you can. Yes, I love you too.'

Chapter Thirty-Five

After he had left the works manager's office Jim found himself under pressure. The capping machine he had just reassembled was still not working properly. Percy Bradley came along to take a look at it and he soon spotted the reason. 'Yer've not connected up the cut-out,' he said, giving Jim a quizzical look.

'I'm sorry,' the younger man said grimacing. 'I should've spotted that.'

'Yeah yer should,' Percy told him. 'By the way, that line couplin' needs tightenin' too or it'll work loose wiv the vibration.'

Jim shook his head in disgust. 'I'm sorry, Percy, I dunno what I must 'ave bin finkin' about.'

'You look a bit preoccupied. Is there anyfing troublin' yer?' the foreman asked him.

'Nah, why?'

'Well, it ain't like you ter be careless,' Percy replied. 'If it was Len Moody I could understand it. 'Is brains are in 'is arse 'alf the time.'

Jim looked around to make sure no one was within earshot. 'There is somefing bovverin' me ter be honest,' he admitted. 'Keep this ter yerself. I was called up ter see Norris a little while ago.'

'Oh, an' what was that for?'

''E got an anonymous message about me an' that secretary of 'is,' Jim went on. 'It accused me an' 'er of 'avin' an affair.'

'Not anuvver one,' Percy said shaking his head slowly. 'There's some nasty people about. Why don't they mind their own business?'

'You know about the first one then?'

Percy nodded. 'You weren't 'ere at the time. It was towards the end o' the war. The news spread all over the firm, in fact the bloke involved went round tellin' everybody,' he explained. 'I fink 'e was proud of it. Bill Crawley 'is name was. 'E was an office clerk. Flashy sort o' geezer. I never took to 'im ter tell yer the trufe. Anyway 'e left soon after.'

'I'm worried in case whoever sent the note decides ter go furvver,' Jim said anxiously.

Percy Bradley stroked his chin. 'Yeah, I can see yer point. Still if yer innocent yer got nuffink ter worry about.'

'It could still cause trouble fer both of us though,' Jim remarked.

'It won't cause Angela any loss o' sleep,' Percy replied. 'She's got no one to answer to. She's bin on 'er own fer a few years now.'

Jim gave Percy a questioning look. 'That's very strange,' he said.

'What is?'

'Well, when I was strippin' those pipes in 'er office she was tellin' me about 'er 'usband Laurie bein' interested in bird-watchin'. In fact she was moanin' about the time 'e spends at it.'

Percy smiled. 'She must 'ave 'ad 'er reasons fer tellin' yer that, but I can assure yer that Laurie Stapleton ain't livin' wiv 'er any more. There was a big bust-up more than five years ago. Laurie used ter work at the railway goods depot in Pages Walk. 'E was on shift work, an' one night 'e came 'ome unexpected an' caught 'er in bed wiv 'is best mate. The reason I know all this is 'cos my wife's related ter the Stapleton family. 'Er an' Laurie are cousins. Accordin' ter my ole dutch, Angela an' that Crawley bloke I was just tellin' yer about 'ave got back tergevver again. She said they'd bin seen tergevver a lot lately.'

Jim tried to hide his shock but he was certain that Percy had seen it in his face. 'Well, that's their business,' he mumbled.

Percy nodded in agreement. 'Take my advice an' give 'er a wide berf. She's trouble.'

Jim set to work again with a horrible feeling in the pit of his stomach. He had been used by the seemingly insatiable woman and had been too naive to see through her little game. Well, it was over now as far as he was concerned, but first he had to confront her. He owed that much to Ruby.

On that Tuesday morning Tommy Lo left the seamen's hostel in Rotherhithe and caught a number 82 bus to Stepney through the river tunnel, and as he made his way towards Limehouse his mind was racing. He would have a chance to make a case for his actions, but he knew Billy Chou had seen to it that there would only be one outcome. It would be a game of bluff, of playing for time, but Tommy Lo knew that he was up against a very dangerous and cunning opponent.

Trolley buses sped past him and laden horse carts trundled over the cobbled road as the young man neared his destination. He could see the buildings in Pennyfields and he hoped and prayed that his mother had left there for the safety of Norfolk. People turned to stare at him and then hurried on with their heads bowed. The cobbler looked up from his work and across the street two traders stood whispering together. Word had already got out and his presence would be noted and reported throughout the run-down area of China in mirage.

Tommy Lo walked purposefully with his shoulders thrown back and a gentle sway of the hips, but the tension was screwing up his insides and he wished himself far away. How nice it would be at this very moment to smell the salty sea, feel the strong wet lash of the sea-wind on his face and counter the rolling movement of the deck beneath his feet. The cobbled streets of Limehouse were hard and unwelcoming and the sun beat down relentlessly as he reached the house of Wu Sung, where the Tong frequently met. The front door was shut tight and the old man would no doubt be sitting in the tea-house a few streets away with his aged friends.

As he turned the corner into Formosa Street Tommy Lo was confronted by Victor Sen and Danny Ling. 'I was expecting you,' he said smiling. 'Is the meeting-place set?'

Victor Sen nodded. 'The warehouse.'

'When?'

'Now.'

'I was on my way to the tea-house,' Tommy Lo told them.

'There's no time,' Danny Ling said quickly.

'One hour's grace is little to ask.'

'We've been told to bring you right away,' Danny Ling insisted.

'Billy Chou will have his day, but he'll have to wait until I've been to the tea-house,' the young man replied calmly. 'Unless you wish to use force.'

The two Tong members looked at each other uneasily and Victor Sen shrugged his shoulders in resignation. 'We'll tell Billy Chou that you'll be at the warehouse in one hour.'

'You do that,' Tommy Lo said with a magnanimous smile.

The pair stepped aside to let him pass and they watched until he reached the end of the narrow street before hurrying off.

Wu Sung was sitting with two friends in the tea-house, and as soon as Tommy Lo walked in he mumbled something to them and they moved to another table.

'Is Wu Sung willing to spend a few minutes in the company of a Tong fugitive?' Tommy Lo said with a smile as he reached the table.

The old man motioned him to sit. 'This is a day of harmful elements, but until you face your accusers I am doing no wrong in talking with you,' he replied.

'I am grateful, Wu Sung,' Tommy told him. 'Let me refill your bowl.'

The shopkeeper was beckoned over and she gave the young man a curious look as she poured hot green tea into two fresh bowls.

'You're at a disadvantage having Billy Chou as an enemy,' Wu Sung said. 'He's ruthless and eager for power.'

'My disadvantage is having Danny Ling and Victor Sen

as full members,' Tommy corrected him. 'They're both too weak to stand up to him.'

'New members should have been recruited from the juniors this year as allowed,' Wu Sung remarked. 'It was a mistake not to have them.'

Tommy Lo nodded in agreement. 'Limehouse is a small area and we felt that it didn't warrant an army to control a few. You hosted the meeting, you must have heard the arguments against it. It seemed right at the time.'

'It's too late now, but it's not too late for you, Tommy Lo,' the old man said in a low voice. 'Your standing is high amongst some of the junior members. Use them to regain control by force. Only Billy Chou will pose a problem.'

Tommy Lo smiled at him. 'You're a bloodthirsty old man.'

'It's a good thing sometimes for the young to listen to the voice of age and experience,' Wu Sung replied. 'Unfortunately there's little time for talking now, so I'll remind you of your instructions to me and ask you if they still apply.'

The young man nodded. 'I want you to remember the name of Paul Neal. It's possible that you and he will meet very soon. The young Englishman is trustworthy and ready to act on my behalf. Give him what help you can should it be needed.'

Wu Sung nodded his head slowly. 'You should not delay any longer,' he said solemnly. 'Already doors are being bolted against you.'

Tommy Lo stood up and bowed slowly. 'I pray that we will be able to continue our conversation, Wu Sung.'

'I hope so too,' the old man replied as he returned the bow.

The sound of a tug whistle shattered the silence as Tommy Lo walked along Canton Street. Up ahead the old warehouse loomed ominously and beyond it the tall chimney of the Beckton power station belched yellow smoke and fumes into the clear blue sky. Few people were about, but Tommy Lo knew that soon the junior members would be on the streets, in doorways, shadows and alleys, ready to seize their moment of glory.

At the warehouse entrance he came face to face with two young men dressed in black trousers and shirts, wearing red bandannas tied tightly round their heads. 'We're the appointed escort,' one said.

Tommy Lo bowed stiffly and stepped into the gloom, walking slowly between them. Their feet echoed on the wooden planking as they went down the long narrow passageway, and Tommy blinked against the darkness as they entered a large musty-smelling room.

Billy Chou and Danny Ling sat at a table covered with a black cloth, and Victor Sen was seated to one side amongst some junior members. Billy Chou stood up and placed both hands down on the table. 'The meeting of the special vote is now in session,' he said in a loud voice.

Tommy Lo looked at the two small piles of mah-jong pieces and the folded black bag next to them, then his eyes strayed to the long knife lying with the hilt towards him at the other end of the table. When the decision was called each of the senior members would take one ivory piece from each of the piles. The fate of the accused rested literally in their hands. East wind or west wind? One east wind piece placed in the bag would be enough to turn the proceedings into a full-scale manhunt. Just a short ten minutes to pick up the knife and make a dash for survival. After six hundred seconds the sleeping tiger would stir and the power of the Tong would be awesome.

'Tommy Lo. You have been accused of betraying the trust of the Sons of Heaven Tong. What have you to say?'

The young leader looked into the eyes of Billy Chou and replied in a clear voice. 'Guilty!'

Chapter Thirty-Six

Legend had it that in the thirteen-year rule of Kiang Hsi, the second Manchu emperor, a monastery of fighting monks were recruited to defeat a rebellion in Fukien, receiving imperial power as their reward. These Buddhist monks were then seen as a threat themselves, and an army was sent to suppress them. Five monks survived, founding five monasteries and five secret societies dedicated to overthrowing the Manchu and restoring the previous Ming dynasty, which was remembered as a golden age.

During this period the societies were often believed to be protectors of the people against the repressive and sometimes vicious regime of the emperor, but their secrecy and martial arts training eventually drew them into criminal activities. Tong, meaning 'hall' or 'meeting-place', were set up in China and abroad to guide the local populace and give voice to the traditional wisdom of village elders, but they too were very often corrupted by the lure of power and money, and their loyalties to one side or another shifted like the wind.

In Limehouse, on that June Wednesday morning in a riverside warehouse, the plea of guilty at the Tong inquisition was recorded with disbelief. The junior member nearest the door was able to whisper the plea to a colleague outside and word spread. A runner in the pay of Wu Sung breathlessly relayed the plea to him and the old man shook his head. A special vote was like last year's harvest of the fields, it was invariably cut and dried. The argument was always short and useless, but at least the victim was allowed a brief few minutes to make his bid for freedom before the wrath of the Tong descended upon him and tore him to pieces. With a plea of guilty the ten-minute respite was automatically waived. What was Tommy Lo thinking of, he wondered? All he could hope for was leniency, an alien word in the creed of the Tong. The truth was, should one east wind piece tumble from the black bag then the Tong members would immediately fall upon the accused and dispatch him before he could reach for the knife lying a few feet away.

Billy Chou leaned forward with his hands clenched on the table and glared at Tommy Lo. 'I have to remind you of the consequences of pleading guilty,' he said.

'There's no need. I'm aware of the consequences,' Tommy Lo replied.

Billy Chou looked around the gathering and then turned back, fixing his eyes on the young man before him. 'You have betrayed the trust of the Tong by misappropriating funds held in lieu of payment of a gambling debt. The funds, in the form of a valuable set of pots, are missing. If you are to expect clemency you will need to tell us where the pots are. It's our contention that they are in the possession of Vu Ping the dealer, who is at the present time on his way to the Far East to sell the pots. Is that not true?'

A low mumbling rose in the large dusty room and when

Tommy Lo cleared his throat it subsided. 'I do not deny that I betrayed the trust of the Tong,' he began. 'To that charge I plead guilty. But I challenge the accusation that I misappropriated funds, namely a valuable set of ginger pots. They are not in the possession of Vu Ping. His swift departure was merely coincidental. He had urgent business to take care of in Hong Kong. I saw to it that the pots were re-directed and at this moment they are concealed in a place of safety, and I intend them to remain there until they are redeemed by Li Fong the owner, or until a buyer can be found. Acting alone and without agreement can be seen as a betrayal of trust, just as acting alone to kill someone who has already been punished by the Tong can be seen as a betrayal.'

'What are you saying? That one of our number killed the candlemaker?' Billy Chou asked.

'I didn't mention the candlemaker,' Tommy Lo said in reply.

The mumbling started again and Billy Chou raised his hand for silence. 'The question remains unanswered. Why did you hide the pots without consulting us first? If for some reason you die their whereabouts might never be discovered.'

'I did make provision for such an eventuality,' Tommy Lo said smiling slyly. 'I gave instructions that should I die, as you put it, by violent or mysterious means, then the pots would remain where they were until they could be sold, the proceeds of the sale used to reimburse the debtor and the creditor. To the question, why did I act alone, the answer is simple. The set of ginger pots is priceless, and such wealth coming into the hands of a Tong could corrupt, as happened to the Wu Hsing Tong in Glasgow two years ago. My contention is that I acted to prevent a recurrence of what happened there. If in so doing I betrayed the trust of the Tong, then so be it. I have pleaded guilty so it is for you to decide whether to excuse my actions, or to kill me here and now. The choice is yours.'

The mumbling rose in a crescendo and Billy Chou struggled to be heard. 'If there is nothing more you wish to say we will leave to consider our verdict,' he announced loudly, picking up a piece of ivory from each of the piles.

Victor Sen and Danny Ling did likewise, followed by the four junior members nominated to take part in the vote, and as they all left the room the noise increased. Tommy Lo sat back in his chair and stared up thoughtfully at the cobweb-covered beams in the roof. The plea of guilty had taken Billy Chou completely by surprise. It was obvious his intention had been to pronounce him guilty and after the customary ten minutes' grace he would have led the hunt and delayed the killing just long enough to torture the whereabouts of the pots out of him. The ways and means of breaking someone were various, and it was certain that sooner or later the threshold would have been reached and Billy Chou would have won. The guilty plea had served to forestall him. He knew that one piece of the east wind in the black bag would be the end of his adversary. He would die on the spot and take with him the secret of the pots' location.

The members filed back into the room and a hush descended. Billy Chou carried the black bag and before he tipped the contents out on to the table he fixed Tommy Lo with his cold eyes. It was a look of defeat, but there was something else too in the dead stare, and it reaffirmed what the young man on trial already knew. This was just the first act of the drama.

The ivories spilled from the bag and Danny Ling slowly turned them over one by one to expose the coloured figuring. 'They're all of the west wind,' he said solemnly.

Loud noise erupted as Tommy Lo stood up and some of the junior members smiled over at him.

'You are free to go,' Billy Chou said above the din. 'The Tong will convene tomorrow.'

Tommy Lo smiled as he turned to leave. Billy Chou, Danny Ling and Victor Sen would now be required to swear a new allegiance or stand down. Either way they had lost face and the door was now open for junior members to press for entry into the cadre.

The afternoon streets of Limehouse were back to normality once more. Front doors were open again and people stood chatting together in the warm air. The shopkeepers placed their wares out on the pavement and in the tea-house on Formosa Street Wu Sung waited.

Paul Neal hurried home through the quiet turnings, knowing what to expect even before he turned into Cater Street. The scribbled message on the door of the laundry seemed to burn itself into his head. Closed until further notice. He knocked on the side door, willing the sound of Mei Li's footsteps on the stairs, but it was quiet. He stood for a few moments, his heart leaden and cold anger building inexorably inside him. The Tong had driven them away in fear of their lives and he was left with nothing but memories. The bastards would have to answer for this, he vowed, and answer for it soon.

Surely Mei Li and her guardian would not have left the country already though. They would most likely be staying with friends, or at a hotel while they arranged passage on a ship. He must find them, speak to Li Fong and make him see that Mei Li would be happy here in England with him, not trapped in a marriage with some stranger thousands of miles away.

'It's no good you knockin', son, they've gone away,' an old man called over.

Paul hurried across to him. 'I don't s'pose yer know where they've gone, do yer?' he asked quickly.

The old man shook his head. 'Bit sudden it was. My ole woman took two o' me shirts ter be cleaned an' pressed an' the Chink wouldn't take 'em. She said somefing about goin' away, but my ole gel couldn't get the rights of it. Mind you, she's a bit 'ard of 'earin' an' inclined ter get fings arse-up'ards at times. I should fink they've all gone back ter China. Best place for 'em if you ask me.'

Paul walked out of the street racking his brains. Perhaps Mei Li would contact Kay or make a point of meeting her after work to give her a message. Surely she wouldn't leave it like this?

When he walked into the house Kay met him and the look on her face made his heart leap. 'Come upstairs, Paul. I've seen Mei Li,' she whispered.

'You saw 'er this evenin'?'

Kay closed the bedroom door and sat down on the edge of her bed. 'They left 'ere last night. Mei Li was waitin' for me at the bus stop. 'Er an' Li Fong 'ave gone to an 'otel until they can get fixed up wiv a ship.'

'What 'otel? Where?' Paul asked eagerly.

'She wouldn't tell me. She said it was fer the best, but she did say she'd get in touch wiv yer frew me an' see yer before she leaves the country.'

'Charmin'. Bloody charmin',' Paul growled. 'I don't believe it. It's that ole Li Fong. 'E can't wait ter leave an' 'e's put pressure on 'er. 'E knows she wouldn't argue wiv 'im.'

Kay looked sad. 'I'm very sorry, Paul, but it's somefing yer can't change. She's still Chinese an' finks like one, even though she's bin 'ere fer some time. People like you an' me say what we fink an' do whatever we want, almost, but yer can see 'ow be'olden she is ter that guardian of 'ers. It's years o' growin' up that way I s'pose, an' she can't undo it all in a matter o' weeks, much as she'd want to.'

'Did she give yer any indication 'ow long it'd be before she leaves?' Paul asked.

Kay shook her head. 'She didn't get on my bus. We just 'ad this brief chat before she dashed away. She must be stayin' somewhere over the water. I would fink so anyway.'

'Well it wouldn't be anywhere near Lime'ouse that's fer sure,' Paul replied. ''Ow can I find out?'

'Face it, Paul, yer can't,' Kay told him kindly. 'Just wait fer Mei Li ter contact me an' then take it from there.'

'Fanks, Kay. Sorry if I jumped at yer,' he said with a brief smile.

She stood up and laid a hand on his shoulder. 'Fings'll work out some'ow, I know they will,' she said softly. 'Just keep yerself tergevver, an' don't go gettin' no crazy ideas. I got enough wi' Joey wivout you worryin' me sick.'

'What's wiv Joey?'

''E's all fer goin' over Lime'ouse an' sortin' 'em out.'

Paul shook his head slowly. 'I bet 'e's already lined up 'is army.'

Kay smiled. 'Butch Wheeler, Sonny Rowland an' 'alf the bloody market men. Sonny told 'im 'e'll rope in some o' the boxers from the gym an' Butch reckons 'e could pull in a few of 'is mates too. Joey said they only want the word from you.'

'They're good mates, Kay,' Paul told her. 'The best. Joey's a brick an' 'e'll make yer a good 'usband, as long as yer keep 'im on a tight rein.'

'Don't worry, I've got 'im taped,' Kay replied. 'Now come on, let's get downstairs an' face the music. Muvver'll be all ears.'

The sun was dipping down behind the rooftops as Ruby finished the washing up. She could see Jim at the bottom of the garden tidying up the scattered flowerpots and she brushed a strand of hair from her forehead with the back of her hand as she went out to him. 'I'm worried about Paul,' she said. ''E's 'ardly ate anyfing an' 'e's gettin' ready ter go out. Kay told me that Mei Li's gone.'

'Gone?'

'Yeah, they've all gone, 'er an' 'er guardian an' the laundryman an' 'is wife too.'

'That was sudden,' Jim remarked as he stood upright.

'I could see this comin',' Ruby said sighing. 'I feel so sorry fer Paul. 'E must be feelin' terrible.'

Jim shook his head sadly, then he gazed steadily into her eyes. 'I know yer must be worried. I am too, but you don't deserve all this. I've bin an idiot an' I've caused yer nuffink but pain, but it's over now, Ruby. I swear on our children's lives. God knows what possessed me. I 'ad everyfing a man could want an' I couldn't see it. I've bin weak, but it's gonna be different from now on. I'm gonna fight as 'ard as I know 'ow ter win back yer love an' respect, if yer'll just give me the chance.'

Ruby brushed away a tear. 'You didn't fink I was gonna let some tart come on the scene an' take yer from me wivout puttin' up a fight, did yer?' she said resolutely. 'I've 'ad ter take a good look at meself ter find out where I was goin' wrong, what I'd done that made yer go off me.'

'You didn't do anyfing wrong, Ruby,' he said quietly.

'Oh yes I did,' she replied. 'I made yer lives a misery, the way I was goin' on. It was Bel Allenby who finally put me right. She could see what I was like, the way I was carryin' on, but I've changed, yer know I 'ave.'

Jim reached out and took her hand in his. 'I know it'll take time, but believe me, Ruby, our marriage'll be stronger than ever, an' we'll be 'appy again, as God is my judge.'

They walked back along the garden path, with Jim still holding her hand, and as they stepped into the scullery Ruby turned to him. ''Old me tight, Jim,' she whispered.

Over the river in Limehouse as night descended Tommy Lo sat in the house of Wu Sung. The old man had cooked a meal by way of celebration, and now as the two sipped their tea the notorious river mist began to swirl into the narrow mean streets.

'It was no gamble, as long as I pleaded guilty,' Tommy Lo said smiling. 'How could they kill me? They'd never have found the pots.'

'It's not over though,' Wu Sung remarked. 'Wealth corrupts, and Billy Chou would sell his soul to be able to lay his hands on them.'

Tommy Lo nodded. 'They're safe where they are for the time being.'

Wu Sung stroked his chin. 'You must be vigilant. I spent a lot of my younger years at sea, and I've witnessed at first hand the seeds of corruption growing inside men's hearts. In San Francisco the Shao Lung Tong grew rich very quickly in the twenties. They drove around in limousines and wore expensive clothes, and the charity they supplied to the deserving was a pittance. It was the same when coolie labour was used to build the railroads across America. The Green Tong recruited impoverished peasants and took a nice cut from the company bosses. They were ruthless with anyone who dared to challenge working conditions and wages, and the coolies worked as veritable slaves.'

Tommy Lo nodded. 'It's for those sorts of reasons that I decided to hide the pots.'

'You should stay here tonight,' Wu Sung advised him. 'It's becoming misty and you'd be ill advised to walk the streets alone.'

Tommy reached down and tapped the bulge where his knife was strapped to his thigh. 'I have my trusty friend with me,' he said smiling.

Wu Sung refilled the tea bowls. 'Where will you go then?'

'I have to make a phone call and then I'll stay at the seamen's hostel in Stepney.'

'And tomorrow?'

'I'll receive the oath of allegiance from the members,' Tommy Lo said with a grin.

Wu Sung sipped his tea. 'I'm an old man and I've seen much in my life,' he remarked quietly. 'An old man very often develops a sixth sense for things and it's wise for the young to take heed in such circumstances. I can foresee only pain and suffering if you remain here in Limehouse. You would be better advised to take the pots and disappear.'

Tommy Lo was about to answer when there was a loud knocking on the front door. 'Sit tight, Wu,' he said urgently as he reached down through the hole in his trouser pocket and pulled out his flick-knife. With a quick movement he depressed the safety clip and the razor-sharp blade shot out. The knock was repeated and as Tommy cautiously opened the door he saw Ti San the young waiter standing there looking distraught.

'You must come quickly,' he gasped. 'It's Victor Sen. He's been stabbed.'

'Where is he?' Tommy Lo demanded.

'I found him in the alley behind the Peking Club,' Ti San said breathlessly. 'He wants to speak with you. Please come quickly, there's very little time.'

The two men ran through the thickening mist and as they turned the last corner they saw the glow of light from the club sign softened and distorted in the damp air. They turned into the back alley and heard a muffled groan. Victor Sen was propped up against the wall holding his hands over his stomach, a dark red pool of blood spreading out from under his body.

Tommy Lo bent down and saw from the size of the gaping

wound that there was little time. 'Who did it, Victor?' he asked quickly.

The ashen-faced victim tried to speak as a trickle of blood dribbled from the corner of his mouth. 'Billy Chou,' he mumbled. 'Gone crazy.'

'Take it easy, I'll get an ambulance,' Tommy told him.

Victor Sen tried to shake his head. 'It's too late. Watch out. For Billy Chou. At Kano's gambling house, and we argued. I told him wrong, what he's doing. Pulled a knife on me. Frightened, he was . . . possessed. Left quickly, but . . . Followed me. Caught me outside Peking Club, and . . . stabbed me.' He coughed and blood ran down his chin. 'Tong's finished, Tommy. You . . . right, what you did . . .'

'Should I go for the police?' Ti San asked.

'No, go back inside the club,' Tommy told him. 'I'll take care of Billy Chou. You know nothing and you've seen nothing. It'll be safer for you that way.'

Victor Sen's body tensed and his dark eyes glistened like cut glass as the last breath rattled in his throat.

'Is he . . .'

'Yes, he's dead,' the Tong leader replied. 'Now *go*!'

As he walked swiftly along the quiet street Tommy Lo glanced at his wrist watch. It was nine fifteen. He would have to make the call to Paul Neal first and then deal with Billy Chou. He passed the black walls of the bomb-damaged cane factory, unaware of the figure that emerged silently from the darkness of the doorway. Tommy did not see the blow coming, only a searing flash of light, and then nothing.

Kobi the big Korean looked down at him and smiled. 'He'll be out for some time,' he growled to his colleague.

'Help me get him into the van. This is one bastard I wouldn't want to be, once Billy Chou starts on him.'

Chapter Thirty-Seven

Butch Wheeler eased his lanky frame on the bar stool and leaned on the counter. 'He's so bloody mysterious,' he moaned to Joey Westlake. 'What's goin' on, Joey boy?'

'Gawd knows,' his friend said shrugging his broad shoulders. 'It's serious though. You know Paul. 'E ain't one ter make much out o' fings, an' when 'e said it's a matter o' life or death yer can bet it is serious.'

Reg Donaldson was busy polishing the glasses and Joey beckoned him over. 'Get us the same again, sport,' he ordered, 'an' one fer yerself.'

'Cheers, Joey,' the barman said smiling.

''Old up,' Butch said quickly as the phone rang.

The barman picked up the receiver and then looked around the bar. 'No 'e ain't in yet,' he said, putting it back down. 'It's all right, it was someone wantin' ter know if Mutton-eye's 'ere.'

Sonny Rowland walked into the public bar and ambled over. 'Ain't Paul arrived yet?' he asked.

'Evenin', Joey, evenin', Butch. 'Ow are yer?' Joey said sarcastically.

'Them bloody brains of 'is are scrambled,' Butch remarked. 'We're all right, fank you fer askin'.'

Sonny ignored the banter. 'Are you gonna tell me what this is all about, or shall I guess?' he growled.

'I couldn't say too much terday while I was servin',' Joey replied. 'You know 'ow those ole gels get chattin'. We don't want 'alf o' Bermon'sey knowin' our business.'

'What business?' Sonny pressed him.

Joey sipped his drink. 'Now look,' he explained. 'Paul's waitin' on a very important phone call from over Lime'ouse. If it don't come 'e's gotta go over there termorrer.'

'What for?'

'I don't bloody well know. Ter sort fings out I s'pose.'

'What fings?'

'Important fings.'

'It's all ter do wiv this Chinky sort 'e's bin seein' I should fink,' Sonny remarked.

'It could be,' Butch added.

'Well, it's gotta be serious if 'e's willin' ter lose a day's work ter go over there.'

'Why ain't 'e 'ere?' Sonny asked.

''E's already bin in,' Joey told him. ''E's gone down the library ter look at all the newspapers.'

'Newspapers? What for?'

'Ter check the times o' sailin's.'

'What, ships?'

'Well it wouldn't be bloody trains, now would it?' Joey said, grinning.

'This is all over my 'ead,' Sonny sighed as he picked up his drink.

Twenty minutes after eight o'clock Paul walked into the Swan looking anxious. 'No phone call?' he asked.

Joey shook his head. 'There's still plenty o' time.'

The evening dragged on, and Paul gradually got more and more uneasy.

'I don't fink yer gonna get this call,' Joey remarked. 'It's turned ten.'

'There's anuvver 'alf hour yet,' Paul replied, eyeing the clock.

'Now listen, Paul,' his friend said quietly. 'I dunno what's goin' on 'ere, except that yer gotta go over Lime'ouse termorrer if yer don't get this call yer waitin' for. D'you mind tellin' me who yer gotta see?'

'The police,' Paul answered.

'I'd be very careful if I was you,' Joey warned him. 'Yer gonna stand out like a sore thumb in Chinatown. S'posin' any o' those Tong blokes recognise yer from when they was over 'ere. They could drag yer down some back alley an' cut yer open. I fink I should come wiv yer. I could get a pal o' mine ter run the stall till I get back. Butch could come too. It'd be no trouble fer 'im.'

Paul smiled. 'I'm grateful fer yer concern, but there's no need ter worry. I've only gotta pass on a message.'

'What sort o' message?'

The young man looked around at the enquiring faces of his friends. 'Look we can't talk 'ere, it's too noisy,' he said. 'Wait till the pub turns out an' if there's bin no phone call I'll put you all in the picture.'

'Yeah, we can go ter Ted's coffee stall fer a meat pie,' Sonny suggested.

'Don't you ever fink of anyfing else but yer belly?' Butch said, rolling his eyes.

'I gotta keep me strength up don't I,' Sonny replied indignantly.

The bell finally sounded and Paul was on tenterhooks. It looked like Tommy Lo had failed in his quest and he said a silent prayer for him. Come on, make that call, he willed him, you've got ten minutes yet.

The four friends lingered over their drinks as the customers drifted off home, and Paul sighed sadly as Reg Donaldson came over. 'Now come on, lads,' he said irritably. 'If the law put their 'eads in 'ere an' see those glasses they're gonna nick me.'

The young men made their way along Tooley Street to the junction with Tower Bridge Road and strolled up to Ted's coffee stall. They took their hot meat pies and mugs of steaming tea over to a low wall that surrounded the statue of John Bevington, a well-known character in Bermondsey's commercial history.

'You don't mind if we sit down 'ere do yer, John?' Joey said looking up at the iron effigy.

They squatted on the brick wall and Butch took a large bite from his pie. 'I fink yer'd better let us in on this, Paul,' he spluttered with his mouth full.

'Yeah, I fink so too,' Joey agreed.

'Look, there's no need fer you lads ter get involved,' Paul told them. 'It's a straightforward business. I fink yer makin' too much out of it.'

'That's fer us ter decide. Now come on, pal,' Joey urged him.

Paul took a deep breath. 'All right then, but this stays wiv us. It's very important. OK?'

His friends listened intently while he told them about the conversation he had had with Tommy Lo and when he finished Joey whistled through his teeth. 'One fing's fer sure. We ain't lettin' you go over there on yer own,' he said adamantly. 'We're comin' wiv yer termorrer like it or lump it. I'll get my pal ter run the stall, an' you can manage it, can't yer, Butch?'

'Sure fing,' the big man replied.

'What about you, Sonny? Can you get up in time?'

'Don't be stupid,' Sonny growled. 'I go runnin' before six every mornin'. I'll be there.'

'That settles that then,' Joey said smiling. 'Shall we piss off 'ome?'

'I fancy anuvver pie,' Sonny announced. 'Anyone else want one?'

They all shook their heads and Joey grinned as the boxer ambled up to the coffee stall. 'Sonny's a diamond, but 'e's as silly as a box o' lights,' he remarked. 'I went down the gym ter watch 'em all trainin' last Thursday afternoon an' they 'ad Sonny in the ring against this young Jewish lad from Whitechapel. It was s'posed ter be a sparrin' session but I could see what they were up to. This Jew-boy's in against the southern area champion next week an' they was givin' 'im a full work-out at Sonny's expense. I tell yer, lads, I felt like gettin' 'old o' that trainer of 'is an' puttin' one right on 'is chops. Sonny don't deserve that sort o' treatment.'

'Once we get termorrer over we should try an' do somefing for 'im,' Butch said with feeling. 'I know I take the piss out of 'im but I love the geezer. It breaks my 'eart ter see the way people take 'im on.'

'I could fix 'im up wiv a stall but yer know what 'e's like,' Joey sighed. ''E'd be givin' the stuff away.'

'I tried ter get 'im on the winder-cleanin' game wiv me

419

but 'e's scared of heights,' Butch told him. 'I couldn't get 'im ter climb up the bloody ladder.'

Sonny came back with his second pie and the four sat together in the coolness of the summer night, watching the activity at the stall. Finally Butch yawned. 'Well, lads, I dunno about you but I need me beauty sleep,' he declared.

They strolled home along the Tower Bridge Road and Joey eased back to walk beside Paul. 'I 'ope you ain't gonna try an' pull a fast one on us,' he said.

'Would I do that?' Paul replied innocently.

'Yeah. So what time are we leavin'?'

'I need ter go early.'

'What's early?'

'About 'alf eight I reckon.'

'We'll all meet at 'alf eight at the bus stop down by the tunnel then.'

'Yer on,' Paul said grinning.

Tommy Lo opened his eyes and immediately winced at the pounding in his head. A wave of nausea swept over him and he breathed deeply, suddenly remembering that he had to make a phone call. Had he managed to, he wondered? No, it was all coming back now: turning the corner to make his way to the phone box, then a blinding pain. He realised he was sitting with his back against a damp wall and as he tried to move away he felt the tug of cold metal against his skin. He had been tethered by an ankle and a wrist to chains fixed in the wall. A dim light shone through a dirty fanlight high in the facing wall and the stark reality dawned on him. He was being held in the cellar at the riverside warehouse.

Tommy Lo cursed his carelessness. Wu Sung was right,

he should have stayed at the house. But he needed to make the call, and then there was that knock at the door. Suddenly the sickening sight came back to him: Victor Sen lying in a pool of blood, his stomach opened up with a knife.

The young Chinese man tested the chains and knew that it was hopeless. They would let him sweat for a while and most likely come tomorrow morning early. Billy Chou would be impatient to get his hands on the pots, and after the information had been screwed out of him he would probably be dumped in the river. Danny Ling would be involved too. He had always sided in with Billy Chou.

The young man worked away at the chains for a while in despair, finally accepting that he was getting nowhere. His only hope was that Paul Neal would report the information early enough. Kennedy would be sure to come to the warehouse and search the place. Footsteps outside made him start and the heavy door creaked open.

'I brought you some soup and bread,' Danny Ling said coldly as he crouched down and placed a bowl by the captive's foot.

'You're in this too, then?' Tommy Lo sneered.

'You tried to be too clever,' Danny Ling growled. 'You did what you did because you couldn't trust us, but we couldn't trust you. You would have sold those pots the first chance you got.'

'I'll tell you one thing,' Tommy Lo said as he reached his free arm out to pick up the bowl of soup. 'Those pots are cursed. They'll bring nothing but evil to anyone holding them except Li Fong.'

'You talk stupid,' Danny Ling remarked. 'Tomorrow you had better see sense and tell us where the pots are hidden.

It's your only chance. If you tell us right away you'll go free, but if you try to resist you'll end up begging to die, I warn you.'

'Do you really think that Billy Chou will let me walk away from this place?' Tommy Lo said with a patronising smile. 'As soon as he has the pots in his possession I'll be killed.'

Danny Ling did not answer and he averted his eyes as he stood up straight. 'You'd be well advised to think hard. And get some sleep. Tomorrow could be a very wearing day.'

'Nice work your lord and master did on Victor,' Tommy taunted him before the loud slam of the door sent waves of pain reverberating through his concussed head. Why wait till morning, he thought angrily as he dipped the stale bread into the watery soup. Billy Chou was enjoying every minute of this. He was giving him time to think, to visualise in his mind what was planned for him, and the realisation of his utter helplessness sent a shudder of fear through his very bones.

Chapter Thirty-Eight

Tommy Lo awoke once more from a fitful sleep and tried to ease his aching limbs. The chains had restricted his movement and raw patches were beginning to show around his wrist and ankle where the fetters had rubbed during the night. The light filtering through the high fanlight told him it was morning, and from the faint rumble of traffic he guessed that the docks were open for business which would make it after eight o'clock. Paul Neal had seemed a sensible man and he would lose no time in going to see Inspector Kennedy, Tommy told himself. Kennedy could be expected to take a look at the warehouse, and he might even suspect that he was being held there, if he wasn't already floating down the river with his throat cut.

Footsteps outside made the young man sit up straight against the damp wall and he looked up as Danny Ling entered carrying a mug of tea.

'I trust you slept well?' he said sarcastically.

'Very well thank you,' Tommy Lo replied, 'everything considered.'

Danny Ling put the tea down near the prisoner and backed away. 'Billy Chou should be here soon,' he said. 'It was a very profitable night for him at the gambling house and we celebrated with a few drinks too many I'm afraid. It's a pity. You know how nasty Billy Chou can get when he's recovering from a hangover.'

Tommy Lo did not take his eyes off him. 'Yes, I saw some of his handiwork at the back of Husi Kang's club. What was the point of killing Victor Sen? He would never have been a problem to you.'

Danny Ling hunched his shoulders. 'Victor Sen was against us coming for you, and he tried to persuade Billy Chou to accept the outcome of the vote and get back to us working together as a Tong once more.'

'That was good thinking,' Tommy Lo replied. 'And he was killed in cold blood for voicing it.'

'It's too late now,' Danny Ling said shaking his head. 'The Tong's credibility had disappeared and there were other aspects to consider.'

'Like finding the pots and becoming very rich.'

'Yeah. The temptation was too great to ignore.'

Tommy Lo sipped his tea. 'So this Tong goes the way of others, whose members sold their souls for riches,' he said with distaste. 'I've already told you those ginger pots will bring you nothing but grief and misfortune. Think hard, Danny Ling. Let me loose and help me finish Billy Chou once and for all. Just remember, you'll end up the way Victor Sen did when you're no more use to Billy Chou. He's mad and he's going to end up destroying himself and anyone associated with him.'

Danny Ling backed to the door. 'You're wasting your time,' he replied. 'You think hard and make it easy on yourself. We'll get to the truth eventually and you'll suffer for your obstinacy.'

The door slammed shut behind him and Tommy Lo looked up at the fanlight. 'What's keeping you, Kennedy,' he said aloud.

Joey Westlake reached the bus stop at the Rotherhithe Tunnel entrance and saw Paul already waiting there. 'I went ter the market early,' he said. 'I got Big Fred ter run the stall terday. 'E's well pleased. 'E could do wiv the shekels after bein' banged away fer a year.'

Paul smiled. 'I came in me work gear,' he remarked, opening his coat to show the boiler suit sporting the initials GPO on the breast pocket. 'I told the foreman I'll try an' get in ter work this afternoon.'

Five minutes later Sonny Rowland trotted up wearing a loose green cardigan over his grey trousers and a navy blue scarf wrapped around his neck. 'I done a five-mile run this mornin',' he announced, wiping the sweat from his face.

'I 'ope Butch ain't gonna be long,' Paul said anxiously.

Ten minutes later the gangly figure of the window cleaner turned the corner. 'Sorry I'm late, lads,' he said cheerfully. 'The bloody tram in front got stuck on the points.'

'Yer should 'ave got off an' walked,' Sonny told him. 'I run five miles this mornin'.'

'That's what I did do, yer dozy git,' Butch growled at him.

The number 82 bus pulled up full of dockers and the four young men jumped on.

''Ere, while we're over Lime'ouse can we take a look in the Cutter?' Butch asked. 'It's s'posed ter be a really famous pub. I was talkin' ter this geezer the ovver day an' 'e was sayin' that 'e goes over the water ter drink. 'E reckons the pubs over there are much livelier than our ones. 'E was tellin' me about the Cutter. Full of all sorts it is.'

'Yeah, I can just imagine,' Joey said pulling a face as the conductor came along the aisle.

''Old up, I'll get these,' Paul said, putting a hand in his pocket.

Sonny tapped Paul on the shoulder from the seat behind. ''Ere, while I fink of it. D'yer want some tickets fer Manor Place Baths next week?' he asked. 'I'm on the bill. It's the supportin' bout ter Sammy Goldberg an' Basher James fer the area title.'

Joey gave Paul a quick glance before turning round in his seat. 'Who yer fightin', Sonny?' he asked.

'Dave Becket.'

'Dave Becket? 'E's tipped as the next cruiser-weight champion,' Joey said quickly.

'Yeah that's right. They reckon I'll give 'im a good scrap,' Sonny replied casually. 'I might even come out best, who knows. I'd be next in line then.'

'Yeah, yer will, won't yer,' Joey said sarcastically.

The bus emerged from the tunnel and turned right into Commercial Road, pulling up outside the seamen's hostel by Salmon Lane.

'Come on, we get off 'ere,' Paul told them.

The young men made their way along West India Dock Road towards the police station. Up ahead they could see the dock gates and on the right-hand side of the road the Cutter public house.

'That's the pub I was tellin' yer about,' Butch said as they hurried up the few steps into Limehouse police station.

'What can I do you gents for?' the desk sergeant asked with a grin.

Paul glanced quickly at the clock which showed five minutes after nine. 'We've gotta see Chief Inspector Kennedy urgently,' he announced.

'All of yer?'

'Yeah all of us.'

'I'm afraid 'e's not in,' the sergeant told him.

'When will 'e be in?'

'I dunno.'

'Well yer better find out, 'cos if we don't get this message to 'im on time 'e's gonna be spittin' fire an' brimstone,' Paul said sharply.

The anxious look in the young man's eyes prompted the sergeant to take him seriously. 'Is the inspector due in this mornin', Bert?' he enquired.

The constable sitting behind him shook his head. ''E's goin' straight ter the council meeting.'

'Can't you reach 'im?' Paul said quickly.

The sergeant picked up the phone. ''Ello, Mary. Sorry ter trouble yer at 'ome, but 'as the inspector left yet? Good. Could I 'ave a word wiv 'im please? 'Ello, sir. I've got four young men 'ere an' they said they've got some vital information that won't keep. Yes they do seem genuine. Right. That's fine.' He put the receiver down and turned to Paul. 'The inspector said 'e'll look in on 'is way ter the meetin', in about fifteen minutes. This info better be pucka.'

'Don't worry, it is,' Paul said confidently.

'If you'll take a seat then.'

'Disbelievin' git,' Butch mumbled.

''E reminds me o' Laurel an' 'Ardy,' Sonny remarked.

'What, both of 'em?' Butch asked with a grin.

'Nah, the fat one.'

'Oliver 'Ardy yer mean.'

'Yeah that's 'im.'

'If 'e 'ad a moustache 'e would.'

'Yeah an' a bowler 'at.'

'That geezer be'ind 'im reminds me of Peter Lorre.'

'Yeah 'e does.'

''Old tight, 'ere comes Sidney Greenstreet,' Butch said grinning as a large policeman walked into the station.

Sonny laughed aloud and the policeman spun round quickly. 'What you laughin' at?' he said aggressively.

''E just told me a joke,' Sonny replied amiably.

The policeman pushed his way through the swing doors and Joey leaned back against the wall and crossed his legs. 'D'you know somefing? I got a funny feelin' about terday.'

'What d'yer mean?' Butch asked him.

'Well, d'yer remember when we all went on that beano from the Swan last year?'

''Ow could I ferget it,' Butch replied, with a rueful smile.

'It started off somefing like this, wiv you an' Sonny talkin' in the pub about who people reminded you of, an' then when that big geezer come over an' asked who you was laughin' at Sonny told 'im we thought 'e looked a bit like Clark Gable, if 'e'd 'ad a moustache, an' dark 'air, an' a face that wasn't so ugly. If I remember rightly that was the point when all 'ell broke loose an' we was lucky ter get out o' that pub in one piece.'

'We wouldn't 'ave done if Sonny 'adn't floored the geezer first,' Butch replied.

'Yeah well 'e did get stroppy,' Sonny said frowning.

The front door opened and a tall, heavily built man wearing a dark suit walked into the reception area. He gave the young men a curious look and then turned to the desk officer. 'Are these the gentlemen who want to see me, Sergeant?' he asked. 'Right then, lads, if you'll just follow me.'

At the end of a long corridor Chief Inspector Kennedy opened a door and stood back for them to go in. 'If you'll just give me two minutes,' he said courteously.

Paul looked around the office and noticed the framed photograph of the inspector standing in the midst of a group of young Chinese men. Next to it was a framed citation, and as he started to read it the inspector entered the room along with another officer. 'This is Detective Sergeant Murray,' he announced. 'Pull up some chairs.'

When they were all seated comfortably the inspector leaned on his desk and looked around at the four in turn. 'I understand you have some important information for me,' he said expectantly.

Paul introduced himself and gave his address. 'The information concerns Tommy Lo,' he began.

'You know Tommy Lo?' Kennedy said frowning.

'Frew my gelfriend,' Paul replied.

'Is she Chinese?'

'Yeah.'

'From this area?'

'No, Bermon'sey.'

'Go on.'

'Tommy Lo came ter see me on Tuesday evenin',' Paul explained. ''E told me 'e was in trouble wiv the Tong. I dunno 'ow bad it is but 'e seemed ter feel that 'is life was in danger, an' 'e told me that if I never 'eard from 'im by last night I was ter come an' see you this mornin' as early as possible.'

'And you came mob-handed,' the inspector said smiling.

'These are me friends,' Paul replied. 'They didn't want me walkin' round 'ere on me own, considerin' what I know.'

Kennedy smiled. 'How was Tommy Lo going to contact you?' he enquired.

'By phone.'

The two policemen exchanged quick glances. 'Right then, you'd better tell me everything you know.'

Paul recited the information word for word, and when he spoke about the *Honi Maru* arriving that evening at the King George the Fifth Docks Kennedy looked very serious. 'As a matter of fact we know about the *Honi Maru*. It arrived early and at the moment it's moored in the Reach,' he said with a quick glance at his subordinate. 'It'll dock early this afternoon at high tide. We also know about the shipment of opium. You telling us that it's bound for the Peking Club confirms our suspicions and we're very grateful.'

'Do yer suspect that Tommy Lo's bin killed?' Paul asked.

'It's quite likely I'm afraid,' Kennedy replied. 'The Tong have allies everywhere. When someone upsets them retribution comes quickly. At least you'll have helped in no small measure to avenge his death. We now have something to go on and you can be sure that Billy Chou and the other Tong members will be picked up for questioning. I'm indebted.

Now I'd suggest that you leave the area right away. This can be a dangerous place for strangers.'

The four filed out of the police station and Sonny rubbed his midriff. 'There should be a decent caff round 'ere somewhere. I'm bleedin' starvin',' he groaned.

'Let's try that one over there,' Joey suggested as they made their way back along the West India Dock Road.

Chief Inspector Kennedy went into action as soon as the young men had left. 'I want Billy Chou brought in right away,' he growled. 'And send a team to impound that van of Ling's, and I want you to visit Husi Kang at the Peking Club. Don't be too heavy-handed. We don't want to frighten him off now that the opium shipment's arrived. He'll be expecting us to call on him anyway, considering that the victim was killed in the alley behind his premises. Just take the usual statements. I'm going to personally grill that bastard Billy Chou as soon as they bring him in.'

Revitalised with egg, bacon, sausage and fried bread, and a large mug of tea, the intrepid four decided that even though the detective had advised them to leave the area right away it might be better to look around first and get the feel of the place, which until then they had regarded as somewhere to avoid at all costs.

'It ain't too bad when yer fink about it,' Butch remarked as they strolled along Pennyfields. 'They've gotta live somewhere after all.'

Sonny smiled at a shopkeeper who was putting his stock outside his premises and the man bowed politely.

Joey stopped to look in a tea room and the owner

beckoned him to come in. 'They must fink we're off the ships,' he said, giving the man a large grin.

They turned into Canton Street and Paul grabbed Joey's arm. 'This is where the ware'ouse is,' he said quickly. 'That looks like it down the end o' the road. Let's take a gander.'

As they neared the warehouse they could see some men milling around at the entrance and Paul nudged Joey. 'Take this turnin',' he said urgently.

'What's wrong?' Joey asked when they were safely out of sight.

'We don't wanna alert 'em do we,' Paul told him. 'The police are gonna raid the gaff ter find that van.'

'I reckon we should go an' see what the Cutter's like,' Butch remarked. 'It ain't far from 'ere.'

They found the pub, which had just opened, and when they stepped out of the morning sun into the dusty gloom they saw the large landlord Kipper Joe smiling at them with his hands resting on the polished counter. 'You're the first terday,' he boomed out. 'Yer not off the ships I can tell,' he said, pointing to the GPO letters on the overalls beneath Paul's unbuttoned coat.

'We bin on business,' Butch told him, 'an' we've 'eard about this place so we decided to 'ave a butcher's.'

'Yeah, well we are pretty well known. So what'll it be, lads?'

Paul gave him the order. 'D'yer get many Chinese in 'ere?' he asked as Kipper Joe filled the glasses.

'Quite a few, yeah. Why d'yer ask?'

'I just wondered if yer knew a man by the name o' Tommy Lo,' Paul replied. ''E's a friend o' mine.'

'A friend o' yours?' Kipper queried.

''E's got 'imself in some trouble an' I was 'opin' 'e was all right.'

'Tong trouble?'

'Yeah.'

'There's a lot o' talk on the streets but I can't afford ter make comments or take sides, not in my position,' Kipper Joe said firmly. 'The Tongs don't trouble me an' I don't trouble them. They're welcome ter drink in 'ere same as anyone else. All I ask is that they be'ave themselves.'

'It makes sense,' Paul said as he picked up his glass of beer.

The big publican studied him for a while and then leaned forward on the counter. 'Where d'yer come from, son?' he asked.

'Bermon'sey.'

'I'm known as Kipper Joe by everyone round 'ere,' the big man told him. 'What's your moniker?'

'Paul Neal.'

'An' 'ow comes yer a friend o' Tommy Lo?'

'It's a long story,' Paul replied. 'I got ter know 'im frew my gelfriend. She's Chinese yer see. Tommy Lo's a decent bloke. I'm really worried about 'im.'

Kipper Joe stroked his large chin for a few moments. 'Look, I know a Chinese geezer who might be able to 'elp yer, but whatever yer do, don't tell 'im I sent yer. When yer leave 'ere turn left an' . . .'

The four drank up quickly and made their way into the backstreets of Chinatown. Wu Sung looked nervous as he peered through the half-opened door. 'Yes I am Wu Sung,' he said. 'Is one of you the man who goes by the name of Paul Neal?'

'That's me,' Paul told him, looking very surprised.

'I have been expecting you,' the old man said as he opened the door and stood back for them to enter. 'If you will be seated I will bring some tea.'

'I 'ope it ain't too milky, on top o' that beer,' Sonny said pulling a face.

'I can guarantee it won't be milky,' Paul replied with a grin.

The young men watched intrigued as Wu Sung laid out the bowls and filled them with clear green liquid from a tall thin pot.

'Any friend of Tommy Lo is welcome in my humble home,' he said, holding out the bowls in his bony fingers.

'Is Tommy Lo dead?' Paul asked anxiously.

Wu Sung shook his head. 'I do not think so, not yet, but I think he will be soon if something is not done.'

'You mean the Tong are 'oldin' 'im?' Paul asked.

'The warehouse on Canton Street is the place, I would guess,' Wu Sung told him.

'We've already bin ter the police an' they're gonna raid the place,' Paul told him.

Wu Sung smiled, shaking his head slowly. 'I know the warehouse. It has many places to hide someone. They will move him through the underground tunnel when the police go in. The tunnel once went to another warehouse, but that one is gone. It was destroyed in the war. Now the tunnel opens near the water and there are many ways to disappear from there. There are many alleys, and there is the river. They could move him by boat.'

434

Paul sipped the bitter tea. 'First we need ter know fer sure if Tommy Lo is there,' he said thoughtfully.

''Ow we gonna find out?' Joey asked, pulling a face and putting his bowl down on the table.

'I got an idea. See 'ow this strikes yer,' Paul said, smiling slyly.

Chapter Thirty-Nine

Ruby left the house on Wednesday morning and glanced along the alley to see Lizzie Roach rocking away contentedly, her head slumped down on her chest. No one else was about and as she hurried out into Grange Road she thought about what Jim had said that morning before leaving for work. 'Everyfing's gonna be fine, gel,' he had told her with a reassuring kiss on the cheek.

Just a few encouraging words, but she knew what they meant. Today he was going to put things right and she had not known whether to rage at him or hug him. Instead she did neither. Her smile was brief and forbearing, but inside she felt a surge of expectation. She was missing him, missing his arms around her and his soft caress. Her vow to make him suffer for his transgression was weakening already and she sighed with equanimity. Some women would give their men hell and others would totally ignore them or throw them out of the house. For her the family was everything. Happiness was togetherness, and today she had a spring in her step as she made her way to the surgery.

The four young men from Bermondsey walked to the corner of Canton Street and Paul took off his coat. 'Now listen,' he said handing it to Joey, 'keep out o' sight. If I'm not out in 'alf an hour yer better come lookin' for me.'

'Good luck, pal,' Butch said as Paul strolled off.

''E's got some bottle, I'll give 'im that,' Joey remarked.

Paul ambled up to the telephone junction box near the warehouse entrance and pulled a notebook from his breast pocket as he leaned forward to read the number on the metal cover. He whistled blithely to himself as he scribbled something down then he walked on, his eyes searching the brick wall of the warehouse. He spotted the lead sheathing which ran up to a window and he took out a penknife to scrape it, all the while observed by two junior Tong members who were lounging against the wall. He walked up to them and smiled. 'I'm from the Lime'ouse telephone exchange,' he said calmly, pointing to the letters on his overalls. 'I've gotta check on the wirin'.'

'There's no telephones here,' one of the young men said peremptorily.

'Yes I know. They were cut off some time ago an' that's the trouble,' Paul replied, scratching his head. 'Yer see, the lead cables should be capped, but a lot weren't due to the war an' the result is that rats tend ter gnaw at the ends o' the wires an' short 'em out. Then there's the dampness. That causes shortin' out too. Look, I know it's a bloody nuisance but I gotta do a survey. I need ter get in the ware'ouse. Can yer let me in?'

'No one goes inside,' the Tong member said menacingly.

Paul raised his hands in resignation. 'OK, lads, I'm only tryin' ter do me job. Yer see it's all linked up wiv that junction box over there. The wires from this ware'ouse go in there an' they're shortin' out the rest. Unfortunately the local police station is on the same circuit an' 'alf their phones are down. They're creatin' merry 'ell an' they've bin on to us ter get somefing done quick. Still, if I can't get access it's not my fault.'

'You wait here,' the young man said quickly.

Paul nodded and leaned against the wall in a nonchalant manner, although his heart was pounding in his chest. He felt sure that Wu Sung was right about Tommy Lo being held there at the warehouse and he crossed his fingers while he waited.

The young man came back out. 'You come with me,' he said, waving his hand impatiently.

Inside the entrance Danny Ling stood talking to another young man and he turned to stare at Paul. 'All the telephones are gone,' he said. 'Only the wires are left. You can see they run along the ceiling and up on to the other floors.'

'That's a big 'elp,' Paul replied, giving Danny Ling a smile as he took out his notebook. 'I shouldn't be very long once I locate the fault.'

Danny Ling continued talking to the young member and Paul cast his eyes round quickly before he trotted up the long flight of stone steps. The large open area of the first floor was empty, and the other two levels were the same. Windows were missing and debris littered the stone floors. It was pretty apparent that Tommy Lo was not being held up here, Paul thought.

'Did you find the fault?' Danny Ling asked as Paul hurried down the stairs.

'There's quite a few loose ends, it could be any one of

'em causin' the short,' Paul replied. 'Mind you, it won't take 'em long ter cap 'em.'

'Can't you cap them?'

'Nah, yer need an engineer. I could do it but they won't let me. I'm on inspectin' yer see. It's two different departments. Never mind, if I can just take a look down these stairs.'

Danny Ling looked anxious. 'That's the cellar. No phones in the cellar.'

'Nah, but I gotta take a look, just fer the record,' Paul told him with a smile.

Danny Ling switched the light on at the top of the stairs and led the way down. 'You can see there's no wires,' he said impatiently.

'That's fine. If I can just take a look in this room,' Paul said, reaching for the handle of a heavy-looking door.

'It's locked and I don't have the key,' Danny Ling told him irritably.

Paul stroked his chin as he looked around the large cellar area. The room behind the locked door had most likely been used as an office and it was the only secure room in the warehouse. 'Well, if yer sure there's no loose wires in there I won't need ter see inside,' he said, raising his voice a little. 'I'll get someone down right away ter cap the wires an' then we won't need ter trouble you any more. A nice stout door this,' he remarked, giving it a kick. 'Elm I would say. Don't make 'em like that any more. Anyway I shouldn't worry about the cappin'. It'll only take a few minutes.'

As he walked out into the sunlight Paul took a deep breath. It had gone off like a dream and he had guessed right. Tommy Lo was imprisoned in the cellar. The kick on the door had been answered by the faint rattle of a chain.

'What's the score?' Joey said anxiously as Paul turned the corner.

'Tommy Lo's in there. In the cellar,' he replied excitedly.

'Do we get the rozzers, or get 'im out on our own?' Butch asked.

'There's two men outside the ware'ouse an' two more inside at the moment,' Paul told them.

'The place might be swarmin' wiv Chinkies by the time we fetch the coppers,' Sonny said. 'Let's get 'im out now.'

Butch looked a little apprehensive. 'I'll go along wiv the rest of yer,' he offered.

Paul turned to Joey. 'What d'yer fink?'

'Let's do it.'

'Come on, we're wastin' time,' Sonny urged them, banging his large fist into the palm of his hand.

'Look, I've told 'em that the wires need cappin',' Paul explained. 'We'll walk down there casual like an' bluff it out. You lads are the engineers, OK?'

As they reached the warehouse entrance the two young Tong members stood in their way and Paul smiled at them. 'We've come ter do the cappin',' he said calmly.

'You wait,' one of them ordered.

As he turned to enter the warehouse Paul jumped him from behind. The other member reached into his coat but Sonny was too quick for him and a swift right hook followed by a knee in the groin and a vicious uppercut laid him out cold. Paul had his hand over his opponent's mouth to stop him shouting out as they struggled violently and Butch grabbed his legs. As he hit the floor with Paul beneath him Joey kicked him in the head and Sonny bent down to finish the job with a few quick punches. It was over very suddenly and Paul eased himself from beneath the prone Tong member and staggered to his feet gasping. Butch and Joey bent down to drag the two unconscious men into the doorway but Paul shouted to leave them as he saw a group of young Chinese running towards them from the end of the turning. The friends dashed headlong into the warehouse ready to tackle whoever stood in their way and Sonny turned to shut the heavy door, leaning his bulk against it. There was no sign of Danny Ling nor the other Tong member and Paul noticed the heavy iron bar standing in the corner near the entrance. The men outside began hammering on the door and Sonny was having trouble keeping it shut. Joey leant his weight against it while Paul grabbed up the bar and dropped it into the slots. 'That should 'old it fer the time bein',' he gasped.

Suddenly Danny Ling appeared at the head of the stairs alerted by the noise and he crouched and moved to one side, his hand reaching into his coat pocket. Paul sprang at him but he twisted sideways and threw him over his hip. The young man looked up at the flash of a blade and heard Butch roar like a madman as he dived at the Tong member. Boots, fists and heads flew everywhere and Danny Ling was battered into oblivion before he had the chance to use Paul as a shield.

Joey breathed hard and wiped away a smear of blood from his lip. 'Bloody 'ell, that was close,' he coughed.

Butch Wheeler had surprised himself by his actions and he stood trembling, a wide smile showing the gap in his teeth. Paul struggled to his feet and the front door started to splinter. 'Come on, lads,' he shouted, leading the way down the stone stairs. 'That's the door! We'll 'ave ter break it down.'

Sonny put his shoulder to it but it stood firm. Joey tried kicking it to no avail. Then they heard Tommy Lo's voice. 'It's too thick! Get the keys,' he yelled out.

Paul and Joey sprinted up the stairs and rolled the unconscious Danny Ling over on to his back while they went through his pockets. 'These could be 'em,' Paul said excitedly.

Joey pointed to the front door. 'They're almost frew,' he shouted as they ran down the stairs again.

The largest of the keys fitted the door and when they bundled their way into the room Tommy Lo grinned at them. 'You took your time, Paul Neal,' he said calmly.

Joey tried each key in turn on the shackles, his hands shaking, and finally he gave a triumphant shout as he found the right one. They helped Tommy Lo to his feet and he rubbed his wrists briskly. 'We'll need to go out through the tunnel,' he told them. 'This way, and be careful. It might be guarded.'

They heard angry shouting as the men finally broke the front door down above them, and as they dashed across to the far side of the large cellar Tommy Lo picked up a piece of iron piping before opening the metal door. A gust of sour air hit them and huge black spiders scurried off into the shadows. Tommy pushed them into the low dark tunnel closing the door behind him and wedging the piping through the handles. 'That should keep them for a few minutes,' he remarked.

They picked their way through the blackness towards the

faint outline of light up ahead. 'Let's hope the door's not barred,' Tommy said.

When they reached the end of the tunnel the door opened with ease. It was quiet in the narrow alley, and down below the swirling river was moving in on the tide.

'What a sight,' Joey said, holding his arms wide.

Butch put his arm around Sonny's shoulder. 'I fink we did well.'

'Yeah we did, didn't we?' Sonny replied with a grin.

Tommy Lo led the way along the alley and into another narrow alleyway with houses on either side.

'Fancy livin' 'ere,' Paul remarked.

'No fanks,' Joey replied with a quick look over his shoulder.

Sonny Rowland was bringing up the rear, and as he passed by a front door it suddenly flew open. A young man in black leapt out into the alley brandishing a long knife over his head. He brought it down in a circular movement and thrust out with a shout as Sonny spun round. The boxer's quick reflex saved his life but the blade pierced his upper arm and he fell backwards on to the cobblestones with a cry of pain.

'Tommy Lo, the Tong has spoken,' the man said, waving the bloodstained knife. 'There's no escape for you. Today you will die, and I have the privilege.'

'Stand back!' Tommy Lo shouted. 'He's pilled up.'

The wild-eyed young man moved forward menacingly towards Tommy Lo and they crouched, circling each other in the alley.

'Kneel and die quickly,' the junior member snarled.

Tommy Lo feinted forward and ducked swiftly as the

knife whistled through the air above his head. It missed him by no more than an inch but it threw his attacker off balance, and before he could recover Tommy Lo had grabbed his arm. He spun the man round and planted a knee in his back, grasping the knife by the hilt and forcing the edge of the blade against the man's throat. The young men from Bermondsey shuddered and looked away as Tommy jerked the knife hard and sliced open his neck, spurting blood on to the cobbles and they hurried out of the alley, glancing back to see the crazed assailant lying twitching in the gutter.

The early afternoon sun was still high in the sky as the men rested in the safety of Wu Sung's house. Sonny Rowland looked pale-faced as he sat back in a comfortable chair with his arm in a sling, having been expertly tended to by Dr Lee, who was quite used to treating knife wounds.

'My house is at your disposal until it is safe to leave,' Wu Sung reassured them.

'I have a contact at the Peking Club,' Tommy Lo explained. 'As soon as the arrests have been made he'll let me know, then I'll make sure you get a police escort out of the area. I am very grateful to all of you,' he told them, and he bowed solemnly.

Chapter Forty

Jim Neal walked home from work on Wednesday evening feeling that a heavy load had been lifted from his shoulders. It had been much easier than he imagined. He and Angela had sat together in the riverside pub at lunchtime and to begin with she was her usual bubbly self.

'Whoever's responsible for the letter is just a frustrated little idiot. Let it die a natural death, Jim,' she said.

He felt in control for the first time since his association with her began but he did not want to gloat. She was a sad figure, if what he had heard about her was true, and now she would have to face up to the truth, just as Ruby had forced herself to do in a brave attempt to get her life back together.

'The original anonymous letter, Angela. It concerned a man called Crawley.'

'Yes that's right.'

'Do you still see 'im?'

'No, of course not.'

'What about Laurie?'

'What about him?'

''E's not wiv yer any more, is 'e?'

'You seem to know a lot.'

'I 'appen ter know that 'e left yer a few years ago, after catchin' you an' his best mate tergevver.'

Angela's composure slipped enough for him to notice. 'It's a . . . No it's not true,' she faltered.

'Let's stop the play-actin'. Laurie left yer, an' you an' Crawley are still seein' each ovver. Don't try an' deny it. Yer've bin seen tergevver, recently.'

Angela's face flushed and she downed her drink in one gulp. 'I don't have to sit here and listen to you whining on,' she said sharply. 'If you don't believe me you can go to hell, or anywhere else you like. You were on a good thing and you didn't appreciate it. You could have had it all, a wife, a lover. In fact the best of both worlds, but you chose to tell her. You're pathetic.'

'Yeah I did, Angela,' he said quietly. 'I chose ter tell 'er. I can't live life wiv two faces, an' if you can then good luck ter yer. I just wanna close the book on us.'

'I've already done so,' Angela said with venom as she stood up and stormed off.

Jim watched her leave, and then aware that eyes were on him he left too. Now as he strolled home he smiled to himself. It had been easy, easier than he had anticipated. The hard part was in front of him, but he felt that the signs were good. As he walked in the house he heard Ruby's voice. 'That you, Jim? 'Ere come an' take a look at these marigolds. They've all come out tergevver.'

Wu Sung entered the room and looked around at the lounging figures. 'Can I get you some more tea?' he suggested.

'No it's OK,' Joey said quickly.

'Perhaps you would prefer beer.'

Butch looked up quickly. 'That sounds good,' he said smiling.

The old man left the room and came back carrying a stone flagon. 'It keeps cold in here,' he told them. 'My good friend Kipper Joe at the Cutter supplies me with a regular flagon of ale.'

Paul smiled to himself, recalling that the publican had asked him his name. Wu Sung had obviously warned him to be on the look-out, realising that a pub would be the first place someone would visit to make enquiries in an unfamiliar area.

Wu Sung brought in some glasses and poured the drinks. Joey took a grateful gulp and nodded towards a small oblong box inlaid with ivory and gold leaf. 'That's a smashin' piece o' craftsmanship,' he remarked.

'It's a mah-jong case,' Wu Sung told him. 'Do you play mah-jong?'

Joey shook his head. 'You blokes play it a lot, don't yer?' he replied.

Wu Sung smiled. 'We all have time to spare. Would you like me to teach you the game?'

Joey rubbed his hands together. 'Yeah, why not.'

Paul shook his head when Joey waved him over. 'I'm not up to it at the moment,' he said with a serious face.

Wu Sung opened the box and took out all the pieces, to the surprise of Joey, Butch and Sonny. 'I didn't fink there was all this much stuff fer mah-jong,' Sonny remarked.

'Cor! Look at the patterns on these pieces,' Butch said incredulously.

Tommy Lo looked over and smiled. 'They'll be experts

before long,' he said to Paul. 'Wu Sung is a master at the game.'

Paul nodded and glanced back through the net curtains into the quiet street. 'I was just wonderin' about Mei Li,' he said quietly. 'Would it really be that 'ard for 'er ter defy 'er guardian?'

'It depends,' Tommy replied.

'I mean by stayin' 'ere in England an' refusin' ter marry a man she 'ardly knows.'

'I'm half Chinese and half English,' Tommy told him, 'but I have a strong sense of being Chinese and I understand how hard it must be for her. It would probably be impossible for Mei Li to defy her guardian. The obligation, the duty Chinese people are bound by in such situations is stronger than death. It's not a question of making a choice. For Mei Li there is no choice. If she loves you, and I'm sure she does, part of her will stay here for ever, but she will still go home and marry the man Li Fong has picked for her.'

'I've not given up,' Paul said firmly. 'Wiv luck we'll meet before she an' Li Fong leave the country, an' I'm gonna try an' get 'im ter see sense.'

'Well I wish you luck, Paul Neal,' the young Chinese man said sincerely.

With the *Honi Maru* safely docked and cleared by Customs the courier left the ship to make a phone call on the quayside. Briefed on what he had to do, he then phoned for a cab and went back aboard to collect his large canvas bags. When the taxi arrived he was waiting, and after brief instructions to the driver he clambered in, unaware that a signalling wave from the after deck was noted by a watcher in the quayside shed, who took his cue and picked up his phone. The taxi drove into Pennyfields and stopped outside the Peking Club, and as soon as the courier entered the building Chief Inspector Kennedy gave the word to go from his vantage point inside a bomb-damaged house along the street. Police cars squealed to a halt and uniformed officers ran into the club and down the adjoining alley. Kennedy strolled along the street in no apparent hurry with a satisfied grin on his face. 'Is the building secure?' he asked the uniformed sergeant.

'Tight as a drum, sir.'

Sergeant Murray was already in Husi Kang's private office and as soon as he walked in Kennedy could see that something was wrong. Husi looked aggrieved as he stood beside the courier, who sat passively holding a large packet on his lap. 'What is the meaning of this intrusion without a search warrant?' he demanded to know.

Kennedy ignored him, taking the opened packet from the smuggler and scooping out a handful of mint tea-leaf, and his face grew black with anger. 'We've been taken on, Murray,' he growled. 'Go and see if anyone bothered to take the number of that cab.'

'Cab, sir?'

'The cab,' Kennedy almost shouted. 'This is a decoy. The driver was obviously instructed to deliver the shipment elsewhere.'

Murray hurried away and was soon back. 'No I'm afraid not,' he reported.

At six o'clock Ti San came to the house of Wu Sung looking very worried. 'There have been no arrests,' he said breathlessly. 'The carrier brought only mint tea.'

Tommy Lo looked puzzled and he sat down to think for a moment or two then he spoke quietly to Wu Sung. Finally he turned to the four young men. 'You must stay here for the time being,' he told them firmly. 'The streets will be dangerous after what's happened.' He addressed Ti San in Cantonese and the young man bowed and went out, followed by Wu Sung.

'It seems that Billy Chou was released this afternoon without charge,' Tommy explained. 'He'll be at the warehouse gloating, but now he'll have to answer to me and me alone.'

'You can't go back there,' Paul said quickly, 'they'll kill yer fer certain.'

'I have no choice,' Tommy replied, 'but I want you to stay here. If things go wrong and I don't return Wu Sung will know what to do.'

'Yer'll stand more chance if there's two of us,' Paul insisted.

'If yer fink I'm waitin' 'ere while you two go pissin' off yer got anuvver fink comin',' Joey declared. 'Your Kay would never fergive me if I let yer go on yer own.'

'OK, OK,' Paul said, turning to Butch. 'You stay 'ere an' look after Sonny an' Wu Sung. Yer've earned yer corn terday, anyway.'

Butch smiled, a gap-tooth smile that touched Paul. 'Don't you worry, they'll be all right wiv me,' he said proudly.

Canton Street was deserted as the three men made their way towards the warehouse, and when they turned into the narrow backstreet that ran beside it they saw a taxi-cab parked a few feet ahead. 'Christ! They've killed the driver!'

Paul exclaimed as he saw the blood splattered over the windscreen, steering-wheel and seat.

'They've dumped him in the river that's for sure,' Tommy Lo said through gritted teeth.

They passed quickly through the deathly quiet street and into the narrow lane that ran parallel to the foreshore. When they arrived at the tunnel door Tommy Lo held up his hand. 'Be as quiet as you can,' he said, tapping his thigh to reassure himself that his knife was still in place.

With their backs to the light they were forced to feel their way along, and when they finally reached the warehouse and crept across the chamber to the passage Tommy held up his hand. 'They'll be in the room opposite,' he whispered.

'Do we charge in?' Paul asked in a hushed voice.

Tommy Lo shook his head and smiled. 'Let's go in nice and easy.'

Paul and Joey looked at each other not knowing what to expect, but the sight that greeted them as they stepped into the room surprised them all. Billy Chou was sitting at the table with his head bowed. Beside him was Husi Kang and Kobi the large Korean. The bruised and battered Danny Ling sat nearby, and lying in the centre of the table were two large canvas bags. Standing over the prisoners and at strategic points around the room were armed men. A tall thin man with grey wavy hair stood in the middle of the large room and he smiled amiably. 'Good evening. Do come in,' he said cheerfully. 'If you'll just take a seat and be quiet you won't be harmed, but should you try to leave, my men have orders to shoot. Is that understood?'

At that moment a man hurried in and whispered something to him, and he nodded quickly. 'It seems that the gentleman we've been waiting for is on his way,' he announced.

Paul glanced anxiously at Joey and he pulled a face as they found a chair, while Tommy Lo sat down next to Billy Chou. Heavy footsteps sounded outside and the door opened. Chief Inspector Kennedy's eyes widened with surprise as he looked around. 'I thought I'd find the consignment here,' he growled.

'You took your time,' the tall man remarked.

'What's going on? I don't understand,' Kennedy replied. 'I'm here to make an arrest.'

'I'm afraid not,' the grey-haired man answered grimly. 'It's all over, Kennedy.'

One of the guards moved behind the policeman and pushed him into the room.

'Allow me to introduce myself,' the grey-haired man said. 'I'm Divisional Inspector Craig of Scotland Yard, working in co-operation with the Hong Kong police force. Chief Inspector Kennedy, you are under arrest for drug dealing, conspiracy to murder and perverting the course of justice. There will be other charges, I have no doubt, but those will do for a start. Read him his rights, Miller.'

'This is ridiculous,' Kennedy said quickly.

'I beg to differ,' Craig replied calmly. 'We've had your personal office phone tapped for some time now. We've got it all nicely recorded on a boxful of tapes. It's all there, your messages to the drug carrier, your order to kill the taxi driver as soon as he handed over the bag, and instructions to Husi Kang the club owner to meet you here for the share-out. As a matter of fact the taxi driver was substituted by one of our men at the dock gate, and I have to tell you that the young

Tong member who was ordered to carry out the killing was himself shot dead. It was unfortunate but totally necessary, I assure you. I expect you saw the taxi parked in the lane. We didn't want to alert you on your way here so we decorated the cab with something I acquired from a friend of mine who works at the film studios. Very realistic, but rather a messy concoction actually.'

Kennedy slumped down in a chair and Craig walked over to where Paul and Joey were sitting. 'And how do you fit in to all this?' he asked.

'We're Tommy Lo's friends,' Paul told him.

'Oh I see,' the policeman said, a ghost of a smile playing around the corner of his mouth.

As he turned to address Kennedy again Tommy Lo saw his chance. He slid from his chair and grabbed Billy Chou round the neck, his knife held against Chou's throat.

The guards moved forward, their guns pointed at the pair as Tommy Lo lifted Billy Chou from his chair and backed him towards the door.

'Now don't be silly, young man,' Craig said sternly. 'Let him go. My men can drop the two of you.'

'It's your choice,' Tommy Lo said calmly. 'This is Tong business. We have a score to settle. Now open the door and stand away.'

The guards looked anxiously at Craig, and finally he held up his hands in resignation. 'Do as he says,' he ordered.

Tommy Lo pulled his prisoner out into the passage and slammed the door shut with his foot. Billy Chou started to resist but the knife bit into his neck and drew blood. 'If you struggle I'll cut your dirty throat right now,' Tommy Lo snarled as he dragged him along the passage to the end door that led on to the quay.

He leaned on it and it creaked open heavily. As they staggered out on to the quay Tommy suddenly pushed Billy Chou away from him violently, quickly slamming the door shut and sliding the bolt into place.

'Would you kill me without giving me the chance to defend myself?' Billy Chou scowled.

Tommy Lo smiled as he reached inside his coat and withdrew a sheathed knife which he tossed to his adversary. 'You've always wanted to test yourself against me, Billy Chou,' he said coldly. 'Well, you've got the chance now.'

Inspector Craig smiled as he looked around at his team. 'I fear we'll be picking up the pieces,' he remarked. 'Handcuff the prisoners, Miller. We don't want any more attempts at escape. Johnson, Burley, follow me.'

He led the way along the passage and pushed on the door. 'It's locked,' he said quickly. 'We'll go via the yard. Hurry, chaps.'

As they reached the quayside and clambered up over a stack of oil drums on to the raised quay itself they could hear the sound of steel on steel, and then Craig saw the back of Billy Chou. He was holding his knife at his side and leaning over Tommy Lo who was on one knee. Chou turned slowly and staggered forward a pace, his opponent's knife buried up to the hilt in his chest. He fell forward, dead before he hit the concrete, and Tommy Lo staggered to his feet.

'It's over, Tommy!' Craig called out to him.

The young man smiled and suddenly stepped up to the edge of the quay. 'No it's not,' he replied. 'I've no intention of rotting in one of your prison cells. I'll take my chance in the river.'

'Don't be foolish. It's running full. You'll never make it with those currents,' Craig shouted.

Tommy Lo raised his hand in a farewell gesture and then dived headlong into the muddy water. The men behind Craig rushed forward and leaned over the quay, waiting for the fugitive to surface, but the turbid water flowed past powerfully, its dark surface unbroken.

One hour later the two shocked and saddened young men from Bermondsey sat telling their story to the police chief.

'Well, you're free to go,' he told them finally. 'I'm sorry about your friend. Tommy Lo was involved in handling drugs at the beginning, but he's been helping the police for some time now. In fact it was he who first alerted us to Kennedy's double dealings. He should have stayed around and taken his chances. I don't think any court would have convicted him, taking everything into consideration.'

Chapter Forty-One

On Saturday evening Paul Neal stepped down from a bus in the Strand and made his way to Trafalgar Square. It had always been one of his favourite places to visit as a child, and now his heart was pumping fast with anticipation as he walked up the wide steps of the National Gallery. From the porch he looked down on to the fountains and up at the figure of Lord Nelson, trying not to appear too conspicuous. He was early, eager to see Mei Li again, and while he waited the young man went over in his mind the words which would make her understand that to leave him was the same as killing him slowly. He had written the words down in the quietness of his bedroom, recited them like an actor learning his lines, and then torn up the scribblings and started again.

Kay had brought him the message on Friday evening and he had smiled at the location for the tryst. It was inside the imposing building that he had first laid eyes on Mei Li and immediately fallen in love with her. Now, just a few short weeks later she was going to walk out of his life for ever. Tonight he must make her see how much she meant to him but he was afraid that the words would somehow stick in his throat.

He saw her coming towards him, her long raven hair rippling in the light breeze, her long sleek olive-green dress hugging her exquisite figure. She saw him and smiled, and he hurried down the stairs two at a time to wrap her in his arms, oblivious to all that was going on around them.

'It's been so long, Paul,' she whispered.

He felt the softness of her body and sighed deeply. 'Too long,' he replied. 'I've missed yer like mad.'

They linked arms as they left the Square and found a small café in St Martin's Lane. Mei Li gazed lingeringly at him across the table. 'We'll be sailing some time next week, Paul,' she told him with sadness in her eyes. 'But I have some good news too. I have a girlfriend who works with me, from Shanghai. She has a sugar-daddy, a very rich man who's set her up in a flat in Bloomsbury. It's a very grand flat in a block with a porter and a reception desk, all very smart. My friend, Mollie Chan, has gone away for the weekend and she said I could use her flat. She knows about you and me, and she feels very sad for us. She's given me two tickets to the review at the Plaza for this evening too. Isn't that nice?'

Paul laughed aloud. 'It's wonderful,' he said. ''Ave we got time fer anuvver coffee? There's so much I've gotta tell yer.'

The evening had passed like a beautiful dream and Paul was still pinching himself as he gazed out of the bedroom at the crescent moon. He tightened the belt of his dressing-gown and glanced down into the wide, almost deserted thorough-fare. The words he had composed had all gone, flown like wild birds from his mind the very moment Mei Li came into sight, but now it didn't matter. They were together once more, however briefly it might be.

'You look funny in that gown,' Mei Li giggled as she came into the room wrapped in a bathrobe almost as big as his. 'I think Mollie Chan's sugar-daddy must be very fat.'

He held out his hands and she came to him, pressing herself close and he stroked her hair, kissed her neck and tiny ears and felt her shiver with pleasure. 'I love you, Mei Li,' he whispered.

'I love you too, Paul Neal,' she answered.

Their lips met in a tender kiss and very gently he slipped the robe from her shoulders to kiss her bare skin. He met her gaze and saw the same look she had given him during the review, when she stroked the inside of his thigh and held him with her expressive almond eyes. They were tempting him, luring him like a traveller to chambers of unearthly beauty never seen before and fleeting moments of forbidden promise.

He moved just enough to loosen the cord and the bathrobe dropped to the floor. Her shapely body was ravishing and he shook with excitement as he leant down to kiss her firm pink nipples. She held her head back, slightly arching her body and slipping her fingers through his wavy fair hair. Suddenly he picked her up in his arms, holding her like a baby, and very gently he laid her down on the bed covers. She smiled up at him, her cheeks hot and flushed, her eyes wide with expectation and he slipped off his robe. The feel of his passion made her gasp as he lowered himself next to her and she groaned to feel his hands moving upon her, his fingers exploring the roundness of her soft small breasts, her flat belly and the mound of her sex. She willed him on, her hand on his wrist encouraging him and he felt her eager wetness. She moaned and coiled against his caress, and then unable to bear the waiting any longer she guided him into her. The pain was brief, and desperate not to lose control he clenched his teeth as he thrust his hips against her, her sharp nails biting into his back and her hot panting breath on his throat as she made love for the very first time.

High in the night sky the horned moon had disappeared behind a dark cloud and the tired lovers heard the distant roll of thunder. Mei Li turned over to face him and he slipped his arm around her nude body. 'Storms frighten me,' she whispered.

'You're safe wiv me,' he said softly, kissing her forehead.

'Will you always keep a place in your heart for me, even when you're married with lots of children and very rich?' she asked.

'I'll never marry, Mei Li,' he replied. 'I'll make a lot o' money though, an' then I'll come ter Singapore.'

'Don't, Paul,' she said sadly. 'Just let us enjoy tonight, and tomorrow, and then when we part we'll have these precious moments to remember for the rest of our lives.'

He kissed her cheek and her wet eyes, tasting her silent tears. 'There was so much I wanted ter say when we met this evenin',' he sighed, 'but seein' yer comin' terwards me left me speechless. You looked so beautiful.'

The thunder rolled again, louder this time and she nestled into him. He held her tight, and then as she drifted off to sleep he eased over on to his back and closed his eyes. The clock at his elbow seemed to be ticking louder, mocking him, and it was breaking dawn before he finally managed to fall asleep.

It had been a glorious sabbath and they had strolled through the Royal parks, over the narrow Serpentine bridge which Mei Li said reminded her of her childhood in China, and sat sipping coffee in a small café near Piccadilly Circus before going back to the flat where she cooked him a traditional Chinese meal. She had become anxious as the evening wore on and now it was getting late. They talked of mundane things, both reluctant to face the inevitable, and then as the lounge clock struck nine Mei Li slipped from under his arm and stood up. 'I must go now, Paul,' she said, her voice almost a whisper.

'Yeah I know,' he replied, the words sticking in his throat.

They left the flats, eyed by a curious porter, and Paul hailed a taxi. It had better be quick, he thought, longing to clasp her in his arms and carry her off.

She hugged him, her body shaking as she sobbed quietly. He kissed her lips, her neck and her downcast eyes, and she pulled away from him. 'I'll always love you, Paul Neal.'

'I'll always love you, Mei Li.'

She slid her hand slowly out of his and climbed in the taxi. He watched, etching into his mind the final sight of her beautiful face as the vehicle pulled away from the kerb, taking from him the only woman he would ever love.

Sonny Rowland shrugged his shoulders as he sat with Joey in the Swan on Thursday evening. 'The quack told me it's never gonna be 'undred per cent, an' when I asked 'im if I'd be able ter box again 'e nearly 'it the roof.'

'Still it's fer the best, Sonny,' Joey remarked. 'Let's face it, yer wasn't goin' anywhere. Bein' a punchin'-bag fer the up-an'-comin's ain't exactly the best deal, is it. You'll be all right. Just remember ter watch me on the stall, an' when yer get used ter the business I'll see about lettin' yer work that barrer up on the station. A couple o' weeks an' yer'll be goin' like the clappers.'

'D'yer fink so?'

'I know so.'

'What d'you reckon, Paul?'

There was no answer and Joey shook his head. 'Leave 'im, 'e's bin in anuvver world since last weekend.'

Sonny glanced over at the forlorn figure of his friend and nodded. ''E's certainly took it 'ard,' he said quietly. 'I don't fink 'e's said more than two words all week.'

Joey and Sonny sat shoulder to shoulder at the counter trying to bring Paul into the conversation, but finally they had to admit defeat. The young man sat hunched over his beer hardly touching it, and even the barman felt compelled to make a comment. 'Is 'e gonna sit cuddlin' that bleedin' pint all night?'

It was a dull, listless evening in the Swan, until Butch burst his way into the bar looking like he'd seen a ghost. 'Charlie Wong the bloody knife grinder's van's just drawn up outside,' he blurted out.

Paul swung round on his stool. 'Do what?' he said in disbelief.

'Go an' take a look,' Butch spluttered.

Paul hurried out with Joey and Sonny on his heels. Of the

van there was no sign, but in the back of a waiting taxi they saw the grinning face of Tommy Lo staring out through the lowered window.

Butch had played his part and he stood back displaying his distinctive gap-toothed smile as the others embraced the young Chinese man.

'We thought you was dead,' Joey gasped.

'I never expected ter see you again,' Paul said, his eyes wide with surprise.

'Never mind all that,' Tommy Lo said quickly. 'You've got one hour, Paul Neal, before Mei Li's ship sails. Jump in.' He leaned forward towards the driver. 'King George the Fifth Docks, fast as you can.'

'I can't get over it,' Paul laughed as the taxi sped towards Rotherhithe Tunnel.

'After I hit the water I swam under the quay and held on to a stanchion for ages,' Tommy explained. 'Climbing out was a problem, but I managed it, as you can see.'

Paul shook his head slowly, still in shock. ''Ow did yer find out when Mei Li would be sailin'?' he asked.

'I've got a contact in the shipping office,' Tommy Lo said grinning.

The taxi sped along East India Dock Road and through Canning Town to the docks. Tommy Lo moved the bag by his feet and stretched out his legs. 'I have to see Li Fong and I thought you might like to say a last goodbye.'

The cab pulled up by a ship called the *Southern Star* and Tommy Lo paid off the driver before leading the way up the gangway carrying his bag. 'Visitors for Li Fong and party,' he told a steward.

'If you'll just follow me, sir,' the man replied. 'We're

sailing in thirty-five minutes. All visitors must disembark ten minutes before.' He led the way to the upper deck and knocked lightly on a cabin door. 'Thank you, sir,' he said as Tommy Lo put a half-crown into his open hand.

Mei Li squealed with delight and rushed into Paul's arms, and Tommy Lo stood back to admire. 'They make a lovely couple, don't they,' he remarked to Li Fong.

'I don't understand,' the old man replied. 'What's the reason for this visit? We sail very soon.'

'Let's walk a bit,' the young man suggested.

They found a seat by the rails and Tommy Lo unzipped the bag. 'In here are the pots you put up as security,' he said smiling. 'I don't think they'll be needed now, so I'm returning them to you.'

The old man started to shake as he stared down at the parcel. 'I never expected to see them again,' he croaked. 'This is wonderful. You're very kind to consider an old man in such a way.'

Tommy Lo shrugged his shoulders. 'It was nothing. At least your journey home will be a happy one, which is more than can be said for Mei Li.'

'How so?'

'You are going home, she's leaving it.'

'But she is going home, to marry a respectable business-man who has much standing on the island. She will be happy, given time.'

'How much time? Twenty years? Thirty?' Tommy said disdainfully. 'This is the only place she'll be happy, here in London, with the man she loves. You saw them. Don't tell me it didn't move you. If it didn't then you are a cold-hearted, foolish old man. Let her go, Li Fong. Give her the freedom she's desperate for. Don't trade on her duty and loyalty to you. Give her what she can't ask for. Release her from the promise, the promise you made to someone she doesn't know or want to know. Take a look at these precious pots, and think of the legend they enshrine. Try to remember the days of your youth when you sought to light the lantern in a young woman's soul. Don't tell me you never did, Li Fong. Look at Mei Li. Look into her eyes and see how her soul's on fire. It won't even glimmer if she's to spend her youth in the arms of a fat businessman with nothing but dollar signs in his eyes. She belongs to Paul Neal, freely.'

'Will all visitors disembark now please,' a voice boomed out over the loudspeaker.

The old man picked up the bag and walked back to his cabin, with Tommy Lo at his shoulder. 'Do it now, Li Fong,' the young man urged him anxiously.

Mei Li was standing holding hands with the broad-shouldered young Englishman, but she moved away self-consciously with an imploring look in her eyes as her guardian came up to her.

Li Fong held out his arms. 'I have underestimated the feelings shared by you and your young man,' he said in a voice of quiet dignity. 'I can see that you love each other and I've decided to discharge you from your obligation to a foolish old man.' He cast a cutting glance at Tommy Lo. 'If you so wish you have my blessing to marry the young man of your choice. Cherish her, Paul Neal, and may you both be very happy and have many children.'

The goodbyes were feverish and tearful, and as the gangway was hauled up and the tug took up the strain Li Fong leaned over the rail and waved as the young people climbed into a taxi. He could still feel the warmth of Mei Li as she embraced him and he remembered long ago, when he took the tiny baby still covered with blood from the womb of her forsaken mother and the mud of the field and held her next to him, keeping her warm as he hurried to the mission. The parting had cracked open his heart but it was good to feel sunlight shining again in the dusty corners of his soul, and deep inside him he felt as if someone was laughing.

The taxi drew up in Grange Road and Tommy Lo said his farewells. 'We'll keep in touch,' he said. 'With luck I'll be back in England in time for the wedding. Oh, and in case you're interested, Wu Sung was minding the ginger pots. Under the stairs would you believe. Farewell, Mister Just-in-time. Farewell, Mei Li. And now I've got a ship to catch myself. Euston Station, driver, and hurry.'

Epilogue

In July 1950 Kay married Joey Westlake, and eight months later their first child was born. It was a boy, and the choice of names was easy. The baby was christened Tommy Joseph. Ruby worried at first over what her neighbours might think about the somewhat quick arrival of the baby, but her old friend Bel Allenby administered some more sound advice. 'Kay's completely unconcerned, so who gives a toss?' she said with a big smile.

Sonny Rowland never boxed again and Joey, true to his word, allowed him to help out on his stall, eventually giving him a stall outside London Bridge Station to manage. A national newspaper carried the story of the boxer's retirement from the ring, due to an injury sustained whilst acting as bodyguard to an undercover officer investigating drug running in Chinatown, and his fame grew. People came from far and wide to buy from his stall and have their picture taken with him. Elstree Film Studios used him as an advisor for fight scenes, and he was given a few walk-on roles. This was followed by a speaking role in the award-winning film *Night of Splendour*, in which the exciting new star Rachel Grimes shimmied out of a limousine in the pouring rain and Sonny, looking splendid in his doorman's livery, held up an umbrella and uttered the immortal line, 'Nasty night, Ma'am.'

Sonny was happy with his new-found fame, but Joey had the practicalities of running the stall to think about and he was finally compelled to persuade Butch Wheeler to manage it. The arrangement worked well. Sonny paraded round the stall, bringing in the trade and posing for all and sundry, while Butch smiled indulgently as he weighed up the produce.

The Limehouse business was concluded when Kennedy, Danny Ling and Husi Kang all received long sentences. Wu Sung and the young waiter Ti San, who had once worked in the Bermondsey laundry, each received an invitation to Paul and Mei Li's September wedding, and word came from Tommy Lo that his ship would be docking in Liverpool two days before the big day, and yes, he would be honoured to act as best man. Paul and Mei Li visited Wu Sung in Limehouse and succeeded in convincing him that in the absence of Li Fong no one was more suited than he to give Mei Li away.

Percy Bradley finally retired from Madeley's, and much to Len Moody's chagrin Jim Neal was promoted to maintenance foreman. The writer of the anonymous letters was never discovered, but Angela Stapleton left the company in August and the last anyone heard of her she was managing a country pub with Bill Crawley.

Jim and Ruby Neal were up to their ears in weddings, as Bel put it, and they had become very close. Neither of them was prepared to talk about Jim's infidelity and they decided that the subject was now dead and buried, both taking heed of Bel's proverbial remark: 'After a storm the sun usually shines again.'

The Anglo-Chinese wedding attracted much attention locally and Lizzie Roach treasured the photograph of her holding on to Wu Sung's arm as they tripped out of the church. Connie Wilson, Myrtle Thompson and Nora Mason joined with their long-suffering husbands to make the day go with a swing: Jack Mason managed to get some coloured lights from the brewery stores which he strung along Tanners Alley. Connie Wilson produced some Chinese lanterns from a source she refused to reveal, on orders from her husband George who was now back at work in the King George the Fifth Docks. The wedding feast went on into the night and Tommy Lo was mildly amused at being followed everywhere by the Wilsons' son Freddie, who told Paul that the young Chinese man reminded him of the number one son in the Charlie Chan films.

The balmy night wore on and it was almost time for Mei Li and Paul to leave for their wedding-night hotel in the Strand. She slipped her arm round his waist and gazed into his eyes. 'This is like heaven,' she said sighing happily.

Paul cuddled her shoulders and looked up at the row of Chinese lanterns glowing against the deepness of the velvet sky. They burned brightly, but as far as he was concerned none so vividly as the flame shining in Mei Li's almond eyes.

Down Milldyke Way

Harry Bowling

When Kate Flanagan's husband is sentenced to seven years for armed robbery, she knows that now is the time to be free of him and make a new life for herself and her two children.

Forced to quit her house, Kate must first take the unpalatable step of moving to a slum tenement block in Milldyke Street, Dockhead. It's a street with no corner shops and no familiar terraced houses – just a bleak turning with a reputation for housing the dregs of Bermondsey. Yet people are people wherever they live, and Kate soon settles in among the Milldykers, sharing their gossip, heartache and laughter.

But then Kate stumbles over the murdered body of an old woman who lived in the next block – and realises that she, herself, could be a target. When she turns to the attractive and sympathetic Sergeant Cassidy for protection she finds that her emotions, as well as her life, are in danger . . .

'What makes Harry's novels work is their warmth and authenticity. Their spirit comes from the author himself and his abiding memories of family life as it once was lived in the slums of south-east London' *Today*

0 7472 5543 1

HEADLINE

The Glory and the Shame

Harry Bowling

On the night of Saturday 10th May 1941, amidst the carnage and devastation caused by enemy bombers, Joe Carey and Charlie Duggan risked their lives to save those trapped in an air-raid shelter. Yet six men and women perished, including the popular George Merry – a man whom the Totterdown folk believe was the hero of the hour.

By 1947 the inhabitants of the street are rebuilding their lives – but the legacy of war is a powerful one and for the families of Joe and Charlie, the future seems to be inextricably bound to the past. And then young Sue Carey meets Sam Culkin, an ambitious journalist, determined to further his career through a series of articles on the heroism of the people in wartime London. Already faced with both a violent factory strike and the frequent street fracas between the Barlows and the Sloans, the inhabitants of Totterdown Street must now cope with news which exposes not just the glory of the past but the shame as well.

'The king of Cockney sagas' *Publishing News*

0 7472 5544 X

HEADLINE

If you enjoyed this book here is a selection of other bestselling titles from Headline

LIVERPOOL LAMPLIGHT	Lyn Andrews	£5.99 ☐
A MERSEY DUET	Anne Baker	£5.99 ☐
THE SATURDAY GIRL	Tessa Barclay	£5.99 ☐
DOWN MILLDYKE WAY	Harry Bowling	£5.99 ☐
PORTHELLIS	Gloria Cook	£5.99 ☐
A TIME FOR US	Josephine Cox	£5.99 ☐
YESTERDAY'S FRIENDS	Pamela Evans	£5.99 ☐
RETURN TO MOONDANCE	Anne Goring	£5.99 ☐
SWEET ROSIE O'GRADY	Joan Jonker	£5.99 ☐
THE SILENT WAR	Victor Pemberton	£5.99 ☐
KITTY RAINBOW	Wendy Robertson	£5.99 ☐
ELLIE OF ELMLEIGH SQUARE	Dee Williams	£5.99 ☐

Headline books are available at your local bookshop or newsagent. Alternatively, books can be ordered direct from the publisher. Just tick the titles you want and fill in the form below. Prices and availability subject to change without notice.

Buy four books from the selection above and get free postage and packaging and delivery within 48 hours. Just send a cheque or postal order made payable to Bookpoint Ltd to the value of the total cover price of the four books. Alternatively, if you wish to buy fewer than four books the following postage and packaging applies:

UK and BFPO £4.30 for one book; £6.30 for two books; £8.30 for three books.

Overseas and Eire: £4.80 for one book; £7.10 for 2 or 3 books (surface mail)

Please enclose a cheque or postal order made payable to *Bookpoint Limited*, and send to: Headline Publishing Ltd, 39 Milton Park, Abingdon, OXON OX14 4TD, UK.
Email Address: orders@bookpoint.co.uk

If you would prefer to pay by credit card, our call team would be delighted to take your order by telephone. Our direct line 01235 400 414 (lines open 9.00 am–6.00 pm Monday to Saturday 24 hour message answering service). Alternatively you can send a fax on 01235 400 454.

Name ....

Address ....

....

....

If you would prefer to pay by credit card, please complete:
Please debit my Visa/Access/Diner's Card/American Express (delete as applicable) card number:

Signature .... Expiry Date..............